Praise for M

and

"With passion, romance, and revealing moments that will touch your heart, Emily March takes readers on a journey where mistakes are redeemed and a more beautiful future is forged—one miracle at a time."
—*USA Today*

"A brilliant writer you'll love creates a world you'll never want to leave."
—Susan Mallery, *New York Times* bestselling author

"A heartfelt story of family, community, second chances, and the power of love . . . Don't miss it!"
—Susan Wiggs, *New York Times* bestselling author

"Heart-wrenching and soul-satisfying. For a wonderful read, don't miss a visit to Eternity Springs."
—Lisa Kleypas, *New York Times* bestselling author

"A heartwarming tale of courage and redemption . . . that will have readers cheering." —*Publishers Weekly*

"Fans of Debbie Macomber's Cedar Cove series and Robyn Carr's Virgin River series will find much to enjoy in the start of this new series." —*Booklist*

Also by
EMILY MARCH

Eternity Springs: The McBrides of Texas

Tucker

EMILY MARCH

St. Martin's Paperbacks

This is a work of fiction. All of the characters, organizations, and events portrayed in this novel are either products of the author's imagination or are used fictitiously.

First published in the United States by St. Martin's Paperbacks, an imprint of St. Martin's Publishing Group.

ETERNITY SPRINGS: THE MCBRIDES OF TEXAS: TUCKER

For information, address St. Martin's Publishing Group, 120 Broadway, New York, NY 10271.

www.stmartins.com

ISBN: 978-1-250-31493-2

Our books may be purchased in bulk for promotional, educational, or business use. Please contact your local bookseller or the Macmillan Corporate and Premium Sales Department at 1-800-221-7945, ext. 5442, or by email at MacmillanSpecialMarkets@macmillan.com.

Printed in the United States of America

St. Martin's Paperbacks edition / March 2020

10 9 8 7 6 5 4 3 2 1

For TJ and John.

Thanks for giving me Elvis.

Acknowledgments

I am blessed to have many fabulous people working with me to bring my books to readers. My most sincere thanks to everyone at St. Martin's Press. Leading the way is my phenomenal editor, Eileen Rothschild, whose insight and instincts are unsurpassed. Thank you so much, Eileen, for helping me make the books the best they can be. My thanks to the rest of my St. Martin's team, including Tiffany Shelton, production editor Laurie Henderson, production manager Jeremy Haiting, copy writer Elizabeth Wildman, senior marketing manager Marissa Sangiacomo, Naureen Nashid with digital marketing, and Sara LaCotti with publicity. A special thank-you to Danielle Christopher for the fabulous cover design. I have the best covers!

I also need to thank Meg Ruley and Christina Hogrebe with Jane Rotrosen Agency for all you do on my behalf, year in and year out.

And to Mary Dickerson. I cannot begin to express my appreciation for your unfailing guidance, generosity, and friendship. These books are as much yours as they are mine.

I have the best job in the world and I appreciate the efforts of everyone who makes it possible for me to spend my days lost in Eternity Springs and Redemption, Texas.

Chapter One

Tucker McBride fed coins into an ancient soft drink machine, heard the *clink clink clink* as they fell into the box, opened the door, and pulled out a frosty glass bottle. After positioning it beneath the opener, he yanked, and the metal cap clattered into the box. Seated on a stool behind the gas station's counter, an old man with a tobacco chaw in his cheek watched him intently.

Tucker lifted the bottle to his lips and sipped. Sweet, syrupy, black cherry flavor exploded on his tongue, and instantly took him back to childhood. "Dublin Dr Pepper. Man, I haven't had one of these in twenty years."

The ingredient that made the particular variety of Dr Pepper bottled in the small town of Dublin so special was Texas's own Imperial Pure Cane Sugar. It made the soft drink sweeter, to be sure, but a Texan would tell you Dublin Dr Pepper just tasted different. Better.

"Well, you ain't having one today either." The gas station owner turned his head and spat a stream of tobacco juice into a spittoon. "You must not be from around here if you don't know that the corporate

suits out of Dallas put nails in the coffin of Dublin
Dr Pepper a few years back. Sued the little guy, they
did. Not allowed to make Dr Pepper anymore. What
you're drinking is a Dublin Original. Twenty-four flavors instead of twenty-three."

No, he hadn't known. That wasn't the sort of news
a man usually picked up in the desert of Iraq, the
mountains of Afghanistan, or the swamp of Washington, DC. "A knockoff, then. Damned good one."

His second sip took him back to summer days
spent with his cousins, Jackson and Boone, at their
grandparents' lake house at Possum Kingdom. Nothing tasted better on a hot summer day than Dublin
Dr Pepper. They'd consumed the soft drinks by the
caseload until they'd grown old enough to switch to
Shiner beer.

The man behind the counter shifted his tobacco
chaw from his right cheek to his left, then said, "Yeah.
Can't get Original anymore either. Big city reporter
stirred up trouble by writing about the situation, so
the family pulled the plug on the flavor. Couldn't af-
ford another lawsuit from Goliath. I hauled two truck-
loads of Original back here. Worked our way through
about half of it." He gestured toward the bottle in
Tucker's hand and said, "You be careful who you
share my location with, you hear? I don't believe in
wasting the good stuff on folks who can't appreciate
what they got."

"You have my word. I appreciate you offering me
access."

"I always offer to the military. I'm a vet myself.
Vietnam."

Tucker gave him a look of surprise. "I'm not in uniform." Not anymore.

The man shrugged. "You got the look, son. So, where you headed? Fort Hood?"

Tucker took another long sip of his drink. "No. Not this time."

He'd left the huge, Central Texas army base for the final time earlier today on his H-D Road King without a firm destination in mind. Now, he turned his head and looked through the store's ancient screened doors toward the motorcycle parked at the gas pump. "I'm possibly on the road to Redemption. Or maybe Ruin. The jury's still out on that one."

"Huh." The gas station owner rubbed his grizzled chin stubble. "Well, I reckon most of us stand at that crossroads sometime in our lives. You want some jerky to go with your Coke? It's made locally. You won't find better."

In Texas, all soft drinks were Cokes, not sodas or pops or even Dr Peppers. Glad to be home, Tucker paid for his gas, his Original, and three different flavors of beef jerky, thanked the man behind the counter, and headed outside. He leaned against his motorcycle, sipping the drink and chewing on a piece of jerky as he scrutinized the intersection before him. Wonder how many farm-to-market road intersections existed in Texas? He knew the two-lane farm roads numbered over three thousand and made up over half of the state's road system. Bet Boone would know the answer to the question. He knew useless facts like that.

Tucker blew an airstream over his bottle to make it *whoo* just like he'd done when he was a kid, in no real hurry to move along. He was on no time clock. Nobody knew he'd come home to Texas. This was the first time in a long time he'd had the luxury to lolly-gag while traveling.

For the majority of the past decade, he'd operated on a ticking clock while finding his way in and out of jungles, deserts, mountains, urban fortresses, and just about anywhere else someone needed the services of his specialized Army Ranger unit. The work had suited him. He'd excelled at the job, aided by his natural talents and traits—tenacity, endurance, the ability to make quick decisions, and an uncanny sense of direction. It also helped that he'd had more than his fair share of good luck and, according to his late father, a head as hard as the granite dome of Enchanted Rock.

Tucker had been little more than a boy when he'd decided on a military career. Having plotted that course early on, he'd never strayed from the path.

Until now. Now, he'd not only veered from the trail, he'd burned his map, smashed his compass, and shattered his satellite phone on the way into the wilderness.

He'd left the service. He'd quit the military. This was the first time in his life that he'd ever quit anything, and he didn't have a clue where to go from here.

He was lost.

Figuratively speaking, that is. Tucker knew he stood at a farm-to-market crossroads where the prairies and lakes region of Texas transitioned to the Hill Country. Where he was lost was inside himself. He'd lost his identity, his sense of self. He'd grown up, and he no longer knew what he wanted to be. Helluva thing for a man in his mid-thirties.

"So, which way are you going?" he asked himself. He could turn north, head for the family ranch outside of Fort Worth and do some catching up with kin. His parents were both gone now, and he'd been an only child, but he still had plenty of family.

Family who would pepper him with questions and ask for explanations.

He wasn't ready for that. He would not take FM 486 north toward Thorndale and weave his way up toward Fort Worth.

Instead, he could head southeast, mosey on down to the coast and Port Aransas, and rent a fishing boat. Or, he could make a real ride of it and go west, way out west toward Big Bend. Hiking and camping and communing with nature sounded appealing to him.

That's what Tucker liked best of all. He belonged outdoors, where the air was clean and fresh, and the people along the trail were generous and good and forthright and kind.

He did not belong on special assignment behind a desk in the nation's capital, surrounded by vipers— duty that revealed the political underbelly of institutions he had always revered. Duty that darkened a man's soul.

Swamp didn't begin to describe it. *Slimy cesspool* was more appropriate. They'd made him responsible for one tiny little area of it, no bigger than a broom closet in the grand scheme of things. He'd made a valiant effort to clean up his space, but the vipers and rats had blocked him at every turn. He'd finally admitted he was fighting a losing battle. His only choice was to surrender to the filth or leave.

Tucker had left, but doing so damaged something inside him. He needed to heal. He needed to shed the film of slime he'd acquired. He was counting on clean country air and crystal clear spring water to do the trick.

That crossed the Gulf of Mexico off his list. He wouldn't take FM 112 south toward Old Dime Box either.

So . . . what would it be? The Piney Woods? The Davis Mountains? Big Bend National Park?

No. Tucker didn't truly have a decision to make. He'd known his ultimate destination ever since he'd exited the Fort Hood gate, even if he'd pretended otherwise and followed his nose on the road for a while.

From here, he was going to head southwest toward the Texas Hill Country. Toward Enchanted Canyon, to be exact. The air blew clean and fresh there, and the water ran sweet and crisp and cleansing. The only vipers he'd likely run across slithered on their bellies or coiled and shook their rattles in warning. The people there, well, they didn't come any better than his cousin Jackson. Tucker could tolerate that much family, at least. Jackson wouldn't press him with questions he didn't want to answer.

He drained his soft drink, placed the empty in the wooden bottle crate sitting on the ground beside the pumps, then swung a long leg over the saddle and started his bike.

He'd probably take a ride to Big Bend and another to the coast and do a trek up to the Piney Woods in the coming weeks and months, but today, for now, he'd take the scenic route toward the little tourist town of Redemption. He'd look up Jackson and share the salient pieces of his story. Jackson would give him the space he needed right now. Plus, he could be counted on to smooth Tucker's way with the rest of the famdamly.

While Tucker had been waging war in Washington, Jackson had taken point in dealing with a family windfall, the inheritance of Enchanted Canyon from a distant relative. He'd overseen the remodeling of the nineteenth-century brothel and dance hall that stood at the halfway point between Redemption and the ghost town and former outlaw conclave of Ruin, snuggled at the back of the canyon. The cathouse had been converted to a bed-and-breakfast, and the Fallen Angel Inn had recently opened to great success. Many of the guests it welcomed came to hear music at the Last Chance Hall, which was Jackson's pet project.

Jackson was the perfect person to run interference for Tucker. No stranger to turmoil after a contentious divorce and child custody fight, he would be a sympathetic ear for whatever parts of Tucker's story he wanted to share. And maybe, just maybe, Jackson could help Tucker find his way to . . . somewhere.

So Tucker headed for the Hill Country and took pleasure in the ride through a fertile stretch of rolling plains along the way. The afternoon was overcast, but the temperature hovered in the mid-seventies. A mild breeze carried the lingering scent of morning rain. The cotton harvest was underway, some of the fields stripped bare, others white as snow. Fat Angus, Herefords, and Holsteins populated the pastures. Seeing them made him hungry for a good steak. A short time later, as he rode through a bottomland pecan orchard, he added pecan pie to the menu.

He would need to decide where he wanted to stay overnight before long. He could step up his pace and make it into Redemption tonight, but camping held greater appeal. Today's weather forecast called for a cold front to blow through around sunset, taking the clouds with it. It had been way too long since he'd camped beneath Texas's starry sky.

As was his custom, Tucker carried essential gear with him. He simply needed to find a place to build his fire and a shelter. In his mind's eye, he pictured the map he'd studied before heading out from Fort Hood this morning and reviewed the landmarks he'd noted along his meandering today. Bastrop State Park wasn't too far away. He could alter his direction a skosh and go there. Finding a vacant campsite this time of year shouldn't be a problem. Tomorrow, he could take a morning hike through the park, then circle around Austin and arrive in Redemption mid-afternoon.

Decision made, he took the next southeast turn, and a few minutes later, zoomed past a figure before he registered what he'd seen.

A woman.

A vision with mile-long legs and glossy waves of hair the color of rich mahogany that fell almost to her waist. She had finely drawn features: her face heart-shaped, her nose straight, her lips lush and full. A sleeveless red dress hugged her voluptuous curves, its narrow tab shoulders revealing the strap of a red bra underneath. Her full hips enticingly swayed as she walked on the shoulder of the road in a pair of red high heels.

No car was in sight. No house was in sight. No other human being was in sight.

Former Army Ranger Tucker McBride had just spied a long-legged damsel in distress.

Gillian Thacker was having a wretched day.

She'd had a fight with Jeremy, the worst they'd ever had. It had started out over a relatively little thing—wedding details—and escalated quickly. Before she knew it, they'd had the row of their relationship.

The trip to Bastrop for an arts festival and two nights at a historic B&B was supposed to have been a romantic getaway for the two of them, a surprise he'd popped on her earlier this week. She'd been thrilled. She'd needed both a break from work and to spend some quality time with her fiancé. The entire month of August had been ridiculously busy at Bliss Bridal Salon, the wedding gown shop in Redemption, Texas, that she owned in partnership with her mother. Due to her workload, in the past three weeks Gillian had had to cancel two dates with Jeremy in addition to her plans to accompany him to Houston last weekend for a banking industry symposium at which he was a speaker.

They'd no sooner arrived in Bastrop this afternoon and begun unpacking when the bickering began. Really, why did Jeremy have an opinion about the reception china Mom wanted to use, anyway?

Gillian threw the small stone as hard as she could off into the cotton field, then continued to brood as she walked down the narrow two-lane road. In three-inch heels. Thinking about the wedding and the argument, so that she wasn't dwelling on her current predicament.

She was starting to get a little scared. "But I won't think about that."

She couldn't believe this all started over china, the lovely mismatched service for two hundred that her mother had been collecting for years in anticipation of using for her only daughter's wedding reception. Although, to be precise, the china had only been a part of today's explosion. What really set Jeremy off was the fact that Gillian had asked for her mother's opinion rather than his about what flatware to use with the china. Never mind that the man neither knew nor cared anything about table settings, and her mother loved nothing better than setting pretty tables.

It was a control thing with Jeremy.

Gillian and her mom enjoyed a very close relationship. In addition to being parent and child, they were partners in a business and friends. Gillian was beginning to suspect that Jeremy was threatened by it. He needed to assert power, which was silly because he wasn't in competition with her mother. Gillian loved them both, she needed them both, but in totally different ways. Why couldn't he see that?

He'd gotten his feathers ruffled rather often of late. She had always tried her best to soothe them, but today, when he'd wanted to veto the flatware selection, she reached her limit.

He'd been mean about it.

The ensuing argument had spiraled from china to flowers to sparklers to signature drinks to photo booth props—and then it got out of control. By the time she'd stormed from the B&B in Bastrop where they had planned to spend the weekend, she and Jeremy had fought over some idiotic things, and some very serious ones.

Did he honestly believe she was too devoted to her work? She was a small business owner. If she wasn't devoted, the salon wouldn't be successful!

And the new event-coordinating business they were planning to start after their wedding was something for the two of them to do together. As partners. Her mother wouldn't be involved at all in Blissful Events beyond making referrals.

Jeremy had always said he'd liked the fact that Gillian was ambitious. Why was that all of a sudden a problem?

Then he'd leveled some truly hurtful claims. Gillian could admit that she could be too stubborn and single-minded on occasion. Maybe sometimes she was blind to what Jeremy needed from her and their relationship. But where in the world had he come up with the whole "too friendly with his friends" accusation? She'd never—never once—acted in any inappropriate manner with any other man, much less one of his friends. That he'd accuse her of that had taken her breath away and blown the lid off her temper.

At the time, she had been thankful she'd had the means to leave the B&B. She needed to be in Dallas for a meeting early Monday morning, so in order to save her some travel time, she and Jeremy had driven to Bastrop in separate cars. On Sunday afternoon when he headed west to return to Redemption, she'd planned to go north.

Now, she wasn't so glad she'd had a getaway car.

She glanced up at the sky. Still heavy clouds. Was it supposed to rain today? She hoped it wouldn't rain today. That was all she needed.

"It'll be okay," she told herself. Everything would be okay. The sun would come out, and then she would at least be able to determine in which direction she walked.

She was lost. Completely, thoroughly, totally lost.

She couldn't believe she'd acted so foolishly. It wasn't like her. Not at all. She was organized and attentive and intelligent—but not too friendly. She didn't do things like run away from an argument, jump into her car, and drive blindly away. She was a careful driver. She didn't speed, and she paid attention to the road. She hadn't received a traffic ticket since college, and that hadn't been for speeding or reckless driving. She'd forgotten to renew her registration!

But this afternoon, she'd left her mind behind in the Katherine Suite at Lost Pines Inn. By the time she'd pulled over and plugged her destination into her car's GPS system—something she seldom used so wasn't all that familiar with—the route it had plotted took her on a series of farm roads. Rather than go the fifteen miles to the interstate highway, she'd followed the GPS woman's voice like an automaton. She'd driven east and west and north and even south, through tiny towns she'd never heard of before. And she'd grown up in Texas, little more than one hundred miles from where she'd started in Bastrop!

She hadn't seen another vehicle in well over an hour. Two hours, probably. She couldn't know for sure because her phone had died, and she couldn't recharge it because she'd loaned Jeremy the charging cord she kept in her car. She didn't wear a watch. The only jewelry she regularly wore were earrings and the diamond solitaire that Jeremy had given to her last New Year's Eve.

She glanced down at her ringless left hand. Had she really taken it off and flung it at Jeremy while shouting they were done, before storming out of the B&B? She wasn't a drama queen. She didn't do scenes like that.

She had today.

She hadn't meant it. Well, maybe she'd meant it at the time, but that was in the heat of the moment. Her feet were killing her. Tears stung her eyes. Again. She wasn't ordinarily a crier. She'd cried more today than in the past ten years put together.

She needed to get a grip. Every couple fought. This was not a big deal. So what that Jeremy had hurt her feelings? She'd surely hurt his too. She should have stayed and talked it out, not let herself get angry and scared, and leave. Leaving never solved problems.

Although, she'd had a right to be angry. Jeremy had been in a mood, himself. Words were weapons, and he had certainly wielded his words like a sword. He could be an actor on *Game of Thrones* or *Outlander*. Sir Jeremy of Lost Pines Inn. He'd wounded her, left her bleeding from a thousand cuts, so she'd probably been right to walk away. Not that she'd walked. She'd run down the stairs and dashed to her car and spun her tires upon pulling away from the inn.

Gillian *never* spun her tires.

"If only—" She broke off, halting her steps to work another pebble from her shoe. Maybe she should try going barefoot for a bit. At least the farm road was clean. She probably wouldn't step on broken glass. Or a rusty nail. When had she last had a tetanus shot? How soon did one die from tetanus, anyway? Did tetanus kill people? She wasn't sure. If only she'd grabbed her bag before leaving the B&B, she'd have had a change of shoes, the cute sandals with the rhinestones. If only—

Stop it!

If and *only* were the two most useless words to use together in a sentence. If only Gillian had paid attention to where she was going. If only that stupid feral hog hadn't run across the road right in front of her. If only she hadn't swerved to miss it and hit a pecan tree instead.

It was a beautiful tree. Probably a hundred years old. Gillian hoped her little crossover SUV hadn't hurt it.

She sniffled. Whimpered. Whined aloud. She was lost. She couldn't believe she was lost!

Then, she heard something. She straightened and turned an ear toward the sound, listening intently. Help? Finally?

An engine. Not a car engine. Not a pickup driven by a kind, gentle, friendly cotton farmer.

Gillian heard a motorcycle headed her way. Coming fast.

A motorcycle. Roaring down a two-lane road.

She pictured the driver. He'd be a big man covered in tats, wearing a black leather vest over a wife-beater shirt, with a chaw of tobacco stuck in his cheek. Huntsville prison wasn't too far from here. He probably just got out of the pen where he'd done twenty years. For murder. And he hadn't had a woman in twenty years.

She really needed to stop listening to those true-crime podcasts.

What to do? What to do?

She couldn't very well hide. She was wearing red and surrounded by cotton fields. If she tried to hide, she'd look like a dead body lying in a field, and she didn't want to give him any ideas.

She needed help. She was lost, had no water, no shelter, and she really needed to pee.

He was coming fast. He'd be here in moments. Should she attempt to wave him down? He didn't *have* to be a convict fresh out of Huntsville. He could be a doctor or a lawyer from Austin who rode Harleys as a hobby.

She hated this. She couldn't believe she'd put herself in this position. *How could I have been so stupid?* It was embarrassing. She hated being embarrassed. And, she was frightened too. Scared down to the Big Apple Red polish on her toes. This was definitely the second most horrid day in her life, headed toward first.

What to do? What to do?

In the end, she did nothing but wear her best deer-in-headlights look. The man was dressed all in black, a full-face helmet obscuring his features. Darth Vader on a Harley. He blew past her like a proton torpedo.

Gillian released the breath she'd been holding. "Okay. Okay. I'm lost, but at least I'm alive."

For now.

Up ahead, the motorcycle had slowed. The driver started turning around.

Chapter Two

Tucker was a sixth-generation Texan, small-town born and bred. Certain behaviors were stamped into his DNA. A real man tipped his hat to the ladies, opened doors for females of any age, and never, ever failed to stop and assist a woman in distress.

So, of course, he had to turn around.

That this particular woman in distress was a total smoke show dressed in fire-engine red only made playing the role of Texas gentleman that much sweeter.

He wondered how she'd managed to find herself out here in the middle of nowhere, no car in sight, not a house anywhere around, and the closest town a good ten miles away. Unfortunately, hot looks and a bright mind didn't always go together.

He pulled to a stop beside her and flipped up the visor of his helmet. His assessing stare met a wary gaze shining from big, periwinkle-blue eyes that were swollen and red-rimmed with tears. She had an abrasion on her cheek just above her chin. Had someone hit her? When his quick visual sweep of her body revealed additional redness on both of her arms, he reconsidered. Airbag deployment, most likely. "Do you need some help, ma'am?"

He watched her intently and saw her quietly repeat the word *ma'am*. After a moment's hesitation, she licked her lips, swallowed hard, and said, "Well, um, I, um. May I borrow your phone?"

Her voice was smooth as Tennessee whiskey with just enough Texas in her drawl to sound like home to ears too far away for too long. "Yes, ma'am."

She took a small step backward as he set his kick-stand and climbed off his bike. *She's scared of me.*

It was a perfectly natural reaction and showed some sense, but Tucker didn't like scaring women, so when he pulled off his helmet, he was scowling. Her eyes widened, she took another step back, and he realized he'd made the situation worse. *Well, hell.*

He reached deep inside him for the charm that had grown rusty with disuse, made a stab at a reassuring smile, and addressed the elephant in the cotton field. "Don't be scared. I won't hurt you. I came back to see if I could help. That's all. I give you my word, and a McBride's word is his bond."

"That's so old-fashioned," she said.

"Yes, well, that's how we roll. Now, I'm going to reach into my pocket and pull out my phone."

Her gaze dropped to his hand, and she gave a nervous little laugh. "No gun?"

"No gun." That was in a different pocket.

Tucker unzipped his jacket and reached into an inner pouch for his phone while trying his best to look unthreatening. Their fingers brushed as he handed it over. Her fingernail color matched her dress.

"Thank you," she said.

"You're welcome. My name is Tucker."

"I'm Gillian." Her teeth tugged on her bottom lip as she stared at the phone. "Do you have Google maps? I need to send a pin of my location to my—"

She broke off abruptly, and her head came up. Those glittering blue eyes—puffy and swollen from tears and framed by long, thick lashes—went round and big. Distracted, he fell into them. "Tucker Mc-Bride? Your name is Tucker McBride?"

He blinked and pulled slightly away. Now it was his turn to be wary. "Yes."

She gave him a once-over, and some of the stiffness melted from her spine. "I know Jackson. Boone too. You're the third cousin, aren't you?"

Well, this was unexpected. "Yes, Boone and Jackson are cousins of mine. Have we met?" He didn't think so. He'd damned sure remember her.

"No."

"I'm surprised you'd connect me to them. We're a long way from Redemption."

"Are we?" She gave a short, strained laugh. "I wouldn't know. I'm lost. But you look just like them, and Tucker McBride is an unusual name. Plus, I remember when the three of you arrived in Redemption the first time. You all rode motorcycles. My friend Maisy laughed that you had your own little McBride gang, so you were perfect for Ruin."

Tucker grinned. "If you only knew." He extended his hand toward her for a handshake. "Nice to meet you, Gillian . . . ?"

"Thacker. Gillian Thacker." Her grip was firm, her smile filled with relief. "I'm a friend of Caroline Carruthers. Are you on your way to visit Redemption?"

Caroline was the woman Jackson was seeing, Tucker knew. He nodded. "Yes, I am. So now that you know I'm not a serial killer, want to tell me what you're doing standing in a cotton field in a sundress and stilettos? Not exactly apparel for farming."

She glanced down at her feet. "Technically, I'm not

in the field but on the shoulder of a road. A narrow, two-lane, never-ending road. And no, cotton is not my thing. I'm all about satin and lace."

Satin and lace? A vision of Gillian in lingerie the same shade of red as her dress flashed in Tucker's mind as she continued, "I sell wedding gowns at a bridal shop in Redemption. Bliss Bridal Salon on Main Street."

He tore his thoughts from the fantasy and listened when she began babbling about a pig and a pecan and a purse without a phone charger. When she finally wound down, she left Tucker shaking his head at her foolishness. He held up his hand. "Let me get this straight. You weren't joking about being lost? You literally don't know where you are?"

"No. Not exactly." She lifted her chin, and her voice sharpened defensively. "I know I'm still in Central Texas. I'm somewhere between I-35 and I-45. I'm north of Austin. I think."

He slowly shook his head. "Where is your car? How far have you walked?"

"That way." She hooked her thumb over her shoulder. "Maybe two or three miles. I've been walking a while."

"In those shoes?"

She gave a rueful smile. "They're all I have with me. I left in a rush. I waited for quite some time at the scene of the accident, but nobody ever came along. I went looking for a farmhouse or a town. I never guessed I'd have to walk this far. This isn't West Texas. It's not even the Hill Country. I thought for sure I would have found help before now." She paused a moment, then added, "Do you by chance have any water with you that you wouldn't mind sharing?"

"I do." Not by chance, but because he was prepared.

Tucker was always prepared. He retrieved his stainless steel water bottle and offered it to her.

"Thank you. I was starting to get really thirsty. I usually carry some in my car, but today . . ." Her eyes filled with fresh tears, and she rapidly blinked them back. "Today hasn't been a good day. I've done a bunch of stupid things today."

Tucker could have agreed with her, but he didn't like to pile on. While she quenched her thirst, he said, "I have a first aid kit. Why don't you let me tend to your scrapes and take you back to your car? We can note its exact location for the tow truck, and then I'll take you someplace where it's comfortable to wait while you make arrangements to get to wherever you need to be."

"That would be great." She handed him his phone. "Thanks. I really appreciate it."

"My pleasure. Glad I can help."

He retrieved his kit and cleansed the abrasions. The wounds were minor, but marred a tanned, flawless complexion.

"Am I going to get a black eye?" she asked as he smoothed an antibiotic cream over a scrape below her right eye.

"Hmm?" Tucker murmured, distracted by the soft, silky texture of her skin.

"It's tender. Is it bruising?"

"Oh. Not sure. Fifty-fifty, I'd guess. Your cheekbones did their work." Great cheekbones. Really great cheekbones. Bet she had a bit of Slavic blood in her DNA. Or maybe Comanche or Apache, if her people were from this part of the world.

Tucker finished his ministrations, stifled the urge to kiss her boo-boo, and stepped away. Five minutes later, when she sat behind him on his bike, her arms wrapped around his waist, he decided it really was his pleasure. When was the last time he'd been held in any manner by a woman? Too long ago to easily recall. How depressing was that?

Gillian directed him to the site of the accident, a wooded section of land divided by a creek. Upon seeing the crushed front end of the silver crossover SUV smashed into the trunk of a huge pecan tree, Tucker grimaced. The vehicle was definitely not drivable. She was lucky to have walked away with only minor injuries.

He glanced at her and advised, "Next time, hit the hog."

Having pinpointed her vehicle's location, Gillian called first her auto club to arrange for a tow and then a brother named Mike to come pick her up. When it turned out that her brother was on a bird hunt with her father in South Texas, Tucker offered to drive her all the way home to Redemption.

"Oh, no. I couldn't possibly put you out that way."

"I was headed that general direction anyway. No bother."

"That's terribly kind of you, Tucker, but there's someone else who will help me." Then, with obvious reluctance, she placed a call to someone named Jeremy.

The gentleman in Tucker told him not to eavesdrop. The scoundrel listened avidly. It quickly became apparent that Jeremy was her boyfriend, and the pair had argued, which probably accounted for her tears and inattention to her driving. Tucker had to give the guy credit, though. As soon as she mentioned wrecking her car, the tone of the conversation changed. Jeremy was obviously concerned about her.

The brittle mood that had clung to Gillian since

he first spotted her eased somewhat. She shifted the phone away from her mouth, looked at Tucker, and said, "My friend says we're about twenty minutes east of Temple. He's at a golf resort about half an hour south. Would you mind taking me to the Buc-ee's on I-35? Or if it's too much out of your way, he'll meet me here."

Buc-ee's was a quirky convenience store chain with a cartoon beaver as its logo, whose stores boasted hundreds of parking spaces, dozens of gas pumps, and the cleanest bathrooms in America. With less than fifty stores, Buc-ee's had developed a cultlike following in Texas and beyond. "I'll be glad to take you to visit the big beaver. I try never to pass up the roasted nuts."

"The banana pudding is spectacular," she advised before returning to her call to establish a meeting place inside the large store with her friend. "Thank you, Jeremy," she said. "I appreciate the help."

Whatever Jeremy said in reply caused her to stiffen. Her tone held some bite when she responded. "With any luck, you'll still be able to get in nine holes before dark. I'll see you at Buc-ee's."

She ended the call and handed Tucker's phone back to him while wearing a false smile. Her eyes glittered with pique.

Trouble in paradise, Tucker concluded as he slipped his phone back into his pocket. Had her boyfriend complained about leaving the golf course to aid the damsel in distress? Ol' Jeremy must not be very bright.

Gillian used her key fob to open her vehicle's rear door. She removed a purple nylon backpack. Curious, Tucker observed, "Something tells me that isn't a well-stocked go bag."

"It's my gym bag. I carry all my essentials with me."

Tucker snorted. "Like a compass? Fire starter? Water purifier? Maps?"

Her chin came up. She held her bag open to display its contents. "Moisturizer. Shampoo. Sunscreen. No sneakers, unfortunately, but I do have a pair of shorts, which will make riding a motorcycle while wearing a dress less, um, awkward."

Tucker gallantly resisted the urge to drop his gaze to the short hem of her skirt. "The sunscreen is defensible. The rest, not so much." He reached into the bag and checked the SPF number on the label. Fifty. Then his tone grew serious as he added, "Seriously, though, Gillian. I hope this incident has shown you the importance of keeping basic supplies with you when you travel. Have you realized that we haven't seen another vehicle since I stopped to help you? You have no water, you walked away from the shelter of your car, and there's a cold front on its way. You very easily could have been stranded overnight, and feral hogs aren't the only wild animals around. At the very least, you should have water and a decent pair of shoes with you."

"I know. I know. Believe me, I've learned my lesson. I can't thank you—" Gillian looked up at him with a rueful smile on her face. Their gazes met and held. "Enough."

In that moment, sexual awareness flashed between them. Her eyes subtly widened. Nervously, her tongue moistened her lips. When she ever so slightly leaned toward him, Tucker took it as an invitation. His fingers drifted under her chin, lifting up her face. He bent his head and brushed her lips with his, gently, tentatively at first. When she responded, he let his fingers delve into that glorious hair of hers and angled her head to allow him to deepen the kiss.

She tasted of spearmint and smelled faintly of pumpkin spice, the air freshener he'd spied hanging from her rearview mirror, he deduced. When her arms snaked up and clasped around his neck, Tucker slipped his free hand around her waist and pulled her tighter. *Sizzle. Pow. Boom. Welcome back to Texas, McBride.*

Abruptly, the moment ended when she pulled away. Her blue eyes were wide and panicky, and she brought her hands up to cover the cheeks that had gone as red as her dress. "Oh, no. No. No. No. I'm sorry."

"I'm not."

She took another step back, her hands extended palms out toward him. "That shouldn't have happened. I'm engaged. Well, maybe technically I'm not still engaged because I threw his ring at him and told him we were through and to grow up, but it wasn't a real breakup. I don't think. We had a terrible fight, but he *is* coming to get me. And he had a tee time."

"Such sacrifice," Tucker drawled.

"I'm so sorry. I'm not myself. I don't do things like this. Never mind that he accused me of it. I'm not that kind of woman. This has been a really, really bad day, and I'm truly not myself."

Taking pity on her, Tucker attempted to reassure her with a grin. "Well, damn. Why is it the goddesses are always taken? No harm done from my perspective. Consider it a friendly little thank-you kiss."

"I'm never that friendly. Honestly, I'm not."

"Don't forget the thank-you part. I deserved a big thank-you."

"Yes, you do, but I usually send a little gift to say thank you. A bottle of wine. My favorite barbecue seasoning. Local honey."

"Sweet and savory." Tucker nodded. "Same thing, just a different delivery method."

"I think maybe it's time to change the subject." She closed her eyes and visibly gathered herself before looking up and offering him a friendly smile. "So, you lectured me about my go bag. Educate me, Mr. McBride. What do you keep in yours?"

"Water filter. Flashlight. Matches. A stick of fatwood." Tucker hesitated. His lips twitched. He shouldn't . . . he *really* shouldn't . . . but she did ask. "Condoms."

Following a beat of silence, she asked, "Fatwood?"

"Tinder. It burns . . . hot."

"Ah. I see." She licked those bee-stung lips again and cleared her throat. "Jeremy keeps a supply bag in his car."

I'll just bet he does.

"I'll have to ask him what he keeps in it."

"You do that." The fun had gone out of this particular game, and Tucker took another step back. "You have everything? We should probably get going. Don't want to keep your maybe-still-a-fiancé waiting."

Gillian winced. "Yes. Yes, I'm ready." This time when she climbed behind him on the bike, she held herself away from him as much as possible.

Nevertheless, Tucker sensed her presence like warm sunshine on a cold winter's day. The drive into Temple passed in a flash, while at the same, the minutes dragged by. When he made the turn into the parking lot at Buc-ee's, he admitted to himself that he'd be sorry for this little adventure to come to an end.

He also knew he wasn't really in the mood to meet

ol' Jeremy. So, he pulled up at one of the sixty-plus gas pumps, switched off his motor, and prepared to say goodbye to his passenger.

"There's Jeremy's car," she said, pointing toward a line of parked vehicles, a mix of pickups, SUVs, and a few sedans. "He beat us here."

"Good. My Good Samaritan work is done."

"A Good Samaritan indeed. I can't thank you enough, Tucker. Here." Gillian started to reach into her purse. "Let me buy you a tank of gas."

Tucker laid his hand over hers. "No. Absolutely not."

"But you went out of your way—"

"No, I didn't. Like I told you, I want a bag of roasted nuts." Roasted nuts seemed an appropriate choice at the moment.

"Okay, then. Come inside and let me buy you those."

"You've already thanked me, Gillian."

"Don't remind me!" She cast an anguished gaze toward the man who'd just emerged from inside the building, a blond, pretty-boy prepster, who wore a pink golf shirt tucked into black slacks and designer sunglasses propped atop his head.

Jeremy. Tucker suddenly wanted to put his fist through the fellow's pearly whites. At the same time, he wanted to soothe Gillian's troubled soul. Quietly, he said, "Don't fret yourself. Don't make it out to be a bigger deal than it was. I'm a soldier home from the wars and feeling a little lost. It did me good to rescue a damsel in distress. You have been a nice welcome home to me."

She tore her gaze away from Jeremy and looked at Tucker, a faint smile flirting with her lips. "Has anyone said that to you yet? Welcome home?"

"No. Not yet."

"In that case, let me be the first." Then, in front of the drivers and passengers of the dozens of cars lined up at the gas pumps to buy fuel, her maybe-ex-fiancé, and the big beaver Buc-ee himself, Gillian Thacker went up on her toes and planted a kiss on Tucker's mouth. "Welcome home, soldier. Welcome back to Texas."

She turned around and dashed toward the Buc-ee's front door and the man who apparently owned her heart.

Tucker pumped gas into his motorcycle and watched Gillian and Jeremy exchange an embrace before climbing into a late-model BMW sports car. Moments later, it swung out of its parking spot and turned his way. The gas pump clanked and the hose nozzle shut off as the car stopped in front of him.

The driver's side window slid down. Jeremy called out, "Hey, man. Thank you for your service."

Tucker smiled and gave a little salute. The extension of his middle finger was so slight, he doubted the other man noticed it. *Asshole.*

The window rose. The car pulled away and turned onto the service road. As the Beemer merged onto the interstate highway headed north and disappeared, Tucker felt like it took the sunshine away with it.

Gillian Thacker had been a nice diversion, but that was over now. She'd ridden off into the sunset that was traffic on I-35, and now the gloom that had been riding his shoulders for months returned. He shoved his hands into the back pockets of his jeans and silently compiled a sitrep.

Currently, he stood at a gas pump at a Buc-ee's in Texas. Without a woman. Without a job. Without a purpose.

Crap. What the hell had he done? Who the hell was he now?

The army was his life. His identity. He'd devoted himself to the job, and what he'd done had been valuable. How many people were alive today because he'd been there to put boots on the ground, because he'd had the knowledge and the training and the desire and the balls to do what needed doing? He'd stopped counting years ago. He'd made a difference!

And dammit, he'd let the politicians win. He'd let the bureaucracy win. *Quitter.*

Shame rolled over him like a West Texas dust storm, but it was too late for second thoughts. You didn't get a do-over when you separated from the service. Not that he really wanted one. He just wanted to be able to live peacefully in his own skin again.

Tucker muttered a curse. No sense crying over a spilt bag of Buc-ee's Beaver Nuggets. The deed was done. He'd picked up his marbles and gone home to Texas, and now he'd have to learn to live with the decision.

Tucker gave one last glance toward the interstate where the lovely wedding-gown princess had ridden off with her tee-box prince before he turned and strode toward the convenience store entrance. At least there was one craving he could satisfy. He looked up at the bucked-tooth beaver above the door and muttered, "Nuts."

Chapter Three

On her hands and knees and drowning in a sea of ivory satin and lace, Gillian reached blindly for the tab numbered twelve. Her fingers brushed a cotton rectangle, and she grabbed it tight. She dipped her head below a fan of scratchy tulle and searched for a number. Fourteen. "Grrr."

She shook her head, wiggling deeper, feeling like a dog nuzzling through a bowl of boring kibble to find the prized peanut butter treat. Her engagement ring snagged on a thread. She shook it free and grabbed again. There. A glance revealed a one and a two. Victory! She threaded the button marked twelve through the twelve tab, and then traced her way to thirteen and beyond. Finally, with all eighteen buttons fastened, she scooted out, rolled back on her heels, and asked the bride-to-be, "Well? What do you think?"

Caroline Carruthers couldn't take her gaze off the reflection in the mirror. "I think, maybe, oh, Gillian. This might be the one."

Gillian shared a knowing smile with the other person in the room, her mother, Barbara, before observing, "That's what you said about the first three you tried on, Caroline."

"I know!" The lovely dark-haired, brown-eyed woman who was engaged to Jackson McBride moaned. "This is too hard. All the gowns are beautiful."

"It helps when you have the body of a goddess."

"You're one to talk, Ms. Mile-Long Legs. No way could I wear a body-hugging wedding dress like the one you chose."

Gillian wrinkled her nose. "Wait and see what else Mom has chosen for you to try on. You'll be eating your words."

Caroline looked at her reflection. "Maybe I'll stop at this one. It makes me feel like a princess."

Wearing an indulgent smile, Barbara asked, "Princess Caroline, are you ready to step out and show your ladies-in-waiting?"

"Sure."

Gillian held back the dressing room's curtain, and Caroline stepped into what they called the parlor. The area had a raised dais and mirrors placed to allow the bride to view herself from every angle, adequate seating for twelve—fifteen, if people sat close—and a sideboard for refreshments for the "bride tribe" to sample while they waited. Caroline's tribe was small, but special, and included mutual friends Maisy Baldwin and Angelica Blessing, along with Caroline's late husband's sister, Elizabeth Garner. Pixyish, blond maid of honor Maisy owned the local florist. Angelica worked for the McBride family as innkeeper for their bed-and-breakfast resort in Enchanted Canyon. Despite being at least three decades older than Caroline, Maisy, and Gillian, Angelica had become a dear friend of theirs over the past year. She had a kind heart, caustic wit, and—with her long red hair and affinity for sparkles, bangles, and jangles—a sense of style unlike anyone else in Redemption, Texas.

"Oh, wow," Maisy said, waving a carrot stick for emphasis. "That is spectacular. Love the boat neck."

"It's very flattering," Angelica agreed. "Very princess-y."

Caroline held out the skirt and twirled. "That's what I thought."

"We can't do a ball gown style of bustle with many of our gowns, but it's perfect for this dress," Barbara explained, bracing her hands on her slim hips as she studied the bride with a keen, hazel-eyed gaze.

"You look lovely." Elizabeth lifted her phone and snapped a few photos. "This promises to be a tough choice."

"I know." Caroline's teeth tugged at her lower lip. "Maybe I should stick with something simpler. After all, it is a second wedding for both Jackson and me. I don't want to choose something inappropriate."

"Don't be silly." Elizabeth gave her head a single, definitive shake. "You're the bride. You can wear whatever you want. Besides, you have impeccable taste. You would never choose anything inappropriate."

"Nor have I chosen anything inappropriate for you to try on," Barbara said. "Bliss Salon does have a reputation to uphold." Following a moment's pause, she added, "I have selected a silver gown for you to consider."

"Silver?" Caroline repeated, interest lighting her eyes.

Barbara smiled as she tucked an errant strand of her chin-length, highlighted blond hair behind her ear. "Want to try it next?"

"Yes." Caroline took one last look at the princess

gown, made one more twirl, then headed for the dressing room. Gillian trailed after her, and while her mother went to get the next selection from the rack of gowns she'd set aside for this morning's appointment, Gillian helped Caroline out of the princess gown. They chatted about her choices as the bride slipped into the white satin robe that Bliss provided, and the saleswoman returned the dress to its hanger. Gillian was buttoning the last covered button when her mother swept in carrying an armful of sparkling silver lace.

"Gillian, I've got this one. Why don't you put on your bridesmaid hat and sit in the parlor with the others?"

"Sounds like a plan." Gillian exited the dressing room and took a seat in time to hear Maisy saying to Angelica, ". . . surprised when I ran into Tucker McBride at the lumber yard. First time I've seen him since Thanksgiving."

Gillian's ears perked up. Since his return to Redemption, her erstwhile rescuer had been an invisible man.

"We don't see much of him at the inn either," Angelica replied. "He stops in occasionally for dinner, but mostly he keeps to himself. He's been spending a lot of time exploring Enchanted Canyon."

"Jackson has mentioned that Tucker loves the outdoors." Maisy sipped her champagne, then addressed Gillian. "You've met Tucker, haven't you? The beautiful brown-eyed McBride? Not to be confused with the gorgeous green-eyed McBride or the sexy silver-eyed one."

Gillian hesitated. She'd never mentioned her farm-to-market misadventure last fall to either her parents or her friends. Doing so would have meant admitting to the fight with Jeremy. Since they'd reconciled before returning to Redemption, she hadn't seen the need. As far as she could tell, Tucker hadn't said anything to anyone either. He obviously hadn't told Jackson because he would have mentioned it to Caroline, who certainly would have asked Gillian about it. "Caroline introduced us at the bookstore's Christmas party."

"He was there? I didn't see him."

Gillian shrugged. "I'm under the impression it was a brief visit. It was a packed house, and he didn't seem very comfortable in the crowd."

Angelica clucked her tongue. "That poor boy. It's a good thing his shoulders are so broad. Otherwise, he might topple from the weight of his burden."

Maisy, Gillian, and even Elizabeth, who lived in Austin and wasn't part of the local community, all turned avid looks Angelica's way. Maisy demanded, "What burden?"

Gillian took a celery stick from the crudités tray and nibbled one end, watching Angelica closely. She was curious about Tucker McBride, not only because of what had happened between them the day they'd met, but because he'd been such a recluse since his return to town. At the time, she'd been glad not to run into him on the streets of Redemption—she remained embarrassed to this day over her foolish flight from Bastrop, and she still felt guilty about the first kiss. Nevertheless, she found it curious how he had all but disappeared into Enchanted Canyon upon his arrival.

Angelica brushed a cookie crumb from her orange broomstick skirt. "It's not my place to say."

Maisy narrowed her eyes. "Is this something he's told you, or one of your hunches?"

Angelica lifted her chin. Her large hoop earrings swung. "Darling, my *hunches* are golden. Besides, all one needs do to recognize that Tucker is burdened is to watch his interactions with dear, sweet Haley. It's obvious they are simpatico."

"Really?" Gillian asked. Jackson's seven-year-old daughter, Haley, was dealing with the aftereffects of the recent private plane crash that had claimed the lives of several people close to her, including her beloved Poppins, who'd been more mother than nanny. "Has Tucker lost someone?"

"Not some*one*. Some*thing*."

Anything else Angelica might have said on the subject was interrupted when Gillian's mother swept back the dressing room curtain, and Caroline stepped out wearing the silver lace gown. Following a moment of stunned silence, Maisy said, "Just kill me now. I will never look that good in a wedding dress. On the off chance I ever have the opportunity to wear one, that is."

Elizabeth didn't speak, but simply clasped her hands in delight as her eyes filled with tears. Angelica fanned her face and said, "Ooh la la."

Caroline met Gillian's gaze with a look that Gillian readily recognized after five years of operating Bliss Bridal Salon. Caroline had found her dress. The bride-to-be asked, "Yes?"

"Jackson will swallow his tongue."

Beaming, Caroline studied her reflection from all angles, twirled in a slow circle, and finally said, "It's perfect. I love the color. I love the style. I love the fabric. I love it. I absolutely love it. This is it. This is the one."

Gillian met her mother's gaze. She knew Barbara had three more gowns selected for Caroline to try.

She also knew her mother would return them to stock without saying another word about them.

"Another satisfied bride," Barbara said with a smile.

"Actually, that's what happens when Jackson takes it off her," Maisy corrected.

They all shared a laugh, then Barbara and Caroline discussed a schedule for fittings and the option of a veil. When that was done, Caroline's bride tribe prepared to depart for a local spa where they had mani-pedi appointments to be followed by lunch at an area winery. Gillian climbed the stairs to her tiny office to retrieve her purse, then met her mother in the stock room. "You sure it's okay for me to play bridesmaid? You don't need me here, Mom?"

"Nope. I've got it covered. Aunt Cathy's coming by to help. We have a bride from Lubbock coming in with her mother and grandmother."

"That's good."

Gillian turned to exit through the salon's front door to the sidewalk, where the others waited for her. She was halfway to the door when her mother called, "Just promise me you'll be back in time for our four o'clock appointment."

Gillian stopped. She'd heard a note in her mother's voice that gave her pause. She knew her mother. Something was up. "Who do we have coming in at four?"

When a full five seconds ticked by without Barbara providing the name, Gillian's stomach sank. She had a bad feeling about this. *No. Please, no.* "Mother?"

Barbara steepled her hands in front of her mouth and met her daughter's wary gaze.

"No! Tell me it's not Lindsay Grant!"

"I wish I could."

Gillian groaned aloud. Lindsay Grant was Bliss Salon's most infamous customer. She and Gillian had been sorority sisters at the University of Texas, and her parents owned a vacation home not far from Redemption. She and her mother had visited Bliss Bridal on the day the shop opened and purchased the first gown Bliss Bridal had sold. On the bridezilla scale, Lindsay was a Tyrannosaurus rex, and by the time they delivered the dress, Barbara and Gillian had been ready to close up shop.

Lindsay had come back two years later to buy a gown for her second wedding. The experience had been just as joyous for Barbara and Gillian as the first. Then last month, Gillian and Jeremy had run into Lindsay at a charity ball in Austin, fresh off her second divorce and escorted by a new victim . . . um . . . man. She'd mentioned to Gillian that she'd see her again soon. When sharing the news with her mother the next day, Barbara suggested declaring bankruptcy—never mind that Bliss made them both a tidy profit each year.

"Lindsay and her bridal party are scheduled for four o'clock."

That meant they'd show up at four thirty and be here until eight.

"And since I'm confessing, there is one more detail you should know," Barbara continued. "When Lindsay made the appointment and provided the number of people in her party, she mentioned the name of her matron of honor—Erica Chadwick."

"You are kidding me."

"I'm afraid not."

Gillian closed her eyes. Erica had been another sorority sister of hers, and the two of them had been "frenemies" since the second semester of freshman year when Gillian's superior grade point average earned her the spot in the sorority house that Erica thought should be hers. It hadn't helped things any when the hot guy in their accounting class who was also a back-up quarterback for the Longhorns had turned down Erica's invitation to the spring formal and invited Gillian to the football banquet. After that, Erica made it her mission in life to never lose out to Gillian in any way, shape, or form again.

The woman was smart, pretty, outgoing, and could be as venomous as a baby rattlesnake. After college, Erica had gone to law school and now practiced corporate law in Dallas—the perfect ocean for a quintessential mean-girl shark to swim in, in Gillian's opinion.

Groaning, Gillian brought a hand up to her forehead. She dramatically announced, "I forgot to tell you, Mom. I came down with the plague this morning."

"Ha. Ha. Don't even think about deserting me, Gillian Michelle. I'm not without ammunition here. All I need to do is mention your new business to Lindsay. She was Bliss's first bride. Maybe Blissful Events could—"

"Now, that's just cruel, Mother," Gillian interrupted. "Almost as cruel as failing to mention our four o'clock before now."

"Needs must."

The front door bells jangled, and Maisy stuck her head inside. "You coming, Gillian?"

"In a minute. Y'all go on, and I'll catch up." When the door closed once again, Gillian met her mother's gaze. "You know, Mom, we could both catch the plague."

"It's a lovely thought, but no."

"Want me to bring you back something for lunch? A martini, maybe?"

"Thank you, but I'd better skip it. After we finish with the Lubbock bride, I'm going to close the shop and take Aunt Cathy to the Bluebonnet and get my sugar on."

"A worthy substitute for alcohol."

"I know you'll have a healthy lunch at the spa. Want me to bring back a piece of lemon chess pie for you?"

Gillian pictured herself wearing her own wedding gown, and then imagined Lindsay Grant standing in front of a rack of Bliss dresses. "Sure. I still have eight weeks to watch my calories. If plague is off the table, then pie needs to be on it. Pie drunk might be the only way I make it through the afternoon."

Standing at the base of a century-old pecan tree whose winter-bare branches extended over a spring-fed creek in Enchanted Canyon, Tucker kicked over a piece of deadwood and observed, "This is one of my favorite ways to spend an afternoon."

"Digging for worms?" asked Haley. A look of innocent curiosity gleamed in eyes the same spring-green color as her father's.

Tucker reached down and ruffled the seven-year-old child's blond curls. "Passing time with my best girl."

He pulled his fixed blade knife from the sheath he wore on his belt, squatted down on his boot heels, and used the knife's tip to dig through the soft, loose black soil where the log had lain. Beside him, Haley mimicked his pose and sifted through the dirt with a stick.

The sweet scent of fresh earth rose on the still afternoon air as Tucker flicked aside pieces of decaying wood and plant life, his keen-eyed gaze searching for his prey.

"How deep do we have to dig?" asked Haley.

"That depends on the season and locality. This time of year, the little buggers burrow beneath the frost line, and in some places, that can be very deep. But here in the canyon, we've had a mild winter, so I expect we'll find something pretty easily."

In less than a minute, Haley's small hand shot forward, her index finger extended. "There's one!"

"Sharp eye, sugar bug." He plucked a fat earthworm from the dirt and placed it onto the red bandana he'd spread upon the ground. "Keep looking. We need a few more."

Haley's brow furrowed as she moved the dirt. "If we find a bunch and have extras, you could eat one of them."

Tucker smirked. The child had been obsessed with the idea of unusual sources of protein since she'd watched a television show that touched on the subject not long ago. "If we find plenty of extras, you can eat one too."

She wrinkled her little button of a nose. "No. I'd rather feed the worms to the fish, and then eat the fish. I like fish."

"Smart cookie."

She grinned impishly up at him. "I like cookies better than fish. We should fage for those."

"Forage," Tucker corrected. "The word is *forage*. So, what bait would you suggest for catching cookies?"

"That's easy. All we have to do is ask Miss Angelica and say please."

"Good to know. Although, I probably won't have as good of luck as you do when I go fishing for cookies in the inn's kitchen. I don't have Miss Angelica wrapped around my little finger like an earthworm like you do."

Haley giggled. "That's silly." Then her smile faded and sadness dimmed her gaze. "Poppins always said I had her wrapped around my little finger. She didn't say the worm part, though."

The pain in her voice broke Tucker's heart.

He worried about her. Her parents worried about her. Most of the adults in Haley's life worried about her. Even her grief counselor agreed that Haley's thoughts too often focused on the dark—on death and dying and loneliness and loss. Under the circumstances, it was understandable, but they all hoped to begin seeing some lasting healing of Haley's spirit soon. The grief counselor had suggested that Haley needed tools to feel more in control over her world. Angelica had insisted that Haley needed to spend more time in Enchanted Canyon.

Tucker agreed wholeheartedly. Heaven knew the canyon was doing him a world of good.

He'd arrived in Redemption in September with a chip on his shoulder, self-pity in his heart, and shame on his soul. Almost immediately, the plane crash gave him a reminder of the real problems life had to offer. A job change meant diddly-squat when compared to the upheavals Haley faced.

With Jackson away from Redemption dealing with fallout from the accident, Tucker had spent those first weeks in the Hill Country alone, exploring Enchanted Canyon and living off the land. The place began to work its magic on him, and the turmoil in his spirit slowly eased. Nothing like landing a three-pound bass and cooking it over the friction fire he'd started before going to bed beneath the cozy, warm shelter he'd built to make a man feel competent.

It was that realization that had given Tucker the idea to teach Haley wilderness skills. Hence, this afternoon's outing on a day when school dismissed at noon for teacher in-service.

In less than three minutes, they had five earthworms on the kerchief. Tucker offered the fattest one to Haley. "Okay, sugar bug. Are you ready?"

Her eyes went round as a Bluebonnet Café peach pie. "I was kidding about eating them!"

"I know that. I'm talking about the goal we set when we started on our hike today."

Haley's teeth nibbled at her bottom lip as she studied the wriggling, four-inch worm. "I don't know, Uncle T."

Tucker was technically her first cousin once removed, but he and her dad, Jackson, had always been more like brothers than cousins, so *uncle* fit. "What's holding you back?"

"I'm an awfully girly girl."

"I dunno about that. Girly girls don't talk about eating worms all the time."

"Talking and doing are different." She never took her gaze from the wriggling worm. "I'm the girliest girl in second grade. I never get grubby."

"If you don't want to go through with this, that's perfectly all right." Tucker returned the worm to the bandana. Her teeth tugged at her bottom lip. "But even girly girls need to know how to take care of themselves in a 'mergency," Haley said.

"That's true." He waited, giving her time to make up her mind.

"I saw on National Geographic channel that Yellowstone Park is a volcano even though it's not a mountain. What if it blows up and everybody dies but me? I should learn how to catch a fish, so I could eat and stay alive."

Poor thing. Tucker wanted to take her in his arms and hug her tight and promise her Yellowstone wasn't about to blow, but that wasn't his job here this afternoon. Today was about helping Haley reach a point where she once again felt safe and secure, so she'd stop dwelling on the dark. "Fishing is a basic life skill that's not only useful, it's fun."

"Unless you're the worm."

"Or the fish, for that matter. Lucky for us, we're living life at the top of the food chain."

At that, she finally looked away from the worm and up at Tucker, indecision clouding her eyes. Tucker decided that if he didn't press her a bit, they'd be here until dark. He winked at her and asked, "What's it gonna be, sugar bug? Ready to get grubby?"

After a long moment, she nodded. "I'll do it."

"Let's go get our poles."

On her previous visit, they'd hiked into the woods and harvested branches to fashion into fishing poles. He'd decided against using a vine for line—the girl was only seven, after all—but he'd given her a little essentials pack for her backpack that included monofilament line and hooks. Now, Haley scampered back to where they'd left their poles propped against the trunk of a creek side cottonwood tree near the spot where they'd decided to fish. She picked up her pole and held it out to him. "Do you want to check my knot, Uncle T?"

"Already did. You tied a good clinch knot." They'd

practiced knots over the weekend. He squatted down, opened the bandana, and held it out toward her.

"Okay, so . . ." She exhaled a bracing breath and reached for an earthworm. "Do I just poke it?"

"No. We'll do a worm weave. Watch me." Tucker found the other worm and proceeded to teach her how to properly bait her hook. For the girliest girl in second grade, she did an acceptable job. Soon, two baited hooks floated in the slowly flowing creek.

Less than five minutes after sinking her worm and with her gaze locked on the hunk of bark they'd used as a bobber, Haley asked, "How long does it take to catch a fish?"

"Ya never know. Just have to be patient and keep your eye on the prize."

Thoroughly at peace with the world, his own fishing pole gripped lazily by his right hand, Tucker leaned back against the trunk of a cottonwood hugging the riverbank and watched his cousin's daughter. She had leaves in her hair, a streak of dirt on her cheek, and worm guts on her T-shirt where she'd wiped her hands. Love swept through him, along with a powerful dose of yearning. He'd like to have a little girl wearing worm guts of his own someday.

"What kind of fish do you think we'll catch, Uncle T?" she asked, pulling her line from the water to check the status of her worm.

"None, if you don't leave your hook where it belongs. On these little hooks, I expect we'll catch perch. Then we'll use one of the perch as bait on a bigger hook and try for a cat."

"Cat*fish*," Haley corrected. "You're not fooling me. Catfish are really ugly."

"They sure do taste pretty, though."

"I'm a little scared that we might catch one."

"Why is that?"

"'Cause I'd have to kill it and chop its head off and scoop out its guts, and that's a lot more than sticking a worm. I think if I'm stranded, I'd rather just eat berries."

"Well, for one thing, you don't scoop out a fish's guts or chop off its head when you clean it. Not if you do it right, anyway. Second, that's a lesson for you on down the road. You need to take things one step at a time, sugar bug. Whatever fish we catch today, I'll clean. You can watch the process or not, that's up to you."

She visibly brightened. "Okay. I like that plan."

Not a bad afternoon outing, Tucker decided later as twilight began to fall. They'd caught two black bass, three perch, and two big old cats with plenty of meat. Tucker had planned to run Haley into town and drop her at Caroline's bookstore when they were done, but they'd caught enough to have an old-fashioned fish fry that night. "How about we invite your dad and Caroline out for supper? We can build a bonfire."

"Yes! I love bonfires. Can we roast marshmallows?"

"Of course." Tucker listened with satisfied contentment as Haley used his phone to call her father to request the change in plans. Afterward, they hiked the short distance back to the spot beside the swimming hole where Tucker lived in the Airstream trailer that once had been Jackson's. There, Haley watched the fish-cleaning process with more interest than squeamishness—a heartsick girly girl happily getting her outdoors on.

This is good, Tucker thought. Good for the heart.

Good for the soul. Good, for both Haley and him. Angelica Blessing said that troubled souls could find peace in Enchanted Canyon.

Maybe, just maybe, she was on to something.

Chapter Four

"I take it back," Gillian said as she flipped Bliss Salon's OPEN sign to read CLOSED. "Lindsay isn't the T. rex of bridezillas. She's the Spinosaurus."

"I'm not familiar with that dinosaur," her mother replied as she rehung the gown Lindsay had left piled on the floor.

"I wasn't either, but I googled *most dangerous dinosaur* after she yelled at Erica."

Barbara gave an amused snort. "I hate to defend Lindsay, but Erica deserved it. I'd forgotten how much I disliked that girl. She's very passive-aggressive, isn't she? It wasn't kind of her to constantly call attention to the size of Lindsay's hips. That's not appropriate behavior for a maid of honor."

"That's typical Erica," Gillian said with a shrug. "Lindsay's in love, and apparently, Erica is fresh off a bad relationship, so she's going to have her claws out."

"Jealousy is such an ugly trait. Despite all that professional success she made sure to share with us, Erica is obviously an unhappy woman."

"Bless her heart," Gillian drawled.

Mother and daughter shared a smile, then Barbara glanced at the clock. "All in all, it was a successful appointment, and I won't complain. We got them out of here only an hour and a half past closing time."

"You did a brilliant sales job, Mother. I'm proud of you."

"Thank you, dear." Barbara disappeared into the dressing room and returned a moment later with her arms full of a wedding gown. "Want to put this one back on the mannequin for me?"

Gillian frowned. "Are we switching out our display window already?"

"No. I want to display this one in the parlor for a bit. This is my favorite dress in the shop right now."

"It is gorgeous," Gillian agreed. She accepted the dress from her mother and got to work dressing the naked mannequin in the corner.

Aside from Lindsay Grant and Erica Chadwick, today had been a lovely day. Caroline was so happy with her gown. It had been fun to watch—

"Ow!"

Barbara's pained exclamation interrupted her thoughts. "What's wrong?"

"Nothing," Barbara responded. "Poked myself with a pin. How are you coming with the bustle?"

"I may get it fastened by Thursday," Gillian grumbled. For the second time that day, she knelt on her hands and knees beneath yards of satin and lace, warring with the buttons and tabs of a ball gown bustle. When she finally accomplished her mission, she backed out of the skirt and looked up at her mother. "I can't tell you how glad I am that the gown Caroline chose only requires ten tabs to bustle. Makes my bridesmaid's duties much less stressful. This is some bustle, Mom."

"I know," Barbara Thacker agreed. She bent over beside Gillian and gave the satin skirt a fluff. "You have to admit the ball gown bustle is perfect for this dress. Didn't Caroline say it made her feel like a princess?"

"She did. This gown is definitely fit for a princess bride."

Barbara flicked her gaze toward her daughter and casually suggested, "Perhaps you should try it on."

Gillian looked down and dusted invisible dirt off her black slacks. Then, while rolling up the sleeves of her crisp, white cotton shirt, she met her mother's gaze. "Mom, I have my dress. It's a beautiful dress. It's just what I want."

Barbara hesitated a moment, and Gillian braced herself. Her mother was obviously choosing her words with care. So far, the two of them had navigated the treacherous wedding-planning waters with relative ease, mostly because their wishes ran along the same wavelength. But wedding gowns were Barbara Thacker's business, her area of expertise. Her art. She knew every dress in her shop. She knew what alterations could be done to each gown to fulfill a bride-to-be's dreams. And most apropos in this case, she had created the number one rule regarding sales at Bliss Bridal Salon: When it comes to choosing her dream dress, the bride is always right. The mother of the bride's opinion only matters if it matters to the bride.

Gillian sensed that this MOB was about to break the rule.

Don't get defensive. Don't get angry. Mom feels passionately about this, she's the best mother in the world, and you need to let her have her say.

"We've danced around this for months," Barbara finally stated. "Let me say this once, and I'll never bring it up again. Fair enough?"

"Okay." Gillian swallowed hard.

"You are planning a fabulous wedding. Your organizational skills, your attention to detail, your instincts and imagination and eye for design—the planning process plays to all of your strengths. For a year now, you've poured your heart and soul and energy into creating the perfect day for you and Jeremy. It's going to be beautiful, and you're going to be beautiful, and our guests are going to have a spectacular time. Of that, I have no doubt."

And here comes the but.

"But." Barbara reached down and cupped Gillian's cheek in her palm. "All the hard work, all the planning, all the dreaming—I don't want you to look back on your wedding with any regrets. That's why I'm about to break rule number one."

Bingo!

"I'm afraid you will someday regret your choice of wedding gown. Oh, it's a gorgeous dress. I admit that. It fits you and flatters you, and no one who sees you on your father's arm walking up the aisle in church will think you made a poor choice. Jeremy will certainly love it."

"He will."

"But, Gillian, that gown is not your dream gown. You are the bride. You should have *your* dream gown."

"Mom—"

"Don't try to argue otherwise." Barbara stepped away from Gillian and began pacing the room. "I am the keeper of the scrapbooks, remember? Your idea books. You were how old when you compiled the first one? Nine? Ten?"

"Nine," Gillian grumbled.

"When was the last time you looked back at the

beginning of your Pinterest wedding board? Every gown on it has one thing in common. Every gown is a princess gown. Every single one. That's been your dream dress since you were a little girl. You've never wanted to be a boho bride. It was never your style. You chose your wedding gown to please Jeremy, not yourself. You chose it because that's the style Jeremy said he loves. Not because you do."

Gillian rose to her feet. "I *do* love the dress I chose."

"I know. I love it too. Just not for *you* at *your* wedding. It's not your dream dress."

Gillian opened her mouth to protest, but her mother knew her too well. She would hear the lie, so Gillian chose to say nothing.

"Look, I understand making choices to please the man you love, I do. Grooms *should* have input into wedding decisions, but the dress—no." Barbara's gaze turned imploring. "Honey, *you* are the *bride*. It's *your* wedding gown, not Jeremy's. You've worked for almost a year now to create a fairy-tale wedding, and I can't believe you've chosen not to be true to your own vision for the most personal part of it. And your shoes!" Barbara added, holding up her hand in emphasis. "Let's not leave the shoes out of this. Sandals? Seriously? Gillian, it's always—*always*—been rhinestone-embellished heels."

"Sandals will be much more comfortable to dance in."

"That's why Kate Spade makes sparkle Keds!"

Gillian couldn't argue with her, so she didn't try. She could, however, attempt to explain. "Mom, you've seen those videos online where grooms get choked up and teary-eyed when they get their first look at their brides? I want that moment. I want my groom to look at me and see the woman of his dreams and be so overcome with emotion that he'll get misty eyed."

"Oh, Gillian." Barbara sighed. "How is it that you and I can be so much alike but at the same time so different? I don't understand young women today. From my perspective, that's like walking down the aisle saying 'Am I good enough for you?' instead of 'Here I come, you lucky bastard.' Honestly, this is not why I burned my bra when I was a teenager. It's not the feminism we fought for. It's all well and good to be the woman of his dreams, but not at the sacrifice of *your* dreams!"

"You burned your bra? I thought that happened in the sixties? You weren't a teenager in the sixties."

"I'm speaking figuratively."

"And I'm being pragmatic. It's not a dream, Mom. It's a dress."

"Well, now." Barbara folded her arms and lifted her chin. "That's a heckuva statement for the co-owner of one of the most successful bridal salons in Texas. And here I thought the reason we've done so well for the past five years is because we sell dreams in the form of dresses!"

Gillian winced. She'd stepped into that one, hadn't she? "You're right. I'm sorry. I guess I'm feeling defensive."

Now it was Barbara's turn to wince. "Oh, honey. I'm sorry too. I didn't mean to make you feel bad. The dress you chose is lovely, and you look fabulous in it."

"It's okay, Mom."

"I won't bring it up again. Those words have been burning a hole in me, and I just needed to get them out."

"I understand, and I appreciate your honesty and the fact that I can trust you to always be honest with me."

Her tone wry, Barbara asked, "Even if doing so broke rule number one?"

"Well." Gillian shrugged. "Maybe we should think of it as a professional lesson. Reminds us both just how important rule number one is in the wedding gown business.

"True." Barbara sighed and added, "If only motherhood had such a clear set of rules."

A note in her mother's voice had Gillian giving her a sharp look. Barbara's teeth nibbled at her lower lip. Not a good sign. Her mother wasn't done yet.

"Well, like the saying goes, in for a penny, in for a pound. Might as well get this off my chest too. Honey, is everything okay between you and Jeremy?"

Gillian bent over and straightened the magazines on the coffee table. Something fluttered in her stomach. Nerves. Normal bridal jitters. That's all.

She met her mother's gaze. "Why would you ask that?"

"I just, well, I've sensed some . . . I don't know . . . tension."

Gillian shrugged and shifted her gaze to the princess gown. She smoothed a wrinkle from the fabric. "Wedding planning is stressful. It's normal for couples to fight. You've been around enough brides to know that."

"So, you two *have* been fighting?"

Fighting wasn't the right word, but yes, something had changed in her relationship with Jeremy since the events in September. When they'd left the Buc-ee's in Temple that Saturday, he'd chosen to take her on to Dallas rather than back to Redemption like she'd expected, and they'd made the mutual decision to wait until they arrived at their destination to have their needed talk. Exhausted, Gillian had slept for much of the drive. After checking into a hotel downtown, they'd ordered room service and a bottle of wine. Gillian didn't drink, but the bottle was two-thirds gone before Jeremy finally opened up.

He'd admitted to getting drunk and kissing another woman while away at the symposium over Labor Day weekend.

Gillian was shocked, hurt, but under the circumstances, she couldn't very well get mad about that, could she?

That led to a heart-to-heart conversation during which she'd told him about what had transpired between her and Tucker McBride. Jeremy had been shocked, hurt, but under the circumstances . . .

Jeremy had apologized. Gillian had apologized. He'd declared his love for her, and she'd responded in kind. They'd both committed to give 100 percent to their relationship, and when he'd offered her the ring back, she'd accepted it.

Nevertheless, the events of September had been an earthquake in their relationship, and they continued to experience tremors. Trust had taken a hit, but they were rebuilding. It had been a wake-up call for them both not to take each other for granted. Gillian was confident they'd end up stronger because of it.

Wasn't she?

"It's pre-wedding jitters," she told her mother. "Most every couple has them at one time or another. It's normal."

Barbara gave her a searching gaze for a long moment before nodding. "Okay, honey. That's good to hear. However, since I started this ball rolling already, I'll say one more thing and get it off my chest, and then we will be done with it. Okay?"

Could I stop you? "Okay."

"You've been planning this wedding for a year. You've put your heart and soul and dreams into it, and I know how much you want it to be a fairy-tale day. I want that for you too. But, sweetheart, being in the industry, you and I both have heard stories of brides who have gone through with weddings they knew they should have canceled. That's a mistake I don't want you to make."

"Mom."

Barbara held up her index finger. "Gillian, if you have serious doubts at any point—even as your father is walking you down the aisle—I want you to promise me that you'll listen to them and act. Don't allow the wedding to prevent you from calling a halt to getting married."

"I won't, Mom."

"Promise?"

"I promise. But you don't need to worry because that's not going to happen," Gillian assured both her mother and herself. "Jeremy and I are fine. There's so much going on, what with the holidays and wedding planning and getting everything ready to launch Blissful Events. We're just stressed."

"Okay, then." Barbara crossed to Gillian and took her in her arms for a hug. "I needed to say my piece, and now I've said it. I only want what's best for you, Gillian."

"I know, Mom."

"Let's call it a night, shall we? Your father is making Tuscan chicken for dinner. Care to join us?"

"My favorite. Of course, I'll join you." Gillian pressed a kiss to Barbara's cheek and added, "And I love you, Mom. To the moon and back."

"And I love you too, baby girl. I love you too."

In harmony with each other once again, the Thacker women locked up and walked out of Bliss Salon and into the crisp winter evening.

The fish turned out fabulous, and Tucker and Jackson staged a mock battle over the last piece to entertain a giggling Haley. Caroline gave an exaggerated roll of her eyes, then swooped in to steal the fillet right off her fiancé's fork.

Afterward, they built a fire in the pit and roasted marshmallows on skewers while Haley continued to enthusiastically share details about her afternoon with Uncle T. As the tangy scent of burning cedar drifted over them, the conversation moved on to a debate between Caroline and Haley about the perfect amount of marshmallow char needed to create the perfect s'more. Tucker and Jackson stood back from the crackling fire and watched. Softly, Jackson said, "She's happy tonight."

"She did great today."

"She really took a fish off her hook?"

"She did. Two of them. Baited the hooks herself too."

"I'm impressed. Thanks for taking Haley under your wing, Tucker."

"Glad to do it. I hope it helps."

"Already has. She was a knot-tying fool last night. Went through the house tying together anything that dangled. Kept her distracted during the hours that her mother was on an airplane."

"Where is our favorite famous pop star off to this time?"

Jackson cut Tucker a sardonic look. His relationship with his ex-wife had improved since the mid-September plane crash, but nobody would call her his favorite anything. As for Tucker, well, he'd never liked the woman even before she'd dragged Jackson to hell and back over custody issues.

"Nashville," Jackson said. "Studio meetings. She'll be back tomorrow."

Both men were distracted when Haley giggled as the marshmallow Caroline was toasting went up in flames. Jackson rubbed the back of his neck. "I love hearing that sound."

"Pretty music, for sure."

"This is the happiest I've seen Haley in weeks. You're really good with her." Jackson gave Tucker a sidelong glance and added, "Maybe now that you're out of the army, you should think about getting married and having an ankle-biter or twelve of your own."

"Twelve!"

"Cheaper by the dozen," Jackson said with a shrug.

"In what universe?" Tucker's gaze fixed on the beautiful little girl and the yearning that he'd experienced earlier returned in spades. "Actually, I've thought about that. I wouldn't mind having a family of my own. You know, you're not married to the lovely Caroline yet. Maybe I should swoop in and steal her away from you."

"Try it and die. Never mind that you wouldn't stand a chance. Caroline loves me."

"But I am the charming cousin. Granddad always said so. If I turned on the charm—"

"What charm? It's been AWOL for a decade now.

Besides, Caroline and I are soul mates. She's my music and my muse. She's the song my heart sings each day I awaken lying next to her."

"Those are some pretty poetic words, cousin. Gonna write 'em down?"

"Actually, I already have." Jackson's jade-green eyes glowed with joy. "She's given me back my music, Tucker. I'm writing some good stuff these days."

"That's awesome." Tucker clapped his cousin on the back. "I'm glad for you, man. Really happy for you both."

As if sensing that she was the topic of the cousins' conversation, Caroline looked away from the marsh-mallow roasting over the fire and smiled brilliantly at the McBride cousins. Tucker added, "Your lady sparkles. You are one lucky man."

"Don't I know it. Caroline bought her wedding gown this morning. She's been dancing on air ever since."

"What is it about women and weddings?" Tucker asked. "A woman I worked with in DC had a daughter getting married last year. The two of them were on the phone half a dozen times every day talking about everything from swizzle sticks to bridesmaid's robes to playlists. And the money involved . . . it's crazy."

"I don't think Caroline's one to worry about swizzle sticks, but she's been all about the dress for a while now. Wedding gowns are big business. Took her three weeks to get an appointment at Gillian Thacker's dress shop, and Gillian is one of her bridesmaids!"

Tucker gave Jackson a doubting look. "Seriously?"

"Seriously. That shop does a bang-up business. Gillian's mother is apparently some sort of wedding gown guru, and women come from all over the state to buy their dresses from her."

"I met Barbara Thacker. She and her sister spent a weekend at the inn last month. Seems like a nice lady."

"Barbara is good people. So is Gillian." Jackson hesitated a moment before adding, "Not so sure about the guy she's marrying."

Tucker's interest went on high alert, but he kept his tone casual. "I don't think I've met him."

"You will. Once Jeremy Jones finds out that you play golf, he'll be your new best friend."

I doubt that. "What don't you like about him?"

"I'm not sure. Can't quite put my finger on it. I may be totally wrong about the guy too. Caroline likes him a lot. Maybe I just don't like him because I can't seem to beat him on the course."

"You've never beaten me."

"Proves my point. I don't like you either."

The conversation was interrupted when Caroline approached. "It's a school night, so it's best I start herding Haley toward home. I need to stop by the Fallen Angel on the way and drop off some books Angelica has ordered for Christmas presents. Do you want me to take River with us?"

Caroline and Jackson had both come from work, so they'd arrived in separate vehicles. River was Jackson's yellow Lab. "I'll bring River with me."

Listening to the conversation, Haley asked, "But you'll put him in my room when you get home so he can sleep with me, right?"

"Of course. Days with me, nights with you is our deal."

Caroline said, "Gather up your things, sweetie. Angelica is expecting us."

"She'll give me a cookie!"

"You just ate s'mores," Jackson pointed out. "You don't need cookies too."

"Sure I do. Cookies make me happy."

Tucker grinned. It was an argument he knew his cousin couldn't resist. He winked at Haley and said, "You're a smart little cookie, sugar bug."

"I know."

"Now, give us a hug good night."

Haley ran first to her father, hugged and kissed him good night. Then she went into Tucker's arms. "Thank you so much, Uncle T. I had a super time. It was the bestest day."

"I had fun too," Tucker said, returning her hug and meaning it. He picked her up and spun her around. "Next time, we're going to work some more on fire building."

With the women departed, the cousins fell silent for a time, enjoying the peace of the chilly winter evening, the crackle of the campfire, and the soft snoring of the dog lying nearby.

Tucker's thoughts returned to Gillian and her beau. So, Jackson didn't care for the fiancé, hmm? Interesting. Wonder just how good a golfer ol' Jeremy was? Tucker might have to see about getting up a game with him. The idea of whipping the man's butt on the links had a real appeal, which was saying something. He hadn't wanted to play golf since his last round at Congressional. He'd played with some Congress critters at the order of his CO, and he'd hated every minute of it. Those snakes had—

"Maybe you should think about doing more of this," Jackson said, interrupting Tucker's musings.

"Family fish fries?"

"Well, yes. That was damned good fish. But that's

not what I'm talking about. I'm talking about the lessons with Haley."

Tucker picked up a branch to stir the fire. "You know I'm happy to spend as much time with her as you guys want. I do think it's helping her."

"I do too. Haley's time with you here in Enchanted Canyon has been great for her. But the thing is, I believe it's been good for you too. Listen, I have an idea."

"That's always dangerous."

"Yeah, well, I can't argue that. Especially in light of what's happened since I mentioned my idea to Boone."

Tucker tossed the cedar branch onto the fire and shot Jackson a wary look. "Why do I think I'm not going to be thrilled about the direction this conversation is about to take?"

"Probably because you've known Boone all your life. Bossiest sonofagun on the planet."

The gentle breeze switched directions, and smoke drifted toward them. Tucker savored the scent. He did love the smell of burning cedar. "What have you two done?"

Now it was Jackson's turn to get a stick and poke the fire. "It's kind of a long story, although it's only been a couple of weeks. But you know Boone."

"I know Boone. I repeat. What have you two done?"

"Okay. Here's the deal." He jabbed a log and sparks rose into the winter night. "At the risk of bringing up a touchy subject, this is quite the extended vacation you've been taking. It's not like you."

Tucker shrugged. "I'm still trying to figure out what I want to be when I grow up. Thinking about joining the circus."

"Bad news for you there, cuz. I think the circus has gone out of business."

"Seriously?"

"I think so. The circus with animals, anyway. Issues with animal cruelty."

"Huh."

"Anyway, unless you've completely changed personalities, you're gonna get tired of not having anything to keep you busy. Angelica said you taught her how to make a friction fire?"

"Yeah." Tucker smiled at the memory. "She came by the trailer out of the blue one evening and asked me to teach her. It took us a while, but we eventually got the job done."

"She enjoyed it. Said you were a patient, excellent teacher."

"I enjoyed it too. Angelica is a hoot."

"Well, she mentioned it to Celeste."

"Boone's friend?"

"Yes."

Tucker knew of Celeste Blessing, but he'd never met her. She was the owner of a resort in the Colorado mountain town where Boone now lived. She'd been the person who suggested her own cousin, Angelica, for the innkeeper position after the McBride cousins inherited Enchanted Canyon and decided to remodel the long-abandoned brothel into the Fallen Angel Inn.

Jackson continued, "Anyway, Celeste—"

He broke off abruptly at the sound of an approaching engine. Both men looked toward the road as a Jeep Wrangler made the turn toward the Airstream. Jackson muttered, "Finally."

"Finally," Tucker repeated. "You expecting company, cousin?"

"Yep."

"Let me guess. Our bossy cousin has traveled from Eternity Springs to grace us with his presence."

"Got it in one. He's running late, though. He was supposed to be here in time for supper."

The Jeep stopped next to his own truck, and a familiar figure emerged. Boone McBride strode toward them wearing dress slacks and a long-sleeved white shirt, cuffs rolled up midway on his forearms. He was half an inch taller than Tucker's own six foot two, something he'd always lorded over him, and older by two months. They shared the same prominent McBride cheekbones and slim, mostly straight nose, each sporting a bump from a break, Tucker's from their teen years and Boone's since his move to Eternity Springs. He had dark hair and a shark's smile, and tonight, his silver-gray eyes glowed with purpose.

Tucker repressed a heavy sigh. Obviously, his cousins were on a mission, and it involved him and his future. A month ago, he'd have reacted by turning around and heading into the woods, not to return until they'd decamped. Tonight, he realized he wouldn't mind hearing what they had to say.

Progress, I guess. Enchanted Canyon doing the work.

After they all exchanged greetings, Boone turned to Jackson. "Have you told him?"

"Was just getting around to it."

Tucker asked, "What's this all about?"

Jackson nodded toward Boone, who said, "It's an intervention. We get together and gang up on you. The women in Eternity Springs swear by it, so here we are."

"I'm honored," Tucker said in an exaggerated drawl.

"You should be. I canceled a date with a long-legged brunette to attend this little soirée."

Unbidden, an image of Gillian Thacker flashed through Tucker's mind. "That's quite the sacrifice. So, this sounds like something I'll need to endure with a drink. Whiskey, anyone?"

"Definitely."

"Absolutely."

Tucker went into the Airstream, and when he emerged a few minutes later carrying three glasses and a bottle of bourbon, he saw that his cousins had set up lawn chairs around the fire pit. Jackson tossed another log onto the fire while Boone talked to River and scratched the contented yellow Lab behind his ears.

Once they all had drinks and had taken a seat, Boone launched the first salvo. "You're right, Jackson. Mr. Spit-and-Polish has gone to seed. When was the last time you got a haircut? Your mane is almost as long as Ponytail Boy, here."

Jackson gave his hair a taunting wave toward Boone. "I didn't say he'd gone to seed. I said he needed a job. His longer hair looks good. Caroline says so."

"The legal beagle is just jealous of all the jack we're saving at the barbershop."

Jackson scoffed. "Boone hasn't set foot in a barbershop for fifteen years. He goes to"—Jackson lifted his fingers to make air quotes—"the salon at the spa."

"Hey, if you got a chance to have Penny Watson run her fingers through your hair once a week, you'd go to Angel's Rest spa yourselves. But I digress. Jackson is right. Tucker, you need a job. You've sulked in the canyon long enough."

"I haven't been sulking."

"No? What do you call it?"

Brooding. "Reassessing."

Jackson snorted, and Boone continued, "Well, whatever you want to call it, it's time you stopped. We know you better than anyone. If you keep this up much longer, you're going to wig out on us and do something stupid like join the French Foreign Legion or a knitting club."

"I would never join the French Foreign Legion, and there is absolutely nothing wrong with knitting clubs."

"Might be a good way to pick up women," Jackson added.

Boone ignored them both and pressed on. "Leaving a job is stressful enough, but you left a life, Tucker. It's natural for you to feel anxious and depressed. Knowing you, you probably feel guilty too."

Annoyed now, Tucker snapped, "Well, thank you, Dr. Freud."

"You had good instincts when you made the decision to come here to Enchanted Canyon. You're in your element here. But, it's one thing to take a break and heal, and something else entirely when the healing morphs into hiding."

"I haven't been hiding," Tucker protested.

"Bull," Jackson snapped, his green eyes flashing. "You don't leave the canyon."

"I do too. I went to Caroline's Christmas party just last week. And I went to your place for Thanksgiving."

"Twice. Big damned deal. You get Angelica to buy your groceries, and everything else you order online and have delivered. You're becoming a recluse, Tucker."

Boone tossed a branch on the fire, and as tree sap snapped and crackled and sparks fluttered up into the cold night air, he announced, "You need something to pull you out of your funk. Luckily, we have a plan."

"You always have a plan," Tucker groused.

"Not always," Boone replied in a droll tone. "Otherwise, I wouldn't have ended up in Eternity Springs."

Tucker momentarily considered attempting to follow the dangling bait by leading the conversation toward Boone's personal crisis, but he found he was curious about their plan. "Cut to the chase."

"Okay. We want you to open a survivalist school. Well, more than just a survivalist school. Nothing wrong with preppers, but you need a bigger target market. We think you should teach wilderness skills to adults and children."

"Seriously?" Tucker almost laughed out loud.

"Seriously," Jackson replied.

Tucker hid his grin by taking a sip of his drink and savoring the smoky taste of the smooth Kentucky whiskey. To Jackson, he said, "This was your idea?"

"No. Angelica and Celeste cooked it up between themselves."

Boone leaned forward, an earnest look in his nickel-colored eyes. "I've learned that when Celeste speaks, it's wise to listen. She is a special person with an uncanny way of being around when a person needs help. So, do you want to hear all of our reasons why this is a good move, or can we skip straight to reviewing the business plan? I'll warn you, I'm determined to talk you into this, so I wouldn't bother wasting a lot of breath arguing."

Tucker snorted. One of the perks of this career change of his was that no man alive could make him do something he didn't want to do—not for long, anyway. However, in this case, arguing wasn't necessary. He took another sip of his whiskey, then spoke in a

casual tone. "Sounds great. I think it might be something I'd enjoy. Want to go inside where we have
some light, and you can show me this business plan
of yours?"

"Huh." Jackson scratched his dog behind his ears
and met Boone's gaze. "That was easy."

"Yeah. Too easy." Boone narrowed his eyes. "Explain yourself, Tucker."

He could have done that. Tucker could have told
his cousins that the same idea had occurred to him
over a week ago, that he had contacts in the industry
to whom he had reached out, and that he had the beginnings of a business plan sketched out already. But
Boone looked a little worried and worrying him
was fun, so Tucker simply shrugged and said, "I'm
a reasonable man. Besides, I already tried the knitting
club. Not to ruin the surprise or anything, you might
find a handmade pair of socks beneath your Christmas trees."

Boone snorted. "Right." Still, he looked a little nervous.

"I need another drink," Jackson said, rising from
his lawn chair. "We killed this bottle."

The three big men all but filled the Airstream.
Boone and Jackson claimed seats at the table. Tucker
brought a camp chair in from outside in which to sit.
He was able to continue his joke by producing part
of one of the Christmas gifts he'd ordered for one of
the housekeepers at the Fallen Angel. The look on his
cousins' faces when he showed them a knitting basket
complete with needles and yarn was priceless.

Tucker bedded down that evening feeling more
upbeat than he had since receiving word about his
special assignment to DC. As he drifted toward sleep,
he decided he might just be ready to come out of the

canyon. He'd consider showing up for the McBride family Christmas gathering in Eternity Springs. That'd make his uncle Parker happy. If that went well, he could give Jackson's New Year's Eve show at the dance hall a try. He could flirt a little. Look for a woman to kiss at midnight. Maybe a woman who knew how to knit.

For the first time in a long time, Tucker looked forward to the coming year. He fell asleep smiling, his soul easing toward being at peace.

Chapter Five

The musical superstar and new Redemption resident Coco headlined the New Year's Eve lineup at the Last Chance Hall. Tickets were impossible to come by, but Gillian had an in—she was to be a bridesmaid in the dance hall owner's wedding.

Last year, Gillian and Jeremy had spent New Year's Eve at a swanky hotel in downtown Austin. She'd worn a killer gold dress and a pair of Jimmy Choo's, and after he'd popped the question, they'd danced the night away. She'd been giddy with love.

Tonight, she'd dressed rodeo chic in a filmy, flowing short white dress accented with a sparkling gold belt, gold hoop earrings, and paired with new dress boots. She wore her hair up with curling tendrils escaping at her temples. She knew she looked good. She felt pretty. Jeremy paid her the appropriate compliments when he picked her up for their date.

That didn't allay her unease as they made small talk during the drive out to Enchanted Canyon. Rather than being giddy like last year, tonight she felt nervous and uncertain. Bridal jitters, she kept telling herself.

She wasn't convinced.

They'd been invited to join Jackson and Caroline

for dinner at the saloon before the show started. They arrived to find Maisy already there with a date, a divorced father of two from California named Ben who was in town for the holidays visiting his parents. Gillian liked him right off. He was funny and friendly and good-looking too, with sun-bleached hair and a tanned complexion that suggested he spent a lot of time outdoors. He was sharing a story about teaching his nine-year-old son to surf when Jackson and Caroline arrived.

"Is Angelica joining us?" Maisy asked as Caroline took the seat next to her. The table was set for seven.

"No." Jackson hung his denim jacket on the back of his chair. "Tucker has promised to grace us with his presence."

"Really?" Maisy said. "That's a surprise." She turned to her date and explained, "Jackson's cousin moved to town last fall, but we hardly ever see him."

"He's been working on his recluse imitation while he explores the canyon," Jackson agreed. "Mainly he's been adjusting to a career change. Spent the last year or so in Washington, DC, rubbing shoulders with lobbyists and politicians, and says he needed some time in the wilderness to feel clean again."

"Understandable," Ben said.

Gillian was glad to have the heads-up about Tucker. The only time they'd crossed paths since parting ways at Buc-ee's had been at the Christmas party at Caroline's bookstore. Neither had admitted to a prior meeting at the time.

She'd thought about him a lot in the weeks and months since September. She'd thought about that kiss a lot as she attempted to understand her actions that day.

The kiss had shaken her almost as much as the

argument with Jeremy. Why had she responded to Tucker the way she had when she was in love with Jeremy? Had it been simply the wake of an emotional meltdown during the argument? Had it been heatstroke?

Was it Tucker?

Six weeks before her wedding, she should know the answer, shouldn't she?

She sincerely hoped that neither Jeremy nor Tucker would bring up what happened in September. How would she respond if that happened? How could she explain it to friends to whom she'd never mentioned the meeting with Tucker McBride?

There was another answer she didn't have. Luckily when Tucker joined them and took the empty seat directly across from Gillian, the only sign he betrayed of the September event was the knowing twinkle in his eyes when they shook hands and said hello. The conversation over dinner was easy and interesting.

The McBrides shared an amusing tale about an event that occurred during the recent McBride family Christmas holiday in Eternity Springs. Maisy had everyone laughing with a story about an unfortunate encounter between a trio of raccoons, a shed door left open, and popcorn strings intended for First Methodist Church's Christmas pageant. After that, talk turned to sports, and Jackson mentioned that his cousin was a scratch golfer. Jeremy lit up like New Year's Eve fireworks. "I'm part of a group that plays twice a week over at Tapatio Springs," he said. "You'll have to join us."

Gillian caught the look that passed between the two McBride cousins, but she couldn't interpret it. Tucker wiped his mouth with his napkin and said, "I'd like that."

It turned out that Ben also played golf, so for the next ten minutes, conversation revolved around the various courses throughout the world where the four men at the table had played. Gillian watched Jeremy indulgently. The man did love his golf.

"Do you play, Gillian?" Tucker asked her at one point.

She smiled and shook her head. "No, I don't. I tried a few times, but Jeremy and I decided fairly quickly it's better for our relationship that when we travel, I go to the spa, while he plays golf."

"Good plan," Caroline agreed.

The discussion flowed to travel after that, and they talked about Maisy's upcoming trip to Paris, Caroline and Jackson's honeymoon to the South Pacific, and Gillian and Jeremy's honeymoon in the Caribbean. "I'm not sure just what all is on our agenda," she explained to Ben after they placed orders for dessert. "Jeremy is in charge of the honeymoon."

"You're the planner, Gillian," he said. "Not me."

Gillian frowned at her fiancé as the now-familiar anxiety caused her stomach to take another roll. Jackson broke the awkward silence that followed the comment by pushing back his chair and rising. "I need to get on over to the hall. You all enjoy your chocolate, and Caroline, don't forget to bring my cookies when you come over."

"I won't." Caroline lifted her face for Jackson's kiss.

Do I glow like that when Jeremy kisses me good-bye? Gillian wondered. She didn't think she did. Not anymore. She gave her head a shake to dislodge the unsettling thought and lifted her glass of wine for a sip. Over the top of her drink, she caught Tucker staring at her.

Maisy interrupted the moment by asking, "So is Jackson singing tonight too, Caroline?"

"He's doing one set with Coco, but that's all. He's very excited about the opening band, though. They are some young guys out of Abilene who played a Sunday afternoon at the Last Chance not long ago. Jackson said their songwriter has real talent."

"He should know," Ben said, earning smiles from all the women.

Jeremy didn't respond, and when Gillian glanced at him, he seemed distracted. She followed the path of his gaze and couldn't hold back a groan. "Oh, no. I know tonight's concert is the hottest ticket in Texas so I shouldn't be surprised to see those two, but if either one of them heads this way, I expect somebody to run interference."

Maisy asked, "Who? What?"

"Lindsay Grant and Erica Chadwick."

"Ah." As Gillian stabbed a fork full of the chocolate cake they'd all been sharing, Maisy explained, "They're old college frenemies of Gillian's."

Gillian chastised Maisy with a look, but she couldn't deny it. Maisy took note of Jeremy's expression and asked, "Have you met them, Jeremy?"

He wiped his mouth with his napkin before responding with a hard note in his voice. "I've heard plenty about them."

Gillian addressed the curious looks at the table by expanding on Maisy's explanation. "Lindsay is a repeat customer of Bliss. She's called three times since Christmas trying to convince me to coordinate her April wedding. Erica has called twice."

"Why is Erica calling you?" Jeremy asked.

Gillian shrugged. "Doing her bridesmaid duty, I imagine."

"I thought you sold wedding dresses," Tucker said. "You coordinate weddings too?"

"Not yet, but I will soon. Jeremy and I are starting a new event planning business."

"Oh, really?" Tucker said. "A new business, hmm? From what I understand, there's a lot of that going around in Redemption. Congratulations."

"It's Gillian's baby," Jeremy snapped. "I have my hands full at the bank."

Gillian stiffened at the comment. Deliberately, she returned her fork to her plate and folded her hands in her lap. The jitters inside her intensified to big, black doubts she could no longer deny. It was a very good thing their premarital counseling at church began next week. She and Jeremy needed another heart-to-heart, honest talk.

"The Texas Hill Country has become a popular place to hold destination weddings, hasn't it?" Ben asked.

Jackson nodded. "They're becoming a big part of our business at the inn, that's for sure."

Tucker took a bite of dessert and casually observed, "So, to be an event planner, I guess you must be organized. And of course—" He paused, and a teasing glint entered his caramel-colored eyes as he licked the last bit of chocolate off the fork and then added, "—always prepared."

Very funny, Gillian told him with her eyes.

He ever so subtly winked at her.

Unaware of the underplay, Maisy said, "You should see her notebook for her wedding. Gillian has prepared for every possibility and planned accordingly."

"There's no room for errors in weddings," Caroline observed.

"Tell me about it," Ben said, lamenting. "It's called divorce."

"Speaking of divorce," Maisy said, a note of warning in her voice. "Bridezilla incoming. I'd guess you have ten seconds to make an escape."

"Oh, joy."

Jeremy took Gillian's hand and shot to his feet, pulling her up with him. "We won't allow them to ruin what's been a nice evening up until now. Let's go take a walk."

Gillian didn't hesitate. She grabbed her bag and hurried alongside Jeremy toward the exit. But as they stepped out into the chilly night air and moved far enough away that they were safe from interruptions, she pulled her hand free from his and halted. "Why did you say that about Blissful Events being my baby? We're going to be equal partners. That's why we decided to wait until after our wedding to file the paperwork."

"You decided that. I didn't."

With a quick intake of breath, Gillian took a physical step back from her fiancé. "What is wrong with you, Jeremy? You've been cranky for weeks now."

Jeremy closed his eyes and sighed heavily. "Everything will be fine. It's prewedding jitters, that's all. I'm sorry."

"I think it's more than just jitters." *For both of us.*

He dismissed the comment with a shake of his head, then glanced back toward the door of the saloon. "Look, I'm just in a terrible mood. I don't like that those two women have been pestering you. I'll go talk to them. Like you said at dinner, we are partners. This is something I can do."

"Forget them. It's New Year's Eve. Let's not bring business into our holiday celebration any further. Let's dance and enjoy ourselves. This is a night to celebrate new beginnings."

"Which is why we shouldn't drag old baggage into the New Year," he grumbled. "Go on into the hall. I'll catch up with you in a little while after I've shaken off this . . . funk."

He turned and left her in the middle of the barren rose garden. In that moment, a gust of cold wind sent brittle leaves skittering across the path, and Gillian felt a chill through to her marrow.

Tucker was having an excellent time at his first New Year's Eve party as a single, civilian man. First and foremost, he was so damned happy for Jackson. He'd made his dream happen. The Last Chance Hall was packed to the rafters, and music and laughter filled the air. By all appearances, he'd successfully launched those kids from Abilene tonight, which was precisely the sort of thing he wanted to do when he envisioned reopening the hall.

The man himself had just finished a set to wild applause, and now he was busy scootin' up the sawdust with his ladylove. Jackson had been through more than his share of dark days in the past few years, but as the New Year began, the sun definitely was shining in his sky.

The example Jackson set stirred Tucker's reenergized competitive spirit and gave him hope for some sunshine for himself. His and Jackson's skies were different, to be sure. Tucker hadn't lived with gray, stormy days for years on end like his cousin had during his lousy marriage. But sometimes, all it took was one big old dark thunderstorm to throw off a tornado and blow a path of destruction. For the past few months, Tucker had been in after-the-F-5 cleanup mode. Now that he'd cleared away the brush and rubble, Tucker was ready to shift into the rebuilding phase.

A new place, new job, new life. And, with any luck, new people.

He wanted a little Haley of his own to take fishing and hiking and camping beneath the star-filled Texas sky.

Scanning the hall and sipping a longneck, Tucker noticed Gillian twirling in the arms of a man who likely was family, based on the resemblance the two shared. Regret filled him. Damn, but that woman did it for him. Witty, intelligent, loyal, and loving. Sexy as sin. Too bad the tornado hadn't swept through his life sooner and dropped him into Gillian's path. He'd have done everything in his power to beat Jeremy to the punch and win the beauty's heart.

Jackson sidled up beside Tucker, interrupting his musings. "How come you're not out there dancing, Fred?"

"Fred Astaire?"

"You're as smooth on the dance floor as you are on the golf course."

"True. But I can play golf alone."

"Want me to request a line dance?"

Tucker gave his cousin a chiding look. It was an old argument of theirs. Tucker was old-fashioned when it came to dancing. In his opinion, dancing needed a partner, a man needed a woman to hold and swirl and twirl. "Thanks, but no. I'm content hanging on the corral fence for now."

Jackson narrowed his eyes and gave Tucker a speculative look. "Are we talking about more than two-steppin' here?"

"Yes. Yes, I think we are. I think I'm close to being

ready, though." Without conscious thought, Tucker searched the crowd circling the dance floor for Gillian. He spotted her just as the song ended and applause broke out. As her dance partner led her toward the table where Maisy and her date sat, Tucker asked his cousin, "Did you ever use one of those online dating services?"

"Are you kidding me?"

"I guess not, you being a celebrity and all. It's just that, well, I'm not exactly sure how one goes about dating while living in a small town. There is no anonymity. Everybody knows everybody else's business."

"Life in a Hill Country fishbowl." Jackson shrugged. "It is what it is."

"A small fishbowl at that."

"Still, you are Captain Stealth, aren't you? In and out of dangerous places all over the world without getting caught? I think you could date a Redemption girl on the sly just fine."

"You do have a point."

Jackson waved to get a server's attention, motioned to Tucker's beer, then held up two fingers. He waited until the drinks had been delivered to ask, "What about Maisy? She's single and unattached, unless this date with Ben starts something."

Tucker scowled at his cousin. "Doesn't she date Boone?"

"No. They've never gone beyond flirting."

"You sure?"

"Yes. Well, pretty sure. I think they sparked a bit, but nothing caught fire."

Tucker shook his head. "I'm not going there. Remember Lizzie Hart?"

"Lizzie who? Oh, wait. The girl at summer camp after our sophomore year. Y'all had a fistfight over her, didn't you?"

"More than one. Swore then that I'd never fish from the same pond as Boone."

"Doesn't seem right considering that you're living in this pond, and he's a thousand miles away. Why don't you ask him?"

"I could, but . . ." Tucker shrugged. "I like Maisy a lot, but I have the same sort of sisterly vibe going on with her as I do with Caroline."

"Gotcha." Jackson took a pull on his beer. "I do have one suggestion, but it's a serious step. Once you take it, there's no turning back."

"That sounds ominous."

"It is. Show up at the Wednesday night book club. That will get the word out to every woman in town that you're available."

"Wednesday night book club, hmm?"

"They're reading Diana Gabaldon's *Outlander* series beginning in January. You do a great Scottish brogue. If you can dust off that charm you used to wield so spectacularly, you won't have to lift a finger to get dates. They'll come to you."

One of the dance hall's employees interrupted the conversation with news that Jackson was needed backstage. Tucker finished off his beer and decided he was in the mood to do a little dancing too. He began by asking Caroline to two-step, then continued with a waltz with Maisy. He spied Gillian in the arms of a guy he recognized from the hardware store in town and debated whether or not he should ask her to dance.

He wanted to hold her in his arms more than he should. He wanted to talk to her and spend time with her and, yeah, get naked with her.

He needed to get over that. Not only was she taken with a capital *T*, Gillian was a friend of Caroline's, and

Caroline was about to be family. He wouldn't be able to avoid her, so he needed to crush these inconvenient feelings of his.

Self-analysis wasn't ordinarily his bailiwick, but he wanted to believe that he wouldn't lust after a married woman. He never had before, so chances were good that second ring on her finger would settle his hormones. Right?

Except he'd never lusted after an engaged woman before either.

Yeah, he was a little worried.

His gaze found her in the crowd. Being New Year's Eve, lots of folks had dressed up a notch. Gillian wore understated clothes compared to many. Nevertheless, she glittered. She sparkled. She made the Last Chance Hall come alive.

What would one dance hurt? It wouldn't make him want her more than he already did, would it?

He was saved from making the decision when someone tapped him on the shoulder. Angelica Blessing beamed up at him with a wicked twinkle in her eyes. Her long, fire-engine-red hair swung loose beneath a silver felt hat with a sequined hatband. She wore dangling earrings—one shaped like an angel's wing, the other like a devil's pitchfork—and a blousy silver shirt tucked into jeans the same color as her hair. Her red leather boots had a saucy silver fringe. "Hey, cowboy. Want to dance?"

"With you? Always and anytime."

"In that case . . ." She waved toward the stage and caught the lead singer's notice. A moment later, he announced a step back into classic country, and the first strains of the Western Swing waltz made famous by Bob Wills and the Texas Playboys back in the 1940s, "San Antonio Rose," drifted through the hall.

"I haven't heard this in years," Tucker told Angelica as he led her onto the floor.

"It's one of my favorites," she replied. "Pick up the pace, McBride. I may be mature, but I can dance."

She wasn't lying. Tucker dusted off his old swing moves, and they twirled and spun and even dipped their way around the dance floor. When the song ended, Tucker was breathing hard and laughing aloud. Angelica simply made him feel good.

She winked up at him and said, "Good job, farmer."

"Farmer? I thought I was a cowboy?"

"Remember when I introduced myself to you? I told you I was a plain speaker and that you had a tough row ahead of you to hoe."

Yes, now that she mentioned it, he did recall. It had been a weird moment because she'd looked at him with a strange light in her eyes and some of what she'd said had made no sense. "You said I might break the blade a time or two."

"I did. It's a farmer's reality. However, the New Year is upon us, and harvest blessings are right around the corner." Angelica reached up and touched his cheek. "Just be prepared and remember your Aristotle: 'Patience is bitter, but its fruit is sweet,' and 'Friendship is a slow ripening fruit.'"

"All right." Smiling down at her, Tucker remembered a phrase his mother used to use: *dottie old dear.*

"Happy New Year, Tucker McBride. Thanks for the dance."

The band played the first few chords of "Copperhead Road." Angelica said, "My favorite line dance! Gotta go."

Tucker watched her take center-front stage and

slowly shook his head. He loved her, but sometimes Angelica Blessing was one strange bird.

Someone tapped him on his left shoulder. Gillian said, "Well, now. Don't you know how to trip the lights fantastic?"

"It was all Angelica. She knows how to make a dance partner look good." Unable to stop himself, he gave her a quick once-over. *Pretty as a Parker County peach.* "How come you're not out there on the line?"

She pursed her lips into a pout and shrugged. "I'm not a fan. It makes me feel like I'm in an exercise class, and I can't stand exercise class."

"A woman after my own heart," he observed. Then, because she stood beside him and her fiancé wasn't around, and he'd seen her dancing with over a half a dozen other men this evening, he surrendered to temptation. "May I have the next dance?"

"I'd like that."

When the line dance ended, Tucker took her hand and led her onto the floor. The lead singer in the band announced the next dance as the last of the evening before the start of Coco's show. Gillian's smile faltered just a bit when the familiar chords of Eric Clapton's "Wonderful Tonight" began.

It was slow. It was romantic. It was the type of song that made it almost impossible not to hold the woman in his arms too close. Didn't help that the exotic, woods-and-spices perfume she wore made him want to pull her closer than appropriate for a friendly dance. She moved like a dream, and with those mile-long legs of hers, she fit him perfectly.

If Tucker were Gillian's fiancé, he'd damned sure not let some other guy dance this song with her. It wouldn't matter if she was with the mayor or a minister or a milkman, Tucker would cut in. Forcefully.

Jeremy was nowhere to be found.

So, Tucker closed his eyes, pulled her a little closer, and indulged himself. Sexy, soft, and sweet, she was heaven in his arms. She was glorious.

The band played the full version, and at some point, Coco joined them in the vocals. It was eight minutes of bliss. Impure bliss. Tucker grew as hard as a bois d'arc fence post, and he valiantly resisted the urge to press himself against her.

For a moment when the final notes of the music faded away, stillness came over the crowd. Tucker lifted his head. The temptation to kiss her was almost overwhelming, but it waned when he stared down into Gillian's luminous eyes. "What's this?" He thumbed a tear from her cheek. "Don't cry, sweetheart. What's the matter?"

"I'm sorry. That song is just so beautiful and, well . . ." The crowd broke out in applause, and she stepped away and looked around. "Where is he? I haven't seen Jeremy since our walk in the garden."

Hell if I know. Your fiancé should have been here. He should be here now ripping you out of my arms.

On stage, Coco said, "Happy New Year, y'all! I want to thank the band for allowing me to jump in on that last song. It's one of my favorites."

The applause turned to cheers. Ever the performer, Coco bowed and blew kisses and accepted accolades for almost a full minute. Then she said, "Are y'all ready to get this party started?"

"Yes! Yes! Yes!" chanted the crowd.

"That's good because it's about that time, I believe. Official timekeeper? Where are we?"

"Thirty-eight seconds until midnight," Jackson called.

"Woo-hoo!" Coco waved her arm like a cowboy looping a lariat. "Let's do this thing! Lights! Drum roll."

Gillian was now glancing around the dance hall anxiously. "It's so crowded in here. Do you see Jeremy anywhere, Tucker?"

"No."

Spotlights illuminated the mirrored seventies-style disco ball that Jackson had rigged at the center of the stage for the purpose. Allowed to stay awake and participate in the holiday, Haley manned the rope with her father's help. The crowd laughed and cheered as they began to slowly lower the sparkling mirrored ball. Gillian paid no attention to the stage. Instead, she threaded her way through the crowd toward a nearby table and empty chair. Tucker followed her. When it became clear she intended to stand on the chair, he muttered a curse and grabbed the chair's back to hold it steady.

"I can't believe this," she said.

"Thirteen. Twelve. Eleven," counted the crowd.

"He was in a lousy mood, so I figured he was sulking in a corner, that maybe he stayed away to spare me. I never thought he'd do this."

"Ten. Nine. Eight. Seven."

She made one full turn around the chair, looking for her fiancé.

"Six. Five. Four."

She wobbled. Tucker cursed again and put his hands around her waist and lifted her down to the floor.

"Three. Two. One. Happy New Year!"

The mirror ball hit the stage, and the crowd went wild. Haley ran to her mother for a hug and kiss. At stage left, Jackson gave Caroline a thorough kiss.

Looking dazed and brokenhearted, Gillian blinked back tears. "I can't believe he ditched me at midnight on New Year's Eve."

Screw Jeremy Jones, Tucker said to himself. As the band launched into "Auld Lang Syne" with Coco leading the vocals, he cupped Gillian's chin and tilted her face up toward his. "His loss is my gain. You can kick his ass later. Happy New Year, Glory."

Then Tucker bent down and stole a friendly New Year's kiss.

Friendly. Dammit.

Chapter Six

With "Auld Lang Syne" ringing in her ears and the taste of Tucker McBride on her lips, Gillian was filled with despair. Everything was wrong. They'd gotten engaged last New Year's Eve. Tonight, he didn't even bother to be with her at midnight? She needed air, so she turned to leave the crowded building. Vaguely, she sensed Tucker following behind her and just as she was about to push into the bleak winter night, a man called her name. He wasn't Jeremy. Gillian recognized one of his golfing buddies.

"There you are. I've been looking for you. Jeremy called me. He said you didn't answer your phone."

Gillian's phone was in her purse and tucked safely away in the dance hall's office. "Where is he?"

"He said he got sick and left. He asked me to drive you home."

"Oh." She immediately felt concerned and contrite. He hadn't ditched her. He'd gotten sick! "Oh, no. What type of sick, did he say?"

"No. Just that he didn't want you to catch it."

Now Gillian felt guilty. She should have gone looking for him long before midnight.

Jeremy's friend continued, "Want to meet at my car when the party's over? I'm in my truck. Last row, underneath the lamppost. Can't miss me."

Two more hours? Wonder if I could get an Uber this far out?

"I'll take you," Tucker offered. "I'm about ready to leave."

Gillian looked up into his warm brown eyes and realized she wanted to go with him. More than she probably should. "Thank you."

She was quiet during the twenty-minute drive into Redemption. Sensitive to her mood, Tucker didn't fill the silence with small talk. She appreciated that. Her focus was on Jeremy and the events of the evening. When she checked her phone, she saw that he'd called around eleven. He'd texted, too. Why had her first reaction been that he'd ditched her? He probably had been feeling unwell all night. That's why he'd been grouchy at dinner.

And yet, why did she sense there was something more going on here? Why did she wonder if Jeremy was truly ill? And why hadn't she really missed him until almost midnight? Until the dance with Tucker? This was wrong.

As they approached town, Tucker asked, "Do you want to check on him? I'll take you by his place."

"Yes, but he probably won't want me to stay. I'll need my car, and it's at my house."

Tucker shook his head. "Let me wait and see you home, Gillian. I'll sleep easier tonight knowing you're home safe and sound. Redemption might be a small town, but this is still the most dangerous night of the year to be out on the streets."

Tucker isn't concerned about Redemption drunk drivers, Gillian thought. He was offering her his silent support in case this was something other than illness like her fiancé had claimed.

Gillian gave him Jeremy's address and moments later, he pulled his truck to a stop in front of the house. Jeremy's car was in the drive. "I won't be long."

"Take your time. I'm happy to wait for you."

She hurried up the front steps and used her key to let herself inside. "Jeremy?"

He was in his bedroom sitting on the side of his bed, wearing only his boxers. His face was buried in his hands. "Go away, Gillian. You shouldn't be here. I'm sick. Go home."

Ignoring him, she approached the bed. "What are your symptoms? Do you have a fever?"

She reached out to feel his forehead, but he jerked away from her and headed for his bathroom. "I'm about to throw up again. Go, Gillian. I'll call you when I'm better."

He didn't look well. He was pale and his eyes were glassy. "You shouldn't be alone," she called as he shut the bathroom door. "Let me stay. I'll bunk in the guest room and—"

"No. No, I want you to go. I want to be alone."

The vehemence in his voice told her he meant it. She listened for sounds of retching, but the only thing she heard was the sound of water running in the sink. She sighed. "All right. I'll go. I'll check on you tomorrow. Promise me you'll call if you need anything before then."

"Okay."

She turned to leave, but hesitated when a question occurred to her. "Jeremy, did you ever get your flu shot?"

"Good night, Gillian."

Well, that was her answer, wasn't it? They had a

flu season wedding! Everyone in the bridal party had been instructed to get their flu shots. For the groom to ignore it? What did that say about their relationship?

They seriously needed the premarital counseling they had scheduled. She hoped this illness of his wouldn't delay it, because she could no longer deny that these jitters were serious doubts.

She'd planned to pay another round of deposits this week. Maybe she should hold off on that until after she and Jeremy met with the counselor. If they called off the wedding . . .

The thought made Gillian feel a bit fluey herself.

"You okay?" Tucker asked as she climbed back into his truck a few moments later.

"I'm tired. I'm just really tired." Physically and mentally. "Thanks for waiting for me, Tucker."

"Like I said, I'm happy to do it. Can't think of anyone I'd rather ring in the New Year with."

She gave a sad little laugh. "This isn't much of a ring."

He drove half a block before replying, "Actually, for me, it is. I'm in a good place, have some good plans going forward, and I'm making some good new friends here in Redemption. You and I can be friends, right?"

She cut him a sidelong glance and scolded, "No more kissing."

"Hey, it was New Year's Eve at midnight. And I kept it friendly, didn't I? That's well within the allowable lines."

He reached over, took her hand, and gave it a squeeze. "Happy New Year, new friend. I've been told by someone who claims to be in the know that it's gonna be a great one for you and me both."

"Someone in the know?"

"Angelica."

Gillian smiled. "In that case, I'm not going to worry. Angelica knows things."

The innkeeper's comment really did make her feel better, and as she unlocked the front door of her house and turned to give Tucker a wave, her smile was genuine.

Two weeks later, her smile was nowhere to be found. She stood beneath the threshold of Jeremy's bedroom door with her arms folded and her foot tapping. He'd used his illness to keep her away for two full weeks. They had not seen the counselor nor had the heart-to-heart talk they desperately needed, and their wedding date was now only a month away. "I think you should go back to the doctor."

He lay in his bed, on his stomach, and spoke into his pillow. "Don't worry. I'm better."

Then why was he still in bed? *You'd think the man had the plague.* "If you're feeling better, then we have some things we need to discuss. Our premarital counseling needs to be—"

"Leave it alone, Gillian," he snapped. "I don't have time for this. I have to go to work today, and I need to get ready."

Hurt by both his words and tone, and out of patience with the patient, she snapped back, "Fine. I won't bother you anymore. You call me when you're feeling more yourself, and we can discuss our future."

She left the house in a full-blown snit. She did not spin her tires as she pulled away from his house, and she gave herself a gold star in self-restraint. She drove to Bliss with her radio blaring hard rock, grateful to have the distraction of work. She had window design on her calendar, and she dove right into it.

Shortly before the shop opened at ten, her mother

joined her in the courtyard outside of Bliss Salon. The two women stood side by side with their hands on their hips and gave the display window a critical study. "What do you think, Mom?" Gillian asked. "I was going for subtle Cinderella."

She'd used a backdrop of shimmering silver and added a Louis XIV chair upholstered in snowy velvet to the scene. Rhinestone embellished Jimmy Choo shoes sat beside a chair leg, the right shoe tipped over on one side. A fingertip veil was draped over the chair, a tiara propped crookedly atop it. Fanned across the chair's seat was a trio of books: *The Princess Diaries, The Princess and the Pea*, and *The Princess Bride*.

"You might have overshot subtle," Barbara observed. "But I love it."

"Should I have used a wire dress form instead of the new mannequin? It might be a little more romantic that way."

"No, I don't think so. The clear molded plastic is sleek and elegant, and the silver neck finial is classy. This window is very Princess Grace. I think it's perfect. You have such an eye for design, Gillian."

"Thanks, Mom. I got it from you."

"We make a good team."

Hearing a peculiar note in her mother's voice, Gillian gave her a sidelong look. Barbara's hazel eyes had filled with tears. *Oh, no. I'd hoped I was done with drama for today. And no way was she going to voice her concerns before she had a chance to talk with Jeremy.*

"That's not going to change, Mom," Gillian said as she slipped her arm around her mother's waist and gave her a hug. "We're just growing our team."

"I know. I know. Don't mind me. I'm a little emotional this morning. And I'm glad our family is growing. You know I am. I'm excited for you to start your new business—I know you're going to make it a huge success. It's just that, I don't know, this is an ending of sorts and a bittersweet time. Working with you to build Bliss has been a joy."

"For me too, Mom." Gillian's gaze shifted toward the hand-lettered sign beside the shop's door. Bliss Bridal Salon. Proprietors: Barbara Thacker, Gillian Thacker.

Barbara reached into the pocket of her black slacks and pulled out a clean tissue. Dabbing at her eyes, she said, "I'm the mother of the bride. I'm allowed to be a little emotional."

"That you are."

"Thank goodness you have it all together as usual."

Not hardly. Gillian's mouth twisted in a rueful smile. "Hey, I have my bridezilla moments."

"Few and far between, and nothing like She Who Will Not Be Sold Another Gown."

Gillian winced. Yesterday's fitting appointment with Lindsay and Erica had been even more awful than the last. They'd stayed until almost nine. Lindsay had been a terror, unhappy about everything. When she'd snapped at Barbara over a zipper that wouldn't zip due to the holiday pounds she'd put on since the previous fitting, only a warning look from her mother had stopped Gillian from poking the witch with a straight pin. Erica hadn't helped the situation one bit either. Rather than attempting to soothe the bride's nerves, she'd sat like a sullen lump in the corner, saying no more than a dozen words the entire time.

Barbara continued, "Forgive me, sweetheart. I'm on edge today. Feeling a bit, I don't know, lost."

The peculiar look that flashed across her mother's face gave Gillian pause. "Mom, if I've made you feel left out of anything planning-wise—"

"No," Barbara interrupted, stepped toward her daughter, and gave her a quick hug. "I didn't mean that. All is well. I'm having a grand time with the wedding."

"You're sure?"

"I'm sure. Honey, you've managed to hit an almost perfect balance with the trifecta of roles you are performing—daughter, bride, and wedding planner. As a daughter, well, we're almost through this, and you and I are still friends. As the bride, you've been respectful of Jeremy's wishes and vision, and of your own, too, without stepping on anyone's toes too hard. As a wedding planner, you've excelled. Event planning fits your skill set to a tee, and I'm so glad I need not concern myself with all the details."

Barbara gestured toward the window and added, "I love the display design, sweetheart. You are really very good at everything you do."

"Except nursing a fiancé sick with the flu," Gillian replied with a bite in her voice.

"Oh, honey." Barbara threw her arm around her daughter's shoulders and gave her a squeeze. "Don't take it to heart, and remember your grandmother's always appropriate marital advice: *This, too, shall pass.*"

Gillian smiled wistfully at the mention of her grandmother, gone now for almost four years. "You know who sort of reminds me of Nana, despite being her total opposite in most regards?"

Barbara didn't hesitate. "Angelica Blessing."

"Yes." Gillian gave the window one last look. "Angelica predicts I'm going to have a fabulous year this year."

"I'm going to agree with her. I think you're gonna be happy as a clam, Gillian. You just need to get past this fluey start first."

"What is wrong with this picture?" Jackson asked as he toted a box past Tucker to set near a stack of them sitting beside the checkout counter.

"I'm taking a break," he replied.

"Obviously. You're standing around staring aimlessly out the window when there's plenty of work to be done."

Tucker wasn't staring aimlessly. He was watching Gillian Thacker. This was the first time he'd seen her since New Year's Eve. Well, if he didn't count seeing her in his dreams, that was.

That dance and that kiss had been a big mistake.

"Move your butt, cousin," Jackson said. "There's still half a trailer yet to unload. It needs to be done before lunch because I'm not coming back after the meeting at the bank."

"What meeting at the bank?"

"You need to start checking your email now that you're a businessman. Boone sent an email about it yesterday. The bank needs signatures for our accounts, and apparently, Jones likes to do the meet-and-greet for any new business. He's going to take us to lunch afterward. Goodwill gesture and all of that."

Jeremy. Wasn't that just ducky? "Well, I guess as long as the banker is buying, I'd better work my ass off so I have an extra big appetite." Tucker cast one last glance toward Gillian, then returned his attention to the boxes. "Remind me why we're doing all the work when this whole storefront thing is Boone's idea?"

"Because we're idiots. And Boone is . . . Boone."

Tucker simply sighed. For the next two hours, he and Jackson hauled and opened boxes, assembled shelves, and hung pegboard. They unloaded the trailer filled with the antique desk, chair, and bookcases they'd stored since remodeling the Fallen Angel Inn and wrestled them upstairs. Slowly, the space began to take shape. A little after eleven as curses flew while they worked together to level a shelf, Jackson grumbled, "This would be easier with another set of hands."

"Maybe we should ask the banker to help us over here instead of buying us lunch," Tucker suggested.

After much effort, ten minutes before they were due to leave for lunch, they finally managed to fix the shelf properly to the wall. They stood observing their handiwork with their hands shoved in their back pockets when a voice spoke from behind, "It needs to come up some on the left."

Tucker and Jackson both hung their heads and then shared a look. Simultaneously, without turning around, they both lifted a hand and shot the speaker the bird.

"Now, isn't that a nice way to greet a visitor," Boone said.

Tucker scowled at Jackson. "He's here again? It's not that easy to get here from Eternity Springs. Why is he here again?"

Jackson shrugged, then his brows winged up. "Are you seeing Maisy Baldwin?"

"What?" Boone asked. "No. She's awfully cute, and she thinks I'm cute too, but there wasn't any sizzle. We're friends."

"I think Maisy is sweet on the guy from New Year's Eve," Tucker told Jackson. Then he arched a brow toward Boone. "How long have you been skulking around outside while we've been in here working?"

"Hey, that's insulting." He waited a beat and added, "Ten minutes, maybe. You guys were a hoot."

"Jerk." Tucker shot him the finger again for good measure, then observed, "This *is* a surprise. Is anything wrong?"

"No. All is well. Mark and Annabelle Callahan have been in Eternity Springs visiting Brick and his crew, and they flew back to Texas last night. I hitched a ride on their plane, and drove down from Brazos Bend this morning." He shrugged and added, "I was feeling left out."

Tucker snorted. "I don't see how. You're in my business every time I turn around."

"That's because I'm a businessman, not a recluse."

"I'm not a recluse, and you're not a businessman. You're a damned lawyer."

"I'm both a damned lawyer and a businessman. Luckily for you, I'm willing to share my expertise in both areas." Boone folded his arms and made a slow inspection of the room. "This is gonna be great. Even better than I expected. Have you tackled anything upstairs in the classroom area yet?"

"No," Jackson drawled. "You can help us haul the benches upstairs after lunch."

Boone's brows arched. "The delivery guys didn't do that?" Jackson and Tucker shook their heads. "Why the hell not?"

"The guy who arranged for delivery didn't spring for the upcharge," Tucker explained with a smirk. "Tightfisted S.O.B."

"Damn. Sorry." Boone winced, then shrugged it off. "Oh well. We're manly men. We can handle it."

Jackson checked his watch. "After lunch. It's almost time to head over to the bank."

"Excellent," Boone said. "Before we go, I have one little task to accomplish. Have you noticed the flagpole brackets on the canopy out front?"

"No," Jackson said, glancing toward the Main Street entrance.

"Not that front," Tucker corrected. "The other front. The courtyard entrance. I noticed them. There are three of them."

Boone nodded. "I noticed them on the real estate photos. Flagpole brackets need to hold flags. I got us an American flag, a Texas flag, and . . ." He strode toward the front of the shop, where he picked up one of three flagpoles. He unfurled the flag with a flourish. "This!"

Tucker read it and snickered. "Seriously?"

"We need a slogan. It's perfect. You say it all the time."

Jackson nodded. "He's right. You even have Haley saying it. Grab the ladder, Tucker, and let's do this thing."

Ten minutes later, the three McBride cousins stood shoulder to shoulder, hands on their hips, staring at the flags fluttering in the gentle January breeze. Tucker grinned. Something told him Gillian was gonna love this.

"Thank you so much, Shannon. We enjoy doing business with you." Upstairs in the cramped, second-floor room that she used as an office, Gillian ended the call with one of their suppliers. She set her phone onto her desk beside the twenty-year-old *Princess Bride* lamp she kept burning while she worked because the converted storage room had no window or natural light. The Christmas gift from Aunt Cathy, along with the foul ball Gillian had caught at an Astros game when she was eleven and the bowling trophy she'd won last year, were the only personal items she kept here. The rest of the space was filled from floor to ceiling with files and folders and fabric swatches.

Luckily, Gillian was organized by nature, so she managed to work in such a confined setting. However, she did look forward to having a real office once she and Jeremy worked past this rough spot, married, and launched Blissful Events from the mercantile building across the courtyard. She had her office space already picked out. It had four windows and plenty of room for a desk and filing cabinets and the personal touches that would make it hers. She had her eye on a cabinet over at Anderson Antiques that was perfect for displaying some of the hand-painted teacups she collected but had no room for here at Bliss.

She crossed the supplier call off her to-do list and went to the next item. She managed to keep her mind on business and off her personal concerns until she finished up just before noon. She headed downstairs whistling one of Jackson McBride's songs and broke off mid-note upon finding her mother sweeping up broken glass in the shop's entry. "What happened?"

"Just clumsy me," Barbara replied, disgust lacing her voice. "I was digging for my sunglasses in my purse and didn't watch where I was going. I tripped over my own two feet."

Gillian gave her mother a quick once-over as she took an automatic step forward. She didn't see any sign of injury, thank goodness. "Did you fall?"

"No. The yoga classes are paying off. I managed

to keep my balance, but unfortunately, I bumped the entry and broke the crystal vase I scored at the garage sale last week."

"Thank goodness."

Barbara scowled at Gillian. "It was Waterford!"

"Thank goodness that you didn't fall," Gillian clarified. Her mother had a history of taking tumbles. "I'm glad the vase was the only thing broken."

Barbara wrinkled her nose. "Well, I murdered the poor daffodils too, I'm afraid. Broke their delicate little necks. That's what I get for bragging about scooping a piece of Waterford out from beneath Belinda Parson's nose."

Gillian stifled a smile. Her mother and Mrs. Parson had been Friday morning garage sale shopping partners for more than a decade. The competition to snag the good stuff was serious business. "Hand me the broom and dustpan, Mom. I see some pieces you missed."

As Gillian swept up the last of the glass shards, Barbara stood with her hands on her hips and made a slow circle, studying the salon's greeting area. "I hate not having flowers to greet our clients. The room isn't nearly as warm."

"I can stop by Blooms on my way back from lunch and pick an arrangement up from Maisy. She always keeps a few made up. Or, if you have another vase, she told me a few minutes ago that she'd got some gorgeous calla lilies in this morning."

"Callas?" Barbara brightened at the thought. "I love callas. Mini or standard?"

"Minis. Pinks and whites."

"Oh, beautiful. Get some of both. A dozen. They'll look lovely in your grandmother's trumpet vase. I have it tucked away in the back. Tell Maisy I said hello, and don't forget the flower food!"

"Yes, ma'am."

"Now, I'd better run. You know how my sister gets when she has to wait on me." Barbara picked up her handbag and headed out the door, calling over her shoulder as she went, "No need to rush your lunch, dear. Our MOB called, and they're running about twenty minutes late. There's a road closed in Austin."

"There's always a road closed in Austin," Gillian replied as the door closed behind her mother.

She put away the broom and dustpan, made one final adjustment to the bustle of the gown in the front display window, and then grabbed her purse, flipped the OPEN sign to CLOSED, and stepped out into the bright sunshine of a beautiful winter day.

The weather forecast called for temperatures in the mid-seventies this afternoon, with a partly cloudy sky and a slight chance of rain in the early evening. Poor weather certainly wouldn't prevent anyone from enjoying outdoor activities today.

The mouthwatering aroma of grilling meat seasoned with Mexican spices perfumed the air and reminded Gillian that today was Taco Tuesday. The Miguelitos' food truck parked in the Marktplatz at lunchtime on Tuesdays. Ordinarily, she ate a salad at home during the week, but on Tuesdays, she treated herself to Miguelitos' fish tacos with hot peach salsa and a side of guacamole.

After locking Bliss's front door, she turned and walked at a brisk pace across the courtyard, headed for the passageway at the back of the U, which offered a shortcut to the market square. She had a smile on her face and joy in her heart—until fluttering off to her left attracted her attention.

Fluttering, where there wasn't supposed to be fluttering.

She halted abruptly. Across the courtyard that Bliss shared with the empty mercantile building, three flags flew from the canopy above the front doors—the Stars and Stripes, the Lone Star, and a third with brown lettering on a field of forest green that read GET GRUBBY.

Gillian blinked, then looked again. Why was her building flying a flag that said GET GRUBBY?

A bad feeling washed over her. Her heart began to pound, and her mouth went dry. Gillian's gaze zoomed to the lower right-hand corner of the display window next to the entrance. It was empty. Bare! Bare, but for the rectangular residue of tape that for years—literally, for years—had fastened a black-and-red sign to the window. A sign that read FOR SALE.

The sign was gone.

Chapter Seven

Tucker sauntered back toward Enchanted Canyon Wilderness School a happy man. He'd eaten tacos, or a variation of tacos, in cities and towns and villages all over the world, and nothing tasted as good as Tex-Mex, in Texas, on a warm and sunny winter afternoon.

He'd managed to beg off the business lunch with Jones too, which added to his enjoyment of the day. Not only had he thwarted Boone's plans for him—always a positive—he'd also avoided having to spend at least another hour with Gillian's banker over German food. Exceptional German food, admittedly, but the quality of the cuisine couldn't overcome the sour taste that being in Jeremy's company put in Tucker's mouth.

He didn't like his male model handsomeness or his charming, confident manner or the fact that he wore Italian loafers and French sunglasses and drove a German car. He especially didn't like the fact that ol' Jeremy would get to have breakfast with Gillian every day for the rest of his life.

So after listening to the banker's spiel while he and his cousins signed papers for almost an hour, Tucker had had his fill of the man long before Jeremy suggested they walk on over to Otto's for lunch. He'd prepared an excuse about an expected delivery that required a signature and abandoned his cousins to the wurst in favor of Marktplatz and Miguelitos' Taco Tuesday.

Damn, but those carnitas had been delicious.

As he sauntered back toward their new building, his thoughts turned to this change of course upon which he'd embarked. During the weeks he had spent alone and exploring Enchanted Canyon, he'd come to terms with the loss of his career, and he'd dealt with his disillusionment in his dreams and ideals. Bottom line—he'd been an excellent warrior. A bureaucrat, not so much. A politician, not worth a damned lick. His army career going forward would have required that from him. He'd had no choice but to make the change.

He'd quit, but he wasn't a quitter. He didn't need to rag on himself about that. His time in Enchanted Canyon had helped him to accept that the job, the mission, had evolved over time. Recognizing his limitations and acting on them wasn't quitting if, bottom line, the army and his country were better off with another man in the position. Tucker could hold his head up knowing he'd made the right choice. He'd done the right thing.

And now, change, here I come.

So what kind of teacher would he make? That was the question before him, wasn't it?

He had a fair amount of experience instructing soldiers. He spoke with authority, and people listened to him. People who attended his classes would be there to learn, having paid a significant fee for the opportunity. The kids would be the wild card, but based on his afternoons with Haley, he thought he'd be good with them.

He strode back toward the shop in no real hurry since he figured Boone and Jackson would be at the very least another half an hour. No sense tackling the work all by himself when he had cousins to help. Besides, unloading boxes was the perfect time to chew Boone's ass about some of the inventory choices he'd made.

Since he wasn't in a hurry, Tucker detoured to the ice cream store for a mint chocolate chip. "Cone or cup?" asked the matronly woman behind the counter with a smile.

"Cone, please."

He'd also decided the time had come for him to put away the reserved, unfriendly attitude he'd adopted over the past decade or so. It worked okay for a recluse hiding away in the Hill Country, but as of today, he was officially out of the canyon. He needed to dust off his charming and put on his friendly. So while the server finished fitting the ice cream into the cone, he pulled out a rusty, flirtatious wink and rascal grin. "Pretty skin like yours makes me think of peaches 'n cream. Why don't you add a dip of that flavor too? I'm in the mood to splurge."

"Go on with you now," she said with a laugh, her cheeks coloring prettily. "That line may work on the young'uns, but I have your number."

Yet, when she handed over his cone, Tucker couldn't help but note that the second scoop was bigger than the first. *Catch more flies with honey . . .*

Stepping out onto the street, he turned toward the mercantile building, his stride long, and his thoughts on the afternoon ahead. With three sets of hands, they should be able to knock out most of the unpacking. Maybe he'd let Boone and Jackson stock the shelves while he set up his office on the second floor. It was a great space with lots of windows, which he liked. He could do most of what needed doing for the business side of the wilderness school on his laptop and phone, but if he had to be stuck indoors in an office, he'd be glad to have windows. The windowless cubicles of his special assignment time had drained his soul.

Tucker took a lick of his cone and added his office's proximity to the ice cream parlor to the list of things that made him happy. He liked ice cream even better than Tex-Mex.

When his gaze snagged on the swaying hips of the woman in front of him, he admitted he liked eye candy best of all.

Gillian Thacker had just exited Bliss Bridal Salon and turned to walk away from him. It gave him the perfect opportunity to ogle her ass without getting caught.

She had the sultry sexiness of a WWII pinup girl, tall and curvy with an unconscious way of walking—a hippy, come-hither sway—that absolutely did it for him. Today, she wore her long mahogany hair loose. The wavy curls bounced to and fro with her every step in a way that called to a man saying, "Touch me. Touch me."

A glance around showed he wasn't the only man watching her walk either. Of the six guys within line of sight of Gillian, four of them had their eyes peeled. *She shouldn't be allowed out in public.*

Tucker wondered if Jones realized just how lucky he was. The banker talked plenty this morning, but his only mention of Gillian had been as an aside while yammering on about golf. Somehow, Tucker and Jackson had gotten roped into playing a round with the bridegroom-to-be next weekend. Never mind that Tucker hadn't played golf once since leaving

DC. He'd have to find time before Saturday to visit the driving range. It was bad enough that Tucker had to surrender the field where Gillian was concerned. It absolutely would not do for good ol' Jeremy to kick his butt on the golf course too.

Tucker was jealous of the man. He could admit it. Jeremy had what Tucker wanted.

Gillian ticked off a number of Tucker's boxes. He liked her spunk, her style, her honesty, and her humor. And of course, there was that physical appeal—the supermodel body, smoky voice, and sexy smile. And the walk. That luscious, provocative, glorious walk that could lure a man into trouble.

The walk that twenty yards in front of him abruptly stopped.

Gillian's purse slipped out of her hand and thudded onto the courtyard's winter-dead grass. She stood frozen like a new tub of peaches 'n cream fresh from the freezer. Then she began to weave.

Damn. Hope there's nothing wrong with her. Tucker picked up his pace, and in a dozen strides, he'd caught up to her. "Gillian, you okay?"

Her head whipped around. Her big blue eyes looked a little wild. "Tucker?"

"Can I help you, honey?" He took her elbow in support. "Are you ill? You look pale. Did you catch Jeremy's flu?"

"No. I'm not ill. Well, maybe I am. Maybe I'm hallucinating. This can't be right. There must be a mistake."

"What can't be right?" Tucker frowned and followed the path of her gaze. She was focused on his flags, so he gave them a quick study. US, Texas, and Boone's slogan. "You have something against our slogan?"

"Your slogan," she repeated. Her eyes widened, and then narrowed. "*Your* slogan?"

Tucker nodded. "Boone thought the school needed a slogan. *Get grubby* is a little saying Haley and I use when we're doing our wilderness thing."

"The school." She blinked and gave her head a shake. "What school? I don't understand. Caroline mentioned something about you becoming a teacher. I thought you'd be at Redemption High."

"Me? Teach at a high school?" Tucker scoffed. "I might have spent more than a decade in the military, but I'm not near brave enough to teach at a high school. No, we're opening a wilderness school."

"A wilderness school," Gillian repeated. "For like, preppers? Survivalists? People who eat bugs and grubs and grasshoppers?"

Tucker rolled his eyes. "We are going to teach wilderness skills and preparedness to people who are interested in the outdoors. *Preppers* is a pejorative term. I don't use it, and before you climb too high on your horse, maybe you should ask the people in Houston if they were glad they had basic supplies on hand after Harvey hit, or even the people of Austin who owned five-dollar water purification filters last summer when the city told them to boil water for two weeks."

"Okay. Okay. You're right. That's snotty of me. So, the slogan for your school is: *Get Grubby*?"

"Yes."

"All right, then." She dragged a hand down her face, then asked, "Tucker, why is your slogan on a flag that is flying from my building?"

"*Your* building?" He turned his head and looked toward Bliss. He didn't see any flags flying from the salon's canopy. That left the McBride family's latest purchase. "You mean the mercantile building?"

"Yes."

"Well, Gillian, the mercantile is *our* mercantile— the McBride family's. We bought it earlier this week. Wrapped up all the paperwork this morning."

"No." She let out a soft little moan. "Why? You own an entire canyon. And an inn and a dance hall and a ghost town. Why did you buy my building?"

Tucker was a little confused himself. He didn't think she'd owned the building. The former owner's name was Ayers if he recalled correctly. "Because Boone decided that Enchanted Canyon Wilderness School needed a presence in town, so we're now your new neighbor."

Tucker found the fact that she looked so appalled about it more than a little insulting. He hooked his thumbs in the pockets of his jeans and observed, "Kind of appropriate, don't you think? A survival school across from a bridal salon? Heaven knows surviving marriage takes skills. Maybe we could do a cross-promotion sometime."

"A cross-promotion?" Color flooded back into her cheeks, and the pitch of her voice rose as she repeated, "A cross-promotion?"

Innocently, he asked, "What? You don't think that's a good idea?"

"I . . . I . . ." She held her head in her hands and accused, "You stole our building!"

"Stole?" Now, that didn't sit well. He was a lot of things, but he wasn't a thief. He arched a brow, looked pointedly at his new purchase, then back at her. "Sweetcheeks, Enchanted Canyon Enterprises paid a pretty penny for this place."

"*Sweetcheeks*? Did you just call me *sweetcheeks*?"

Tucker wouldn't have been surprised to see smoke pouring from her ears. Okay, so that word had been politically incorrect, but Gillian brought out the— what was that term they use these days? *Masculine* something. No, *toxic masculinity*. That's it. Gillian Thacker sent Tucker's testosterone off the charts. And that walk . . .

"Call 'em as I see 'em," he murmured, before raising his tone and asking, "What am I missing here? Why are your panties in such a twist over the fact that we are neighbors?"

"Do not talk about my panties, you misogynistic jerk!"

"I am not misogynistic. I happen to love and respect women. I might be a little behind the times when it comes to my metaphors, but you can deal with it. And tell me why you're so upset that we're opening our school in the mercantile building."

"Because." She closed her eyes and gave her head a shake. In that instant, the temper in her tone drained away, leaving only woebegone in the words she spoke next. "Because the expansion is our plan. It's our big dream."

Tucker felt a shimmer of unease. Gillian was a partner with her mother in the wedding gown shop. Barbara Thacker and her sister, Cathy, had spent a weekend at the Fallen Angel Inn not long ago, and he'd guided them on a hike through the canyon. Tucker liked Gillian's mother very much. He would hate it if he'd inadvertently trampled on her big dream by going along with Boone's big idea.

Gillian's next words doused the guilt flickering to life inside him. "We talked about it on New Year's

Eve. Blissful Events is the wedding and event planning business he and I are starting."

Oh, yeah. The one that's all your baby.

"The mercantile building is the perfect location for it. We're just waiting until after the wedding to make an offer. The building has been for sale forever. Literally years. I never dreamed someone else would buy it out from under our feet." She paused and shook her head. "The listing agent knew our plans. He plays golf with Jeremy every Saturday morning. Why didn't he tell us you were interested? We would have made a counteroffer."

Since this big dream wasn't Gillian's and Barbara's, but hers and Banker Boy's, Tucker had to wonder. All the talking Jeremy had done during their meeting this morning, one would think he would have mentioned the death of his big dream. He hadn't.

Jeremy had known about the sale ahead of time too. The McBrides hadn't financed the purchase through his bank, but the bank had handled paperwork for the seller. So why keep the news from his beloved fiancée? *Not your circus, not your monkey, McBride.*

Tucker shrugged. "Well, the sale has closed. That ship has sailed. I guess all is fair in love and real estate."

She shot him an annoyed look. "Bad metaphorical speaking."

He smiled and took another lick of his ice cream cone and waited, watching her, as she spent close to a minute in contemplative thought before nodding briskly. "You're right. We made a mistake by waiting to secure the property once we decided on it. The challenge now is to make the best of the current situation.

I'm prepared to discuss lease arrangements immediately. Would you care to join me for lunch?"

Having worked his way down to the ice cream
cone, Tucker took a bite. The woman didn't waste any
time, did she? Knock her down, she gets right back
up. Another check of one of his boxes. He'd always
thought perseverance was sexy.

"Thanks for the invitation, Gillian, but I've already
had my lunch. Taco Tuesday, you know." He hefted
his cone. "This is dessert."

"That's fine." She glanced toward Marktplatz. "My
lunch can wait. I'm honestly not that hungry. Why
don't we talk in the building? I'll show you what we
plan to do with the space."

"I'm happy to have your company, Gillian, but I
think you've misunderstood. We're not seeking ten-
ants. It's going to be my storefront."

"But—"

"Come on, I'll show you."

He pulled his keys from his pocket as he led her
toward the store. He unlocked the door, opened it,
then stepped back so that she could precede him. Gillian walked into the room still piled high with boxes
and made a slow circle, taking it all in. She turned a
stricken gaze toward him. "You've put up shelving
already."

"Apparently the former owner recently did some
sprucing up, painted the walls, refinished the floors,
and replaced all the bathroom fixtures."

"In October. Mrs. Ayers told me to consider it my
wedding gift. She died right before Thanksgiving.
Doesn't it take time for an inheritance to get settled?
How could Johnny sell the building so fast?" Hope
entered her eyes. "Maybe the sale wasn't legal. You
might have caught a break if that's the case, Tucker.

You'll do better at the other end of Main Street. This isn't a good location for foot traffic. It's the slow end of the street. Tourists don't come down this far except on the weekends when Marktplatz is open."

Tucker didn't believe there was anything wrong with the paperwork. "What is it you wanted to do with this space?"

"I plan to create a wedding district, encompassing the entire U around the courtyard. A bakery. Photography studio. Invitation design and paper shop. A jeweler. Lingerie store. I plan to use the courtyard for vendor showcases. Maisy might move her flower shop once her lease is up or else open a small space that focuses only on wedding floral."

Tucker gazed out of the display window that faced the courtyard and focused on the Cinderella bride display in the window facing his. He could picture what she was describing. The idea made a lot of sense too.

"So." Gillian licked her lips and squared her shoulders. "You see, Tucker, while I appreciate your unusual expertise, *Get Grubby* just doesn't fit. What has been unpacked can be repacked. I'm sure we can find you a location for your storefront much more suitable to your needs."

"This location is perfect for us. It's gonna be more than a retail storefront. We plan to go beyond selling hand axes and knives. We're turning the upstairs into a classroom."

"Weapons? You're going to sell weapons?"

Tucker rolled his eyes. "Tools and teaching. This building is a great spot for us. There's plenty of parking. The courtyard gives us a place for some outdoor demonstrations."

"Outdoor demonstrations? What kind of outdoor demonstrations?"

"What kind do you think?" he asked, exasperated by the appalled expression on her face. "I'm going to string up a dead deer and teach my students to dress it. We'll have your dresses on your side of the courtyard and my kind of dressing on mine."

The woman actually went pale, and he hastened to say, "I'm kidding, Gillian. I'm talking about fire starting. It's—"

"You can't start a fire in the courtyard! These buildings are all made of wood! I'm sure that's against zoning regulations."

"It's not. We checked."

"Well, I'll go to the town council and have some passed."

"I don't think it works that way. Look, we're not fools. Our main purpose is to teach skills, the number one of which is safety. We're not going to set your little shop on fire."

Insult flared in her eyes, and she sucked in a breath. "My little shop? My little shop!"

"My *unusual* expertise," he countered. Damn, but the woman got under his skin in more ways than one. Didn't he deserve a little respect?

After all, hadn't he played knight in shining armor and rescued her from a bad situation last fall? Hadn't he kept his mouth shut when it became apparent that she didn't want news of their meeting to go public? Hadn't he stayed by her side when Jeremy deserted her at midnight on New Year's Eve?

Okay, maybe he shouldn't have kissed her again, but he was only human. A male human. And she attracted him like a buck to a mineral lick.

"What's your price?" she asked abruptly.

"Excuse me?"

"Every person has a price. What's yours? I want this property. What will it take for me to get it?"

A dozen different thoughts flashed through his mind. A dozen different suggestions hovered on his tongue. None of them were appropriate. He cleared his throat. "Gillian, I don't think it's—"

"Think!" she interrupted. "That's the word that needs to concern you before you say anything. Now, while you're doing that, why don't you show me what you've done upstairs?"

Without waiting for his response, she headed for the staircase. Tucker started after her, only not too fast. He wasn't stupid. Watching her climb stairs was a bigger treat than his double-dip cone, and enjoying it somewhat soothed his ruffled feathers.

Beyond placing the furniture for his office, they'd done little more than haul a handful of boxes upstairs since the tables ordered for the classroom had yet to arrive. Gillian went straight to the spacious corner room that would serve as Tucker's office. "I love the light in here," she murmured when he joined her. "Four windows. East and north facing, so it doesn't fight the western sun." She glanced up. "I'd thought to raise the ceiling. The lines of the attic are fabulous."

Distracted by the idea, Tucker considered it. "I'm partial to high ceilings myself."

She pinned him with a keen-eyed gaze. "But you live in an Airstream trailer."

"Technically, yes. I prefer to sleep under the stars. For the most part, that's what I've been doing in the canyon."

"It's the middle of winter."

He shrugged. "You can usually find a protected

spot in Enchanted Canyon. So, what exactly were you going to do with all this space?"

The gleam of hope that entered her eyes made Tucker regret his question the moment he asked it. She launched into a detailed description beginning with his office, expanding to her plans for subdividing the classroom space, and then creating a client conference room and showroom downstairs. "It'll be like a home builder's design center. I'll have the ground floor divided up into areas showcasing the basic vendor categories—photography, music, catering, linens, etcetera. For example, I'll have sizable samples of linens displayed similarly to the way upscale furniture stores display upholstery selections. But the centerpiece of the space will be—wait." She waved a dismissive hand. "Come downstairs. It'll be easier to explain."

Once again, Gillian headed for the staircase, and Tucker followed along, closer behind her this time. She'd taken four steps down when the sound of male laughter exploded from below. Then Tucker heard good ol' Jeremy say, "I think you'll be very successful here, Boone. I'm delighted I could help y'all get this building."

Gillian missed a step and tripped. Ever the hero, Tucker reached out and broke her fall. Unfortunately, he couldn't do anything about the shattering of her heart.

Chapter Eight

Gillian would recognize Jeremy's business laugh anywhere. It was just a tiny bit too jovial, although she doubted anyone else ever picked up on it. Jeremy was good with people, charming and sincere. He sounded sincere when he said, "I think you'll be very successful here, Boone."

Here. Surely, Jeremy meant in Redemption. Not in this building. Not in *their* building. What was he doing here?

"I'm delighted I could help y'all get this building."

Her heel caught on the stair, and she teetered. Tucker grabbed her, steadied her. Feeling light-headed, Gillian made sure to hold onto the railing as she finished descending the stairs. She only vaguely noticed that Tucker didn't let her go until she'd planted both her feet firmly on the ground floor.

Now, all of her attention was directed at her fiancé. He wore his gray suit and the green tie she'd given him for Christmas. "Jeremy?"

His green eyes widened when he spied her, and a brief instant of alarm flashed across his face. "What are you doing here?"

"I'm wondering the same about you. This morning you were still sick in bed with the flu."

He lifted his chin slightly. "I told you I intended to go into work today. I had a lunch scheduled."

And . . . ? Gillian waited.

"I'm delighted I could help y'all get this building."

How could he?

Jeremy didn't elaborate beyond his lunch statement. Not verbally, anyway. But she knew this man well. She recognized the gleam that had come into his eyes. She noticed the way he smoothed his blond hair, adjusted his cufflinks, and subtly widened his stance. He was on the defensive, and that's when he usually got aggressive.

Gillian's temper began to seethe. *He'd* betrayed *her!* And now he was spoiling for a fight? Did she want to give him one?

Maybe. Maybe so. That depends. "Jeremy, how long have you known the McBride family intended to purchase this building?"

"I got the news sometime before Christmas."

Yes. Yes, Gillian did want to give Jeremy a fight. However, she wouldn't do it in front of the McBrides. So she lifted her chin and smiled a smile that could have cut glass. "Speaking of lunch, I'd better get along on my way. I need to get home to let Peaches out for her lunchtime potty break. If you gentlemen will excuse me?"

Without waiting for anyone's response, Gillian sailed out of the mercantile. Her home was an eight-minute walk away. Today, she made it in six and managed to hold off her angry tears until she walked inside and was met with excited puppy yips. Releasing Peaches from her crate, Gillian sank down onto the floor with the puppy in her lap.

Peaches was ten weeks old, a little mop of a Bichon–
Shih Tzu mix with floppy brown ears and a white
face and a little pink tongue that even now licked at
the tears flowing freely down Gillian's cheeks. The
puppy had been Jeremy's Christmas gift to her, presented with a red bow around her neck and nestled in
a wicker basket he'd set beneath Gillian's tree. Gillian's beloved collie, Princess, had died the previous spring, and she'd nursed a hole in her heart ever
since. She'd been ready to adopt a new pet from the
animal shelter last summer, but Jeremy had lobbied
against it. He didn't want a dog. He preferred cats.
They'd debated the subject for weeks and eventually
agreed to wait until after their honeymoon to adopt
any pet.

The Christmas surprise had melted her heart.

She heard the front door open and recognized Jeremy's footsteps as he headed for the laundry room
where Gillian kept Peaches' crate. Without looking
up, she asked, "Peaches was a guilt gift, wasn't she?"

"Yes."

"You were never going to agree to buy the building, were you? Why didn't you just tell me? Why
weren't you honest?"

"Would you put down the damned dog, and stand
up, so I don't feel as if I'm looming over you?"

Holding Peaches close, she rose gracefully to her
feet and headed for the kitchen door. "She needs to
go out."

Jeremy sighed, shoved his hands into his pants
pockets, and followed her. At the edge of her back
patio, Gillian set Peaches down in the yellow winter
grass. The puppy dipped her head and started sniffing. Gillian folded her arms and waited for Jeremy to
speak.

"You are right. I didn't want to buy the building. It's ridiculous to invest that much on a new, unproven business. I was watching out for us."

"What *us*? You made the decision all by yourself! Without discussing it with me."

"Sort of like you and all the wedding planning."

"I included you in the wedding planning."

"Did you? Or did you inform me of the decisions you made with your mother? You're all about the wedding, Gillian, and this wedding has been more hers and yours, than yours and mine."

Gillian's seething temper became a rolling boil. She recognized this tactic. He was attempting to divert her attention from the subject of the building betrayal. She wouldn't allow him to attack her mother. "That's not fair, Jeremy, and it's not true. The wedding is two parts—the ceremony and the party to celebrate the service. The ceremony is the important part, and you and I have done all the planning and made all the decisions for that. As we should have done. But my parents are hosting the reception. You and I have picked the photographer and the band and menu and a million other details. My mother loves flowers. She loves to set a pretty table. If flowers are important to her, then she gets to pick the reception flowers! That's not too much to give her when she's paying for it!"

"See, you've proved my point. The wedding is all you care about. You're marrying me. You're supposed to put me first. I wanted roses, not those fluffy things. You sided with her."

Gillian rounded on him. "They're hydrangeas, not fluffy things, and that argument is ridiculous. What is this? What is really going on here? It's not wedding floral. It's you and me. Things haven't been right with us for months. I thought it was premarital jitters, but it's bigger than that. What are you trying to say, Jeremy?"

"I was scared, okay?" He waved his hand wildly, frightening the dog, who scuttled to Gillian's side. "I didn't want to start a new business. I didn't want wedding planning to become our lives. You weren't paying attention to me. You shut me out."

"So you sabotaged me! You sold our dream!"

"Not our dream. Your dream." He folded his arms and lifted his chin pugnaciously. "When I learned the McBrides had made an offer on the mercantile building, I took it as a providential sign and declined the opportunity to counteroffer."

"*You* declined. *You* decided. You decided our future all on your own." A white-hot storm of rage blew through her. "How dare you. How dare you! This isn't the 1950s, Jeremy. I'm not a little woman who you get to pat on the head and say, *Make me a sandwich and bring me a beer.* Marriages today are partnerships. You don't get to make unilateral decisions that affect both of us. If you felt this way about my dreams, then you should have manned up and been honest and started a conversation about it."

"Maybe so, but that's water under the bridge now. I'd do it differently if I could. If I could go back in time, I'd do a lot of things differently. But I can't." The fight seemed to go out of him then as he added, "What's done is done."

He gripped the back of one of Gillian's patio chairs. His knuckles were white. He wouldn't meet her gaze. A long silence stretched between them before he nervously licked his lips and said, "Gillian, I can't marry you. We need to call this thing off."

Never mind that she had been working her own

way to this same realization, hearing him say it was a fist to her solar plexus. "Wh-wh-what? Y-y-you what? You want to . . . to . . ."

"Cancel the wedding."

Gillian swayed. She stared at the man she'd loved, so handsome in his favorite suit and the tie that matched his eyes, eyes now staring back at her with misery in their depths. She locked her knees to keep from sinking to the ground. "Wait. Just wait. I don't understand. Why do this now? Tucker bought the building. My design center dream isn't happening. You won."

"No, I didn't. Not really." He shoved his hands in his pockets and looked away. Long seconds passed before he straightened his spine and looked at her. The misery was gone. He'd made a decision. "I've had time to do a lot of thinking these past two weeks. Seeing your reaction to the news today crystallized things for me. This business of yours is more important to you than I realized. It's more important to you than I am."

"That's not true."

"Isn't it?" he challenged. "Look, Gillian, if our basic goals and dreams are incompatible, that makes us incompatible. Oh, it probably would have worked between us for a few years, but the entire time, resentments would be bubbling beneath the surface. Eventually, they'd blow us apart. Better it happens now before we have a kid or two who'd get caught in the explosion."

"So, you decide to make a preemptive strike," she said bitterly. "You make this decision today all on your own based on an expression on my face."

"No, I'm making it now because I finally have the guts to do something I've known needed doing for at least the past four months. Marriage between us wouldn't work, Gillian, and I think deep down, you know it too."

Bridal jitters. She'd told herself it was bridal jitters. "We have that counseling—"

He cut her off. "It's too late for that."

"Why? Shouldn't we at least try?"

He shoved his hands in his pockets. "Our problem isn't fixable, Gillian. I tried. I loved you. I didn't want to hurt you. But then New Year's Eve . . ."

When he didn't finish his sentence, Gillian narrowed her eyes. "What about New Year's Eve?"

He dragged his hand down his face. His voice was tight as he said, "I knew I couldn't fix it. I knew this had to happen."

"And rather than talk to me, rather than be honest with me, you decided to act by letting Tucker McBride buy my building? Did you even have the flu, Jeremy?"

"No."

I knew it. Gillian closed her eyes. "You need to leave."

"I wish . . ." He let the sentence trail off and then sighed heavily. "It's better this way."

Then Jeremy turned around and left through the backyard gate.

She was glad to see him go, she realized. Except, he took her dreams with him.

Gillian sank to her knees on the brittle grass. Sensing her turmoil, Peaches bounded toward her. She wrapped her arms around her puppy and held on as if the pup were a life preserver flung from a sinking ship. As Peaches' rough pink tongue covered her cheeks in kisses, Gillian broke.

* * *

For Tucker, growing up in a small town west of Fort Worth in a ranching family meant a yearly trip to the Fort Worth Stock Show and Rodeo, a three-week-long event held annually at the end of January and first part of February. Invariably, the Stock Show ushered in the coldest weather of the year, often accompanied by an ice storm that all but shut the city down. When Jackson told him yesterday they had "Stock Show" weather on the way, he'd decided to revisit another McBride tradition. He'd pulled deer meat from the freezer and whipped up a big old pot of venison chili, his dad's recipe. He took it to the shop and invited friends and family to drop by for a bowl of red. Now, it simmered on the stove in the break room and filled the air with a spicy aroma that made him nostalgic for home.

Sorting through the morning's UPS deliveries in the Enchanted Canyon Wilderness School headquarters stockroom, he decided he might just make a run up to Fort Worth this weekend. Check out the rodeo.

Tucker was thinking about reconnecting with his roots when he heard his soon-to-be cousin-in-law say, "I'm so worried about Gillian."

His head came up, and he went as still as a guard dog on alert, listening intently. Caroline and Maisy had stopped by for chili and to pick up Maisy's special order that had arrived yesterday.

"It's been two weeks since the breakup, and she's hardly left her house," Caroline continued.

Curiosity guided Tucker's footsteps closer to the stockroom door as Maisy replied, "She's a mess, for sure, and I'm afraid it won't get any better until her wedding day has passed."

"Yep. It will be a painful weekend for Gillian."

"We'd better plan on spending it with her—whether she wants us there or not."

"I know. I haven't known Gillian nearly as long as you have, Maisy, but still, this is worrisome. I saw her last night at the twenty-four-hour drugstore. At midnight."

"Midnight?"

"Uh-huh. I had to run in to pick up some hydrogen peroxide because River tangled with a skunk and we had none in the house."

"That stinks," Maisy said.

"Tell me about it. It was loads of fun. Anyway, I'm walking up to the counter, and I see Gillian standing in front of the freezer section. Wearing pajamas and a robe and house slippers."

Tucker almost dropped the box in his hand. Maisy made a scandalized gasp. "Gillian? Our Gillian?"

"Yes!"

"No. Oh, no. Gillian Thacker did *not* go out in public wearing pajamas and house shoes."

"She did. It's true. I saw her standing in front of the freezer case staring at the ice cream. She had a coat on over the robe, at least, but I don't think she'd combed her hair all day, much less put on makeup."

"I can't believe it."

Tucker couldn't believe it either. Gillian Thacker was the most put-together woman he'd seen this side of a North Dallas trophy wife. Even that first time they'd met, after hiking in heels across cotton fields, she'd taken care to touch up her lipstick.

Maisy continued, "In that case, this situation is even worse than I thought. Did you talk to her?"

"I tried," Caroline replied with frustration in her voice. "I called her name as I walked toward her. She startled, then waved and muttered something about needing to buy cat food and sort of scurried away."

"She doesn't own a cat."

"I didn't think she did, and she didn't have any cat food in her basket that I could see—just toilet paper, tissues, tampons, and dog food. And three bags of Cheetos."

"The necessities. Cheetos and ice cream are Gillian's stress eating go-to. She doesn't keep them in the house. She had three bags, you say?"

"Yes, and she might have doubled back for ice cream. I didn't stay around and watch her check out. It was obvious she wasn't happy that I'd spotted her." Caroline hesitated a moment, then added, "Depression can be a serious condition."

"I don't think she's had time to become seriously depressed yet," Maisy replied, her voice strained with concern. "She's still in shock. She's mourning. You know Gillian, she does everything in a big way. She's going to mourn with a capital *M* for a little while."

Tucker slid his box onto a shelf and then moved closer to the storeroom door as Maisy added, "I think she needs to get angry. That's the next step in the mourning process, isn't it? Anger?"

"Depends on which model you use," Caroline replied. "But yes, anger is part of the process."

"Hmm." Following a few moments of thoughtful silence, Maisy continued, "Remember at the soft opening weekend for the Fallen Angel Inn last summer when Celeste and the Eternity Springs' wives talked about their interventions? It's something they do when someone in their circle has a romantic crisis and they believe she needs some straight talk?"

"I do."

"Well, I don't know that Gillian's at the point of needing the big guns of an Eternity Springs level intervention, but I think she could use a little girlfriend support. Barbara told me yesterday that Gillian had promised to come into work today. If she didn't show, Barbara was prepared to go to her place and pile on the guilt."

"I'm glad to hear that."

"She'll need to eat something other than Cheetos and ice cream or she'll be the one who is sick. We should drag her over here for a bowl of chili. We don't need to mention Jeremy or the wedding or grill her about how she's feeling. Just give her a distraction."

"That's a great idea," Caroline agreed. "Tucker's chili is fabulous, and a bowl of Texas comfort food on a cold winter's day would be good medicine for Gillian. However, I doubt she'll agree to come over here. I don't think she'd be comfortable around Tucker or any guy right now."

"True."

At that point, having located Maisy's special order of a knife for her father's upcoming birthday, he snagged the package and sauntered into the kitchen. "I've been eavesdropping. Tell her I'm not here and I left you in charge, Caroline. Since you are family now and all. I'll make myself scarce."

"You sure?" Caroline asked. "You don't mind?"

"Not at all. What are neighbors for if not to offer the comfort of a good bowl of chili?"

"You're a good man, Tucker McBride." Maisy kissed him on the cheek.

He handed over her order and completed the sale. A few minutes later, having donned his coat and grabbed a go pack, he took up a sentry position behind the cigar store Indian in front of the antiques store across the street and watched Caroline and Maisy march into battle in Bliss.

Almost fifteen minutes passed before they emerged from the salon with Gillian in tow. Seeing her, Tucker did a double take. He almost didn't recognize her.

Wanting a closer look, he fished his field glasses from his pack and focused on her face. Gillian was a ghost of her former self. Her complexion was wan, her long brown hair had lost its bounce and sheen, and the spark of life in her eyes had been extinguished.

If Jones were to cross his path right now, Tucker would whip his ass.

He watched the trio disappear into his shop. For a long few minutes, Tucker stared at the GET GRUBBY flag fluttering in the bitter breeze and brooded.

He tried to be honest with himself as a rule. However, until now, he had avoided self-analysis of his reaction upon hearing the news about Gillian's broken engagement.

He'd felt a rush of elation, but on its heels came a wave of reality. It was one thing to get all yearny when the woman was out of reach, but something else entirely when she was no longer off-limits.

Was he ready for this? Did he really want to make a play for Gillian Thacker?

It's true that she was as hot as the Rio Grande Valley in August, but he'd outgrown the looks-matter-more-than-character stage before he'd finished college. Yes, she checked his boxes, but that was definitely a preliminary survey. He didn't know Gillian well enough yet to judge her character.

Don't you?

He pondered the question for a bit. Actually, he did know quite a lot about her. He knew that she'd returned to her hometown after college and built a business with her mother. She had a good friend she'd known since childhood, Maisy, and one who she'd welcomed into her life fairly recently in Caroline. She'd dreamed big, and when thwarted, refused to abandon her dreams. She taught Sunday school at her church and volunteered her time reading to the elderly at a local nursing home. She was partial to bright nail polish and dangling earrings, and she wore heels when other women wore flats. She'd been wearing a red bra the day he rescued her from the road. What did those things say about her character?

Gillian was kind, generous, loyal, and loving. She was faithful to her promises and persistent in her goals. She was confident and proud, often practical, but also a bit daring and adventurous.

She was the kind of woman he wanted to be with. The kind of woman he would fall hard for. She was the kind of woman he wouldn't allow himself to reach for when he lived a military life.

Well, that was then, this was now. He was a civilian. And Gillian was single.

Tucker's gaze drifted away from the school's front door and across the courtyard that separated his shop from hers, lingering on the pots of purple pansies and rustic bent-willow benches and chairs that were arranged around a garden fountain and birdbath at its center. Finally, he fastened his stare on Bliss's front door.

Tucker knew what he wanted. He wanted the chance to change Gillian's relationship status. He wanted Gillian for his own.

He would need to give her time for her broken heart to heal, of course. Gillian wasn't the sort of woman to jump from one relationship directly into another. He was in no rush. He could bide his time and when the moment was right, make his move.

But in the meantime, he hated to see her so blue. He wished he could do something to help her. Maisy thought she needed to get angry. Maybe so. She definitely needed something to take her mind off her troubles, something to get excited about. But what?

He drummed his fingers against the wooden figure's shoulder and thought about it. Gillian's friends were probably right that nothing was going to get her mind completely off her canceled wedding until after the dreaded day came and went. He could understand that. It didn't help matters that her career revolved around brides and weddings. He wondered how the breakup affected her plans to expand Bliss to an event planning business? He'd been certain that she would overcome the challenge of losing her chosen location, but would the loss of her partner be one blow too many?

Tucker recalled the spitfire she'd been the day she'd seen his flags. Such fire and anger and passion. That's what he wanted to see in her again. She needed her fire back.

His gaze shifted to the fanciful wedding gown display in the window at Bliss. He recalled her reaction to his slogan flag. She'd been pretty fiery then. Adamant that GET GRUBBY didn't fit in the neighborhood.

His mouth lifted in a slow, wicked smile. Gillian needed her fire back. Luckily, fire starting was an elemental life skill, and he was an expert at it. Tucker knew just what tinder this situation required.

After checking traffic, he crossed Main Street and ambled toward Bliss's front door.

Chapter Nine

A week before what was to have been her wedding day, Gillian couldn't drag herself from bed. Her alarm had been buzzing for the past ten minutes, but she'd pulled her pillow over her head and ignored it. Five minutes ago, her phone had started to ring at one-minute intervals. She decided she needed to switch her mother's ring tone from Abba's "Mama Mia" to something more soothing. Maybe a lullaby. Or, better yet, the Miss Gulch/Wicked Witch of the West leitmotif from the *Wizard of Oz*.

At minute number six, Gillian's phone played her father's ringtone, and she closed her eyes. She might as well face the music, face the day. Face her mother. The woman wouldn't give up.

Barbara had been the perfect compassionate, caring mother when Gillian first told her about the breakup. She'd said all the right things and acted exactly the way Gillian had needed. Then about a week ago, something had changed. Her mother had quit coddling and started prodding. She had some secret, special project she'd commenced in her sewing room at home, and she wanted Gillian to run the shop.

Gillian doubted there really was a project. More likely, Barbara had concluded that she had allowed Gillian sufficient time to wallow in her misery and the time had come for Gillian to get over it, to get over Jeremy.

What her mother didn't understand, what Gillian couldn't really understand herself, was that she *was* over Jeremy.

What she mourned was the life she'd planned to have with Jeremy. Losing her dreams hurt worse than losing the man.

That had to mean that she hadn't loved him, not the way she should have loved the man she'd been about to marry. The fact that she'd ignored that truth shook her to her core. She should be devastated over this breakup. Instead, she was relieved. She'd almost married a man she didn't love. How could she have been so blind?

Gillian didn't know where to go from here. Did she want to pursue Blissful Events by herself? Or would she take a pass on that now that the McBrides owned the building and she was solo? Would she find a new dream? Maybe she'd sell her share of Bliss Bridal to her mom and move off to Paris and learn to paint. Except she'd never wanted to learn to paint.

What did she want? *Who am I now?*

She didn't know. She'd been with Jeremy for three years. Three weeks was not enough time to come up with a new plan. *A new me.*

She threw off the pillow and glared at her nightstand and the offensively ringing phone. "Hello."

"So, you'll speak to your father and not to me?" Barbara said with a slighted tone in her voice.

"I knew it was you, Mom. Today is Thursday. Dad's playing golf." Her father believed that phones didn't belong on the course. "It's early for you to be calling."

"I need to be sure you'll be in to open the shop like you promised."

"I said I'd come in, Mother. I will be there."

"On time?"

Gillian clenched her teeth, but then relaxed. Her mother's heart was in the right place, like always. She was just doing what she thought was best for her daughter. Barbara and William Thacker raised children, not snowflakes. "On time."

"You'll wash your hair?"

"Mother! I'm not five. I know how to groom myself."

Barbara let her silence speak for her.

Defensively, Gillian responded, "One day. I ran late one day and I put it up in a bun, and no one but you could tell I hadn't shampooed. Don't worry, I'll wash my hair and brush my teeth and change my underwear."

"Gillian, don't even joke about not changing your underwear. Otherwise, I'll worry myself to death. You've been fastidious since the cradle!"

Gillian looked at her flecked and peeling fingernail polish and thought, *Times have changed.*

Her mother's voice softened as she added, "I don't mean to nag. I just worry about you, sweetheart. I always have, I always will. It's a mother's lot."

"I know, Mom. Don't worry any more than usual. I'll be okay, and I'll be at the shop in time to open at ten. I promise."

"Thank you." Briskly, she continued, "We don't have an appointment until noon, so I want you to use that time to add a few touches to our new display window design. I have a theme I'm going with."

She paused as if waiting for Gillian to ask for information about the theme. Gillian didn't care enough to do so.

Eventually, Barbara continued, "I'm sure you'll have some good ideas once you see it. Now, I'd better let you go so you can hop into the shower. Give Peaches a cuddle from Nana. I'll be in this afternoon and see you then. Bye, sweetheart."

"Goodbye, Mom." Gillian let her phone slide from her hand onto the mattress, then started to pull her pillow back over her head. A yip stopped her. She lifted her head and looked toward the foot of the bed where her dog lay curled in the comforter that Gillian had kicked off during the night. Peaches stared at her with reproach. "You're in cahoots with her, aren't you? You heard your name."

The dog rose, stretched, then padded up the bed and onto Gillian. One of Peaches' hind legs landed in the general area of Gillian's bladder. When the pup followed that up with a sandpapery lick to her cheek, Gillian admitted defeat and rolled from the bed.

Twenty minutes later, with her clean hair wrapped in a towel and while Peaches feasted on her morning kibble, Gillian stared into her refrigerator in search of something appetizing. Nothing appealed to her, but knowing that her mother was bound to ask if she'd eaten, she grabbed one of the cartons of yogurt Maisy had stocked in the fridge when she visited over the weekend. Key lime pie was one of Gillian's favorite flavors. Today it tasted like cardboard.

She did not want to go in to work. She didn't want to look at a wedding gown, much less make nice with a bride. All that white blinded her. The happiness and laughter and excitement and anticipation that were part of every Bliss appointment made

her want to throw back her head and howl at the
heavens.

She needed to get over it, of course, and she
would. Bliss Bridal was her business, her career. She
wouldn't sell her share of the business to her mom.
She couldn't—she wouldn't—let Jeremy take that
part of who she was away from her. But right now,
she didn't want to be around that much white. Walking into the shop was like pouring alcohol on an open,
oozing wound.

The yogurt hitting her stomach made it churn
with nausea. Or maybe just thinking about the tulle
trenches had done it. Whatever. She tossed the half-
empty carton in the trash and returned to her bedroom and connecting bath to get ready for work. She
dried her hair and pulled it into a simple ponytail. She
moisturized her skin, but didn't have the heart to even
glance at her makeup drawer. When she opened the
top drawer of her dresser, she froze. It was empty.
Nothing there but the lavender-scented paper liner.
"Oh, hell."

She'd forgotten to do laundry. Again.

She was entirely out of clean panties.

Her gaze stole toward the corner—nowhere near
her laundry hamper, where she'd kicked her clothes
after undressing last night—and the pair of pink panties. Just how far had she sunk?

No, not that far. Mom would rise up out of her
grave to come after her, and the woman wasn't even
dead yet.

Gillian had to have a clean pair stuck away somewhere, right? An old pair with worn elastic or tattered
lace? Surely, she did.

No, she didn't. Pre-breakup Gillian kept her drawers cleaned out. And her nails done. And her legs shaved.

Not even post-breakup Gillian could wear yesterday's underwear.

"That's probably a good sign, don't you think?" she said to Peaches. Two weeks ago, under similar circumstances, she may well have made a different decision.

So, what choices did she have? Go commando? "Talk about 'getting grubby,'" she muttered, as an image of Tucker McBride flashed through her mind. Why in the world would she think of him at this particular moment?

Probably because he was former military, and she could easily picture him as a commando dressed in camouflage and wearing face paint while he skulked through a foreign city on a moonlit night. He'd have a knife in his belt and a rifle in his hands and—

"Oh for crying out loud," Gillian scolded herself. What was that all about? She must be losing her mind.

Shaking off crazy commando thoughts, she focused on her other choice and opened the bottom drawer on her chest. There, she knew, she'd find an acceptable solution to her dilemma, a gift from Maisy at the lingerie shower her friends had given her as part of her bachelorette weekend. Ten minutes later, wearing black fishnet hose with a built-in panty beneath her Bliss uniform of black slacks and a white shirt, Gillian left her house.

It was another gorgeous winter day, so she chose to walk to work. She'd better be careful when crossing the street. Arriving at an emergency room wearing tattered underwear would be bad enough, but fishnet pantyhose? She'd have to move away from Redemption. Probably out of Texas too. To somewhere that didn't have cell service, so her mother wouldn't call and chew her butt about the embarrassment of it all every single day for the rest of her life.

Of course, that didn't take into account the possibility of afterlife haunting. She'd need to be really, *really* careful when crossing the street.

Thankfully, she arrived at Bliss without incident. She unlocked the door, braced herself, and stepped inside. The atmosphere assaulted her. It smelled like weddings, looked like weddings, and even sounded like weddings—that church bell door chime seriously had to go. The slight lightening of her mood brought about by the walk evaporated, and she spent the next ten minutes going about the usual morning routine in a blue funk.

With preparations completed for opening, she turned her attentions to the task her mother had assigned her. Just inside the display window that faced the courtyard, she found a large square box stacked on top of one of the flat, rectangular boxes that dry cleaners use to preserve wedding gowns. The top box was full of—"What is this?"

Not wedding stuff. Weird stuff. Cordage and a bandana and bandages. Other items she couldn't identify. There wasn't a scrap of satin or lace anywhere in the top box. And the second? She moved the top box and saw that the box underneath was filled with fabric. Fabric in a camouflage pattern. Camo?

These things must have been delivered to the wrong place, Gillian thought, as she reached into the box and pulled out—not a bolt of fabric—but a dress. A gown. *A camo wedding gown?* "Mom has lost her mind."

What was the woman thinking? Gillian found her phone and called to ask.

"Hello?"

"Mom! Camo?"

Like a cheery, chirpy bird, Barbara said, "You found the boxes, did you? How do you like the gown? I had so much fun making it. Have you put it on a mannequin yet? Which one do you think you'll use?"

"Wait. Just wait. I don't understand. You *made* this dress? *That's* the secret project you've been working on the past few days?"

"Yes."

"You made a wedding gown out of camo pattern . . . what kind of fabric is this? Cotton?"

"Cotton broadcloth."

"Why? Why would you do that? We do satin and silk, ruffles and lace."

"Not for the next month, we won't. We're doing a cross-promotion with Enchanted Canyon Wilderness School for the next four weeks."

"A cross-promotion," Gillian repeated.

"Yes. Have you noticed his window? It's gonna be darling when he's done."

Gillian looked outside and across the courtyard and gasped. Loudly.

Tucker whistled "Get Me to the Church on Time" while putting the finishing touches on his window. He'd had a seriously good time with this project. Whether it achieved his goal or not, he was glad to have made an effort.

After enthusiastically agreeing to his suggestion during his visit to Bliss Bridal Salon while Caroline and Maisy tried to force-feed Gillian chili, Barbara Thacker had given him run of her stockroom for his supplies and helped him make selections. When it came to the wedding gown, however, she'd made a request of her own. He had been ready to take anything, but she wouldn't hear of that. Barbara Thacker was serious about wedding gowns. She'd wanted him to choose it and to choose something he'd like to see his own bride wearing. "You're not married yet, I understand?" she'd asked.

"Nope. I'm as single as a person can get."

He'd felt a little foolish and entirely out of his wheelhouse while scanning the racks of wedding gowns—until he'd mentally pictured Gillian wearing one. After that, he made his selection quickly. Romantic and sparkly and feminine. Gillian Thacker would look like a princess in the wedding gown now draping a mannequin in the display window of Enchanted Canyon Wilderness School.

He couldn't picture her having added a five-inch fixed blade knife as an accessory, however.

He added a paracord bracelet to the mannequin's arm, then stepped outside to view the completed project. It caused him to laugh out loud.

Then, because it was a beautiful, sunny winter morning and birds were singing, and the aroma of frying bacon drifted on the air from the Bluebonnet Café, Tucker decided to enjoy the courtyard for the ten minutes or so before he officially opened the shop. Besides, Barbara had told him she intended to ask Gillian to decorate Bliss's window this morning and sitting in the courtyard would give him a front-row seat.

He sat in the center of the bench, stretched out his legs, laced his fingers behind his head, and extended his elbows. He lifted his face toward the sunshine. He did love being home. The Texas Hill Country in

February was hard to beat, having enough winter to notice and enjoy, but not so much that you got tired of it. In DC this time of year, the sky was often gray, temperatures freezing, with snow or ice on the ground. By the time the cherry trees blossomed, he'd inevitably been sick to death of winter.

Of course, some of the sandboxes where he'd been stationed had been damned uncomfortable too. Coldest he'd ever been had been a long, January night in a Middle Eastern desert. Recalling that night sent his thoughts down a memory lane that was full of potholes. He shifted uncomfortably, at first thinking he did so because of a couple of seriously unpleasant mental images, but then he realized the problem was physical. He lowered his arms and shifted his back. Something was poking at his shoulders in addition to his brain.

He glanced down and saw that a nail head had worked its way out of the willow. Further examination revealed a dozen or more similarly protruding nail heads on the bench and surrounding chairs. Tucker started to rise, intending to fetch a hammer from his toolbox and take care of the problem before somebody got hurt, but the violent clang of Bliss's front door chimes stopped him.

Gillian charged out of the salon, headed across the courtyard toward his front door.

Tucker grinned. He could almost hear "Ride of the Valkyries" playing. Bummed-out Gillian had transformed into a battlefield beauty ready to haul his ass off to Valhalla.

He settled back in his seat and readied to watch the show.

She didn't see him sitting in the courtyard. Her gaze never veered from the flags flying above his door. He made a bet with himself whether or not she'd barge right in or stop in front of his window.

The window won. Gillian stood in front of it, her hands braced on her hips. She certainly had some color in her cheeks now.

Satisfaction filled Tucker. Smiling happily, he pulled out his phone, thumbed to the photo app, and hit video. Her mother had been a big part of this. He wanted to be able to show her the fruits of her labors. Then, because he didn't have a good enough angle on her face, he called, "Do you like it?"

She whipped her head around like a hawk on a mouse. Her eyes rounded, then narrowed, and she stalked toward him. *Her mother will love this.*

"What are you doing? What are you doing?! Are you taking pictures of me?" she demanded.

"No." He thumbed the off button and lowered his phone. "Video."

"I'll have you arrested!"

"For what?"

"I don't know. Stalking."

"I'm not stalking anybody. I'm just sitting here enjoying the morning and minding my own business when you bang out of your shop and churn toward my shop like an F1 tornado. Everybody pulls out their phones to take pictures of tornados."

That distracted her. "F1? Why F1?"

"Well, I did have an inner debate between one and two. As defined by the Fujita scale, an F0 causes light damage, an F1, moderate. I didn't think you'd reach considerable, which is a two, but I could anticipate you losing your cool and throwing things, so I settled on one."

"I never throw things!" she indignantly exclaimed.

He shrugged and looked pointedly at her left hand.

He distinctly recalled her declaring that she'd thrown her engagement ring last September.

She folded her arms, which he couldn't help but notice plumped up her breasts. The flush on her cheeks deepened. Her pretty blue eyes were twin natural gas flames.

Atta girl. Kiss the depressed look goodbye. Innocently, he asked, "So, what did I do to get you all hot and bothered?"

"I am not hot and bothered. Hot and bothered is . . . is . . ."

"What?"

"Sexual. There's nothing sexual between you and me."

"Yet. More's the pity. Nevertheless, due to my army training, I am good at reading body language, and I deduce that you're upset with me."

"You deduce that, do you?" she snapped, then added in a sarcastic drawl, "Aren't you smart?"

"I do have an unusually high IQ, yes." Tucker chewed the inside of his cheek to prevent himself from laughing out loud. "So, what have I done to upset you, Ms. Thacker?"

She hooked her thumb toward his window. "As if you didn't know. It's bad enough that you chose to make sport of me in front of the entire town, but to drag my naive mother in on it too? That's shameful. Simply shameful."

"Making sport of you?" Tucker straightened out of his slouch. "I'm not making sport of you."

Gillian braced her hands on her hips and quoted the signage in his window. "'Are you prepared for a wedding day disaster?' And you point it right at my business? You're making fun of me, and what's worse, you've dragged my mother into the middle of it too. Do you know how she's spent the last few days? Sewing a wedding dress. Made out of camo!"

"I know about that. I'm anxious to see it." He reached up, grabbed her hand, and tugged. She plopped down onto the bench beside him, and as she yanked herself free, he continued, "We are not making fun of you, Gillian. Quite the opposite, in fact. You've been letting the dipstick write the narrative. This changes that."

"What? How? What have you heard?" She closed her eyes and dropped her head back. "I've tried not to think about what he's been saying about me. I've tried not to think at all. I've been doing a pretty good job of it."

"So I understand."

"What's he saying?"

"Honestly, I haven't heard anything. Your mom thinks he's out of town."

"Probably golfing," she said glumly as she brushed a white thread off of her black slacks.

"You ex cheats at golf."

"What?" She looked shocked. "No! He does not."

"He does. I saw it with my own eyes."

"When?"

"The Saturday after the two of you broke up, though that news hadn't made the rounds yet. Jackson and I played with him and an insurance agent. Jones used a foot wedge at least three times. Maybe four."

"He cheated?" she repeated, wonder in her tone.

She was beginning to relax. Good. "Damn sure did," Tucker confirmed. "Jackson saw it too. Jones is a good golfer, but I'm better. He didn't like that."

"Jackson says you have a nice swing."

"I do. It's natural. I have a knack for muscle memory that allows me to maintain my skill without constant practice. So, why was Jackson talking to you about my golf swing?"

"Not me. Caroline. He was telling her some family story, and you were part of it."

"Ah. Wonder which story it was. He has a few to tell." Tucker smirked and shook his head. "I have a love/hate relationship with golf. I played on my college team, and I might have made a run at making the pro tour if I hadn't had my heart set on the army."

"And the hate part?"

"The most dangerous ground I ever walked were the eighteen holes of a picturesque country club golf course outside of Washington, DC. Place makes the annual rattlesnake roundup over in Sweetwater look like a stroll through Neiman Marcus."

Gillian rewarded him with a soft chuckle that made him feel like a million dollars. "Why is that?"

"The place literally crawls with snakes—politicians and even worse, career military officers who play the political game. Worst thing I ever did was play to my ability, because once word got out that I had game—" He scowled. "When powerful, competitive men want you on their team, they find a way to make it happen. All but ruined the game for me."

"But you still play. You played with your cousin and Jeremy and an insurance agent."

"Yeah." Tucker rolled his tongue around his cheek and debated taking the next step. He hadn't intended to move this fast, but what would it hurt? The truth might be just the balm her wounded soul needed. "I was ready to pass on Jackson's invitation to play, but then Caroline mentioned that you usually rode along and drove Jones's cart on Saturday mornings, so I changed my mind." He watched her closely as he added, "You probably know I had a crush on you."

He didn't miss the flash of emotion in her eyes. Was it pleasure? Happiness? Gratitude? He wasn't sure. It wasn't horror, anyway. Nor was it the worry that immediately followed.

"If I acted inappropriately on New Year's Eve," she hesitantly began.

"No. Not at all. You always presented yourself as Taken—with a capital *T*—even if a man somehow managed to overlook that oversize diamond on your finger and the way you talked about your wedding every third word."

She glanced down at her ringless left hand. "Was I that obnoxious?"

"You were the way you should have been."

Now, she frowned and asked, "Did you hit on me, and I just didn't notice?"

"Nope. I'm not a poacher, and I kept my crush to myself. But that doesn't mean I didn't enjoy the buzz being around you gave me. Since I wasn't buzzing anywhere else at the moment, I didn't see what it would hurt to spend a few hours on a January morning in your company. I have to tell you, I was terribly disappointed you weren't there. Only thing that made me feel better was beating the socks off your ex—in spite of his foot wedge."

"By how many strokes did you win?"

"Even with his using his foot, I beat him by six strokes, not two."

A smile fluttered at her mouth. "My dad always said that a man who cheats at golf would cheat at anything."

"Haven't had the honor of meeting your father. He sounds like an intelligent man."

"I don't think he liked Jeremy very much. He never said it aloud, but I could tell."

"I repeat. Your father sounds like an intelligent man."

Gillian stretched out her legs and crossed them at the ankles. "I thought he was just being a dad who wouldn't like any man his only daughter chose. Now I wonder . . ."

Tucker tore his gaze from her very pretty ankles to find Gillian studying him with narrowed eyes. "Did you like Jeremy? Before the Saturday morning foursome? I know you spoke with him at Caroline's Christmas party, and then we all had dinner on New Year's Eve. Did you like him, then?"

"Saturday morning foursome sounds like a different sort of sport," Tucker observed, buying time to frame an answer.

"Golf is full of sexual innuendos, and I've heard all the stupid jokes. Did you like him?"

"No, I didn't." Her frown and the strain around her eyes revealed that his answer distressed her, so he elaborated. "But that's on me. It's probably fair to say I prejudged him before I actually got to know him."

She arched her brows. "You don't like bankers who wear custom suits and Italian shoes?"

"Polish doesn't bother me." Recalling the white wingtip shoes, white slacks, and red-and-gray cashmere sweater that Jeremy had worn the day they'd played golf, he added, "Although he did get a little boring name-dropping so often, and I thought the country club fashion plate was a bit much. Never been a fan of white slacks on the golf course."

"He's always been a golf fashion snob," she admitted. "What did you wear?"

"Black slacks. Red polo." Tucker's lips twitched with a grin as he added, "I made an eagle on number six."

"An eagle," she murmured. "I'll bet he loved that."

"Not so much. Looked like ol' Jeremy was munching on a sour pickle when I sank the putt. I believe the quote is: 'You must think you're Tiger Woods on Sunday.'"

Gillian snickered, and then passed a half a minute in silent thought. "So, why did you prejudge him? Was it something I said about him that day you and I met?"

She wasn't letting this go, was she? Tucker thought he could probably understand why. Bet she was questioning her own judgment. "It was nothing you said, Gillian. It was that crushing thing I mentioned earlier. I was a little green because you were his."

She remained silent for a long minute after that before saying, "You're good medicine for my ego, McBride. Thank you."

"All I did is tell the truth. You can count on me for that, Gillian. It's what I do."

She closed her eyes and her shoulders drooped. "I thought . . ."

After she let her sentence trail off, he patted her knee. "You've got this, Gillian. You'll be just fine. This knocked you down, but it hasn't knocked you out. You're a strong, determined, successful woman. You don't need that golf cheat to be happy or anything else you decide you want to be. You're gonna pull yourself up by your bootstraps and get on with your life, and you won't look back unless it's to flip him the bird."

Gillian smiled faintly. "I don't make vulgar gestures."

He shrugged. "Maybe it's time for you to get a little grubby."

Her eyes warmed, her smile widened. She said,

"We probably should be getting back to our shops. It must be close to opening time."

"Yeah. Probably."

"May I ask you one last question?"

"Sure."

"The display window. Why did you really do this?"

Well. Tucker had promised honesty, and he intended to keep that promise. However, he had not committed to a degree of honesty. Choosing his words carefully, he said, "I watched you leave for lunch with Caroline and Maisy. You looked so—" Devastated. Broken. Depressed. "Down. I wanted to cheer you up."

"By strapping a knife to a mannequin wearing a wedding gown?"

"It worked, didn't it?"

The sound she emitted wasn't a full-fledged laugh, but it was definitely a chuckle. Tucker counted it as a win.

Rising, he turned to offer her a hand. Gillian took it and stood, and as she took a step forward, the sound of ripping fabric split the air.

Gillian gasped. Tucker had to look. Her right pants leg had been torn in two from mid-thigh almost to the ankle, revealing a lot of leg. *Well . . . well . . . well. Fishnet stockings beneath her britches? Wasn't that interesting?*

"Shoot," she muttered, grabbing at the tear in an attempt to conceal what lay beneath.

No, don't!

"Stupid furniture. This stuff needs to be replaced. Nails won't stay where they belong!"

He heard embarrassment in her voice, but he didn't see it in her expression because he couldn't lift his gaze from that leg. Damn. A red bra strap and now this. He'd never be able to look at Gillian Thacker again without wondering about her underwear.

"Would you stop that, please!" she demanded.

"What?"

"Staring at me."

"But . . . stockings. Fishnet stockings!"

"It's actually pantyhose and not stockings. I was out of clean underwear, okay?"

"So, no garter belt, then? The fantasy takes a slight hit, but I can work with pantyhose."

"Would you stop that? This is so humiliating."

"*Titillating* is the word that comes to my mind."

She made a growl of frustration, then turned and made a mad dash for the bridal salon. Tucker hooked his thumbs in the pocket of his jeans and watched her. Just before she disappeared into the shop, she glanced back over her shoulder, and caught him watching still.

She flipped him the bird.

Tucker laughed aloud. He sauntered back toward his store, chuckling softly. This had gone even better than he'd hoped.

An hour and a half later when he looked outside across the courtyard, he spied Bliss Salon's display window and gave himself a mental high five. He'd known to expect the camo gown the mannequin wore. The pose caught him by surprise.

Gillian had seated the form in a fancy French chair with its legs crossed. The dress was hiked up to reveal the mannequin's sexy, white satin garters holding up silk stockings that disappeared into ladies' hiking boots laced with white satin ribbon. On the floor beside the mannequin sat a white backpack. Spilling out of the backpack were different types of shoes. He spied a sneaker, a flip-flop, a peep-toe glitter pump with a five-inch stiletto heel, a black leather flat, and a house slipper with feathers on it.

"Atta girl," Tucker murmured. Looked like Gillian Thacker was ready to take on just about anything.

His gaze snagged on the peep-toe pump. He thought about her pretty ankles. He thought about those fishnet hose. For the rest of the day and a good part of the night, he couldn't stop thinking about Gillian Thacker—with the tune of Beyoncé's "Single Ladies" drifting through his mind.

Chapter Ten

On February fourteenth, three days before what was to have been her wedding day, Gillian dawdled in the stockroom at the store feeling grumpy.

Curse Cupid and his stupid bow. If she ever came across the little diaper-wearing cherub, she swore she'd grab the weapon from his chubby little hands and put him out of her misery. Whoever invented Valentine's Day needed to be sliced with cardstock paper cuts from head to toe and then buried under a mountain of chocolate and flower petals.

She didn't want to be here at Bliss. She'd rather be almost anywhere else but here. When she'd opened her eyes this morning, she'd seriously considered coming down with the bubonic plague. Tragically, she couldn't do that to her mother. Valentine's Day was one of Bliss Salon's busiest days of the year. Brides who weren't getting married or engaged on Valentine's Day loved to pick February fourteenth to choose their wedding gowns. So, Gillian had come in to work, and now she was surrounded by satin and lace and giggling bridesmaids and teary-eyed MOBs and giddy brides high on romance.

It all made Gillian nauseous.

She knew she needed to pull herself up by Tucker's damned bootstraps again, to put on her big-girl panties and go out there and sell the fantasy.

"Gillian?" her mother called from the stockroom doorway. "Are you having trouble finding that petticoat?"

"Sorry, I got distracted."

"Hurry, please. We've screeched to a standstill in the dressing room."

"Sorry," she repeated. "I'll be right there." Weighed down with guilt, she scanned the shelves, located the box, and removed a crinoline, which she carried back to the dressing room.

From one appointment to the next, Gillian tried to hide her grumpiness. Apparently, she didn't do a very good job of it because her mother's exasperation grew more evident with every hour that passed. Shortly before the two o'clock brides were due to arrive, Aunt Cathy swept into the shop and declared she'd come to help. Barbara handed Gillian her jacket and said, "Go. We've got this. You're doing more harm than good today."

Gillian's spirits sank even lower. "I'm a terrible daughter."

"No, you're not, but you are useless to me today. I understand why you're in a blue mood, but we owe it to our brides to do better. Since we didn't change our calendar after your breakup, we are already scheduled to be closed for the next three days, so go home and do what you need to do to get your head on straight."

"I'm really sorry. Maybe I should tackle some of the paperwork that's been piling—"

"No," Barbara interrupted. "Go. It'll be better next week, I'm sure. Life will look brighter when you get past Saturday."

"I hope so," Gillian muttered. First her aunt, and then her mother gave her a hug and shooed her toward the door.

Gillian ducked back into the storeroom to grab her purse and happened to glance out the window as she turned to leave. Her gaze fell on Tucker's window, and she hesitated. They hadn't spoken since the day she'd decorated the display window. She'd left the courtyard that morning feeling strong and determined, the way he'd described her. The feeling had lingered, but with the arrival of Valentine's Day and with her aborted wedding day on its heels, strength and determination had dissolved like cotton candy in a puddle of rain. As a result, she'd let her mother down. That only made her feel worse.

Maybe she needed another dose of Tucker to jerk her out of this gloom.

She couldn't go barging into the Enchanted Canyon Wilderness School and ask him to make her feel better. Knowing Tucker, he'd have some suggestive proposal on how to help. Not that she really believed his flattery and talk about a crush, soothing though it had been. He was a nice guy. He'd taken pity on her and turned on the flirt.

It had worked. She'd like it to work again. She needed an excuse to pay a visit.

Her gaze drifted over his display window, and an idea occurred. It was missing something. A veil. His mannequin needed a veil. She knew the perfect one for his model too.

Purse in hand, she headed back downstairs, darted into the stockroom, grabbed the veil she had in mind, then headed out of Bliss. She hurried across the courtyard, moving faster than she had all day. A bell chimed as she opened the door to Tucker's school.

Moments later, he descended the stairs from the second level, and upon seeing Gillian, smiled. "Hello, gorgeous. This is a nice surprise."

"I brought you something." She handed him a small plastic bag emblazoned with the Bliss Salon logo.

"A present!" He peered inside the bag, and his brows arched in surprise. "Net?"

"A veil." *My veil.* "Your mannequin isn't finished."

"Ah." He pulled it from the bag. "Want to help me with it? I admit I'm not experienced with wedding veils."

It was a simple, little flyaway bit of tulle that had been perfect for her dress. As Gillian carried it to the window, curiosity about his lack-of-experience comment caused her to ask, "Does that mean you've never been married?"

"Never even come close. Military life is hard on families. Wasn't a mission I wanted to tackle."

Gillian placed the wedding veil on the mannequin, fluffed the tulle, then stood back, and studied the result. "Perfect. Don't you think?"

When he didn't respond, she glanced over her shoulder and caught him staring speculatively at her slacks. It should have annoyed her. Instead, she secretly preened. "Well?"

"Hmm?"

"The window!"

"Ah. Yeah, much better."

She rolled her eyes. She was pretty sure he hadn't looked at it. Turning around, she folded her arms, and his gaze finally lifted to hers. "A couple of our brides today mentioned the windows. They're a hit."

"I expected they would be." He paused a moment, then added, "Noticed lots of traffic at your place today."

"Valentine's Day is always one of the busiest days of the year for us."

"I'm surprised you had time to steal away and bring me window fluff."

"*Window fluff*?" She smiled crookedly at the term. She couldn't argue with it. "I actually am done for the day. My mom gave me the boot. Apparently, all the Valentine's Day nonsense has made me a bit grumpy."

She couldn't believe she was admitting this to him, but then again, she'd already shown him her fishnets, hadn't she? How much more embarrassed could she get?

Besides, Tucker McBride had a way about him that simply made her feel better. Maybe it was the honest admiration in his gaze. Perhaps it was his gentle teasing. She didn't know. Today, she wasn't going to analyze, but simply accept.

Now, he studied her with a considering look in his eyes. "All the hearts and flowers are getting to you, hmm?" She shrugged, and he continued, "You know what? I've got the perfect medicine for that."

An image flashed in her mind—Tucker McBride naked and kneeling on her bed. *Whoa, Nellie!* Appalled by the direction of her thoughts, Gillian felt her cheeks flush. *With embarrassment. That's all. I embarrassed myself.*

"Do you have hiking boots?"

"What?"

"Boots. Something other than the pair in your display window. If not, we'll grab a pair here, then run by your house so you can change into jeans. What size are you?"

"Jeans and boots? Why do I need jeans and boots?"

"It's Valentine's Day. Your fiancé just dumped you."

"Gee, thanks for the reminder. And to be perfectly precise, it was a mutual dumping. I told him to leave."

"Good for you. You're off work for the afternoon, and I'm the boss, which means I can close up shop whenever I want. I want. You and I are going hiking in Enchanted Canyon."

She frowned. "Hiking? Oh, no, thank you. I went hiking up to the waterfalls in Enchanted Canyon last summer with Boone and Maisy and Jackson and Caroline. It's really not my thing. I'm not really an outdoors person."

"Seriously?"

"Seriously. I appreciate the invitation, but I don't do camping or climbing or fishing or hunting or ticks or snakes or mosquitos."

"Oh, Gillian. That's just sad. What *do* you do?"

"Five-star resorts with infinity pools and spa appointments and yoga on the lawn. And bathrooms. Big, luxurious bathrooms with heated towel racks and soaking tubs and walk-in showers."

"Huh." He folded his arms, tilted his head, and studied her. "Well, I guess that doesn't really surprise me. You are a girly girl. So, I take it you don't own good hiking boots?"

"No, I don't. I wore sneakers when—"

"What size are you?" He studied her feet. "Eight?"

"Nine. I'm tall. I have big feet."

"Proportional feet. Your legs are a mile long, Glory." He disappeared into the stockroom before Gillian could formulate a reply.

Glory. He'd called her that before. He'd said it on New Year's Eve right before he'd kissed her. When he came out of the stockroom a few moments later, she repeated the word. "Why *Glory*?"

"Glorious gams. *Gams* doesn't work because that sounds like a grandma, so Glory will do." He shoved a box toward her. "Here, try these on."

Glory. She liked it. "But I don't need hiking boots. I don't want hiking boots. I'm not going hiking."

"Try these on."

She checked the end of the box. "Whoa . . . I'm not spending that kind of money on something I don't want or need."

"You do need them. You just don't know it yet. And you're not paying for the boots. They're a sales sample. You can test them and give me a review so I know if we want to stock them."

"I don't . . . I can't . . ." She caught the pair of socks he passed her way.

"You do have jeans at home, don't you?"

"Of course."

"Good. Try the boots while I gather a few more things." He strode toward the stairs.

"Tucker!"

Halfway to the second floor, he paused and met her gaze. "You're a businesswoman. I'll bet you know the marketing tagline we use for my family's bed-and-breakfast, don't you? About Enchanted Canyon?"

Gillian knew the phrase immediately. The Fallen Angel Inn used it in all of its marketing. "*Where troubled souls go to find peace.*"

She knew Angelica's cousin Celeste had proposed the tag for the Fallen Angel Inn and strongly insisted they use it. She swore by it. For that matter, so did Jackson and Caroline. Maybe Tucker was onto something.

As Gillian tried on the boots, she considered the

Fallen Angel Inn. It had a lovely pool and garden area. The spa was first class. The food served at the Last Chance Saloon, the restaurant between the inn and the dance hall that was Jackson's baby, was excellent. It sounded like a great place to spend the rest of this Cupid day. The boots fit fine, but she wouldn't need them.

When Tucker returned downstairs moments later wearing one backpack and carrying another, she said, "Enchanted Canyon sounds lovely. This is a great idea, Tucker. The weather today is more like spring than winter. We can sit by the pool and enjoy a bottle of wine. I expect the restaurant is booked solid for tonight, but since you're family, if you can finagle a table, I'll buy dinner."

He pursed his lips, thought about it, and nodded. "That's a good idea. I'll take you up on it. Another day. Today, we're hiking. How do the boots fit?"

"Fine, but—"

"Let's go, Glory. Daylight is wasting." He strode toward the door, held it open for her, and waited.

Well, okay. She'd brought this on herself, hadn't she? It was either do this or go home and plot ways to kill Cupid all alone. Maybe she could change Tucker's mind. She would bring along a dress to wear to dinner just in case.

So, Gillian and her troubled soul headed out the door bound for Enchanted Canyon, looking for peace, and maybe a nice glass of sauvignon blanc.

What she found was trouble.

"For heaven's sake, woman." Tucker lifted his gaze toward the sky. "It's a hill. It's not a damned mountain."

"But there's not even a trail," Gillian whined.

"Sure is." He pointed. "Right there. It's an animal trail."

"I rest my case. I don't like animals."

Tucker laughed out loud. "Oh, yeah? Then explain the thousand dollars' worth of dog toys lying around your living room and kitchen."

"I never spent a thousand dollars on dog toys." Gillian arched an affronted brow. "Two hundred, tops. Besides, Peaches isn't an animal. She's a furbaby."

"Okay. Fine. Don't worry, dear. I'll go first and protect you from all the evil squirrels."

"I'm not worried about the squirrels," she grumbled. "The skunks and the snakes are another kettle of fish."

"Now, that's just bull." They shared a grin over the wordplay, then Tucker continued, "Seriously, you are as apt to run across a snake or skunk in your backyard as you are while hiking this canyon. Now, if I may offer a bit of advice about partaking in the peace of Enchanted Canyon, it's easier to do when you're not complaining."

"Bite me, McBride."

"I fantasize about doing just that, Thacker."

That shut her up, and they finished the climb to his destination, mostly in the peacefulness of quiet. Mindful of her lack of enthusiasm, but primarily due to the early sunset this time of year, he'd chosen a relatively short, easy hike for them. He was taking her to the cave he'd discovered while exploring the canyon last November.

So far, the ordinarily twenty-minute hike had taken thirty, and they were still at least ten minutes away from their destination. Guiding Gillian along the canyon wall was like herding cats. Climb a little, then stop. Climb a little more, stop. Adjust the straps of her pack. Rocks in her shoes and leaves in her hair and ick! She'd broken a spider web. Then, OMG, yuck! Something had been buzzing around her, then it flew into her mouth.

Tucker almost kissed her just to silence her.

However, that wasn't how he'd imagined their next kiss, and he'd imagined it for weeks now. Almost daily. That didn't include the dreams he had at night.

Now that she was single, another kiss *was* going to happen. A real kiss this time. Nothing friendly about it. It would happen soon, but not too soon. Tucker needed to be strategic in his planning, and sure of his actions before he took them.

He wanted to get to know Gillian better. He knew she loved her friends and family and bright nail polish and her little mop of a dog. He knew she was hurting over the breakup, and that her wedding was supposed to have been this coming Saturday. Too bad, so sad, on that one. A better man would be more sympathetic to that particular pain, but Tucker was who he was, and he was damned happy that Mr. Wedgefoot was out of the picture.

Now, Tucker wanted to learn her politics and her prejudices, her passions and her purposes. He wanted to know what her favorite foods were, and which she detested and why. He wanted to discover what sports she enjoyed, what books she read, if she binge-watched TV, and if so, which shows?

It went without saying that he wanted to know what she liked in bed.

Tucker wanted to know if Gillian could be his future, and he aimed to find out. Strategic planning and tactical execution with defined mission goals—he knew how to do this. He'd spent his career doing this.

He should have a campaign name.

His mouth twisted in a crooked grin at the thought. He liked the idea. He could go with something appropriate like Operation Smoke Show. Or Operation Glory Gams. No, hmm, maybe—

Movement on the trail in front of him caught his attention. He held up a hand, signaling for Gillian to stop. He wanted her to see this.

"What is it?" she asked.

Quietly, he said, "Shush. At your two. Sunning atop the rock. Haven't seen one of these in a long time."

"Oh. A horny toad!" Then she surprised him by adding, "I used to love to play with them."

That effectively deflected his interest in the lizard, technically called a horned frog, rather than the common nickname Gillian had just used. Tucker gawked at her. "Wait a minute. *You* played with them? Queen of the girly girls?"

She nodded. "I did. They looked so ugly, but they didn't bite or scratch or sting. They didn't even stick you with their horns if you were careful. There used to be hundreds of them on vacant lots in my neighborhood."

"Wow. This is a new side of you I haven't seen before, and one I never guessed existed."

"I was a tomboy in elementary school."

"What happened?"

"Not what." Her eyes sparkled. "Who. Travis Warren. He was the pitcher on my brother's little league team. I fell head over heels, but he only had eyes for Gayle Simpson. She wore lipstick."

"The hussy."

Gillian flashed a smile he hadn't seen of late, bright as a comet. It warmed him from within.

"I can't remember the last time I saw a horned frog," she said. "What has happened to them?"

"I'm not sure. I think I recall an article blaming fire ants."

Gillian grimaced. "Fire ants are evil."

"Won't argue with you about that." Tucker pulled his gaze away from her and looked to see if the lizard had scampered away. Nope. Still there. "Did you ever see one puff way up and shoot blood from his eyes? It's a defense mechanism."

She pursed her lips. Damn, Tucker wanted to kiss them. "I remember the puffing up. I don't recall eye blood." She let out a little laugh and added, "We used to name them. My favorite was Zeus. I remember I used to turn him over and rub his belly until he went to sleep."

That's it, Tucker thought. He had his campaign name. "Hey, Gillian?"

"Hmm?"

"Don't you think I look like a Greek god?"

She laughed out loud and scared the horny toad away. One of them, anyway.

Tucker whistled beneath his breath as he led her the rest of the way to the cave. At its entrance, anticipating her protest, he reached for his flashlight as he said, "Here we are."

"Um . . . okay. Where is here?"

"Look closely. The entrance is hidden. I imagine that's the main reason why the stuff inside has remained so well-preserved." He switched on the light and pointed it toward the shadows. "See it now?"

"A cave. It's a cave?"

"Yeah. You ready to do some spelunking?"

"In a cave?"

"Well, that is where one goes spelunking. Although, to be honest, I don't know if this one actually qualifies for the activity. No tunnels to crawl through. Once you get through the entrance, it's a pretty large cave, about the size of our classroom at the shop."

"I told you I don't do the outdoors. Why in the world would you think I'd want to go inside a cave?"

"Because there is treasure inside."

She gave him a sharp look, curiosity gleaming in her big blue eyes. "What sort of treasure?"

"Something right up your alley." He said no more after that, deciding to wait her out.

Eventually, she grumbled, "My mother started warning me about men like you when I was ten years old."

"Men like me?" he repeated, protest in his voice. "What do you mean, men like me?"

"Men who try to lure women into places they know they shouldn't go."

Tucker snorted. "It's a cave, not an opium den."

"Well, it's probably something's den, and that something hasn't invited me inside. It's rude to be an uninvited guest."

"The McBrides own the canyon and the cave. I'm a McBride. I'm inviting you inside."

"You're the landlord. What about the tenant?"

"I didn't take you for a scaredy-cat."

"Meow."

He laughed. "Okay. How about I go in first and make sure we're not currently occupied?"

"But—"

"Be bold, Gillian. Trust me. You'll be glad you did."

She folded her arms and tapped her foot, but her gaze had focused on the entrance to the cave. Partially obscured by a bushy sage, the mouth was two shoulders wide, arched at the top, and had straight sides. It was vaguely reminiscent of a church door. The shape had caught Tucker's notice that first day when he'd discovered the cave. After finding what was inside, he figured he wasn't the first person who had thought that.

Finally, Gillian exhaled a heavy breath. "Okay. I'll do it. But you go in first and make sure there's nothing inside that will bite, scratch, sting, or eat me."

"It's a deal."

Tucker slid off his pack, ducked inside, and shined his light around. "No snakes, skunks, or bankers. It's safe to come in, Gillian."

"Snakes, skunks, and bankers? That's the Department of Redundancy Department, McBride. So, will you promise this treasure is worth my being terrified?"

"You're not terrified." Tucker used the fire starter on his keychain to light the trio of lanterns he'd left on one of his previous visits. Together with the sunlight that beamed through the cave's mouth, the candles provided sufficient light to illuminate the space. He was confident she wouldn't notice the animal tracks—bobcat, he believed—in the thin layer of dirt atop the stone floor. She might see the bat guano above. He moved two of the lanterns closer to the knobby stone wall in order to better illuminate the veins of quartz that added sparkle to the walls. Then he leaned against the rock wall, his arms folded, and waited to enjoy Gillian's reaction to the cave. "Come on in, Gillian. It's safe. I promise. Prepare to be amazed."

Loose rocks crunched under her feet as she stepped through the entrance. Tucker experienced a satisfying sense of pride as he saw her gaze skim across the glittering crystals in the walls. "Oh, wow," she breathed. "It's beautiful. The walls look like stars." She took a step forward, but stopped abruptly when her stare landed on the old trunk standing against the back wall. "How in the world did that get here?"

"Apparently a lapsed Methodist."

She laughed. "Who?"

He shined the flashlight toward a line of letters scratched with rock chalk above the chest: *Property of Rev. Frederick Fluesche*. "I did a little research. Seems a Methodist preacher bearing the same name became infamous when he took to robbing stage-coaches in the 1880s. It's not a stretch to think he ended up in Ruin."

"That's a stagecoach trunk?"

"Yes. It's called a Jenny Lind. You can tell by the shape. If you look at the end, it looks like a loaf of bread. This one is in near mint condition."

"Wow. How cool is this? It should be in a museum."

"Maybe. But Angelica is still trying to find an appropriate home for some of the stuff we found when we renovated the inn. I figure this stuff has remained tucked away safe and sound in this cave for a hundred and thirty years, so a little more time won't hurt. Besides, I get a kick out of knowing it's here, and that I stumbled on it."

"So, is it filled with anything? Wells Fargo gold?"

"There is something inside. Like I said, it's right up your alley. Take a look."

Gillian crossed to the chest and went down on her knees. She lifted the lid, and Tucker knelt beside her to reach the hinge that would hold the trunk lid in an open position when fixed.

The items inside lay in the order in which Tucker had initially found them. As he'd expected, she reached for the matching hair combs first. Made of tortoiseshell with gold filigree shaped like leaves that cradled red stones—rubies, Tucker guessed—they must have been a wealthy woman's adornment.

"How beautiful," Gillian breathed.

They glowed like fire. Tucker wanted to see them in her hair.

"These are no everyday hair combs." Tearing her gaze away from the items, she looked at Tucker. "This really is a treasure. You shouldn't leave it unguarded in this cave."

He shrugged. "Again, it's been a hundred and thirty years. It's not like we have hundreds of tourists snooping around the canyon this time of year."

"There are tourists here every weekend. Jackson's show at the dance hall this weekend is sold out, and that's definitely hundreds of people."

"They're all at the Last Chance dancing and drinking beer and listening to music. They're not off hiking obscure animal trails."

"The inn attracts plenty of hikers."

"Who are given trail maps and are accompanied by a guide if they come into this part of the canyon."

"Still . . ." She set aside the combs and picked up the lone other piece of jewelry in the box, a gold watch chain with textured oval links and smoothly moving clasps. "This is pretty too. Is there a watch to go with it?"

"Not in this trunk, but I have one that we found in the inn with some other stuff. It's very cool; the gold case is etched and personally engraved. The face has Roman numerals. Keeps time like a charm."

"What does the engraving say?"

"'To my love.' I have it at the trailer. Remind me to show it to you later."

She shot him a look, and he sheepishly grinned. "I couldn't get a table at the restaurant. Angelica tore a strip off my hide for even asking, but I managed to wrangle a kid to deliver our dinner. It's gonna be a nice evening. We will sit out beside the fire pit and share an excellent meal and not be alone on Valentine's Day."

She nodded. "Okay. That sounds lovely except my offer earlier still stands. I'll pay the check."

"Let me provide the wine, and we have a deal."

She held out her hand for him to shake. Tucker took it, briefly considered, then shrugged. *What the hell.* He tugged her toward him, signaling his intent with a look, and when she didn't resist, he captured her mouth with his.

He'd intended it to be a quick, seal-the-deal smooch, but once he got his mouth on hers, he didn't want to stop. She tasted, well, glorious. Sweet and something else . . . something exotic. Ginger. She tasted like ginger, like his favorite molasses and ginger cookies. Her lips were soft and moist and, *oh yeah*, kissing him back.

Tucker took his time, leisurely exploring with his tongue as his fingers twined through her hair. Thick and silky soft, just like he'd imagined it. He groaned low in his throat and pulled her closer. She fit him perfectly, her curves and mounds an ideal match to his angles and planes. Her arms stole around him, and her fingers laced at the back of his neck. He could have stayed right here, doing this, doing more, for hours. Maybe even days.

But this was a first real kiss, and he'd best not veer from the strategic route he'd plotted on the trail up. So reluctantly, he lifted his mouth from hers and released her. He cleared his throat. "Wow, Glory. You pack a punch."

She blinked rapidly. "I'm a little shell-shocked my-self."

Tucker stared at her. He couldn't help himself. Her lips were wet and swollen. Her blue eyes luminous and soft. It took all his willpower to stop himself from swooping in again.

She fussed with her hair and then returned her attention to the trunk. "So, what else is in here? You said it's right up my alley?"

"Yeah." He folded back the cotton fabric lying atop the trunk's contents and revealed the gown underneath. He picked up the dress by the shoulders and stood. Gleaming ivory satin flowed from the chest like a waterfall.

"A wedding gown!" Gillian exclaimed with delight. The dress had a high neck and long sleeves and a bodice covered in beads and lace. The waist was tiny. The train long enough to cover a good chunk of the cave's floor. "It's beautiful."

"Thought you'd like it."

"Don't you wonder how it got here? I wonder if it was worn at a wedding and tucked away as a keepsake. Or has it ever been worn? Did you see any stains on it?"

"I didn't look all that closely."

"Oh, man. I'd love to know its history!" Gillian began inspecting the gown carefully, studying the seams, wondering aloud about the seamstress who made it and the woman for whom it had been made. "Maybe a young bride was traveling to meet her groom, and your Reverend Fluesche robbed her stagecoach. Or maybe she was a runaway bride who ended up on hard times."

"A fallen lady at the Last Chance brothel on the road to Ruin." Tucker shot her a grin. "My family has been passing down a story about a bad-luck wedding dress for a hundred and twenty-five years."

She looked up from the dress just long enough to grin at him. "A bad-luck wedding dress? Really?"

"Apparently an ancestor was a seamstress who made it. I'll tell you about it over dinner. We should probably start thinking about making our way back. Dark comes on fast this time of year."

"Okay." Gillian gave the gown one last wistful look, then handed it over to him. She watched his pitiful attempt to fold the garment and shook her head. "Let me do it."

"I know how to fold things. I was in the army."

"And I work with trains every day. Is there anything else in the trunk? Show me while I'm folding the gown."

"That's pretty much it. The only other item is a man's shaving kit." He showed her the razor, brush, cup, and strop, then tucked them back away before helping her return the wedding gown to the trunk.

"I can't believe you've just left these treasures here," she said.

"Maybe I'll have the trunk moved now that it's served my purposes."

"Purposes?"

"Lured you up to show you my proverbial etchings, didn't I?"

Her mouth lifted in a crooked grin. "Lured? Browbeat me is more to the truth."

Gillian was digging in her backpack when he slipped the watch chain and hair combs into his own. He didn't do it because he was suddenly worried about Enchanted Canyon tourists stumbling across this hidden cave and stealing from the chest. He did it because he was going to hang his gold watch from this chain and mark the occasion. Then, after dinner when he took her home and kissed her good night on her front porch, he'd gift her with the combs. Not as a bribe to be invited inside. It was way too soon for that.

He hadn't sent her flowers or bought her chocolates. The combs would be his Valentine's Day gift to her. With any luck, they'd be the first of many Valentine's Day gifts he would give to her.

Strategic planning. Tactical moves. Operation Horny Toad, full speed ahead.

Chapter Eleven

In the minutes following *the kiss*, Gillian's four years of high school drama class paid off. Outwardly, she remained calm, cool, and collected. Inside, she was an emotional gob of goo. Tucker had kissed her again. She'd kissed him back. And enjoyed it. A lot.

Whoa. Whoa. Whoa. Stop. This was trouble. She wasn't ready for this.

As they retraced their steps heading back toward Tucker's truck, Gillian ignored all the bounties of nature that she'd noticed on the way in. This time, she didn't hear the sound of the distant waterfall or smell the musty scent of decay as they traversed the wooded section of the trail. She barely took note of the tree roots crisscrossing their path, which required stepping over, and certainly didn't notice the dapple of sunlight and shadow on the forest floor. She was totally lost in thought.

She'd been ready for his mild flirtations and over-the-top compliments. They'd been balm for her wounded heart, and she'd done nothing to shut them down. Were she honest with herself, she would admit she'd encouraged them. But this kiss? This kiss had been way more than mild flirtation or roadside impulse. This kiss from Tucker had blindsided her. It had been ten thousand watts of raw energy that knocked her new hiking boots off and heated her blood and recharged nerves that had been dead since the breakup. Shoot, even before the breakup.

Had Jeremy's kiss ever jolted her this way? If so, it was too long ago to remember.

That truth unsettled her and distracted her. Inattentive to the trail, when her new boot skidded on loose gravel of a rockslide during a section that climbed along the canyon wall, her reaction was sluggish. The next few seconds passed as if in slow motion, though it happened very fast.

"Nyah!" she exclaimed when she lost her balance and knew she was going down. In her peripheral vision, she saw Tucker whip his head around in alarm.

Thud. Pain jarred her shoulder and hip as she landed on her side and rolled and slid downhill until a dusty, windswept pile of brittle leaves slowed her momentum and pillowed her crash into a boulder. "Oomph."

"Gillian!" Tucker scrambled sure-footed down the hill.

She sat up, sneezed twice, and was attempting to stand when he reached her and steadied her with his hands around her waist. "Hold still, honey. Are you hurt? What hurts?"

"My pride." She found her footing and balance.

"Anything else?" His gaze skimmed over her. "Ankle? Arm? Shoulder?"

She wanted to massage her butt, but she wasn't about to tell him that. She pushed his hands away. "No, seriously. I'm fine."

"What happened?"

She wasn't about to explain her inattention either.

With a bit of snippy in her voice, she said, "The green-horn in me surfaced. I told you I don't do the out-doors."

His lips twitched. "Well, yeah, it does appear that the outdoors got the better of you." He flicked some leaves out of her hair, then thumbed dirt off her cheek. "You're a mess. You've scratched yourself."

Then, instead of dropping his hand, he sank his fingers into her hair, cupped the back of her head, and tenderly kissed her cheek. "Better?"

Her mouth had gone as dry as the leaves at her feet. "Mmm."

"Good," he murmured against her face before his lips trailed butterfly kisses across her cheek to her mouth.

Trouble. I am in so much trouble.

Her knees turned to mush, and she swayed a bit and came close to losing her balance again. Tucker's hand returned to her waist and steadied her. The one buried in her hair slid down to her shoulder. He released her lips and lifted his head. "Just so you know, anytime you need someone to kiss your boo-boos, I'm available."

A dozen different protests twirled on her tongue, but the one most insistent made it onto her lips. "A month ago, my wedding day was two days away."

"Scrambled your brains, did you? Did you hit your head on the boulder? Or is it my kiss that does it to you? I like that answer better."

"You can't be kissing me like this. It isn't right."

He frowned at her. "Why not? Your wedding day isn't two days away now, is it?"

"Yes. Well, no. But yes."

"Seriously, did you bump your head?"

"No! Well, maybe a little bit, but not enough to scramble my brains. You did that all by yourself."

"Well, then." Pleased, he tipped his imaginative hat. "Thank ya, ma'am."

"Oh!" she snapped in embarrassment and frustration, then pushed past him and started back up the incline toward the trail. Once there, she began to lead the way.

A few seconds later, Tucker called, "Gillian? You're going the wrong way. The trail to the canyon floor takes an upward jag right here for a short distance."

She stopped and grumbled, "I knew I should have gone for a pedicure instead of a hike."

"So, you like to have your toes played with? I'll have to file that piece of intel away for future reference."

A whip of wintery wind swept over the landscape as she looked at him and fisted her hands at her hips. "Would you stop harassing me, please?"

"Harassing? Whoa." All signs of teasing disappeared as Tucker held up his hands, palms out. "Did I cross a line, Gillian? If so, I apologize. Sincerely. I guess I read your signals wrong. I thought this was a mutual flirtation that you were enjoying."

Shame washed over her. "It is. That's the problem."

She kicked at a stone with the toe of her boot and attempted to explain. "Tucker, it's too soon. My breakup was less than a month ago. For me to be this into you . . . what does that say about me? About my judgment? Was I wrong about what I felt for him? If not, then how can I be so fickle and enjoy you so much this soon? If I was wrong about my feelings, then how can I trust myself about anything? Especially men? I was going to marry him! The day after tomorrow!"

Tucker pursed his lips, folded his arms, and studied her. After a long moment, he said, "I have a few arguments I could make, but they can wait. I do understand where you are coming from. I don't want to make you uncomfortable, and again, I apologize if I've pressed too hard, too fast. A strategic error on my part." His mouth lifted in a self-deprecating smile and added, "I don't make those very often. You knocked me off my game, Glory."

"It's not you. It's me."

His smile went crooked. "The relationship death knell."

Turning her head away, she focused her gaze on the towering wall of layered rock on the far side of the canyon as she searched within herself for words. She needed to get them right.

From out of nowhere, tears stung her eyes. She looked at Tucker imploringly. "Don't you see? I don't need a relationship right now, but I do need a friend. I don't want to screw up our friendship."

It took a long moment for him to respond. His expression was unreadable to her. "You want to be friends. Just friends."

"Yes." *Please, Tucker.* Something within her relaxed when the teasing twinkle returned to his fawn-colored eyes.

"With benefits?" When she sighed with exasperation, he added, "I didn't think so." Nevertheless, his smile was tender, his tone sincere as he stepped toward her and took her hands in his. "I'm pleased to be your friend, Gillian Thacker. Just your friend. For now. Until you're ready for something more."

She swallowed hard. "I may never be ready for anything more, Tucker. You shouldn't count on otherwise."

"Consider me duly warned."

Bittersweet relief eased through her. "Great. Thank you."

He gave an exaggerated sigh, then said, "Just to be clear, does being just friends mean no more kissing?"

She rolled her eyes. "No more kissing!"

The crestfallen little boy's look he teased her with ignited a devilish desire within her. She couldn't help but indulge it. "Although, since it's Valentine's Day, and you saved me from stupid Cupid, maybe we could have one for the road. Or, the trail, as it were."

She went up on her toes, slipped her hand around the back of his neck, pulled his head toward her, and proceeded to kiss him senseless. She felt powerful when she finally released him, and he stepped back dazedly. Off the trail. He lost his footing and fell on his ass. She laughed as she reached out a hand and helped pull him to his feet.

Gillian grinned all the way back to the spot where he'd left his truck. Her happiness lasted through dinner and the ride back to Redemption. There, in the spirit of friendship, she'd insisted he kick her out at the curb rather than walk her to the front door like he'd wanted.

Her good mood lasted, and she remained relatively upbeat even when she awoke on Saturday morning. She didn't get teary until her mother, her aunt, Maisy, Caroline, and Angelica Blessing showed up with plane tickets in hand and abduction on their minds.

Ten hours later, she joined them in hurrying through the frigid evening air on the grounds of Angel's Rest Healing Center and Spa in Eternity Springs, Colorado, headed for the resort's hot springs pools.

"Oh, wow, isn't this fabulous?" Gillian said as she

sank into the steaming water and gazed up at the star-filled sky.

Maisy nodded her agreement as she set a tin tub filled with ice and two bottles of champagne beside the pool. "I'm a warm-weather girl as a rule, but there's something sublime about soaking in outdoor hot springs when the air is freezing cold."

"Sheer luxury," Barbara Thacker added. She went to work filling plastic glasses sporting the Angel's Rest logo with bubbly and passing them around, one for each of them. "This is such a darling little town."

Angelica whipped a tie-dyed caftan over her head and tossed it toward a nearby bench where she'd left her towel. "My cousin calls it a little piece of heaven in the Colorado Rockies."

From out of the darkness, Celeste said, "It is exactly that." She stepped into the light carrying a tray filled with more glasses. "It's a slice of heaven on earth. Now, I want you all to be sure to drink water along with your champagne. Mixing alcohol and hot springs puts one at risk of dehydration."

"Yes, Mother," Angelica said.

"Now now, cousin, don't be snotty. Not everyone tolerates heat and champagne as well as you do." To the others, she added, "I've always assumed that her devilishness factors into her body temperature regulation."

"Cousin?" Angelic drawled. "Like we say in the South—bless your heart."

At that point, Caroline jumped in and played referee by sighing with satisfaction and observing, "I love Eternity Springs when there's snow on the ground. It's like a little Victorian snow village. You feel like you've stepped right into a Hallmark card."

"I'll bet it'll be beautiful here in June too," Gillian said. "On your wedding day."

The words *wedding day* hung in the crisp mountain air like a bubble of sulfur. The love shown her by family and friends had kept her tears at bay all day, but as Gillian felt the weight of the other women's concerned gazes, she could hold them back no longer and her eyes overflowed.

"Oh, baby." Barbara sat beside her and wrapped an arm around her shoulder.

"I'm sorry." Tears spilled down Gillian's cheek.

"Don't be sorry," Maisy said. "You have every right to cry today."

"You need to cry," Caroline added. "Today of all days, you need to cry and curse and grouse and grieve and get the poison out of your system."

"We're here to listen to you, Gillian." Angelica lifted her champagne glass in a toast. "If you want to tell us all what a lowdown, scum-sucking, snake-belly, rat-whisker, roach-knee, louse-liver guy that Jeremy is, well, we're ready to listen. And contribute, if you'd like."

"Louse-liver?" Maisy mused. "I like that one."

Before anyone else spoke up, Celeste handed Gillian a glass of water. "Drink your water, dear, and then sip your champagne, and share what you need from us tonight."

Gillian swiped the tears from her cheeks, drained the water glass as instructed, then sipped the bubbly wine and debated how to answer Celeste's question. Finally, she said, "I'm not crying over Jeremy. Truly, I'm not. Honestly, I'm pretty sure I'd have called the wedding off if he hadn't done it first. I'm crying because, well, I had a dream and it died."

"That's true," her mother, always a tough love champion, said. "Mourn that dream tonight, and tomorrow, start seeking a new dream."

"I'm afraid that's easier said than done. I worry about my own judgment. For a long time, I thought he was perfect for me. I thought he loved me and that he wanted the life I wanted. I thought he and I could build a family and a future together and that we'd be happy. How could I have been so wrong? Obviously, I can't trust my own instincts. Did y'all notice red flags flying that I overlooked? Seriously, I want to know."

Following a moment of silence, Aunt Cathy said, "I never thought you were making a mistake by marrying Jeremy. He seemed to make you happy, and that's what I cared about."

"Mom?" Gillian asked.

"I agree with my sister. Were there things about him I didn't particularly care for? Yes. Of course. You are my baby girl, and no man is ever going to be good enough for you. But I didn't think he would make you unhappy."

Gillian asked, "What about Dad? I don't think Dad liked him."

"That's complicated," her mother replied. "You're his princess. But I think what Dad didn't like about Jeremy is more Dad's problem than his. Dad had some business dealings with Jeremy's grandfather that didn't end well. I think it's more a case of your father unfairly casting sins-of-the-father type of blame upon Jeremy because of that rather than anything Jeremy did. Well, except for the golf."

Gillian straightened. "Golf?"

Barbara shrugged. "Dad doesn't like to play with him."

"Why?"

When Barbara didn't respond right away, Caroline spoke up. "He cheated when he played with Jackson."

Gillian sighed. "Tucker told me about that. Did Jeremy cheat when he played with Dad?"

"Yes. Yes, he did," Barbara said.

"Did he cheat in any way besides golf?"

"Not that I ever heard," Barbara said definitively.

"Me either," Maisy added. "And something like that is hard to hide in Redemption."

Gillian released a relieved breath. That particular betrayal would be the cherry on top of this foul-tasting dessert. She'd never once suspected Jeremy of sleeping with another woman. Scarred by his own father's serial philandering, Jeremy had never hesitated to denounce infidelity.

"Okay, then." Gillian took a sip of her champagne. "So what else? Angelica? I know he led a couple of team-building programs for bank employees at the inn. What did you think of Jeremy?"

"Well, if you want to know the truth, I—"

Celeste interrupted by cautioning, "Angelica, stick to the facts."

Her voice filled with affront, Angelica replied, "I wouldn't lie to the girl."

"Take care in what truths you tell her," Celeste snapped. "Your truth is not always *the* truth."

"Sure it is." Angelica sniffed with disdain. "You may be the wise woman among us, Celeste, but I know things, and you can't deny it. However, Gillian didn't ask me what I know. She asked me what I think of Jeremy. Two different questions entirely."

Angelica looked directly at Gillian and said, "I don't see any sense in dancing around the truth. Yes,

I think Jeremy is a louse. He's a weak, selfish man. Gillian, you missed a bullet."

"Well." Fresh tears filled Gillian's eyes. "I asked, didn't I?"

"Now, now, dear," Celeste interjected. "Perhaps your Jeremy was a flawed man, but we are all flawed individuals."

Angelica lifted her champagne in toast and interrupted right back. "My cousin is right. Jeremy is definitely flawed, but he's not a total villain. He loved you, Gillian. I believe he intended to be a good husband to you. But relationships require honesty, and he gets a big fat F in that."

Warning in her voice, Celeste said, "You're not helping, Angelica."

"Sure I am. Lance the boil and all of that. Jeremy is a carbuncle on honesty's butt. Gillian needs to face that particular truth."

"What she needs is time for her heart to heal."

"I know. That's why we brought her here to Eternity Springs. This is where broken hearts come to heal, right, cousin?"

"That is correct."

"And healing happens fastest after you pop the pimple."

"That's disgusting imagery, Angelica."

"It's straight talk. It's honesty. That's what Gillian needs. She needs her friends and family to be honest with her, and she needs to be honest with herself. That's the answer to your original question, Celeste."

"Except I'm not asking you, I'm asking her," Celeste snapped back. She visibly summoned her patience, then smiled gently at Gillian. "So, back to my original question, what do you need from your friends and family both tonight and going forward, Gillian?"

Gillian glanced at Angelica, who rolled her eyes and then winked at her. Suddenly, Gillian's tears evaporated. From deep down inside, laughter bubbled up and broke free. "This. This is what I need. My family, my friends, and the nicest gesture of support I could possibly have imagined."

She found her feet on the bottom of the hot springs pool and rose. The cold night air made her shiver, but the love in her heart kept her warm.

She lifted her champagne glass and spoke. "This is not the speech I had intended to make tonight, but maybe this is the one I'm supposed to make. I want you all to know how much you mean to me. How much I appreciate the caring and the effort and expense to make this trip happen. Celeste, I love your home. Angel's Rest is a fabulous place, your hospitality is divine, and nothing beats a hug from you. It warms me from the inside out. Angelica, Maisy, and Caroline, I wouldn't have made it through this past month without your friendship. You were there for me during the wedding planning and now in the breakup. I don't have words to express how grateful I am to be your friend. I love you dearly."

"We love you too," Maisy replied.

Gillian turned toward her family. "And finally, Mom and Aunt Cathy. My mother and bonus mom. I could talk for hours about all the wonderful things you've done for me throughout my life, but then everyone would turn into prunes. You are my champions. You are my most fearsome supporters. Your love has sustained me and strengthened me throughout my entire life. Thank you. I love you."

Gillian lifted her glass higher and finished, "To

you, my friends and family. My tribe. Y'all are the most magnificent women in the world. I adore you. Cheers!"

"Cheers!" they all exclaimed.

Angelica added, "Somebody open another bottle of champagne."

Later, Gillian and Angelica brought up the end of the line as the group walked back to their guest rooms in the main house of the resort, wrapped in the warm, fur-lined robes Angel's Rest provided for the short journey from the hot springs to the house. Slipping her arm through Angelica's, amazingly mellow for a jilted bride on what was to have been her wedding night, Gillian observed, "People say you have an uncanny instinct about the future."

"It's true. I do. It's a gift."

"About that happy year you predicted?"

"It's gonna happen."

"How do you know? What do you know?"

"Oh, my dear. I'm glad you asked." She halted and brought up her free hand to cover Gillian's and give it a squeeze. "I know because it's my gift. I know that this broken engagement needed to happen. Marriage to Jeremy would have brought you tepid happiness, but never unbounded joy. That is meant for another. I know Eternity Springs will help your heart to heal and your soul will find peace in Enchanted Canyon. It will not happen overnight, but it will happen. Only then will you be ready."

"Ready for what?"

"Your soul mate, dear. He is there waiting for you."

"There? Where?"

"Why, at home, of course. Deep in the heart of Texas."

Gillian felt a flutter of anticipation as an image formed in her mind. Tucker McBride.

No. No no no no no. It was too soon. Way too soon. How could she be thinking about Tucker tonight of all nights?

No, Angelica was sweet as can be, but this fortune-teller thing she had going on was silly. She couldn't predict the future. A soul mate? Did Gillian even believe in such a thing? Soul mates?

Probably not. However, the idea was lovely. A pleasant dream. Eternity Springs had an atmosphere about it that this was a place where dreams came true. Where broken hearts healed. So for tonight—this big fat hairy monster of a night—when she climbed into her comfy bed in Eternity Springs, she would believe in pleasant dreams. In soul mates.

She dreamed about Tucker McBride.

Chapter Twelve

Weeks passed, temperatures rose, and thunderstorms built and blew across Texas as winter transitioned to spring. Deep in the Hill Country, wildflowers nurtured by a healthy amount of rainfall and blessed by a mild winter painted the land in a riot of color. As usual, the show of nature's glory brought out the tourists. Cars and trucks clogged the roadways with visitors ready to participate in the Texas rite of spring—plopping children and pets down in patches of bluebonnets for photographs.

The new season also brought a change to Tucker's schedule. To use one of his grandfather's old sayings, spring had him busy as a long-tailed cat on a porch full of rocking chairs at a family reunion. Interest in the Enchanted Canyon Wilderness School had exceeded expectations. He'd had full classes each weekend for more than a month now, and business at the shop in town had been good enough to justify hiring full-time help. Thank goodness.

He'd needed to spend less time across the courtyard from Bliss. If sexual frustration could kill a man, Gillian Thacker's friendship might well be the death of him. Operation Horny Toad, indeed. He couldn't

have picked a more appropriate operation name if he'd
debated the choice for a decade.

Following their Valentine's Day outing, he'd seen
her almost every day. She would drop by the shop
for a visit, or he'd join her for her lunchtime walk
with Peaches or stop by Bliss to filch an afternoon
snack before heading for the canyon to do some prep
work for the classes. Somewhere along the way, he
tumbled from wanting to needing, and from liking
to caring. He wasn't making much progress in the
impatient-to-patient department, however. The need
for self-restraint just might kill him.

They hadn't kissed since Valentine's Day. She went
out of her way to keep things light and friendly. He
watched like a hungry hawk for a signal that she
was ready to take their relationship up a notch from
friends, but so far, she seemed content with the status quo. Dammit. He was beginning to second-guess
his strategic decision to allow her to set the pace. It
might be time to call an audible, and the next forty-
eight hours or so could present the perfect opportunity
for it.

She and her BFFs had registered for his Wilderness Survival 101 class and dubbed it the "Girls Getting Grubby Weekend." She'd even had pink T-shirts
made. Tucker wasn't sure that Enchanted Canyon
Wilderness School was ready for the "Dirty Girls."

The campus sat on forty-two wooded acres nestled
in the northwest section of Enchanted Canyon that
had lain unpopulated since the Comanche roamed the
land. Within its boundaries, the spring-fed Blanchard
Creek flowed year-round and meandered through a
bottom area that included some massive old-growth
pecan trees. Together with the bottomlands, rolling
hills covered in white oak, cedar elm, and mesquites

provided a natural habitat for an abundance of wild-life including white-tailed deer, axis, turkeys, bob-cats, raccoons, foxes, coyotes, and rabbits. In the sky, one could spot red-tailed hawks, barred owls, pi-leated woodpeckers, and numerous other species of birds. Native edible and medicinal plants included turk's cap, chile pequin, prickly pear, wood sorrel, sugarberry, dewberry, cucumber plant, toothache tree, wafer ash, pokeweed, and more. In other words, it was an undisturbed Eden—perfect for Tucker's pur-poses.

He'd put quite a bit of thought into what structures he should erect on the campus. He wanted to keep it minimal, but within days of launching their website, they identified a strong demand for children's pro-grams. He'd expanded that part of his business plan due in large part to his enjoyment of working with Haley over the winter. Working with kids, how-ever, required amenities he might have skipped had he planned to work only with adults. So by March, ECWS boasted two indoor bathrooms with attached showers, two covered outdoor classrooms, and a two-room building with an office and a dedicated first aid room. Not surprisingly, he'd discovered that having indoor restroom facilities increased demand from female students by about a million percent.

Indoor plumbing was the only reason why he ex-pected the Dirty Girls' arrival at any moment. Gil-lian had made it quite clear she was not a porta potty person.

"She's not much of a dirty girl either," he muttered as he stacked wood in the fire pit down in the pecan bottoms. The idea to attend his Survival 101 class had been Caroline's, not Gillian's. Caroline had come to him seeking help not long after she'd returned from the "Distract Gillian" trip to Eternity Springs.

"She's lost confidence in herself," his soon-to-be cousin-in-law had shared. "That's the worst thing Jeremy has done. She's getting over her broken heart, but her self-doubt continues to grow. I think she doesn't trust herself—her intelligence, her instincts, or her emotions. Unfortunately, it's only getting worse instead of better. She second-guesses every decision she makes. I've seen how your wilderness lessons have helped Haley be more confident. I think Gillian would similarly benefit."

"I don't know, Caroline. I took her hiking in the canyon a few weeks ago, and she was very vocal about not liking the outdoors."

Caroline's eyes brightened, her curiosity piqued. "You took her hiking?"

He shrugged and deflected. "It was Valentine's Day. We both needed something to do."

She assessed him with a look, then apparently decided not to pursue the subject because she continued, "I don't think it's a case of Gillian not liking the outdoors as much as she's not comfortable with it. She didn't go camping when she was growing up, and she simply has no experience. I think that learning a few outdoors skills will help her self-confidence."

"Hey, I'm not opposed to the idea at all. If you can talk her into it, then go for it."

After they'd kicked the idea around a little more, Tucker had agreed to add Caroline, Maisy, and Gillian to his class scheduled for the third weekend of March, and Caroline had set about arranging it. Gillian had resisted the idea at first, as Tucker had expected, but her girlfriends wouldn't take no for an answer. Exactly how she'd gone from reluctant student to Queen of the Dirty Girls, he wasn't quite sure.

"Dirty Girls," he murmured, his mouth twisting in a crooked smile as he placed the last log, checked his watch, then knelt to start the fire. Students for this weekend's class would begin arriving any time now. He hoped they had sense enough to wear more than just their T-shirts. A cold front had blown in overnight bringing unseasonably low temperatures along with a drizzling rain that was forecasted to continue throughout the day. Well, if they didn't come prepared, they'd learn. Preparedness was what this weekend was all about, wasn't it?

He expected Gillian to at least bring a jacket. When he'd met her at Miguelitos' food truck for lunch on Tuesday, she'd already seen the weather forecast for the weekend. She'd been less than enthusiastic, except when discussing the names and T-shirts. Apparently, Maisy had declared that they needed a name for their group in addition to one for the weekend. Angelica had offered up "Dirty Girls." Tucker grinned every time he thought about it.

He had a good fire going when he heard the crunch of gravel that indicated the arrival of the first vehicle. Tucker grabbed his clipboard and started up the hill toward the parking area with a combination of anticipation and nervousness rolling through him. The nervousness caught him by surprise. He wanted this to be a positive experience for Gillian. He wanted her to like the school and what it offered. He was proud of what he was building here at ECWS. He wanted her to appreciate it.

Damn, but he wished the weather were better.

No. He couldn't, shouldn't, look at it that way. He

wasn't running a five-star resort. He was teaching wilderness skills, and the wilderness included inclement weather. Today would be an authentic experience—whether Gillian was comfortable or not.

Upon cresting the hill, he saw the Dirty Girls had arrived first and were lifting the folding chairs they'd been instructed to bring from the back of Maisy's truck. Maisy and Caroline both looked worried. Gillian wore a sucking-a-sour-pickle expression. Tucker winced. This was not the way he'd hoped to start the weekend.

He pasted on a smile and said, "Hello, Dirty Girls. Ready to get grubby?"

Gillian offered a crooked smile. "Tucker, if you only knew."

"We are all ready to get down in the muck and start slinging," Caroline added. At Tucker's curious look, she explained. "We met for breakfast at the Bluebonnet Café, and while Gillian was in the ladies' room, we discovered a rat had been sitting at the counter eating biscuits and gravy."

"Seriously? That's the cleanest restaurant I've ever seen."

"The two-legged kind of rodent. Triple J has returned to Redemption."

Maisy defined the term before Tucker could ask. "Jeremy Jones the Jerk. Or, the Jerk, Jeremy Jones. It depends on how you like the words to roll off your tongue."

"Ah." Word around town had been that following his round with Tucker, Jeremy had taken advantage of his trust-fund baby, working-for-daddy status and had decamped to Florida in order to do some intensive work on his golf game with a renowned instructor.

Now, Tucker understood the unhappiness in Gillian's gaze. He didn't like that Jones still had the power to hurt her. It made him angry. Made him jealous. So he had a bit of a bite in his tone when he said, "Well, you knew he had to return sometime."

Maisy nodded. "I think we all hoped he'd run into the *Caddyshack* gopher and get rabies from a bite. Instead, he stops by our table and starts yammering on about the new house he's going to build over near Fredricksburg and acting like nothing has changed. I'm telling you, it was all I could do not to stab him with my fork."

Tucker met Gillian's gaze and asked, "Did you talk to him?"

"Luckily, he left before I returned to our table. I'll admit this was not the way I wanted to begin my day, but at least I don't have to worry about running into him in Enchanted Canyon." She paused a moment, then her eyes rounded worriedly. "Right?"

"Right."

"Good." She dismissed the topic of Triple J by glancing around and asking, "So, where do we put our chairs?"

Hearing the gravel crunch from more arriving vehicles, Tucker glanced toward the road as he answered, "We're using the pecan bottoms site this weekend. Follow the path down to the fire pit. Set up opposite the whiteboard so you can see it. I'll be down once everyone checks in."

"Aye aye, captain!" Maisy saluted.

The women started down the hill. Just before Gillian dropped out of sight, she stopped, set down her lawn chair, unzipped her backpack, and reached inside. She ran back up the hill carrying a shiny red apple.

"What's this?" Tucker asked when she handed it to him.

"I almost forgot. I brought an apple for the teacher."

He laughed. "Suck up."

"It's a good thing to be teacher's pet."

Thoughts of Eve in the Garden of Eden swam through his mind. Tucker polished the apple on his jacket sleeve and thought, *Glory, you can pet this teacher any time you want.*

"It's pretty here," Maisy observed as the three women reached the bottom of the hill. "Rustic."

Gillian shot her a sardonic look. "Ya think?"

"This is the first time I've been to this part of the canyon," Caroline said. "These pecan trees are fabulous. I wonder how old they are?"

"More than a hundred years, I'll bet," Gillian guessed. "It is pretty. Peaceful." She could use a little peace. Or a lot of peace.

Jeremy was back in town.

Maisy said, "I'm glad to see Tucker has a good fire going. It's cold today! Lucky we got here early, so we get a good seat by the fire."

A blue tarp hanging high above them protected the spot from the drizzle weeping from the sky. Gillian set up her chair beside Maisy's. Caroline placed hers next to Gillian. They each set their backpacks beside their chairs, then stood before the fire, warming their hands and making small talk as other students began to join them.

Fifteen minutes after they'd arrived, Tucker loped down the hill toward them, carrying a clipboard and chatting amiably with a couple who appeared to be in their early sixties. While the final arrivals set up their chairs, Tucker introduced himself and his assistant, a student at the University of Texas who helped him during weekend events, and he shared a little bit about his background and how he'd come to be the founder of a wilderness training school. Gillian learned a few things about him that she hadn't known. For instance, in college he'd spent summers working in three different national parks on search-and-rescue teams. And he was deathly afraid of public speaking.

Gillian wasn't sure she bought that last bit. He certainly appeared comfortable enough speaking in front of this group of mostly strangers. He grinned, poked fun at himself, and seemed perfectly at ease—and deliciously scruffy. He wore a fleece-lined, plaid flannel shirt over a plain gray T-shirt and dark olive cargo pants. He hadn't shaved this morning, and his stubble made her fingers itch to feel it. He'd allowed his military haircut to grow out and now his hair brushed the collar of his shirt. The ball cap he wore sported the Enchanted Canyon Wilderness School logo.

Jeremy had been wearing his blue Italian suit at the Bluebonnet Café. The two men couldn't be more different. Today, she viewed Tucker as infinitely more attractive.

Distracted by the direction of her thoughts, she missed hearing Tucker ask them to introduce themselves. "Gillian, want to start?"

"Start what?"

"Introduce yourself."

"Oh. Sure. I'm Gillian Thacker. I live in Redemption and—" She hesitated, the words *I own a bridal salon with my mother* hovering on her tongue. The ones that emerged from her mouth surprised her. "I am an event planner and co-owner of a bridal salon."

Maisy and Caroline both looked at her and beamed. Tucker winked at her, then said, "Maisy?"

The group of students was an eclectic crowd of a dozen people and included a doctor and wife from Dallas and an attorney and his son from Fort Worth. There was a fourth-grade teacher, a sales rep, and an engineer who worked for NASA, a man who owned a car dealership in East Texas, and a widowed grandmother of six whose late husband had played middle linebacker for the Dallas Cowboys. The middle-aged couple from the Texas Panhandle proudly declared themselves preppers-in-training, and the wife asked Gillian where she could get a Girls Getting Grubby T-shirt.

"You'll be able to order them through the store on the Enchanted Canyon Wilderness School's website in a few weeks," Gillian assured her.

Tucker frowned. "Um, Gillian, we don't have a store on our website."

"You will," she fired back. "Poor planning on your part not to have one."

"Hey, that's not my job," he said with a defensive note in his voice. "That's office related, so that's all on Boone." For the benefit of those that didn't know the McBrides, he added an explanation. "He's one of our partners. I'm the guy in charge of fieldwork, which is a nice little segue. Let's get to it, shall we? Everybody find a seat, and I'll explain how the day is going to work."

Tucker broke the weekend into seven sections, beginning with Survival Mentality and Priorities and ending with Land Navigation and Lost Prevention. "Our purpose here this weekend is to teach you life-enhancing skills that will make you feel comfortable in the outdoors and give you a richer experience when you get out of the cities and suburbs and commune with Mother Nature. The goal is that you'll leave here tomorrow afternoon feeling more competent and confident with new skills to practice when you're not in the middle of an emergency. Okay? Everybody ready?"

"Let's do it," called the engineer.

Tucker nodded and went to stand in front of his whiteboard. He picked up a marker saying, "So, let's jump right in. Your life is at risk. Your survival is under threat. You are in a high-stress situation where resources are not normal. What are you going to do?"

"Probably pee my pants," Maisy jokingly offered.

Tucker, however, took her serious. "Fear is actually an important survival skill. The trick is to use fear as a tool to keep you safe and not as a barrier that holds you back."

Caroline leaned toward Gillian and whispered, "That sounds like something Celeste Blessing would say."

"Remember that in a survival situation, your brain is the most important tool in your toolbox," Tucker continued. "We are not the fastest or strongest creatures on the planet, but human intelligence gives us an advantage—as long as we use it and don't let our primal mind take over and make decisions based on emotion rather than logic. Survival often depends on the ability to keep a cool head. So, here we are, the zombie apocalypse is approaching. Your primal mind might be telling you to turn around and run like hell. You need to listen to your lizard brain, but you shouldn't act on it."

He used a black marker to draw a number one on the whiteboard and then wrote the words: *Calm down.*

Determine your need and develop a solution. Aloud, he said, "I have a problem. I need to fix it. How? A little later we will get into the survival triangle and learn about need priority, but for now, I want you to think about this. Life is full of all sorts of survival situations, some more life threatening than others. Fear of public speaking is the same fear as being eaten by a lion. This survival rule helps in all sorts of situations. Collect yourself, identify the problem, and think about how you're going to fix it. Don't simply react or make an impulsive decision because impulsive decisions often make matters worse."

Listening to Tucker, Gillian's thoughts returned to that morning at breakfast. The moment her gaze had landed on Jeremy, her blood had run cold. She'd reacted impulsively and turned around and hid in the bathroom until he left, which only made matters worse because his mother was in the restaurant too, and she saw her do it. By now, Mary Ann Jones undoubtedly had spread the news all over town and made Gillian look pathetic.

"Any questions?" Tucker asked. When no one responded, he continued. "Okay, then, next."

He wrote the number two on his board along with the words: *Continually work to improve your circumstances.* "I call this the extra blanket phenomenon. Have you ever been camping or lying in bed in the dead of winter or even napping on the couch beneath an air-conditioner vent in July and you're cold? There's a blanket nearby that would improve your circumstance if you'd only get up and get it."

"But it's too much work to get up and get it, so you stay cold?" asked the car dealer.

"Exactly. It's too much work, or you're too lazy or too comfortable to roust yourself out of bed to get the extra blanket. As a result, you don't sleep well. You're not comfortable. Survival rule number two is to empower yourself as a problem solver, not a sit-around-and-whiner. Get up and get yourself another blanket. If something's not working, fix it. Work to improve your circumstance."

Okay, Gillian thought, *that one could apply to relationships too.*

"Third, don't make your situation any worse."

"That's pretty obvious," Maisy said.

"It is," Tucker agreed with a nod. "But it's also easy to do. Act on emotion instead of logic, and you might end up—"

Hiding in a bathroom, Gillian thought.

"Jumping from the proverbial frying pan into the fire. Attitude is vital. Start feeling overwhelmed or sorry for yourself or lose your cool, and things can go south fast. If you convince yourself you're going to die, you'll die. Decide you are going to live, and your chances of staying alive are a whole lot better."

"Wilderness karma," observed the teacher.

"Life karma," Gillian offered. "Honestly, Tucker, everything you've said applies to everyday life, everyday relationships." *Where were you two months ago?*

He flashed her a grin and nodded. "Most everything we'll discuss this weekend comes back to common sense and preparation. Utilizing those two things will carry you a long way toward your goal, whether it's surviving the zombie apocalypse or navigating your way through, I don't know, say, planning a wedding. Caroline, you're planning a wedding now. How do you deal with it when you're feeling overwhelmed?"

"That's easy," Caroline said with a laugh. "I call Gillian. She is the planning pro. She takes care of everything."

Tucker grinned at Gillian. "All right, then, pro. What do you do when the zombies are bearing down upon you from every direction?"

"I focus on the task in front of me and work on solving one problem at a time."

He nodded approvingly. "Exactly. Do that, and you'll hold the zombies at bay. When you get in a tight spot, battle against the desire to feel sorry for yourself. Relish your victories, no matter how small, and do your best to keep your sense of humor. It's amazing how much maintaining a bit of irony can help in desperate situations."

Maisy quoted the famous line from the movie *Jaws,* "'We're gonna need a bigger boat.'"

"There you go." Tucker turned back to his whiteboard, wiped it clean with his shirtsleeve, then drew a triangle. "Now, let's talk about the survival triangle."

In the three corners of the triangle, he wrote the words *Body Temp, Hydration,* and *Energy.* At the center, he wrote *Fire.*

Fire. Yes, she could use a little more heat. The dampness of the morning seemed to have seeped into her bones, and she wished she'd packed a warmer pair of socks than what she wore. Guess she got an F in preparedness. Gillian nudged her chair closer to the fire pit and listened distractedly as Tucker began to lecture about understanding and prioritizing problems.

The cold didn't appear to bother him at all. In fact, even as the thought occurred to her, he slipped off his flannel shirt. The man was comfortable and confident and in his element. Her gaze lingered on his broad shoulders, drifted to his muscular arms. He wore his T-shirt tucked into his cargo pants. When he casually unsheathed his wicked-looking knife as he approached the fire, hunkered down on his heels, then used the knife tip to . . . do something . . . she really wasn't paying attention . . . her gaze drifted to his crotch.

Stop that!

The wanton woman inside her fired back. *Why?* Why did she need to stop it? She was free, wasn't she? Single, with a capital *S*. Why couldn't she have a casual affair with Tucker McBride and enjoy some no-strings sex?

Because she lived in Redemption, that's why. The sex always came with strings because small town affairs were never casual. After they ended, they weren't over because they might just follow you into the bank or sit in the same row at church or take the table next to you at the Bluebonnet. A woman couldn't live her entire life in the ladies' room.

Her gaze drifted to the glowing orange embers of the campfire. She was cold, and she wanted to move closer to the heat. The people around her laughed, and judging by Tucker's mischievous grin, he'd said something amusing that she'd missed.

Whoa, the man was hot when he smiled like that. Of course, he was hot when he scowled too.

She was cold, and she wanted to move closer to the heat.

Jeremy was back in town and pretending all was well. What was she going to do about it?

Survive. That's what.

She would survive Jeremy Jones.

And she just might let Tucker McBride teach her how.

Chapter Thirteen

"We are going to start a friction fire using a bow drill," Tucker said. "Learning this skill teaches you one invaluable lesson—always carry matches."

The comment got the expected chuckle from the group, and so began the first hands-on lesson of his Survival 101 class. He lectured about materials selection, leading the group through the woods in search of the optimum materials for the task before them. "Due to the rain, we won't be harvesting today—I have dry raw materials set aside. Your first time is challenging enough without adding damp materials into the mix."

Tucker's hearing was keen, so he heard it when Maisy murmured to her girlfriends, "And here *I* always thought that being good and damp made the first time easier."

Caroline and Gillian both giggled. Tucker pretended not to have heard even as the comment sent his thoughts in a distracting direction. Dammit, he did not need to think about sex. Sex might be required for survival of the species, but despite what the average male liked to believe, it wasn't necessary for survival, and it didn't belong at Enchanted Canyon

Wilderness School's Survival 101 class. Tucker was a professional. He needed to keep his mind on professional topics. Nevertheless, he was glad when the dreary sky opened up and drenched his . . . heat.

Once they made their way back to the pecan bottoms site, as his students gathered around the fire and a few of them—including Gillian—complained about the cold, he used the weather to make a point. "Remember that body temperature should be your number one concern. At unhealthy body temperature levels, your level of consciousness starts to decrease. Your ability to think clearly disappears, and you're unable to help yourself. That will kill you long before thirst or hunger does. As I said at the beginning, your mind is the most important tool in your toolbox."

The woman from Amarillo said, "My mind is telling me I should have paid closer attention to the weather report. I didn't bring adequate rain gear."

Tucker nodded. "Prevention is the most important survival skill, so if you left our shelter here inadequately prepared, you've learned a lesson. However, now that you're chilled, let's see about teaching you how to tend to the center of the survival triangle—fire. Tomorrow, we'll cover shelter construction."

He gave them an overview of the bow drill process as he set out his demonstration kit, intending to use the teaching technique of telling his audience what he was going to do, then doing it, and finally, telling them again what he'd just done.

He went down on his knees and then picked up the bow and the spindle and explained, "It's all about duration, pressure, and speed."

"That's what I tell my husband," quipped the doctor's wife.

That one everybody heard. Instinctively, Tucker's

gaze shifted to Gillian at the same time hers moved toward him. Their gazes held, and in that instant, the switch flipped in Tucker's primal mind, and from that moment on, everything he said during his fire-making lecture took on a sexual undertone.

"Softer wood doesn't polish," took on a new meaning that had nothing to do with wood selection for the spindle.

He saw something other than a hunk of mesquite branch in his hand as he said, "You want the hardest wood for a handhold."

When he said, "Lubricate your handhold," he wasn't thinking of soap or grease.

"Use the whole bow." *Sex.* "Take long strokes." *Sex.* "Slow and steady until your notch is full, then speed up to light the coal." *Sex. Sex. Sex.* "For tinder, look for something fluffy and flammable." *Just kill me now.*

By the time he transferred his coal to his tinder and blew a flame gently to life, Tucker wondered if he'd survive the attempt to teach Gillian Thacker how to build a friction fire. He was about to spontaneously combust.

He hoped the situation would improve once the students began attempting to make their own fires, but Gillian's natural grace and competent manner apparently didn't transfer to wilderness skills. The woman was an absolute klutz. She handled her knife okay to make her handhold, but she couldn't tie knots worth a damn, and so she'd needed help stringing her bow.

She'd worn perfume. Who the hell wears perfume to survivalist school?

By the time she had her bow strung, holes drilled in her handhold and fireboard, tinder prepared, and fireboard notched to catch the coal when it formed, half the class already had their fires. She went down on one knee, placed her tools, and began working the bow.

Dammit, he wished she'd worn a thicker coat that better camouflaged the swing of her deliciously full breasts.

She made very little progress before her spindle launched out of the bowstring and she had to start again.

Her second effort was no more successful than the first. She tossed her bow down in frustration. "I can't do this. I give up. I'm a fire failure."

"C'mon, Gillian," Tucker chided. "You never really fail at something until you're dead."

"There's something else Celeste would say," Caroline observed.

Maisy shook her head. "Actually, that sounds more like Angelica to me."

Gillian scowled at Tucker.

He encouraged her with a steady, confident look. "You can do it."

Around her, three other students got their fires. She exhaled a heavy sigh and picked up her bow, twisted the spindle into position, and went back to work, moving her arm in a sawing motion.

"Atta girl," Tucker said before turning to help first the lawyer, and then the car dealer. Afterward, he returned his attention to Gillian. He hunkered down beside her. "Keep a straight back and bowing arm. Keep that bow flat and level. Like this." He reached out and adjusted her tools. "Remember to use the whole bowstring. Speed isn't as important. Slow and steady."

"My arm is going to fall off," Gillian complained. "My knee is killing me.

She pouted like a schoolgirl. He wanted to nip at

that bottom lip of hers. "Apply more and more weight on the handhold, Gillian. Keep your back straight. Arm up."

"I am."

He moved behind her, reached around her, and repositioned her bow. He placed his left hand atop hers on the handhold, his right hand over hers on the bow and demonstrated the proper pressure, the slow and steady pace. He smelled the spicy scent of her perfume, and the silky texture of her hair brushed his cheek. Fire flared inside him.

"I see smoke," Maisy cried excitedly.

He hoped she was looking at Gillian's fireboard and not his crotch.

Torture. This was pure torture. With a note of hoarseness in his voice, Tucker said, "You see the black dust that's formed in your notch since you've been bowing? You're making progress."

He released her and backed away. "If it keeps smoking, you may have a coal."

"I won't be able to lift my arm for a week."

"But you'll be warm." Tucker watched the thin wisp of smoke rise from the notch in her fireboard. "Okay, Glory. I think you have your coal."

"I do?"

"Think so. Set your bow drill aside and fan it with your hand." As she followed his instructions, he added, "There you go. See how it holds together in a clump? That's your coal. Now, gently transfer it to your tinder. Hold it up and blow gently. Gently. See, it's glowing red. Keep blowing, Glory. Long, sustained gentle breaths. There you go. There you go."

The tinder in her hands burst into flame. "I did it!" she exclaimed. "Look, I have fire! It's gonna burn my hands!"

"No, it won't. Gently add it to your fire lay." When she did so, he added, "Now, kneel over and blow. Not from the top. Keep it low. There you go."

She was down on both knees with her chest on the ground and her round ass in the air. Tucker had to jerk his gaze off that sweet temptation when she looked up at him, her blue eyes glittering with pleasure. "Thank you. I didn't think I could do it."

"My pleasure. I knew you'd do it." *Smoke comes naturally to you.*

Gillian survived Survival 101. Just barely, and only because Tucker's was one of the few wilderness schools around that didn't require overnight camping, and she had reserved a room at the Fallen Angel Inn and taken advantage of their hot tub.

That night, she'd dreamed of a jungle and Tucker playing Tarzan to her Jane.

Sunday afternoon, she'd trudged toward the car at the end of the day with her thoughts a whirlwind. She was exhausted, yearned for a bath and her bed, but at the same time, she dreaded returning to Redemption and reality.

She needed to put her disturbing Tarzan dreams aside and deal with Jeremy being back in town.

At home, soaking in a tub of hot water and nursing a glass of wine, she reflected on the thought that had occurred to her first on Saturday. Maybe she should attempt to adapt Tucker's lessons to coexisting with her ex in a small town. He'd used the acronym *S.U.R.V.I.V.A.L.* at the end of class today. It might do her good to adapt it to her situation.

"*S*," she said aloud. "Size up the situation." Well, she'd been doing that ever since the breakup. Nothing new to size there.

U was: *Use all your senses.* Guess she could try to be aware whenever she was out and about in town so he didn't take her by surprise, and she ended up back in another bathroom. She could look for him, listen for him; she knew his scent. Be hanged if she'd taste him or touch him, though.

R: Remember where you are. That was easy and paired with *U.* Out in public in Redemption, she'd need to be sniffing, seeing, and listening.

V: Vanquish your fears. Now, that one was more of a challenge. She had to recognize and acknowledge her fears to vanquish them, and she hadn't managed to do that. Her gaze shifted to her glass. Maisy would say that was what wine is for. Gillian lifted her glass and took another sip.

I was for *Improvise.* She frowned, unable to relate it to her situation, so she skipped to the second *V* for *Value living.* According to Tucker, that meant focusing on at least one of your reasons for living and not giving up. That was easy to do in a survival situation, but in a relationship one? She'd have to think about it.

Next, *A: Act like a native.* Tucker's theory there was that natives were best of the best, that the fittest—us—had survived. That the very fact we walked the earth instead of our line having died out meant we had the right stuff to survive. "Another one that needs thinking about," she muttered before taking another sip of wine.

That brought her to *L: Live by your wits*, which Tucker had said meant feeding inspiration and thinking outside the box. Gillian thought he'd gone a little Zen by the time he got to the second part of the acronym, and she came up dry on *L* too. So that left her with *S.U.R.*

"Batting less than .500," she muttered in a glum

tone before lifting her feet and allowing herself to slide down the tub and sink beneath the surface of the bathwater.

Just as the water closed over her head, she heard the echo of Tucker's voice in her mind, clear as a bell. *You've never really failed at something until you're dead.* On its heels came her mother's voice. *If at first you don't succeed, try, try again.*

Hmm. Maybe *S.U.R.V.I.V.A.L.* wouldn't help her with Jeremy, but perhaps the life lesson here was to climb back on the proverbial bicycle and give another relationship a go. It was something to think about.

She levered up from the water and reached for her shampoo and remembered Tucker's kiss in the cave. She wasn't ready. She still wasn't ready.

But maybe she would be ready someday. Maybe if she could figure out the rest of the word, the *V.I.V.A.L.* part of *S.U.R.V.I.V.A.L.*, she could move on.

She finished shampooing, conditioned, rinsed, and climbed from the tub. Twenty minutes later, with her hair dry and wearing her Next Chapter Bookstore sleep shirt, she climbed into bed and patted her mattress. Peaches accepted the invitation and jumped up onto the bed. Meeting her puppy's loving gaze, Gillian spoke in a solemn tone. "One thing is for certain. The first step in my *S.U.R.V.I.V.A.L.*, Peaches, is to not hide in the bathroom the next time I see my ex."

Then she turned out the light and went quickly to sleep. This time, she dreamed about Tucker and a desert island. And beach sex.

An uneventful week went by, and on Friday morning—April Fool's Day—she arrived at Bliss an hour before opening with a smile on her face and a spring in her step, having made the public walk from home to the bridal salon with her senses on alert. No rat sightings whatsoever. Her mother had her annual checkup and wasn't due in until the afternoon, so they had not scheduled any fittings or bridal appointments this morning. Gillian planned to spend an hour or so on display window redesign. She wanted to do something outdoorsy.

She was deep in design mode half an hour later when a pounding on the front door pulled her from her thoughts. *Wonder what this is about?* She was expecting a delivery from UPS, but they always came to the back door.

Jeremy. Could it be Jeremy? Had he come to get the awkward first meeting over with privately? It wasn't a bad idea. She could see him doing it.

She should have anticipated this. She heard the echo of Tucker's voice in her mind saying, *Preparation is your most important survival skill.*

Pound. Pound. Pound. Pound. Gillian's stomach dropped to her knees. No, it sank all the way to her ankles. "*S.U.R.*," she murmured as she rose from her seat in her tiny office. The time had come to get her *V. Vanquish your fears.*

Her legs only trembled a little bit as she made her way downstairs and to the front of the shop. Not Jeremy, she thought, experiencing a wave of relief. A woman. Erica Chadwick.

"Oh, no," she breathed. She'd almost prefer to see Jeremy.

If Lindsay Grant and her bride tribe were on their way in, Gillian was going to duck out the back door. Summoning a smile, she flipped the lock and opened the door. The woman barged inside and sailed toward the parlor saying, "I know you're not open yet, Gillian, but I am pressed for time."

Gillian gritted her teeth, shut the door, and pasted

on a smile. "Good morning, Erica. If you're solicit-
ing prizes for the alumni fundraiser, we already do-
nated."

"Oh, I'm here as a bride." Erica lifted her left hand
and wiggled her fingers, flashing a large diamond solitaire. "I need a gown of my own, and I remember a
dress from when I was here with Lindsay."

Gillian grimly managed to maintain her smile.
"Let me get our appointment book, and we'll get you
set up."

"Oh, no."

Erica rested her right hand on her belly, drawing
Gillian's gaze. Oh. It was an obvious baby bump. She
had to be in her third trimester.

Erica continued, "As you see, we are in a bit of a
rush. At first, I didn't think I wanted to get married,
but as time went on, I changed my mind. Luckily, I
don't need one of your regular bridal appointments
because I know exactly which gown I want. It's a boho
style." She named the designer and described the dress
in detail. "It shouldn't need alterations."

Gillian knew exactly which gown she meant. It was
another gown in the collection from which she'd
chosen her own wedding gown.

If her mother were here, she'd have passed Erica off
to her. She did not want to work with the woman. But
at least, judging by the looks of things, it wouldn't be
a customer experience that dragged on. "I'm pretty
sure I know which dress you mean. Have a seat in the
parlor, and I'll bring out the sample."

In the stockroom, Gillian sorted through the
gowns, until she found the one Erica had described.
Pasting a smile on her face, she carried it out into the
parlor. "Is this the gown?"

"Yes!" Erica shot to her feet and clapped her hands.

She reached for it, held it up against herself, and turned to and fro as she gazed at her reflection in one of the parlor mirrors. "This is it. It's the one I want." She gave a little laugh and added, "Sometimes it takes more time than I'd like, but in the end, I *always* get what I want."

Then she turned around and faced Gillian. The light in her eyes suddenly glittered with triumph that Gillian remembered well from campus days. Erica's smile slowly went stiletto sharp.

Suddenly, before her old sorority sister said another word, the pieces fell into place. Gillian's gaze dropped from Erica's face to the belly swollen with child. Third trimester. Late August, early September. *This. This is what happened. This is why he did it.*

Erica's voice dripped with malice as she said, "Jeremy will love this wedding gown, don't you think?"

When Tucker had a weekend class, he ordinarily took Mondays off. Sometimes, Tuesdays too. Wednesdays, well, it depended on what the next weekend's schedule held. But this Monday he found himself in Redemption, at the shop, counting the minutes down until lunchtime. He intended to take Gillian to lunch and have a serious discussion.

Following this weekend, his patience was at an end. Friction fire on Saturday had almost crippled him. The body temperature and shelter section of the course on Sunday had damned near killed him. The way she'd looked at him when he lectured about the ways heat is transferred from your body had made him a model for that Viagra commercial: *If your erection should last more than four hours.*

Well, he didn't need to seek medical help. He knew exactly what he needed. Judging by the tension that had sizzled through them all weekend, he knew what Gillian needed too. The time had come to do something about this friendship business and make a strategic step forward with Operation Horny Toad.

He had a proposal to make to Gillian over lunch. He had decided that a romantic getaway for the two of them was in order. They had spent the past weekend roughing it, and now he intended to pamper her and ply her with five-star indulgences. He'd drag his tux from the back of his closet and show her a night on the town. He was still debating which city, but he had a handful in mind depending on how much time she could steal away.

He was sitting at his computer researching restaurants in New Orleans when he heard his front bell jangle. Considering that he still had the CLOSED sign displayed on the door, hearing the sound surprised him. Rising, he exited his office and upon seeing his visitor, stopped dead in his tracks. *Oh, hell. Something terrible has happened.* "Gillian, what's wrong?"

Her voice held a note of hysteria. "I tried, Tucker. I got the *S* and the *U* and the *R* and even pretty much got the *V.* I know I'm not supposed to feel sorry for myself or lose my cool or let myself get overwhelmed and maintain my sense of humor, but I can't help it. There is nothing funny about this."

She had a wild look in her tearful eyes. "Gillian, sweetheart." He went to her and grasped her shoulders. "Calm down. Tell me what happened."

The story poured out of her like vomit. Tucker was simultaneously shocked and unsurprised. *Jeremy had Gillian's body and soul, and he cheated on her? What a dumbass.*

She babbled on, repeating enough of his class lecture points that it proved she'd paid attention. "I have sized up the situation like I'm supposed to do," she told him. "I know where I am. I can't be here anymore, or I won't survive! Prevention is the most important survival skill. I need to get out of here. Now. Away from Redemption. Otherwise, I'll probably go to jail for murder, and that would break my mother's heart. Will you take me somewhere, Tucker?"

Me. She came to me. Not her mom, not her friends. Me.

"Will you take me now? Today? Will you help me survive? Not in Enchanted Canyon. I don't need peace. I need people. Lights. Action. Alcohol. Lots of alcohol. Take me somewhere that I can drink and dance and forget. Somewhere I'm not tempted to get a gun and go Roxie Hart on him."

"Roxie Hart?"

"*Chicago.* The musical. 'Cell Block Tango.' Please, Tucker. I've never been this angry in my entire life. Take me away before I do something I'll regret!"

Then her dam burst and Gillian began to cry.

Tucker had never earned the rank of general. However, he did master a general's set of skills. He knew how to adapt his strategy and redeploy his assets amid battle. Therefore, after half a minute of consideration, he said, "Okay, let's go."

He grabbed his wallet and phone and, making a spur-of-the-moment decision, the small flat jeweler's case he kept locked in his desk, and tossed the items into one of his go bags. Slinging the strap of his bag over one shoulder, he flipped the lock on his front door, and then took Gillian's hand and led her out the back. He drove her home, told her to go inside and pack a bag. When she collapsed on the sofa in misery, he did her packing for her while making the phone calls his plan required. One was to Jackson, arranging care for Peaches. Another was to Jackson's ex, who'd moved to Redemption at the end of last year and who had more money than sense. She owned a helicopter and had a pilot on call to ferry her to the airport in Austin. Tucker's relationship with Coco had improved once he'd begun working with Haley on her wilderness skills, so she was happy to help.

Within the hour, they were headed for Austin. Gillian roused herself long enough to ask about her dog, and he explained the arrangements he'd made. By early afternoon, they'd boarded a plane and settled into their first-class seats with the first of the drinks she'd requested. A little less than three hours later, they landed.

Welcome to fabulous Las Vegas.

Chapter Fourteen

Mentally reviewing the past year of her relation-ship with her ex, Gillian paid scant attention to her surroundings. This had been her first time to ride in a helicopter. Under other circumstances, she would have been excited, maybe a little nervous. Today, she hadn't cared. She didn't care how she traveled or where she traveled. All that mattered was that Tucker took her away from Redemption.

Her first Bloody Mary on the airplane took the edge off. The second put her to sleep. She awoke slowly as the plane taxied toward the gate. Hearing the sound of Tucker's gentle encouragement to awaken, she smiled automatically in response. She was leaning against him, her head resting on his shoulder. He felt so nice.

Then everything came rushing back. Gillian opened her eyes and sat up to find Tucker watching her warily.

She would not break into tears. She was done cry-ing over that man. The sleep and maybe the vodka had helped clear her despair. Yet, she was far from empty of emotion. Gillian was still angry, to the marrow, every cell of her body engulfed, extremely, supremely, profoundly, and murderously pissed.

"That bastard," she said. "That lowdown, lying, cheating, Arnold Palmer–wannabe bastard. How dare he!"

"Atta girl," Tucker said with a smile, as relief melted across his face.

The plane arrived at the gate, electronic bells sounded, and passengers began standing and retrieving their belongings from the overhead bins. Gillian gave her head a shake and freed her seat belt. "Gosh, I'm a ditz, but where are we again?"

"Vegas. You wanted lights and action. Can't get any brighter and busier than Vegas."

A smile flirted with her lips. "Vegas, huh? Is it still run by the mob? Maybe I could hire a hit man while we're here."

Tucker grinned, but shook his head. "You'll be too busy to look for a killer."

"I will?" she asked as the door opened and passengers began to file off the plane. Seated in first class, they were one of the first to exit. "What will I be doing?"

"We should have just enough time to check into our suite before you head down to your spa appointment for a massage."

"A massage! Oh, Tucker, I adore you!" She leaned over and went up on her tiptoes to kiss his cheek.

As they entered the chaos and cacophony of Mc-Carran International Airport, Gillian gave her companion a sidelong, speculative look and thought about sleeping arrangements. He'd said "check into our suite." Not room. Not rooms, plural. Suite. It could be two bedrooms. He'd paid for first-class airline tickets. The man apparently wasn't afraid to spend money on this trip.

Tucker didn't hide the fact that he had a thing for her. He was too much of a gentleman to expect her to sleep with him just because he'd dropped a bundle on last-minute airline tickets. He might, however, try to seduce her. Probably wouldn't take much. A wicked wink might do the trick. Or a suggestive smile. Shoot, it might be the other way around. Maybe she'd seduce him. She might grab him by the necktie and drag *him* off to *her* bed.

Not that Tucker wore neckties. She'd never seen him wear one. As far as she knew, he might not even own one. He'd have worn one when he dressed in uniform, of course. She had a hard time imagining him as Mr. Squared Away Spit and Polish. That was so different from the earthy, native wilderness guy. Bet he cleaned up pretty. Grubby, he was to die for handsome.

She wanted him. She wanted to roll around in the sheets with him until she lay exhausted, out of energy, drained of this red-hot fury churning inside her.

That's terrible, Gillian. That would be using him. You are not that kind of girl.

Bet he wouldn't mind.

As they exited the secure side of the airport, a driver waited holding a sign that read T. MCBRIDE. They had no checked luggage, and it dawned on Gillian that they hadn't stopped by his place to pack anything for him. "You don't have a suitcase."

"I'll pick up what I need. No big deal."

The driver ferried them to the hotel, the same one where Jackson and Caroline had stayed with Coco and her crew in those terrible days after the plane crash.

Afterward, Caroline had raved about the hotel's luxury, and the kindness the staff had shown during that trying time. Jeremy had taken Gillian to some upscale places, but this was a big step up from anywhere she'd previously stayed.

They didn't even have to check in but were escorted straight up to their suite. Gillian stood in the center of a small living area, gazing around a little in awe as Tucker murmured something to the bellboy. Then the door shut, and they were alone, and she felt suddenly unsure and awkward.

Tucker said, "It's two bedrooms, Glory. I didn't want to assume. I'm going to take the one here on the right, and you are welcome to join me or not. No expectations. No pressure."

She cleared her throat. "You really are a gentleman, Tucker." *Drat it.* "I want you to know I'll settle up with you at some point. I pay my own way."

"Don't worry about it." He studied her with a long look. "You are wound tighter than a two-dollar watch right now, sweetheart. If I know anything about women, this spa appointment is exactly what the doctor ordered."

"Do you have a massage scheduled too?"

"No. I'm not a spa kind of guy. While you're getting pampered, I'll probably make a run to the T-shirt shop. You might take a look in your bag and see what I missed. I can pick it up while I'm out. Then, to be honest, I'll probably take a nap. I expect we'll have a late night, and I'd hate to fall asleep on the craps table."

"I don't know how to play craps."

"Don't worry. I'll teach you. There's a lot I can teach you while we're here in Vegas. All you have to do is ask."

Gillian couldn't help it. Her gaze stole past the open door of the bedroom he'd claimed as his own. At that moment, thoughts of Jeremy were very far away.

Unfortunately, they returned following a fabulous massage that left her peaceful and relaxed when she sat to enjoy a delicious spa lunch of champagne, chicken salad, and fresh mixed fruit. Her server was the spitting image of Erica, sans the baby bump. The young woman was attentive and sweet as could be, and Gillian left her an excellent tip, but by the time she sat in the stylist's chair for makeup, blow-dry, and style, her mellow mood had disappeared. On top of her encounter with the Erica doppelgänger, she now sat in a salon that was bursting with babbling, bubbling brides.

They were everywhere. When Gillian said as much to her stylist, the woman laughed. "Oh, and this is the slow season for brides in Las Vegas. You should see it on Valentine's Day. You can't throw a bag of rose petals without hitting a bride around here, then. Speaking of weddings, we just got our new polish colors for June. Some beautiful pastels. Would you like to see them?"

"Pastels? I don't know that pastels suit my mood." Gillian went with lady-killer red.

At the end of her spa afternoon, she returned to their suite, propelled by three glasses of champagne and a slow burn. She looked great, she knew, but oh, such ugly emotions churned inside of her. She arrived to find Tucker's bedroom door firmly shut, a long-stem red rose lying atop a note on the coffee table that read: *Meet here at 5:00 for cocktails.*

She glanced at the clock. Ten minutes. All she needed to do was dress. She headed toward the second bedroom, trying to recall what Tucker had packed for

her. Shoes, she remembered, because he'd pulled out
her go-to pair of black heels and her "dinner with clients of the bank" little black dress. Dang it, the bra
she was wearing didn't work beneath that dress. Had
he packed underwear? OMG, had she been so out-of-
control that she let Tucker McBride go rummaging
through her panty drawer?

She stepped into the second bedroom and stopped
abruptly. "Whoa."

A dress lay spread upon the bed with a flat, black
velvet jewelry box and a folded note beside it. Her
mouth went dry when she read Tucker's bold, masculine hand. *Red is the color of fire and blood, of
strength and power and passion. You wore red the
day we met. I hope you'll wear it tonight. Red suits
you. —T*

She blew out a breath and reached for the dress.
It was a silken sunset, a bold, rich red shot through
with a golden shimmer. She held it against herself and
turned toward the mirror. The neckline plunged, but
not trashy low. The hem was a little shorter than she
ordinarily wore, but not so short that she'd be uncomfortable. She had to try it.

She kicked off her shoes and pulled off her top and
turned to throw it toward the bedside chair. That's
when she noticed the shopping bag. She murmured,
"More?"

Oh, yes, more. Definitely more. Lingerie. Red.
Perfect for the dress. And shoes. Not just any shoes,
but—OMG—Christian Louboutin. Glossy, sleek red
snakeskin with stiletto heels.

Now, her heart began to pound, and she sank
into the chair. She'd never owned a pair of Louboutins. They were wildly expensive and ridiculously
impractical, but how, oh how she'd always coveted a

pair. She never would have spent the money on them. She'd never received them as a gift. Not from Jeremy, and he'd loved to see her in high heels.

Tucker McBride gave her Louboutins. He'd given her the shoes, the dress, and the lingerie. The spa. This hotel. The last-minute trip. Everything first class!

From the man who just two days ago talked about eating worms for fuel.

Red is the color of fire and blood, of strength and power and passion. Red suits you.

"Oh, Tucker."

Finally, she reached for the item she'd saved for last. Her mouth was dry as she opened the jewelry box. "Oh, Tucker," she repeated in a breathy voice upon recognizing the antique hair combs, the ones from the cave. How did he happen to have these with him? Why would he give them to her? She couldn't accept a gift like this. Any of it, really. It was all too much.

And yet, he'd gone to so much trouble, so much thought. Gillian couldn't throw his generosity back in his face either. And Tucker wasn't the type to make a grand gesture like this if it wasn't something he wanted to do.

I'll be gracious and accept his gifts. Maybe insist the combs are simply a loan.

Her conscience appeased, she giggled like a school-girl and dug in.

Everything fit. At two minutes to five, she touched up her lipstick, tucked it, her ID, a credit card, and a couple of tissues into the bra pocket she always carried in her luggage and gave her reflection one final look. "Fire and strength and passion," she murmured. Yes. Tonight, Tucker was right. Red suited her mood.

She opened the bedroom door and stepped out to

meet her date. Tucker stood at the bar, mixing what appeared to be martinis. Seeing her, he froze. "Holy hell, Glory."

She gave him a slow once-over. A suit. A gray three-piece suit, a white shirt, and a necktie! Red with black stripes. The Spit and Polish Tucker far exceeded her fantasy. Her fingers itched to reach for that tie. "Holy hell, yourself. The T-shirt shop, Tucker?"

He flashed a grin that she felt clear to her Louboutin-shod toes. "The dress was in the window. I couldn't pass it up. Great decision I made, by the way. You look incomparable."

"Thank you. For the compliment, the dress, the shoes—oh, the shoes! And, for—" She touched one of the hair combs, then waved her arm around the suite. "For all of this. It's too much. Way too much."

"It's my pleasure."

"But the expense! I didn't—"

"Enough. There's oil and gas on my family's ranch, Gillian." He handed her a drink. "You are welcome. I enjoyed shopping, and the shoes were for me as much as for you. I intended to give you the combs on Valentine's Day, but the timing was never right. Now, tell me about the spa. Did you run into anyone famous?"

She sipped her drink. Funny how Jeremy never missed a chance to let people know he had money, but Tucker came from generational wealth and never let on. That was so much more attractive.

"Gillian? Famous folk?"

She shook away the thoughts of her ex. "If I did, I couldn't see them for all the brides."

"The brides?"

She told him about the bundles of bubbling happiness in the salon. Tucker frowned. "I didn't think about all the weddings when I chose Las Vegas for your escape. That was bad planning on my part."

Gillian shook her head. "Are you kidding? All of this? This is a fairy tale, Tucker. You've given me a fairy tale just when I needed one."

It was true. She did feel like Cinderella on the way to the ball when he escorted her to a limo that took them to the restaurant where he'd made dinner reservations. The food was fantastic, the wine sublime, and the company ever so entertaining. Tucker kept her laughing, mostly with stories about the shenanigans he and Jackson and Boone had created during their youth. When they debated whether or not to have an after-dinner drink, he checked the time with the pocket watch he wore on a chain on his vest.

"Tell me about the watch," Gillian asked as she sipped a cognac a few minutes later. "Is that the one you mentioned you found in Enchanted Canyon?"

"It is. And the chain is from the trunk in the cave." He reached up and readjusted the comb in her hair, then let his fingers trail through her curls. "I took it from the trunk the same time I removed your combs."

"I've never noticed you wearing it before tonight."

"I haven't worn it before." He removed the gold watch from its vest pocket, unhooked the chain, and handed it to Gillian who flipped it open and read the engraving. *To My Love.*

Tucker said, "I wore it this morning because Angelica left a strange note on my door last night."

"Strange?"

He nodded. "She suggested I start wearing the watch and then quoted some French guy who said, 'Everything comes in time to those who can wait.'"

"I've heard that quote. I don't know the French guy, though."

"Me either. But I decided to get on my woo-woo and listen to Angelica. Her hunches are uncanny, so I figured I'd wear the watch."

"It's beautiful," Gillian said, handing it back.

Tucker returned it to his pocket, and conversation drifted toward upcoming summer events at the Fallen Angel Inn and Last Chance Hall. Gillian relaxed and enjoyed the moment, though she never completely rid herself of the anger toward Jeremy that simmered beneath everything. Like Tucker said, red suited her. Anger was red, but so was strength and passion. She was strongly, passionately furious with that lying, cheating duffer, and she was absolutely, positively going to enjoy herself tonight in the company of this handsome, generous, witty, sexy-as-sin guide to her survival, Tucker McBride.

If her gaze kept straying to the three sets of brides and grooms also dining at that time, well, she was simply practicing her survival *S: Size up the situation*, before taking another sip of cognac.

After dinner, they walked to the nightclub where he'd reserved a table. The place was loud, the drinks strong, and the music classic rock. It was just what she'd asked for, just what she'd thought she'd wanted, but after half an hour of dancing, Gillian realized that rather than easing her simmering temper, the music and movement fueled it.

Being surrounded by literally dozens of members of bachelorette parties didn't help anything.

When the live band took a break, she suggested they head somewhere else.

"I'm game for leaving. Want to try the casino for a while?"

"Why not? I'm feeling lucky!"

She meant it too. She would have to be a real witch

not to feel lucky with a man like Tucker at her side, having given her this fairy-tale escape. She gave him a sidelong glance and found him staring at her with warm admiration in his eyes. She smiled at him, and he took hold of her hand.

They strolled through the shopping mall toward the casino, pausing to window shop when something caught their eyes. Tucker wanted to buy her a necklace, but she refused to allow it. When he admired a tacky Fat Elvis T-shirt, she bought it for him and had it sent to their hotel suite. They were laughing at a risqué coffee cup he'd purchased as a joke for Jackson when Gillian looked up to see even more brides headed her way.

She ducked into a shop that sold Judith Leiber purses to avoid them, and a bag brought her up short. It was a novelty clutch, a princess castle, covered in crystals. She wanted it beyond reason. Unable to help herself, she picked it up, opened it, and checked the tag. *Holy Moses!*

She quickly set it back down. A middle-aged sales clerk asked in a perky tone, "May I help you?"

"No, thank you. Just looking."

"Let me know if I can show you anything." The clerk turned to another customer and repeated her question.

"You like it?" Tucker's tone of voice told her all she needed to do was ask, and he'd buy it for her.

"No. I just thought of how cute it would've looked in the princess window I did for Bliss. Remember? This bag is perfect for a princess bride."

"You want it."

"No, I don't."

"Yes, you do. I can tell. Don't lie to me."

"No. I'm not lying." She smiled wistfully and

added, "I'll admit if I were a bride and wearing a princess-style gown, and I had a billion dollars to waste, I'd buy it for my wedding purse. It's definitely a special occasion bag, the sort of thing that would become an heirloom."

"Why a billion dollars?"

She smirked and showed him the price tag. Tucker's eyes bugged out. "For a purse shaped like a castle?"

Reverently, she said, "It's Judith Leiber."

She wandered away from the castle bag to another display featuring more classically styled purses. When she paused to flip through a catalog, Tucker stopped, tilted his head, and studied her. Absently, he pulled the watch from his vest pocket and rubbed it with the pad of his thumb. "Gillian," he began. "I have an idea. I think we should—"

"Reeeeeeee!" squealed a customer in a loud, shrill voice. "I have to have this!"

Dressed all in white, wearing a little puff veil and a beauty pageant ribbon that spelled out *Bride*, the woman appeared to be younger than Gillian, and she was surrounded by a group of five chattering girl-friends. A bachelorette weekend, most likely. Suddenly, unexpectedly, tears welled in Gillian's eyes and started spilling. She turned around and blindly fled the shop.

Tucker caught up to her moments later. "Whoa, there. Gillian, what did I miss? What just happened? What made you cry?"

"Nothing. Everything. I'm having a meltdown!"

"Okay, yes, that I can see. Why now?"

"It's so stupid. I'm so stupid. It's all these brides. They're everywhere. They're happy and excited, and I'm jealous. I'm here with you wearing thousand-dollar shoes, and you're ten times better looking than he is, and it's a fairy tale, and I'm so lucky but . . . but . . . he got my sorority sister pregnant while he was engaged to me!"

"Honey," Tucker began.

"I don't care. I don't love him anymore. Maybe I never did really love him. And why am I still thinking about weddings? I look at a six-thousand-dollar purse, and I think I want it to carry on my wedding day? How crazy is that? That's the price of a good used car, and I'm single!"

As Tucker took hold of her arm and guided her toward a bench beside a nearby fountain, she continued to rail. "I don't really care about the purse. I care about the baby. A baby is the main reason we scheduled our honeymoon for three months after the wedding. We wanted to make a baby on our honeymoon, and we wanted to be a couple for a year first before being a trio."

"That's a lot of family planning," Tucker observed.

"I plan! That's what I do! I want a baby, and now my eggs are just getting older and older. Before you know it, I'll be thirty-five and classified a geriatric pregnancy. That's even if I find someone who will make a baby with me."

She flopped down onto the bench, folded her arms, and declared, "Jeremy was wrong. It was about the dream. It wasn't all about the wedding!"

Tucker licked his lips. Blew out a breath. Then, he went down on his knees and took her hand. "Prove it to him."

"Prove what?"

"That it's not all about the wedding. That you don't care about the planning—the music, food, playlist, invitations, and all the other sprinkles."

She blinked. Swiped the tears from her cheek. "How the heck would I do that?"

"Marry me. Now. Tonight."

Gillian gaped at him. "What?"

"Marry me. This is Vegas. It's easy."

"It's crazy, that's what it is," she replied with a little laugh. "You've lost your mind, Tucker."

"Maybe. Maybe not. I think you and I have as good a basis for a marriage as a lot of people. We like each other. We're friends. I know as sure as Las Vegas is hot in July that we will be great together in the sack. We have similar values. I want kids. You wouldn't have to worry about geriatric eggs. We could get to work on that project tonight. I'll share your dream, Gillian. Marry me."

"Tucker. This is crazy talk. If this is about sex, I've already decided I want to sleep with you tonight."

"That works out great because I want to wait until we're married to make love."

"No, you don't. You want to sleep with me to-night!"

"Damn straight. Right after we get back to our room from the wedding chapel."

He had to be kidding. Gillian started to laugh. "Okay, good joke, McBride. You had me going, but you took it one step too far with the no sex before marriage thing."

"Glory, I am as serious as a heart attack. I've known I was going to propose to you ever since I heard you and Arnie P. broke up. The only surprise about this is the timing. When an opportunity presents itself, I've learned to take it."

"Well, I haven't," she snapped. Her heart was pounding. Her mouth was dry. Her head spun from all of the alcohol she'd consumed. Not because she was considering his harebrained idea. She wasn't doing that.

Married to Tucker McBride.

He rose and pulled her to her feet and spoke in a soft, seductive voice. "You said you were feeling lucky tonight. Roll the dice, Gillian. Bet on us."

Then in front of the fountain with naked nymphs spouting water from their mouths and surrounded by people and brides and bachelorettes, he kissed her, sweet as a summer peach.

Gillian kissed him back. She wanted. Wanted! She wanted to throw caution to the wind and roll the dice and act without thinking. She wanted to marry this man. Tonight.

When Tucker ended the kiss and stared down into her eyes, waiting for her decision, tears welled inside her once again.

"I can't. It's not me. It's not how I roll. I'm a planner. I need time to think."

She expected him to argue. She half hoped he would. He gave her a crooked, bittersweet smile and brushed a tear from her cheek with his thumb. "All right. I can work with that."

He stepped back, took hold of her hand, and said, "Let's go play some craps. I'm feeling lucky, myself."

"You are?" she said, lengthening her strides to keep up with him. "Because I said no?"

"Now, Glory, what did I teach you just last weekend? You've never really failed at something until you're dead."

She walked the rest of the way to the casino with a smile on her face.

Tucker taught her to play craps. He'd offered to stake her gambling, but Gillian insisted on using her own funds. She enjoyed beginner's luck at the craps table, winning time and time again, drawing a supportive crowd to the table. When she'd turned her one-hundred-dollar beginning bet into four thousand dollars, she'd decided to pick up her chips. The crowd pleaded and cajoled for her to continue, but Gillian's instinctive caution ruled her hot streak.

"That was fun," she told Tucker, excitement and probably a tad too much alcohol humming through her veins.

"It was," he agreed. "You were—are—hot hot hot."

She gave her hair a toss and grinned. "Lucky. I'm lucky."

Then her gaze fell on a roulette wheel. *S.U.R.V.I.V.A.L. Size up the situation. Use all your senses. Remember where you are. Vanquish your fears. Improvise. Value living. Act like the natives. Live by your wits.*

Red and black. Red.

Red is the color of fire and blood, of strength and power and passion. Red suits you.

"Tucker?"

"Hmm?" he said. He was checking the time on his pocket watch.

"Can I have my chips back?"

"You're not cashing out?"

"No, not quite yet."

She bet everything on red and on one spin of the wheel, doubled her money.

The excitement humming through her was now a 130-decibel song played by a 200-man marching band. She barely spared Tucker a glance as she cashed out.

"Gillian?" he asked as she led him out of the casino with a particular destination in mind. "Where are we going?"

"I'm still feeling lucky," she replied.

A few minutes later, she glided into the Judith Leiber shop and used her winnings to buy the castle. Only then did she turn to Tucker and ask, "Do you think we could find a wedding chapel that has a Fat Elvis?"

Chapter Fifteen

The door to their hotel suite crashed open as Mr. and Mrs. Tucker McBride spun into the room, locked in a wild, passionate embrace. Tucker had made a strategic mistake when he'd begun kissing her in the limo, but he'd never expected to lose control so quickly. It had never happened to him before. But then, Gillian had never happened to him, had she? Ten months of suppressed desire had coalesced into one raging hard-on.

His fingers scratched for her zipper pull. Hers shoved at the shoulders of his coat. He yanked the zipper. She wrenched her mouth away from his. "Don't rip it!"

"Then get out of it. Now. But leave the shoes on."

She shoved him away and shimmied out of her dress as Tucker shed his coat and vest. His gaze locked on her, and all he saw was red. Red bra. Red panties. The red haze of desire clouding his vision. He reached for his tie to yank it off, and she snapped, "No! Let me!"

Damned if she didn't grab his tie and tug him into his bedroom.

They rolled and wrestled and finally, blessedly, lay

naked. Neither one of them had the patience or desire to slow things down, and they consummated their marriage in a red-hot blaze of passion that didn't burn out until the first rays of sunrise burst upon the eastern sky. Finally, sated, they fell asleep in each other's arms.

Tucker awoke four hours later when the soft, supple warmth snuggled up next to him suddenly transformed to stiff and prickly.

"Oh, God." His naked bride sat up and said, "What have I done?"

He pried open one eye, identified the expression on her face as horror, and quickly shut it again before she noticed. He considered pulling his pillow over his head and going back to sleep.

"My mother will kill me!"

Tucker stifled a sigh. It would have been nice to avoid this, but he couldn't pretend to be surprised. She'd been humming on adrenaline when she'd agreed to his proposal last night.

She grabbed hold of his shoulder and shook him. "Tucker, wake up. We have to fix this. We have to undo this. Tucker!"

He opened his eyes. Hers looked a little wild as she stared down at him. He went up on his elbow. "C'mon, Gillian. That's just mean. I *know* you enjoyed yourself. No way you faked *all* those orgasms."

"What? No. I don't fake it! Well, sometimes, maybe, but not with you. Not last night. I didn't fake with you."

"There you go."

He started to pull her back down to him, but her full breast was dangling inches away from his mouth, so he reached up and took it.

A moment later, she shuddered a breath, moaned

low in her throat, and surrendered. It was well over an hour later, after they'd rolled in the sheets some more, then dawdled together in the shower, and Tucker had confirmed that no, she did not fake it, that she brought the subject up again. She was wrapped in one of the hotel's bathrobes and standing at the window, staring out at the Las Vegas Strip when she softly said, "It's not about the sex, Tucker. It's about the wedding. What we did was insane."

"Why?"

She turned to face him. "You don't just get married on a . . . purse high. You have to think it through, you have to plan, you have to tell your mother and buy a dress!"

Tucker tried somewhat hard not to be annoyed. "So, what's most important really *is* the wedding, not being married."

She winced and closed her eyes. "Ouch. I guess that when it comes to my mother, it *is* about the wedding and the dress. I'm her only daughter. If I eloped to Las Vegas without her there to see me get married, it would break her heart."

"You did elope in Las Vegas, and she wasn't there to see you."

"That's why we have to fix this, Tucker. We had a quickie wedding. Now we need to get a quickie divorce. Or an annulment. I'm sure they do that here."

Now, it was Tucker's turn to stare out of the window and think. Gillian and her wedding gowns and her mother. He shouldn't be surprised or take it personally. This was how they made their livings. This wasn't Jeremy's "all about the wedding" accusation. She'd brought up two aspects of it, two critical pieces that were intertwined with the woman who she loved above all others. This wasn't wedding obsession. It was maternal love. Had he made a poor battlefield decision last night? Was it time to retreat and regroup?

Maybe, but damn. He'd gained ground, and it went against his grain to give it up.

Gillian's voice broke into his thoughts. "What's so horrible about this is that given time, I think you and I could have something special. I don't want to screw that up."

Given time. Tucker turned around. His gaze sought his suit vest still lying on the floor where she'd tossed it in the early hours of the morning. He envisioned the watch tucked away in its pocket.

"I do too, Glory. I think you and I can have something outstanding."

"Do you think we could fall in love?" The yearning in her voice broke his heart.

"I think we're definitely approaching the tipping point toward that, yes. I am, for sure. You turned to me for comfort and support. You came to me when you needed arms to hold you. You made love with me last night like you meant it. It wasn't just sex, Gillian. We are more than friends. Aren't we?"

She nodded. Tucker crossed the room to her, reached out and tucked a strand of silky hair behind her ear. "I'll be honest with you, Glory. I've never been in love before, so I'm not one hundred percent certain what it's supposed to feel like. What I can tell you is that I've never felt this way about any other woman."

She hugged herself and rubbed her arms as if she were cold. "Hearing that makes me feel both fabulous and afraid. It's too soon for me, Tucker. A short time ago, I was ready to marry Jeremy. I thought I was in love with him. I couldn't have been more wrong, so now I don't trust my own emotions."

"Understandable."

"I am certain about one thing, though. I absolutely positively can't go home and tell my mother I got married last night by Skinny Elvis!"

"I'm really sorry it was Fat Elvis's night off."

She closed her eyes and groaned a laugh.

"Maybe this thing between us is backwards from what you had before."

"What do you mean?"

"You weren't ready to marry me, and you're not sure you are in love with me, so that means we're perfect. This wedding was meant to be."

"You're crazy. Tucker, this is no way to begin a marriage. You need to be thoughtful and deliberate and certain. You need to plan."

"Or maybe you need to turn the rules upside down. One thing the military taught me is the power of disruption."

"This certainly was that. Backwards, upside down, disruptive? That's not the way I roll, Tucker. No, this . . . impulse . . . can't stand. We have to get a divorce. Like the saying goes, what happened in Vegas needs to stay in Vegas."

"But—"

She implored him with a look. "Maybe if we take care with one another, we can navigate these waters without anyone being hurt. I want us to stay friends. More than friends. Who knows what will happen in time?"

Tucker bit back a sigh. Time. Strategy. Battlefield adjustments. Sometimes a strategic retreat ensured an eventual victory. *Keep your eye on the prize, McBride.* He gave their situation a few moments' thought, then said, "Okay. We'll do things your way. You oohed and aahed over the bathtub at one point last night.

Why don't you go soak and relax while I make some calls? I'll order up breakfast and see what we need to do to comply with Nevada law."

"That sounds great." She went to him and went up on her toes and kissed him quickly. "Thank you, Tucker."

When she would have retreated to the bathroom, he grabbed her arm and tugged her back to him and gave her a long, thorough kiss. "You're welcome."

His calls yielded some surprises that led to more calls. By the time breakfast arrived and he tapped on the bathroom door to let her know, he had a plan that worked for him and one that he hoped would appeal to her.

Over omelets, he outlined their options, beginning with the most complicated and ending with what he preferred. "In order to divorce here in Nevada, one of us needs to establish residency for six weeks prior to filing for divorce. I have a buddy who conducts intense, advanced survivalist training in the Nevada desert in the summer. He's willing to switch places with me and take over my classes, so following Jackson's wedding in June, I could move out here for the duration. After we file, I understand that we can get the deed done in a couple of weeks to a month."

"Oh," she said, her teeth tugging on her bottom lip. "Wow. You're offering to spend the summer in Death Valley so that I don't have to tell my mother about Elvis? I don't know if that makes you my hero or an idiot."

Tucker grinned at her and stole a slice of banana from the fruit cup she'd ordered with his fork. "Actually, what it makes me is determined to win."

"Win what?"

"Your heart." She fumbled her fork at that. Tucker

held her gaze and declared himself. "I don't want any misunderstanding. I'm being completely honest and transparent here. I will cooperate with this divorce because I don't want you to feel manipulated or forced into a marriage you don't want. However, I don't want a divorce. I want marriage and babies and Christmas with your family and Thanksgiving with mine. The whole tamale."

"But, Tucker, how can you be so certain that I am—"

"Dammit, Gillian, the only thing I'm certain about is that nothing in life is certain. I was certain I would spend my entire career in the military. I was certain when I met you that you were beyond my reach. But here I am and here you are, and fate and Elvis have dropped you into my lap. I'm going to do my best to keep you. Consider this fair warning. I'm showing you my battle plan. I intend to spend the weeks between now and Jackson's wedding wooing you. I don't really want to spend July in Nevada. A honeymoon in Alaska sounds much nicer."

"Alaska!"

"Remote. Beautiful days. Nights made for snuggling."

She lifted her chin and gave her hair a toss. "I will not spend my honeymoon in a tent around grizzly bears, Tucker McBride."

Ah-ha! He had a nibble at the hook. He shrugged nonchalantly. "I'm open to negotiation on honeymoon destinations."

She took a sip of orange juice before saying, "Tucker, last night was . . . was . . ."

"Fabulous?" he suggested. "Beyond compare? The best you've ever had?"

She gave a little laugh. "Yes, yes, yes. But, we're

talking about marriage here, not sex. We got married on impulse. I'm a planner. I don't do impulsive."

"I'd argue the point, but let's not get sidetracked. I laid out our options. This is the cleanest option we have if we want to keep the process all American. If we do this, we go home. We see what happens. If I can't convince you to stay with me, I deserve to spend the summer with the kangaroo rats."

She grimaced and shuddered, and in that instant, she reminded him of Haley, the girliest girl in second grade. What he wouldn't give to have a daughter with this woman. Tucker held his breath, waiting for her decision, sensing he'd pushed as hard as he should right now. Damn, but he wanted her to say yes.

"How would we do it? Would we, well, date? Out in the open?"

"Why not?"

Her teeth tugged at her bottom lip as she considered. "We'd face nonstop questions. It's life in the small town fishbowl. I know I'm already on top of the gossip charts, but I'm not accustomed to lying. I'm not very good at it. I'll screw it up."

"So, we don't go public. We keep our relationship secret, have a clandestine affair. Although, does it count as an affair if we're already married?"

"You mean have a real affair? Tucker, we can't have a secret affair in Redemption. Small town fishbowl, remember?"

"You forget I am an expert at clandestine infiltration and exfiltration. No one will know, I promise. It might be fun, add a little spice." When she looked like she was going to protest, he said, "Honey, I don't think we can go back to being lunch buddies. Not after last night. We are going to want to share marital relations."

She rolled her eyes at the term, but confessed, "We are good together in bed."

"Dynamite. In the shower too." Tucker reached across the table and took her hand. "Give it a try, Glory. Give me a chance."

"Oh, Tucker. I want to be clear. I don't want to lead you on. It's just too soon for me to know—"

He interrupted. "I'm not asking for promises now, only time. Give *us* time. Let's take what happened in Vegas home with us. It'll be our little secret. And when June rolls around if you still want this divorce, you'll get no pushback from me. You have my word."

"And you don't lie."

"Neither do I cheat. Not at golf or any other aspect of life."

Her lips twitched, she looked down at their clasped hands, and eventually, she nodded. "Okay."

Tucker wanted to shoot his fist into the sky and holler, "Yes." Instead, he gave her hand a squeeze. "Come back to bed with me, Glory. Let's celebrate."

And so commenced Operation Horny Toad, Part Two.

Back in Redemption, Gillian felt more than a little wicked. Twice during those first few days following the Las Vegas weekend, she came close to telling Maisy about what happened there. Once, she almost told Caroline. Each time, she stopped herself. What happened in Vegas absolutely had to stay in Vegas.

No way could she ever tell her mother she got married on a purse whim. Barbara Thacker would be crushed.

Luckily, Gillian didn't face too much of a grilling upon her return. She'd summarized the exchange with Erica in a note she'd left for her mom when she'd fled

Bliss, so Barbara had understood her sudden need to get away for a few days. When she'd pressed Gillian for information, her questions concentrated on Gillian's emotional well-being, not where she'd gone or what she'd done. Luckily, Coco hadn't spread word around town about how Gillian had departed. Caroline had known more details, of course, and when Gillian picked up Peaches from Caroline and Jackson's house, Caroline had offered to listen if she needed to talk. Gillian had appreciated her restraint. Maisy had been more focused on discussing Jeremy's perfidy and Gillian's mental health than where she'd spent her weekend.

According to Maisy, Jeremy and his new fiancée were the talk of the town. Erica had been quick to spread the word that she'd bought the dress for her imminent wedding at Bliss. Gillian received quite a few pitying looks, but no one as of yet had the temerity to bring the situation up to her face.

She took it all with a grace that surprised herself, and she suspected her strength had a lot to do with how she spent her evenings. She'd come home from work on Monday afternoon to find a wrapped gift on her bed. Always a fan of presents, she ripped open the package and discovered new sheets. Red sheets. She'd rolled in them with the gift giver every night this week.

So far, Tucker had lived up to his claim of having secrecy superpowers. Not even Peaches heard him sneaking in at night.

"I think you need a name," she told him on Thursday as she snuggled up against him in the aftermath of lovemaking. "Like the Phantom. Phantom of Fulfillment."

"I appreciate the sentiment, but phantoms don't

work for me. Phantoms are shadowy and fuzzy and airy. If I were going to have a superhero name, I'd need it to be something more corporal. Something strong and manly. Superman is strong. He's the Man of Steel. Iron Man is strong."

"See, I disagree. Phantoms are sexy. And sneaky."

"Sexy and sneaky are good, but you have to get the strong in there too."

He pulled her on top of him and began nuzzling her neck. She felt him harden against her yet again and observed, "I guess Phantom Energizer Bunny doesn't work for you?"

He nipped her neck and slid into her, and she laughed. "The Stone Obelisk Phantom?"

"There's nothing phantom about my obelisk," he declared before proving his point yet again.

Tucker stayed the entire night, and Gillian awoke on Friday morning to the aroma of frying sausage, feeling deliciously rested and at peace. It was early, a little past dawn judging by the soft light beaming through her bedroom window. She rolled out of bed, showered, then strolled into her kitchen to find the coffee made and the makings for breakfast tacos on the kitchen island.

Tucker tossed Peaches a hunk of sausage and gave Gillian a warm smile. "Mornin', Glory."

"Mornin', handsome. You're up early."

"We have a three-day class this weekend, and it begins this morning at eight in the classroom. I need to do some prep work I've neglected." He spooned salsa onto his taco fixings and said, "We'll move out to the canyon campus around midafternoon. It'll probably be late before I'm through tonight, and then tomorrow's class begins extra early. I'm not camping with them, though. Why don't you come out to the canyon and spend the night with me in the Airstream?"

"Sorry, but I can't. It's my dad's birthday. My brother and I are taking Mom and Dad out to dinner, and then we're doing game night at their house. My dad is a Monopoly maniac. I'll probably end up sleeping over there." Tucker made an exaggerated crestfallen face, which caused her to grin. "You'll survive one night without me."

"It won't be easy."

Since he'd cooked, she cleaned up after, while he took a quick shower, kissed her goodbye, and made his stealthy exit from her house. With a couple of hours to kill before she needed to get ready for work, she decided to take Peaches for a walk. Without conscious thought, she selected her red yoga pants and matching shirt to wear. She chose the red retractable dog leash for Peaches and headed outside.

Dew glistened like diamonds on the green blades of Bermuda grass lawns in her neighborhood. Someone was frying bacon for breakfast. About half of the houses she passed had windows open to take advantage of the fresh morning breeze, so the sounds of everyday family activities drifted on the air. *Mom, where's my history book? Honey, have you seen my wallet? Megan, put the dogs outside before we sit down to eat.*

Gillian smiled with pleasure in the morning. Redemption, Texas, really was a nice little town, and she was happy to live here. Somehow, someway, she would figure out a method to peacefully coexist with her ex and Erica and their little bundle of joy. Maybe she'd spend a bit more time in Enchanted Canyon in search of peace for her troubled soul.

Maybe she should try to cut game night short and accept Tucker's invitation, after all.

As far as the situation with her lover went, well, it was way too soon to make any decisions beyond keeping Vegas in Vegas. This whole secret affair thing was a new experience for her, and she was having fun with it. While skittering around the truth with friends and family did not come naturally to her, and the vague explanation she'd given of how she'd spent her weekend didn't roll smoothly off her tongue, she was an adult. Secret wedding aside, she didn't owe anyone all the details about every aspect of her personal life.

She reminded herself of that later when the fiancée of one of Jeremy's friends arrived for her two o'clock appointment at Bliss and spent as much time digging for dirt and flinging sand in Gillian's face as shopping for her wedding gown. Luckily, Gillian had worn red panties beneath her usual black slacks, so she continued to keep her power attitude on. By the time the bride left the shop, Gillian had decided a bit of online shopping was in order. She needed to supplement her limited supply of everyday panties—in the color red.

Later, as she chose her dinner outfit, she debated whether or not to wear the dress that Tucker had given her in Vegas. It was a date-night dress, not an out-with-the-parents dress. Wearing it, knowing its history, would be a little weird, wouldn't it?

She could see it now. Her mother would say, *"Gillian, I know I haven't seen you wear that dress before. Where did you get it? It's fabulous."*

"It's my wedding dress."

Yeah. Right. Not gonna happen. Gillian pulled her usual black number from her closet and laid it out on the bed. Her phone rang as she was finishing her makeup. Maisy. "Hey, Maisy. What's up?"

"Nothing good," her friend replied. "I heard some news and figured I should give you a heads-up. Your dad's birthday dinner is at Otto's tonight, isn't it?"

Warily, Gillian responded, "Yes. Our reservation is in an hour."

"Well, Marilee Hawkins stopped in with a message for you."

Gillian's stomach sank, and she closed her eyes. It was easy to guess what Maisy was about to say. Marilee Hawkins worked as a hostess and handled reservations for Otto's.

"Jeremy has a reservation tonight."

Bingo. Gillian walked out of her house forty minutes later wearing her red underwear—and her red wedding dress.

Strength and power and passion.

Her mother loved her dress. Gillian told her it was a retail therapy purchase and changed the subject. The Thacker family was seated and enjoying drinks and appetizers when Marilee escorted Jeremy, Erica, and another couple to a table on the opposite side of the restaurant. Visiting with her mother and with her back toward the restaurant's entrance, Gillian didn't notice their arrival, but when her father—a man who rarely cursed—muttered an invective, she knew what it meant.

Her brother, Mike, who didn't share his dad's disdain of foul language, spat out a string of colorful words beginning with "that lowdown" and ending with "sorry sonofabitch" before adding, "The guy's been needing an ass whipping for months. Tonight might just be the night."

Barbara Thacker reached out and gave Gillian's

hand a comforting pat. Her father said, "I've lost my
appetite for German food. Why don't we pay our
check and get an early start on Monopoly?"

Running from Jeremy Jones? The very idea of
it made her see red. Feel red. She heard the echo
of Tucker's voice in her mind—*Remember that red
really is your color.*

Strength and power and passion. Gillian lifted
her chin. "No, we're not leaving." She shot back her
chair, rose from her seat, and gave her parents a reassuring smile. "I must go congratulate the happy
couple. If our server arrives before I return, order the
New York strip for me, would you please?"

"Not the duck schnitzel?" her brother asked. "You
always order the schnitzel."

"Tonight, I'm in the mood for red meat." She
turned on her snakeskin stilettos and started across
the room.

Gillian felt the eyes of everyone in the restaurant
on her. A wave of anticipation rippled through the
room. Jeremy saw her and his eyes rounded in surprise, and then went wary. Erica's eyes narrowed to
slits.

Gillian bolstered her defenses by fantasizing Tucker
lying naked in her bed, and then she formed a smile.
She nodded to the mother-to-be. "Good evening, Erica." Meeting Jeremy's gaze, she said, "I understand
congratulations are in order. I wish you much happiness in your marriage and family life."

"Uh . . . uh . . . uh," he stuttered. "Thank you."

Gillian nodded regally, turned, and with her head
held high, and her smile genuine, returned to her table.
Her only regret was that Tucker hadn't been there to
see it.

The Thacker family took their cues from her, and

throughout the birthday meal, conversation remained lighthearted and fun. Gillian's father and brother didn't ignore her ex's presence, but instead, entertained themselves with creative suggestions on ways they could give him his just deserts.

They were lingering over cheesecake and after dinner port when the Jones party of four departed. The Thacker family agreed that for the gossips in attendance, the score was Gillian one, Jeremy zero.

The board game battle lasted until midnight, and as her parents prepared for bed and her brother declared his intention to go home rather than stay the night, Gillian took advantage of the opportunity to do the same. A light was still burning in Tucker's Airstream trailer when she knocked on the door at a quarter to one. He opened the door wearing nothing but a knowing smile. "I've been expecting you."

"I told you not to do that."

"I knew that houses and hotels on Boardwalk and Park Place wouldn't hold a candle to a trailer in Enchanted Canyon." He took hold of her hand and pulled her inside. "You look happy. Did you win at Monopoly?"

"No. Nobody beats my dad. That's why he loves the game so much. I am happy, though, and let me tell you why."

She gave him a blow-by-blow report of the events at Otto's and his "Atta girl" at the end of the telling had her glowing with pride.

Then he put his hands and mouth on her, and she glowed from a different source entirely.

Days drifted into weeks, and Gillian was as happy as she'd been in a very long time. She ran into Jeremy twice, once in the grocery store and once on Taco Tuesday at the Marktplatz. She handled both occasions just fine. She did suffer a bit of emotional angst when he married Erica and honeymooned at the same island destination where they'd planned to stay, but her friends, her mother, and her lover supported her through it, so she managed all right.

Through it all, she and Tucker continued their secret affair. The school kept him wickedly busy, which was a good thing, she thought. It kept him distracted. He wanted to begin dating her publicly, but she simply wasn't ready for that yet.

She liked Tucker very much. He made her laugh, made her think, made her reach. He was funny and smart and oh, so sexy. She had feelings for him, yes, but what label to place on those feelings she couldn't say. She no longer trusted herself to know. After all, she'd believed she'd loved Jeremy, yet here she was less than six months later with her heart all aflutter over another man.

She was daydreaming about said other man the first week of June when he called her to tell her he wouldn't be sneaking into her bedroom that night. "Boone called a little bit ago. He's on his way to Texas, and he asked if I'd camp with him for a couple of nights in the canyon. Something's going on with him. I'm not sure what. He said that Celeste told him he needed a dose of Enchanted Canyon's peace."

"I hope it's nothing serious," Gillian replied.

"Me too. Boone didn't sound at all like himself, and it's beyond strange for him to make the trip when we're all headed to Eternity Springs next week for Jackson and Caroline's wedding." Tucker exhaled a sigh, then added, "Sorry to cancel on you, Glory, especially tonight when we had the season three finale of 'Pretty Cowboy' lined up to watch. If you want to go ahead and watch it—"

"I'll wait." They'd been binge-watching *Justified* together for the past few weeks. "Pretty Cowboy" was Tucker's nickname for the television series, something he'd adopted after hearing Caroline, Maisy, and Gillian fangirl over the actor playing the main character. "It wouldn't be the same without you. You go on and take care of your cousin. Check in with me when you can."

"Will do. Thanks for understanding. Sleep tight tonight, Glory. Miss me a little bit."

"I'll miss you a lot," she assured him.

She would miss him more than just a lot. They spent almost every weeknight together, and she'd quickly grown accustomed to having him in her bed. It still amazed her that they'd managed to carry on in secret all this time. The man truly was a phantom when it came to sneaking about.

However, good as he was, he wasn't invisible. The whole secrecy thing had been fun, but June was just around the corner. She'd have to decide soon.

Maybe the first step was to take their relationship out of the shadows, let her friends know, let her mother know, that she was seeing Tucker.

She was mulling over the idea, inching her way forward to acceptance when the jingle of Bliss's doorbell announced a visitor. An unexpected, unwelcome visitor. "Hello, Erica. What can I do for you this afternoon?"

Chapter Sixteen

Tucker's eyes went round as an owl's when he spied his cousin walking toward the security exit at Austin-Bergstrom International Airport. He looked like an extra on *The Walking Dead*. It was not a good look for him.

"What the hell, man?" Tucker asked when Boone grew close.

He held up his hand, palm out, and said, "Later. I'll tell you everything, I swear. Only later."

Tucker nodded. "Just answer me this. Is there a body somewhere you need help dealing with?"

Boone's crooked smile both answered and relieved Tucker. "No, no bodies." Then the smile faded, and he softly added, "Not yet anyway."

Tucker shot him a sharp look but didn't press him for more. Once they were in the truck, he silently offered Boone a bottle of water. His cousin chugged half of it, then dropped his head back onto the headrest and closed his eyes. Knowing Boone, Tucker bided his time.

They'd been on the road half an hour when Boone finally spoke. "I need a distraction. Tell me something, anything that will give me something else to think about."

Something else than what? Tucker glanced at his cousin. The zombie look hadn't changed, so he decided to lob a grenade. "I got married in Vegas by an Elvis impersonator."

Boone smiled, but he didn't open his eyes. "I've always enjoyed your imagination, cuz."

"Hey, Boot?" Tucker used the nickname he and Jackson sometimes called Boone. "My wallet is in the console. Would you get it out, please? Grab a dollar from inside?"

Now, Boone cracked open one eye to shoot Tucker an annoyed look, but he did as asked. Once the bill was in Boone's hand, Tucker continued. "Consider that a retainer, so I can count on the cone of silence."

"What am I keeping silent about?"

"I'm engaging your professional services. You can write my new will."

"Why do you need a new will?"

"I want to protect my new wife in case something happens to me."

Boone twisted his head around like a startled owl. "You're serious?"

"I need the cone of silence, Boot. Taking it up a notch to professional cone because Jackson can't know about it."

"Now, I'm officially distracted." Boone tucked the dollar into his shirt pocket. "Spill."

Tucker told him the story, beginning with Gillian's long walk last fall and ending with the previous week's misadventure when her mother unexpectedly showed up at Gillian's house while Tucker was in the shower. He'd had to sneak out of a bedroom window and damned near broke his neck after getting tangled in a water hose.

Boone's laughter eased the worry lines in his expression, and Tucker was glad to have shared his secret, not only for his cousin's sake but also for his own. He hadn't realized until today that he'd wanted to share his news.

"An Elvis impersonator. Wow. I am so disappointed to have missed the happy event. It was April, you say? You've been keeping this secret for two months?" At Tucker's nod, he asked, "So where is all this going? Are you serious about your will? Serious about the marriage?"

"Yes, I am. As soon as I heard that Gillian broke up with her ex, I set my sights on her. Didn't plan Las Vegas, but when an opportunity knocks, you act."

"So, you're in love with her?"

"Head over spurs, yeah." Tucker's lack of hesitation shocked even him. Just when he'd tumbled all the way into love, he couldn't pinpoint, but he had no doubt that it was true.

He loved her. He was in love with his lover. He was in love with his wife. When he'd returned to Texas for good, he'd wanted a home and family. He'd figured he'd be able find someone, a companion and a bedmate, with whom he could share a contented life. He'd never expected to find a soul mate.

Gillian Thacker—no, Gillian *McBride*—was his soul mate.

"I'll be damned." Boone gave him a congratulatory clap on the back, then asked, "How long do you intend to keep up the secrecy? Redemption is a small town. Someone is bound to notice eventually."

"I'm good at being discreet. If we get caught, it

won't be because of me. I gave Gillian my word. She's driving this particular bus."

"I could say something about women drivers, but my sisters aren't here to tease, so I won't bother."

Tucker needed a moment to absorb his personal revelation, so he took advantage of his cousin's mention of family. "How are the twins? And your folks? They're coming to Eternity Springs for the wedding, aren't they?"

"Yep. The whole family will be there. Mom and Dad are doing fine as far as I know. They've been traveling a lot. The girls are doing well. Mom keeps trying to talk them into moving back to Texas, but I honestly think she's okay with them living on the West Coast. Until one of them marries and has babies, that is. She'll want to have her grandchildren nearby."

The worry returned to Boone's expression, and he said nothing more.

Tucker gave it a minute before saying, "I'm looking forward to seeing everybody in Colorado. I had dinner with Jackson and Caroline last night. The bride is calm as can be, but he's as anxious as a mouse hiding from a hawk."

"Hmm . . ." Boone responded. His thoughts obviously were somewhere else.

Neither man spoke during the remainder of the trip. When they reached the turnoff onto the private road that led down into the canyon, Boone released a soft, heavy sigh. Tucker's curiosity was about to burst, but he knew his cousin, knew he had to bide his time. Boone would talk when he was ready.

As they approached the Fallen Angel Inn and Last Chance Hall, Tucker asked, "Should I stop at the hall? Is Jackson camping with us?"

"No. His wedding is next weekend. I didn't want to drag him into this."

This what? Tucker wanted to ask. Instead, he said, "Where do you want to camp?"

"Do you have folks out here from the school?"

"No. I didn't schedule anything for this week or next. Didn't know when we'd be taking off for Colorado."

"In that case, how about we use the site on the river near Ruin. It's fitting that I poke around a ghost town while I'm here. I have some old ghosts riding my shoulders right now, Tucker."

"Ready to tell me about it?"

"Not yet. Let me be in the canyon this afternoon. Tonight around the campfire, I'll tell you my ghost stories."

"Sounds like a plan, Boot. Sounds like a plan."

"I need a new plan for today," Gillian said to Peaches as she tossed the pup a dog treat. Ordinarily, on her regular afternoon off, she paid a visit to the nail salon, did her weekly grocery shopping, and sometimes dropped by Maisy's flower shop for girlfriend time. But after today's scene with Erica, she needed something else. Her emotions were in turmoil. She didn't need to sit and soak her feet for a pedicure. She needed to get out and move them.

All because the new Mrs. Jones believed Mr. Jones would rather have been with Gillian on their honeymoon instead of with her.

"She is one unhappy woman," Gillian said, tossing Peaches another biscuit. Really, where did she get off thinking she could wander into Bliss to verbally abuse Gillian any time she felt like it? "Everyone says the last weeks of pregnancy are a trial, but that doesn't give her leave to be a witch to me."

Gillian wasn't about to put up with it again. The confrontation had made her feel lousy, primarily because Erica's jealousy made her feel good, which in turn made her feel petty.

Why? Because she was over Jeremy? Because Tucker was now in her life? Because she was a red-power woman who'd be damned before she'd let any man or former sorority sister push her around again?

"All of the above" was probably the answer, but it needed to be qualified with "It's complicated."

Complicated answers brought her no peace. She'd been coasting along since Las Vegas. The Carruthers/ McBride wedding deadline was right around the corner. The time had come for some deep thinking, for some honest self-examination. "Or maybe we should just go for a hike," she said to Peaches. Maybe she should take her troubled soul and happy dog to Enchanted Canyon in search of peace.

The idea held much appeal. Gillian had wanted to return to the cave Tucker had shown her. He'd offered to let her use the wedding gown tucked away in that trunk in a display window for Bliss. Wonder if she could find the cave on her own? It'd be worth a try. It had been a relatively easy hike. There was no reason she couldn't try to find it, was there?

Not as long as she followed the rules. She knew the rules. Tucker had taught her.

With the decision made, she changed her clothes, grabbed the hiking pack he'd given her from her closet shelf, and inventoried its contents against the checklist he'd stuck inside the backpack. She had a knife, paracord, a small first aid kit, a whistle, a tarp, fire starter, a hunk of fatwood for fuel, water bottle—oh, shoot. She'd never picked up those water purification tablets he'd told her to get from his shop. The two black trash bags and three gallon-sized zipper bags she needed could be snagged from her pantry supplies.

Not that she would need any of this stuff for a short, afternoon hike, but she knew Tucker. He'd darn sure quiz her on the contents of her pack when she told him she'd gone for a solo hike.

She scanned the rest of the list. The tablets were all she was missing. As she transferred her own go bag from her purse to her backpack and bagged up some kibble for Peaches and some snacks for herself, she decided to kill two proverbial birds with one stop by his shop. He had closed for the day due to Boone's visit, but she had a key. He'd left it here at her place, along with some of his things. On her way to Enchanted Canyon, she would stop by his shop, pick up the tablets, and leave him a note telling him where she was going and when she intended to be back. "I'll get a gold star in preparedness," she said to Peaches.

An hour later, she parked her car in the spot where Tucker had parked the day he took her to the cave, and she and Peaches started out. It was a gorgeous, early summer afternoon with spotty clouds and temperatures in the upper eighties. She took her time, letting Peaches dawdle, sniff, and explore. Yellow, orange, and purple wildflowers grew among tufts of grasses, adding pops of color to the canyon floor. She even caught sight of a snake slithering off the trail and took a picture of it, proof to show Tucker that she hadn't freaked out. Much.

She figured she must be about halfway to her destination when she paused to gaze down at a lovely pool of water fed by one of the numerous springs in Enchanted Canyon, some twenty-five feet or so below her.

It was a pretty spot, one she had not noticed on her previous hike along this trail. "Hmm . . ." she murmured. "What do you think, Peaches? I hope that doesn't mean we took a wrong turn."

No, she didn't think that was the case. This was a narrow part of the trail. She'd probably been watching her feet, not the surroundings, when she came this way with Tucker. It wouldn't do to take a spill and go tumbling down that hill.

It was Peaches who discovered the way down, a dry arroyo that snaked its way down the hillside. Gillian debated a short moment. The climb back up would be steep, but doable. Maybe she'd use the knife from her pack and cut a walking stick to help. It looked to be such a pretty, peaceful spot, and she'd always found the sound water made as it tumbled over rocks incredibly soothing.

That's what she'd come seeking in Enchanted Canyon this afternoon, was it not? Peace and soothing for her troubled soul?

She carefully made her way down the arroyo, catching her breath a time or two when her boots slid on loose gravel, but she never lost her balance. Like her mom said: *Yoga classes pay off.*

Her phone began to ring as she traversed the steepest part of the slope. Her mother's ringtone. She didn't attempt to answer and allowed the call to go to voicemail. "Call you back, Mom," she murmured as she tested the sturdiness of a large rock before placing her entire weight upon it.

Moments later, she reached level ground and took a good look around. It was even prettier than the view from above suggested. The pool of water extended around a peninsula of rock and was larger than she'd realized. Water lilies floated on the surface of a placid green pond. Snowy white blooms pillowed on leafy pads caught the snowfall of seeds from a trio of huge cottonwood trees hugging the bank. Gillian smiled with delight at the sound of a bullfrog's croak.

Her phone interrupted nature's peace. This time, she pulled it from her back pocket and answered, "Hi, Mom."

The person who spoke was not Barbara Thacker.

"Damn you, Gillian," Jeremy said. "Are you trying to ruin my life?"

"Jeremy?" She took the phone away from her ear and looked at the display. It *was* her mother's number. Worry washed over her and sharped her voice. "What are you doing with my mom's phone? Is she all right?"

"I knew you wouldn't answer a call from me. You always answer your mother's call. *Always!*"

"Where is she? Is she okay? Why do you have her phone?"

"She's fine. I'm at Bliss. Barbara is in with a bride."

Gillian exhaled a *whoosh* of relief.

Jeremy continued, "I forgot it was your afternoon off, but your mother always leaves her phone right out in the open, so I'm taking advantage of it. I came up to your office so we can have some privacy."

"You have no right—"

"Gillian, you have to leave Erica alone!"

Her spine snapped straight. Anger blew through her as hot as Austin in August. "Excuse me? *I* need to leave *her* alone?"

"Yes! You shouldn't have asked her if she enjoyed *your* honeymoon. It wasn't *your* honeymoon."

"Well, yes, it was. It was on the same island and

the same hotel. I made the reservations and paid all the deposits."

"I reimbursed you," he defended himself. "And Erica and I went a full month earlier than you and I had planned. She's crazy jealous of you, Gillian."

"That hasn't changed since freshman year of college! Look, she came into my store. She verbally attacked me. I'm not putting up with that."

"She's miserable and hormonal because of the pregnancy, and she's insecure because she knows . . . she knows . . ."

"What?"

"That I don't love her! That I don't want to be married to her! I love you, and I wish I were married to you! Sleeping with her that night was the biggest mistake I've ever made, and I'll be paying for it for the rest of my life."

There. That was the declaration Gillian had wanted to hear from Jeremy ever since Erica went wedding gown shopping at Bliss.

However, hearing it now didn't give her a sense of satisfaction like she'd expected. Gillian slipped off her backpack and dropped it at her feet. She crossed to the thick trunk of one of the cottonwood trees and let herself slide down it until she sat at its base. Perhaps sensing that Gillian could use some comfort, Peaches came over and crawled into her lap.

Hollowness seeped through her. "So, why did you do it? Why did you cheat on me?"

"I was scared, okay? You were all wrapped up in wedding arrangements and busy at the shop and planning yet another business to launch. I was feeling lonely and afraid that I was making a mistake."

"So, you went out and *made* a mistake."

"Yes. Yes, I did. It was at the symposium in Houston.

You were supposed to come with me, but you were too busy. I'd been drinking, I had a weak moment, and you weren't there."

"I wasn't there." Gillian grabbed a nearby stone and tossed it into the pool. "So it was *my* fault that you went out and cheated? With my sorority sister!"

"She was a speaker. She's a very successful attorney, you know. We started talking and figured out we had quite a few mutual acquaintances. She came on to me."

"I'll just bet she did."

"If you'd been there, I wouldn't have slipped."

Gillian took her phone away from her ear and glared at it a moment before saying, "You are such a smarmy, self-righteous, self-delusional bastard, Jeremy. I can't believe I ever loved you."

"You didn't love me. I loved you, but I had a weak moment because deep in my heart, I knew you didn't love me."

"How long have you been practicing that line? Your whole life is a weak moment," she snapped, pushing back onto her feet. "You're a cheat and a liar, and I will not allow you to jack with my head or my heart anymore. Leave me alone. And for heaven's sake, make your wife leave me alone. We might have to live in the same small town, but neither of you are welcome in Bliss. Get out of my office immediately. Give my mother back her phone immediately. Leave my shop and never come back. We are done, Jeremy. This time I mean it. I am so over you."

She disconnected the call, and in a fit of frustration and temper, she threw her phone at her backpack.

She missed.

Her aim was off to the left. The phone's protective rubber case hit a nearby rock just perfectly enough that it bounced.

Gillian watched with dismay as her phone disappeared beneath the water lilies.

"Well, now. That was really stupid, Gillian."

The case was water-resistant, so it might be okay if she got to it quickly enough. Though she was tempted to rush into the water as she was, better sense asserted itself. She sat, loosened her laces, and pulled off her boots, then after a second of consideration, shimmied out of her jeans. She waded toward the spot where her phone had disappeared. The water depth reached her upper thighs. Following a relatively short search, she located the case, pulled it from the water, and groaned. The screen had a spider web of cracks.

The device was dead as West Texas roadkill.

"Great," she muttered. "Just flippin' great."

She waded from the pool and stood dripping and glaring down at the ruined phone, mentally running through her lexicon of curse words, the invectives aimed both at herself and at the scumbag who'd set her temper on fire.

Distracted, Gillian didn't practice good wilderness skills. She didn't size up her situation or use all of her senses or remember where she was. She didn't notice that Peaches had gone exploring, dragging her retractable leash with its orange plastic grip behind her. Gillian didn't hear the rustling in the branches of a nearby tree.

The chaos seemed to happen all at once.

Peaches let out an excited yip and darted from beneath a bush toward Gillian. A colossal something exploded from the concealment of dense foliage. Startled, Gillian took an awkward step back as the winged shape with scary yellow eyes shot directly at her. Even as the great horned owl swooped up and away, her feet became tangled in the leash. She stumbled, tripped on one of her boots, and went down hard on her left ankle.

"Ow!" Pain radiated up her leg. Her ankle began to swell. "Oh, man. This is not good. This is *so* not good."

Had she broken anything? She didn't think so. She hadn't heard a pop. Hadn't felt a pop. Tentatively, she attempted to move it. She could do it, but the resulting pain made her eyes cross.

Oh, man. Oh, man. Oh, man. I can't walk on this. My phone is dead. What am I going to do?

She heard the echo of Tucker's voice in her mind: *Your brain is the most important tool in your toolbox. Keep your cool. Don't feel sorry for yourself. Don't make impulsive decisions.*

"Okay. Okay. Nothing impulsive. You can do this, Gillian. Tucker taught you how. *S.U.R.V.I.V.A.L.* Understand and prioritize your problems."

Priority number one was first aid for her ankle. She remembered that from Girl Scouts. RICE. Rest, ice, compression, and . . . what was *E*?

E made her think of Elvis. Wonder how many couples Elvis had married since the night he performed hers and Tucker's wedding? Wonder what Jeremy would say if he knew she'd gotten married before he did? She giggled at the thought until her inner voice scolded. *What the heck, Gillian? Why are you thinking about that golf gopher? Are you going into shock or something?*

No. Her ankle hurt. She was angry. And stressed. Trying to remember what Tucker taught her and not make her situation any worse.

Peaches whimpered and nuzzled at Gillian's hip. She glanced down at her pup and remembered. "Elevate. That's what *E* is. It's all about the acronym, you know."

She had no ice, but the stream was very cool. *Wonder which is more important—the* E *or the* I*?*

She decided to soak her ankle in the cold spring while she formulated a plan. She wasn't going to be able to walk out of Enchanted Canyon on her own. This was an isolated area. Maybe she'd be lucky, and someone would wander along. Who knew, maybe Tucker and Boone's campsite would be nearby.

However, she needed to face the possibility that she'd be here for a while. Possibly overnight.

Overnight, alone but for her puppy. And bullfrogs. And the owl. Whoa, Nellie, the wingspan on that bird must have been four or five feet. What other animals lived in this canyon? Lions and tigers and bears, oh my?

"Oh, my." She was going to cry. Her ankle hurt so badly!

"But it's okay. We'll be okay," she said to Peaches. "I'm a graduate of Enchanted Canyon Wilderness School's Survival 101 class. What can possibly go wrong?"

"That was a mighty fine ribeye," Boone said. "Thanks for the nice meal."

Tucker poured two fingers of whiskey into a cup, then passed the bottle to his cousin. "Camping doesn't mean roughing it. I ordered a quarter cow from your dad not long ago."

"Hard to beat McBride beef fresh from the ranch." Boone poured himself a drink, set the bottle atop the cooler, and returned to his seat in front of the fire. "It's a pretty night. I haven't done this in way too long."

Tucker watched the firelight flicker across his cousin's expression. Boone looked better than he had when he'd walked off the plane, but he was far from himself. Tucker wanted to know why. "Done what? Camped out? Sat in front of a campfire? Dodged questions from your cousin about what the hell is wrong for the better part of a day?"

Boone made a snorting sound, then responded with another dodge. "Too long since I soaked up the peace Enchanted Canyon has to offer."

"What has your soul troubled, Boot? It's about time for those ghost stories you promised, isn't it?"

Boone sat staring into the fire, his elbows on his knees, holding his cup with both hands. "I don't know where to start."

Tucker sipped his drink, and once the smooth, smoky bourbon had toasted its way down his throat, he asked, "I'm guessing that your past has somehow intruded into the nice little present you've created for yourself in Eternity Springs. Am I right?"

"Got it in one."

"What happened?"

Boone tossed back the remainder of his drink, then set down his cup and stood. He paced back and forth in front of the fire, rubbing the back of his neck. "I hardly know where to start. The last time I heard from Waggoner, Thompson, and Cole, I learned we'd inherited this property, so when the firm's name popped up on caller ID, I assumed it had something to do with Enchanted Canyon and I answered. My assumption proved wrong."

"Boone, if Malcolm Waggoner is coming after you again—"

"No. This has nothing to do with the Waggoner family or the law firm. A former colleague had my number, so he called to give me a message."

"About what?"

Boone pinned Tucker with a sharp look. "Cone of silence here too, Tucker. I need some reciprocity until I figure out what I'm going to do. If the family found out before I'm ready . . ." He shuddered. "It wouldn't be good."

Tucker nodded. "Cone of silence. You have my word."

"Okay, then." Boone scooped up his cup, grabbed the whiskey bottle and poured a double shot, then tossed it back in one motion. His voice was hoarse and grim as he said, "It's a kid. I've been named the guardian of a baby boy who was surrendered at a Safe Haven fire station in Fort Worth. The mother told the firefighter who accepted the baby that she wants me to take him and to raise him. She wants me to be his father."

"Whoa. Well, hell, Boot." Tucker didn't know what to say. Boone had a complicated and heartbreaking history with fatherhood. This was a road he probably wouldn't want to travel. "The Safe Haven law doesn't work that way, does it? Where the mother picks a guardian?"

"No, but you know how closely I worked with Child Protective Services in Fort Worth. The social workers all know me. Know the history. They're willing to let me make the call."

"Who is the baby's mom? How does she know you?"

"I don't know. She provided a medical history, but she wouldn't give her name. She gave them my name and told them I was a prosecutor."

"That makes no sense. You left Fort Worth over five years ago."

"I know." Boone shrugged. "That's all I got."

"Wow." Tucker rested his hand on Boone's shoulder, a silent offer of comfort and support. "Do you know what you're going to do?"

"No. Not yet. You know the baggage I have when it comes to kids."

Tucker gave Boone's shoulder a squeeze. "You'll figure it out, man. You always do. You know we'll have your back, Boone. Jackson and me. *Un pour tous, tous pour un.* We're still the Three Musketeers, even if we're all growing our families at the moment."

"I haven't said I'll take the boy," Boone snapped.

Tucker knew his cousin. He might fight against the inevitability, but the conclusion was forgone. Whether he'd admit to it or not, Boone had a baby on the way.

But now was not the time to press the point, so Tucker gave Boone's shoulder a shove. "No, but I'm doing my best to keep my girl."

Chapter Seventeen

Tucker didn't sleep worth a damn and awoke the following morning with a niggling sense of unease that he chalked up to Boone's situation. The two men had stayed up late into the night talking about the past events that had altered the course of Boone's life, and the ramifications that decisions he made today would have upon his future.

Tucker wanted to talk to Gillian, not to share his cousin's secrets because he wouldn't do that, but because he simply wanted—needed—to hear her voice. He'd missed her last night. He'd wanted her in his tent cuddled up next to him in the sleeping bag.

The idea made him smirk. As if Gillian Thacker would ever go tent camping in Enchanted Canyon. She considered his top-of-the-line equipped Airstream to be roughing it.

He waited until her usual wake-up time to phone her, but the call went straight to voicemail. He tried her again after the morning hike he and Boone took up to the waterfalls. This time, too, it went to voicemail.

The niggle of unease grew to something bigger. It wasn't like Gillian not to answer his calls or at least text him back. He sent her a text asking her to contact him, then returned his phone to his pocket and tried not to worry. When noon came and went without any word from her, he surrendered to his concern and called Bliss. Barbara answered on the first ring. "Hello?"

"Hi, Barbara. It's Tucker McBride. I need to speak with Gillian about something, but she's not answering her phone. Do you—"

"I know," Barbara interrupted. "She didn't come into work this morning either."

Tucker's mouth went dry, and he closed his eyes. Dammit, he'd known something was wrong! Why had he ignored his instincts?

Gillian's mother continued, "I just left her place, and her car isn't there. Honestly, I'm worried. I was just about to call her father. This isn't like her."

He shot his question like a bullet. "When did you last speak with her?"

"When we closed the shop the day before yesterday. Yesterday was my morning off and her afternoon off, so it's not unusual that we didn't speak."

The anxiety in Barbara Thacker's voice made him want to soothe her fears, so he said, "I spoke with Gillian yesterday morning, and everything was fine."

"Well, that's good to know. I'm wondering if she decided to go into Austin to shop. Maybe she had car trouble and didn't make it back to town in time to go to work. But that doesn't explain why she didn't call or doesn't answer her phone."

No, it didn't. Tucker sensed Boone's questioning gaze as he rubbed the back of his neck and debated how to proceed. The first step would be to search Gillian's house for clues. Barbara probably had a key, but he'd do a better job of it. He decided that for now, he would attempt to reassure her mother. "I'm sure she's fine. She probably hasn't realized her phone is dead. Have you checked her office? Maybe she decided to take the day off and left you a note."

"No. I haven't thought of that. I'll go upstairs right now and look for one."

"Let me know when you hear from her or find that note, would you, please?"

"Yes. Of course. Thank you, Tucker."

The moment he disconnected the call, he explained the situation to his cousin. "I've had a knot in my gut since I woke up this morning. Something's wrong. I'm going to start by searching her house."

"Want me to help?"

"Please."

Under normal circumstances, the hike back to the truck and drive into town would have taken thirty-five minutes. Tucker asked Boone to drive so he could make some calls, and by the time they arrived at Gillian's home just over twenty minutes later, he'd spoken to both Maisy and Caroline. Neither woman had heard from Gillian today.

Tucker vaulted from the passenger seat before Boone had the truck in park in Gillian's driveway. He didn't try to be stealthy. If someone saw him use his key, well, tough. He was ready to end this secrecy business anyway.

Right after he gave Gillian a severe lecture about scaring him half to death.

He opened the door calling, "Glory? Are you here?"

He wasn't surprised that a quick walk-through revealed the house was empty. He took it as a good sign that Peaches wasn't around either. If someone had abducted Gillian, they wouldn't have taken the dog too.

"What can I do?" Boone asked.

"Look for anything obvious. I'll concentrate on the subtleties."

He started in the bathroom. Gillian wouldn't take Peaches on a walk without wearing her makeup. No way she'd go somewhere overnight without it.

The case she'd filled with stuff when they went to Vegas and any time she stayed at his place sat in its usual spot. He spied no empty spaces in her precisely organized makeup drawer.

He'd look for her suitcase next, but he knew without a doubt that Gillian had not made a solo overnight shopping trip to Austin. His stomach made a slow, sick roll.

From the bedroom doorway, Boone spoke, "Think I have something, Tucker. This list was on the desk in her home office on top of a drugstore receipt dated yesterday morning at 8:48 a.m."

She would have been on her way into work. That meant she'd come home before she'd gone missing. "Let me see the list."

He took one glance and turned on his heel, headed for the closet. Sure enough, her backpack was gone. "What the hell, Gillian," he murmured. To Boone, he asked, "No other notes? Nothing handwritten?"

Like something saying where she was going and when she'd be back—a fundamental lesson that he'd damned well taught her.

"Not so far, but I didn't get past the office."

Tucker took a quick look around the bedroom, then headed for the kitchen. Nothing on the counters, nothing on the table, but as he stood with his hands on his hips and turned in a slow circle making a visual study, something poked at him. Something was off, but what?

Peaches' dishes were where they belonged. "Her leash is missing," he murmured as his gaze landed on the rack beside the kitchen door. But the leash wasn't all. The extra key to the shop that he'd left hanging there was missing too. "Let's go," he told Boone. "She went to the shop."

Eight minutes later, he found her note. "It's an easy hike," he told Boone. "She took her dog. She should have been home by dinnertime. Something happened."

Tucker's career had placed him in some hairy situations on numerous occasions and under live fire more times than he wanted to remember. In the heat of the moment, his training had always kicked in. Never once had he suffered a brain freeze of indecision and inability to act.

In this moment, he'd turned into Frosty the Snowman, frozen in fear. Thank God his cousin was there to kick his ass into action.

Boone grabbed the keys to Tucker's truck from his hand and headed for the door. "Let's go find her."

To Gillian's surprise, she'd ended up sleeping like a baby in the literal woods. When she awoke with the sunrise to birdsong, she took stock of her situation and did a fist pump. She was seriously proud of herself. She couldn't wait to show Tucker what a good job she'd done.

She figured she probably had eight to twelve hours to wait for the opportunity.

"My ankle isn't much better this morning," she told Peaches when she set out the morning portion of the kibble reserve. "If I had to do it, I could get us out of here on my own. However, I still think we're better off waiting for help. Besides, I sort of want Tucker to see our camp, don't you?"

Her attention on her kibble, Peaches didn't react to the question.

Gillian grinned, gave her dog's head an affectionate rub, then hobbled her way to the creek to wash.

The water was a deep shade of green in the morning light, and it drifted along slowly. Peacefully. Gillian filled her lungs with air and exhaled a contented sigh. Six months ago had anyone—even Angelica—tried to tell her that she would have spent the night in the woods with only her dog for company without greeting the dawn as a raving lunatic, she would have chortled with disbelief.

All in all, this misadventure had been a positive experience. So far, anyway.

Yesterday after soaking her ankle in the pool for a bit, she'd wrapped it with the hairband that was part of the personal survival bag that she had transferred from her purse before leaving her house. Then she'd pulled on her jeans, one hiking boot, and a leather ballet flat, one of the pair that she'd carried ever since her cotton field march last fall. Next, she'd hopped and hobbled to a nearby cedar tree, where she'd used the knife from her pack to hack off a low hanging branch, which she'd fashioned into a makeshift crutch.

Over the next few hours, she had set up her camp. Since it was early summer in Texas, she hadn't concerned herself with Tucker's survival triangle and the need to maintain body temperature. However, knowing that late afternoon thunderstorms often blew up in early summer in this part of the state, she'd recognized the need for shelter. She'd used the tarp and paracord from her backpack, and the knowledge she'd learned during the Girls Getting Grubby weekend to construct it. She gathered leaves and vines to use as a mattress, covered them with her black trash bags, collected firewood, and refilled her water bottle from the stream.

Darned if those purification tablets didn't come in handy.

When the storm blew through just before sunset, she and Peaches had remained cozy and dry.

She'd built a fire more for aesthetics than need, though she'd known that if Boone and Tucker chanced to be camping in this part of the canyon, firelight might have led them to her. She'd held out hope for a couple of hours after dark, but when her eyelids got heavy, she didn't fight sleep.

Now refreshed after her morning bath, Gillian hobbled back to camp and tried to figure out something to do to pass the time. Her fitness tracker read 7:22 a.m. She figured she could expect rescue sometime this afternoon, probably after 3:00 p.m., but no later than 6:00 p.m. The earliest her mother would raise the alarm would be noon. She'd call Maisy first, then Caroline. Eventually, the ripple effect would extend far enough that someone would call Tucker. Once Tucker learned she'd gone missing, she was as good as found.

Within an hour, she was beyond bored. She decided to kill some time by trying to recreate the bow drill tools from the GGG weekend, and see if she couldn't start a fire totally on her own. "If I can pull this off, that will really show him," she explained to Peaches when she began eyeing the surrounding trees for appropriate materials.

It proved to be the perfect way to eat up the hours. She successfully made her handhold, her fireboard, and her bow. The spindle, however, gave her fits. She couldn't find an appropriate piece of wood within hobbling distance. When she found a straight bit, it had too many knots, and her knife skills weren't good enough to smooth it out. By noon, she was ready to give up.

"Wonder if I could catch a fish?" she said to Peaches.

She could fashion a hook from a hairpin, but what would she use for bait? She could dig for worms, but did she really want to kill a worm just to pass the time? Not to mention the poor fish. It wasn't like she and Peaches were starving or anything. Now, if they were still sitting here this time tomorrow, she might revisit the question.

"So, what do we do this afternoon, Peaches?"

Yip. Yip. Yip.

She fashioned a ball out of vines, covered it with the sock she wasn't wearing with her ballet flat, and began playing catch with Peaches, who yipped and yapped with delight in the game.

It ended when a sound distracted Peaches, and she stopped, and her ears perked up. Gillian sat up straight. Was that a dog bark?

She reached for her whistle and began to blow.

Tucker heard the whistle seconds after Jackson's dog River took off. *Gillian!*

Relief ghosted through him. If Gillian could blow a whistle, she was alive. Injured, they could deal with. He followed the dog at a jog, and when the whistle's shrill sound ceased, he hollered, "Gillian!"

His voice echoed through the canyon. He listened hard, his pulse hammering in his ears.

"Tucker!" came the faint, fabulous sound. "I'm here."

Thank God. Thank you, God. "Gillian? Are you hurt? Where are you?"

"Over here! Down here!"

The sound reverberated off the canyon wall so "down here" didn't really help. He asked Boone, who was coming up behind him, "Can you tell which way?"

"No."

Tucker yelled, "Keep blowing your whistle!"

Ahead of the two men, River took a fork on the trail that led away from the cave that Gillian's note said had been her destination. Rounding a bend about a hundred yards from the fork, he saw River veer off the trail onto an arroyo. Tucker didn't hesitate to follow. This was why he had stopped by the Last Chance Hall to pick up Jackson's dog. River had roamed the canyon as a stray before attaching himself to Jackson, and he knew the lay of the land. He might be a yellow Lab, but he had the hearing of an owl and soul of a bloodhound. He'd found Gillian. God bless him.

"Oh! River! I see you," Gillian called. "Here we are, boy!"

There. She was there. Safe. Dry. Smiling that beautiful smile of hers and flinging out her arms in welcome, she was the most beautiful sight Tucker had ever seen. As he scrambled to the canyon floor, he took the first easy breath he'd managed all day.

"Glory." He reached her and wrapped her in his arms, buried his face in her hair, and shuddered. "Oh, hell, Gillian. You scared me to death."

"I sprained my ankle, but I knew you'd find me," Gillian continued. "You're earlier than I expected too. Tucker, you'll be so proud of me! I'm so proud of myself!"

Proud. Tucker dragged his hand down his face as

she babbled on. *Proud* wasn't the first word that came to mind.

"I was Anna Acronym, I'll have you know. *S.U.R.V.I.V.A.L.* Queen, that's me. I kept my cool and made good decisions that didn't make the situation any worse. Look at the shelter I built. It kept us nice and dry during the thunderstorm last night."

She continued to talk, parroting back lessons he'd taught her during the Survival 101 class. Tucker knew he should be happy that she'd managed so well, that she'd taken his lessons to heart and put them to use them when she'd needed them the most. But now that his fear was easing, the fog dissipating, temper stirred.

He interrupted. "Where the hell is your phone?"

She winced. "Well, see, the screen shattered, so when it fell into the pond, it died."

He looked from Gillian to the pool then back to Gillian once again. "How?"

"Well, I lost my temper and threw it. Yes, yes, yes, I know it was stupid, and that isn't like me, but believe me. I was provoked."

She rattled off a story about Jeremy and his wife, which only stoked the coals of anger glowing in Tucker's gut.

"Then the owl flew at me, and I jumped about a foot in the air and tripped over Peaches' leash and hurt my ankle."

"How bad is it?"

She gave him a rundown and demonstration that convinced him she would not be walking out of Enchanted Canyon today. He was mentally reviewing their options as she finished, "But you know what? It's okay." She flipped her hands in a voilà gesture and declared, "I am the Wilderness Queen!"

Tucker gaped at her. Wilderness Queen? She thought he'd be proud of her?

She was safe, relatively unhurt, and at the moment, borderline euphoric. Well, yes, he probably would be proud of her. Eventually. Right now, he wanted to wring her neck.

"You scared me to death," he repeated as he pulled his phone from his pocket. He handed it to her and said, "You need to call your mother."

"Oh. Yes. I'm sure she was worried."

Tucker bit back a caustic remark, stood, and walked toward his cousin, who had joined them moments ago, having followed at a slower pace. "Is she okay?" Boone asked, his gaze on Gillian, who was now speaking with her mom.

"Sprained ankle. We could carry her out, but I think the process would be quicker with a MULE." He wasn't talking about the four-legged animal, but one of the four-wheeled utility task vehicles they kept at the Fallen Angel Inn resort.

"Want me to go get one?"

"Think you can find your way back?"

Boone gave him a chiding look, then looked at Gillian. "She is safe if I leave her with you, right?"

"Very funny."

"I've known you all your life, cuz. During a crisis, you're ice. You only get scared when the crisis is over, and then you get pissed. You are royally pissed."

Tucker muttered a curse, and Boone clapped him on the back and grinned. "Let me say hello to your bride, and then I'll be on my way."

"Don't tell her I told you about Vegas. I'm a client, remember? I'll get your ass disbarred."

"Your secret is safe with me, cuz." Smirking, Boone unhooked his water bottle from his belt and took a drink as he waited for Gillian to finish her phone call. Once she hung up and smiled at him, he said, "Hello, Gillian. Fancy running across you here."

"Hey, Boone. Welcome home. How are the wedding plans going?"

"Eternity Springs and the North Forty are ready for Redemption to descend upon us."

"I can't wait. I loved Eternity Springs when I visited there in February." She gave a little embarrassed smile as she added, "The wedding is the main reason I didn't try to do too much on my ankle. I don't want to be the bridesmaid that hobbles down the aisle at Caroline's wedding."

"As long as you're there, I'm sure she wouldn't mind," Boone said gently.

Tucker cleared his throat loudly. "If y'all are done chitchattin', Boone is going to go get a MULE to carry you out of here."

"Oh. Okay, good." Gillian frowned up at the trail above them and said, "That trail is awfully narrow."

"He can come in through the creek bed," Tucker explained. "It's shallow and accessible."

"I'll be back in less than an hour." Boone gave Tucker a pointed look as he added, "Everything okay here?"

"Fine," Tucker snapped. "Go."

That last exchange finally caught Gillian's attention. She stared at Tucker, her eyes widened, and her exhilaration faded. "Tucker? What's wrong?"

He waited until his cousin had disappeared up the trail before turning to her, his voice grim, and said, "You scared ten years off my life."

"I'm sorry, but—"

"Let me talk," he interrupted. "I have something I need to say."

Gillian grimaced and held her head in the palms of her hands. "You really don't need to lecture me. My mom covered everything from soup to nuts. I feel terrible for all of the trouble I caused. Truly, I do. It was stupid to throw—"

"I love you."

Her hands fell to her lap. She stared at Tucker with wide, round eyes.

"I love you, Gillian," he repeated. "I'm all in. No holding back. I want a life with you. What happened today reminded me of a lesson I learned up close and personal numerous times throughout my military career. Life is too short to waste any more time. Be my wife, Gillian. My family. Let's make a home together. Let's forget about this divorce nonsense and go public. Today."

Chapter Eighteen

All the breath seemed to leave Gillian's body. She wondered if she simply hadn't noticed when the mule kicked her in the breadbasket. The kind of mule with four legs, not an engine.

He loved her. Tucker just told her he loved her!

Thrill washed over her like an ocean wave, sudden and fierce, but even as it crested, another more significant wave overtook it. Fear.

She thought she loved him too, but how could she be sure? She couldn't trust herself. She'd been ready to marry and pledge her love and her life to that two-legged sand trap only four months ago!

"You promised to give me time," she said quietly. "No pushback. You gave me your word."

He braced his hands on his hips. "Let me tell you something about time, Gillian. The past three hours took three decades to pass. I was afraid you'd been abducted or murdered or mangled! I thought you might be dead!"

She momentarily closed her eyes with regret. Sincerity rang in her voice as she said, "I'm sorry, Tucker. To the marrow of my bones, I am so very sorry that I caused you and my parents and my friends even a minute of worry. But that's no reason to change everything."

His brown eyes glittered. "Did you miss the part where I told you I loved you? What about that? It doesn't escape my notice that you haven't responded to that declaration in any way."

"You're not being fair, Tucker. You want to change the rules of the game."

"This is no game, Gillian. It's life. Real life. And it can end in the blink of an eye." He snapped his fingers in emphasis.

"That's true. It can. Maybe if you'd pulled this on me yesterday, I would have gone along to get along, but today is today, and I had an epiphany of my own." She pointed her thumb at her chest and announced, "This girl got grubby and learned I will survive. Just call me Gloria Gaynor."

"What?"

"The song. 1980s, I think."

He exhaled loudly, but she barreled on. "I grew strong. You helped me with that, Tucker, not just what you taught me on our wilderness weekend, but what you've taught me since, well, the very first day we met. I am not the woman I was last September or even in January, but I'm only now learning who that woman is."

"I know exactly who she is," Tucker said, throwing out his arms. "She's the Magnificent Mrs. Mc-Bride. Strong. Smart. Sexy. Stunning. When I got here a few minutes ago, you said I'd be proud of you because of how you'd managed. I'm proud because you're generous and gutsy and gorgeous. You're glorious. You're my Glory, and I need everyone to know that you're mine!"

Tears spilled from Gillian's eyes and trailed slowly

down her cheeks. Her emotions were a riot. That was
both the most beautiful thing any man had ever said
to her and the most tone-deaf. "And I need you to keep
your word to me, Tucker."

Temper sparked in his eyes. He dragged a hand
across his mouth as if attempting to hold back his
words, and Gillian knew that she'd offended him.
Well, tough. "You promised me no pressure in Las
Vegas. I'm feeling very pressured. I think I love you
too, but not so very long ago, I thought I loved Jeremy.
I couldn't bear to make another mistake."

"Just so you know, it really chaps my ass when you
compare me to Jeremy effing Jones."

"I'm not comparing you to anyone, Tucker. From
what I can tell, you are incomparable." He snorted,
and she prepared to elaborate, pushing to her feet
because having him stare down at her gave him an
advantage. She needed equality. She needed balance.

"You called me all those *S* words and *G* words . . .
well, now it's my turn. Tucker, you *are* incomparable. I've never known another man like you. You're
adventurous. You're trustworthy and loyal and loving. You're confident. You're intelligent. You make
me laugh."

"I'm a paragon of virtue," he grumbled, shoving his
hands in the pockets of his pants as he scowled at her.

"You are a really great guy. I would say you're the
greatest guy I've ever dated, except we never dated,
did we? We went from friends to spouses without ever
being boyfriend and girlfriend."

"So, is that the problem, here? You want to go out
to dinner together? To a movie?"

"Maybe. I don't know. *That's* the point, Tucker.
You've come at me out of the blue, wanting to change

the terms of our deal, and you want an answer right now."

"So, I'm jumping the gun by a week. One week. I have to pull the trigger on Nevada one way or the other when we get back from Colorado."

It was a valid point, but dang it, he'd given her his word! "Well, a week is a week is a week and I want it. That's our deal. And if you think for one minute that today, of all days, after my poor mother has scolded me like a six-year-old once already, that I could tell her I got married by Skinny Elvis in Las Vegas and not only didn't invite her but didn't tell her for two months afterward that it had occurred, then I have tickets to sell you to this year's Texas A&M versus UT Thanksgiving Day game!"

As any sports-minded Texan knew, the Aggies versus Longhorns gridiron rivalry had ended with the 2011 game, when the Aggies bolted the Big 12 Conference for the greener pastures of the Southeastern Conference.

Tucker balled his fists. "Dammit, Gillian."

She put her hands on her hips and lifted her chin. "No pressure. You promised. I'm holding you to your word. End of topic." She paused to see if he would continue to argue, but the man had the sense to keep his mouth shut, so she continued, "Now, want to help me break down my camp? That's another lesson you taught me. Leave it as you found it."

With a tight-lipped smile, his caramel eyes snapping with frustration, Tucker nodded once, briskly. Gillian knew the subject was far from closed.

Somewhere deep inside herself, she thrilled at the knowledge.

* * *

Back in Redemption, the combatants retreated to their respective corners. For the next week, Tucker walked around with a hundred pounds of torque in his jaw. She had boxed him in, and he didn't see a way out of it.

That's what made him grouchy as a cornered coyote. She had him dead to rights. She was asking for nothing more than what he'd promised her.

That morning in the canyon after he'd told her to stay off her ankle and sit still and let him deal with the camp, they'd exchanged little more than a dozen words before Boone returned with the MULE. Then once he got her home, her mother was there for some fussing and some fuming, so he didn't hang around. That pretty much set the scene for the next few days until what seemed like half of Redemption traveled to Eternity Springs for Jackson and Caroline's big event.

They'd arrived separately, the day before yesterday, Gillian with the "bride tribe" and Tucker with Jackson, Haley, and a passel of relations from Texas. The Callahan family's North Forty could best be described as a private ranch resort that included lakeside property. Each family from that part of the Callahan clan—and there were lots of them—had private homes in the compound. However, it also boasted a large dining hall and sound stage set up for concerts the music-loving family often hosted and opened to the public. Other amenities included floating docks on Hummingbird Lake for boats and water toys and swimming, and a stand of tree houses that were Brick Callahan's pet project. Brick and his wife, Liliana, were full-time Callahan residents of Eternity Springs. Throughout the year, one family group or another could almost always be found at the North Forty.

Upon the McBride cousins' arrival in Eternity

Springs, Brick had put them right to work doing everything from logistical tasks for arriving wedding
guests to mowing a lawn. As a result, Tucker had seen
little of his secret spouse. The women had spent last
night up at Brick's glamping resort, Stardance River
Camp, to be ready for the sunrise bridal portraits
Jackson had explicitly requested. They'd returned
to the Callahan compound twenty minutes ago, and
he was determined to have a private conversation
with her.

He tracked her down in the room she was sharing
with Maisy, and for once, she was alone. "Come for a
walk with me, Gillian."

"I can't. My ankle—"

"Is fine. I watched you all but skip up the porch
steps five minutes ago." The ball of frustration that sat
in his gut these days took a little roll. "I checked the
schedule, and you're clear until the rehearsal. Look,
you and I need to spend some time together. Otherwise, somebody is going to notice this awkwardness
between us."

"All right. Okay. Just give me a few minutes to
change my clothes."

"Good. I'll wait for you below the tree house."

She nodded. Tucker knew he should turn away and
save his question for later, but he couldn't do it. Her
red-rimmed eyes were killing him. "You've been
crying. Why?"

"Allergies. That's all. Something in the mountain
air."

He didn't believe her, but he sensed that now was
not the time to push. He'd wait to wrest the real reason out of her once they were out of sight of any po-
tentially prying eyes, although he was pretty sure he
could guess the reason.

The wedding. Caroline was having a real wedding with a real dress and a real officiant, and Gillian had had Elvis.

"Women." Tucker marched away from the cabin with a real bee in his boots. Women, weddings, and wishes that failed to come true. "Dammit."

He stewed about it for the next ten minutes, working up a real head of steam. He knew what was going on here. He'd run out of damned time. She was going to insist on the divorce, and he would have to give it to her, and it royally pissed him off. Tucker didn't like not getting his way, especially about something so important as staying married to the woman he loved.

When ten minutes stretched to fifteen, he added the sin of tardiness to his general pissed-off frame of mind. After he'd been cooling his heels beneath the Callahans' damned tree house for twenty minutes, he was done. If it took him playing Cro-Magnon man and pulling her off by her hair, he would do it. They were overdue for a walk and a talk. He had a few things he wanted to say about weddings to the secret Mrs. McBride.

He almost marched right past Maisy without stopping when she waved him down, but her words finally made it past the blood roaring in his ears. ". . . bag I left. She asked me to find you, and tell you she'll be back for your walk in an hour."

Wait. "What? I'm sorry, would you repeat that?"

Maisy rolled her eyes. "You're as cloud-headed as the rest of us today, Tucker. We accidentally left Gillian's bag up at the river camp after the photography session. She went to get it and asked me to tell you she'll look for you when she gets back."

Why didn't she come get me? "I'd have taken her up."

"I offered to go with her, but honestly, I think she needed a little time alone. This week is hard on her. It's the first wedding she's been to since hers was canceled."

If one doesn't count Elvis.

"She's being a real trooper, but it didn't help that her mother went all weepy when she saw Caroline in her wedding gown this morning."

Well, damn. "Okay, well, thanks for the heads-up."

Maisy tilted her head and studied him. "You okay, Tucker?"

"Sure. Why do you ask?"

"You seem a little tense. You're not nervous about the wedding, are you? Being a co–best man with Boone and everything? Tell me y'all haven't lost the rings."

"We haven't lost the rings, and I'm not tense," he snapped.

"Well, okay, then. I think I'll toddle off and see if any other happy person needs any help. Haley was talking about digging worms to go fishing." She finger-waved and turned to leave.

Ashamed, Tucker said, "Maisy. I'm sorry. I *am* a little tense, I guess. Just a lot going on."

"Everything will be okay, Tucker. Know how I know? Celeste told me so. Of course, Angelica said Celeste is full of herself and doesn't know *everything*, but she agreed the wedding was going to be fabulous."

He grinned crookedly. "You gotta love the Blessing cousins."

"Don't ya know it?"

Tucker ended up joining Maisy and Haley in the hunt for fishing worms. Throughout the task, he kept an eye out for Gillian's return. The trip up to the river camp and back should have taken an hour a most, an hour and a half if she screwed around.

Two hours after she'd left the Callahan compound, he started calling her. She didn't answer. He called and he called and he called. After the eighth call, Brick's wife, Liliana, came looking for him. "Tucker, I heard the phone ringing in Gillian's bedroom. It was plugged into the charger. Your name is on the display."

"She doesn't have her phone?" he demanded. "She went up to that remote camp without her freaking phone?"

This time, he really would kill her—if the bears didn't get to her first.

Gillian indulged in a few tears on her way up to the river camp in the cute little Mercedes she'd rented to have some independence during the Colorado trip. She snagged her bag and took advantage of the moment to fix her makeup. Her eyes were red as an interstate highway on a road map. No wonder Tucker had guessed she'd been crying.

Bag in hand, makeup repaired, redness-reducing teardrops applied, she returned to her car and began to lecture herself about keeping the tears at bay. This had been an emotional morning, but she couldn't lose her composure every time she turned around. She needed to wrestle her mood changes into submission and remain more even-keeled. Ever since the Enchanted Canyon argument with Tucker, she'd been a pinball bouncing randomly between one emotion bumper and another.

Her thoughts were a million miles away as she drove the winding road through to Stardance River Camp and exited the gate, turning left. Her friends thought she had wedding envy. Caroline, in a sweet

gesture from a caring heart, had even offered Gillian
the opportunity to bow out of her bridesmaid com-
mitment if the activities and events would prove too
painful for her.

They had no way of knowing, of course, that
wedding envy was only a small part of what was
bothering her.

She wouldn't be normal if she didn't regret the circumstances of the Vegas event. She would have liked
the bridal photos at dawn and sharing all the pre-
ceremony fellowship with her own band of sisters.
Caroline's lakeside wedding tomorrow was sure to be
gorgeous, and Gillian didn't doubt that she'd feel a
twinge or two for a beautiful ceremony of her own,
but again, what unmarried woman doesn't feel that
way at a wedding?

Of course, that was the rub, wasn't it? She was *not*
an unmarried woman. She was a *married* woman.

Married by Elvis in a tacky neon wedding chapel
in the middle of the night. Viva Las Vegas.

Married to a tall, dark, handsome hero who made
her knees weak and her heart sing and her soul yearn.

Love. He'd offered her love. Her heart told her she
loved him in return. Could she possibly believe in it?
Believe in him? Believe in herself?

Not this fast, no. Not in only four months. She read
Cosmo and *Allure* and *Women's Health* magazines.
She knew to beware of the differences between infatuation and love. True love took time to develop.
Tucker might be thinking he was in love with her, but
it was more likely to be lust than love. They simply
hadn't had enough time to—

A warning chime sounded in the car, and with a
wave of worry, she sensed not for the first time. Her
gaze flew to the dashboard, where the low fuel sign

flashed, and the gauge's needle pointed toward *E*. "Oh, no. Oh no, oh no, oh no."

She'd forgotten she needed gas. Surely she had enough to get back to town. It was mostly downhill, after all.

The car engine sputtered and died.

Gillian wrenched the wheel clockwise, and the Mercedes rolled to a stop on the shoulder of the road. Sighing, she reached for her purse and her phone.

Her phone. She'd left it on the charger. Tucker had gotten her so frazzled that she'd forgotten to grab her phone.

She muttered an unladylike curse. "Okay, stay calm. Remember your lessons." *S: Size up the situation.* Okay, that one was pretty easy. The man was going to murder her.

Gillian got out of her car, sat on the hood, and took inventory of the supplies in her overnight bag and purse. Well, she could use her makeup mirror to reflect the sun like a signal mirror. Not that she would need to signal anybody. She was right here in plain sight on the side of the road. Lots of people knew where she'd gone. When she didn't arrive when expected, someone would come after her.

Someone named Tucker, no doubt, and this time he'd find her a whole lot quicker.

While she sat waiting, she used the opportunity to fix the smudged polish on her left ring finger. She stroked pale pink onto her nail and thought about the red polish she'd worn when Tucker slipped the simple, thin gold band he'd bought at the wedding chapel's shop onto her finger. When the plane leaving Vegas took off, she'd removed the ring and tucked it into her fairy-tale castle, Judith Leiber purse, which in turn she'd tucked away deep in her bedroom closet.

Like the fact of her marriage. It, too, was in the closet. Now Tucker wanted to drag it all out, make it public, spread it across the road. Like roadkill on the road to Redemption. Or would the road to Ruin be more appropriate?

Actually, he didn't really want to yank their marriage out of the closet. He wanted her to make room for his stuff. He wanted a dedicated hanging rack and drawers in her dresser.

And she wanted to give them to him.

Her thoughts were getting crazy. Maybe it was altitude sickness. She should drink some water. She did have bottled water in her car. Too bad the engine wouldn't run on H_2O.

She slipped from the hood of the car, grabbed a water bottle from her back seat, and took a sip. Not too much, because the need to pee would present a problem.

Problems. Tucker said he loved her. Could it be real love and not just infatuation and lust? Could these feelings churning inside of her be the real deal too? She wanted to think so. She didn't know. Maybe she needed to read more magazines.

She needed to learn to trust herself again.

Damn this divorce deadline! She didn't want him to spend the summer in Death Valley, but she wasn't ready to tell her mom about Elvis either. For a woman in the wedding business, why did marriage have to be so complicated?

She heard the engine long before she saw the truck coming, and it wasn't coming from the direction of town, although perhaps the mountains surrounding her distorted the sound. As a safety precaution, she got back into her rental car, locked the doors, and waited to identify the oncoming vehicle. A white pickup. Not a lot of help, since there were a lot of white pickup trucks traveling in the mountains. Once it grew closer, she identified the driver—Jackson—and his passenger.

Tucker sprang from the truck before it rolled to a stop. She exited the Mercedes to meet him.

"What the hell, Gillian?" he demanded.

She gave him a hesitant smile. "I ran out of gas."

"You ran out of gas," he repeated, his voice just below a bellow. "So, you didn't bother to check your gas gauge before taking a drive in the mountains? Without your damned phone? And getting lost?"

"Wait a minute," she snapped right back. "I am not lost. I drove to the river camp, picked up my suitcase, and I was headed back to Eternity Springs."

"Eternity Springs is *that way*!" He pointed behind her.

"Oh. I must have got turned around when I left the camp. Well, it doesn't matter. I knew you'd find me."

"You knew I'd find you," he repeated. He placed his hands on his hips, and temper sparked in his caramel eyes. If her life was a cartoon, he'd have had plumes of steam shooting from his ears. "I guess I'm good at that, aren't I? Finding you? Finding you and making love. I know you think I'm good at making love. So I'm a finder, but not your love. Not a keeper. You need a keeper."

Jackson shifted uncomfortably, winced, and shot his cousin a warning look. Gillian folded her arms and lifted her chin, but before she could fire back, Jackson spoke.

"Okay, then," the groom said, turning toward his truck. "I don't have a gas can with me, but I'm pretty sure they'll have one at the river camp. Why don't I run to get gas?"

Both Tucker and Gillian held their tongues until the truck made a U-turn and headed off in search of fuel.

Then Gillian said, "Did you really have to bring up lovemaking, Tucker? You've totally embarrassed me. And, you let the cat out of the bag. Thank you very much."

"Cat? Or maybe you mean a mountain lion, like the ones who roam these hills? The hills you decided to roam without so much as a cell phone!"

"Maybe I really mean a weasel who doesn't keep his word about weddings!"

"I didn't tell Jackson we're married. I told him we're sleeping together!" He hesitated a moment and added, "I told Boone we're married."

Gillian gasped. "What about what happens in Vegas stays in Vegas?"

"It did stay there. It had a nice long visit."

"You broke your promise!"

"I hired Boone in the capacity of my attorney. I'm having him rewrite my will to make my wife the beneficiary."

"Your will!" Shocked, she gaped at him. "Tucker, I don't want your money."

"Good. Because I don't want to die. However, if you go missing again, I think the odds are about even that I'll have a heart attack and croak before that divorce you want so bad is final. There are dangerous wild animals in these woods—big ones!"

"I know. I'm looking at a cranky one right now."

Damned if he didn't roar at her.

Gillian buried her face in her hands and slumped back against her car. "Don't, Tucker. Let's not do this again. Please? Not now. Not today. This is Jackson and Caroline's weekend. Let's let them have it."

That took the wind from his sails. He sucked in a

deep breath and allowed a full half minute to tick by before he spoke in a calmer tone of voice. "That was certainly my intention, but I'm not the one walking around weeping and raising questions."

"I didn't weep. I got teary-eyed, and I can't help it. I'm an emotional person, and this is an emotional time. Weddings are emotional events."

"Your eyes have more red lines than an atlas," he scoffed. "Maisy told me your mother said something that brought on the waterworks this morning. What was that all about?"

"Oh." Gillian rubbed her eyes and shook her head. "It was nothing, just a remark about princesses and wedding gowns. That's all."

"But it made you cry."

"We both cried." She shrugged. "My mother and I have a long history together about wedding gowns. Seeing Caroline in hers this morning churned it up."

Tucker shoved his fingers through his hair and muttered a string of curses beneath his breath. "All right. You're right. This isn't doing either one of us any good. This is not the time or the place to hash out how we're going to go forward. We need to figure out how to get through the rest of today and tomorrow without making things worse."

Gillian felt the tears building behind her eyes once again. Damned if she'd let them spill.

She was relieved that he was willing to postpone their talk. Wasn't she? Then why did she want him to wrap those strong arms around her in a hug? *Gillian Thacker, you are a hot mess.* Frustrated with him and with herself and faced with the prospect of ruining her makeup for yet another time today, she snapped, "I suggest we start by staying as far away from each other as possible."

"Fine by me," he replied.

"Good," she declared. "I'll wait in the car where I'm safe from . . . angry bears."

Twenty minutes later, refueled with a gallon of gas from a red plastic can, Tucker opened the driver's side door of her car and told her he'd drive her back to the Callahans'. "You can't. You're not on the rental agreement."

"We're living on the wild side today, aren't we?"

They arrived back at the North Forty in a slide of tires crunching on gravel. Both front doors flung open. He shot from the driver's seat, she from the passenger side. The doors slammed, and the pair marched off in opposite directions.

Sitting in rockers on the front porch of a nearby cabin, Angelica glanced at her cousin and said, "Looks like we have our work cut out for us."

Celeste smiled beatifically. "Don't fret a single long red hair of yours, cousin. I have a plan."

Chapter Nineteen

"Destination weddings certainly have their unique challenges, don't they?" Barbara Thacker observed as the wedding party watched Jackson attempt to calm his daughter down later that afternoon. Following the discovery that the socks she'd chosen for her rehearsal outfit hadn't made it into the suitcase, a meltdown had commenced.

Tucker's gaze flicked over and met Gillian's. They shared a moment of silent communication before Gillian replied in a subtly dry tone, "They certainly do."

The wedding party had gathered at the lakeside site of the ceremony, where rows of white wooden garden chairs had been set in two columns with an aisle down the middle. At the water's edge along a narrow strip of sand, an arched arbor waited for attention from the florist tomorrow. Tonight, they'd tied ribbons on it in Caroline's colors of dusky pink and gold that complemented the primary decoration, which had been God's work—a crimson and gold sky against purple mountains rising above a sapphire lake.

It was a great evening, cool enough to remind them they were in the mountains, but not cold. A mild breeze swept the scent of honeysuckle in their direction. Jackson and Caroline had lucked out wedding-wise on the weather.

Now if the harried dad could figure a way to calm the storm that had become Hurricane Haley.

"She's a little anxious," Angelica said as Jackson knelt in front of his sobbing daughter and wrapped his comforting arms around her. "She'll be better once she's run through the rehearsal. She's been so fired up about the wedding for so long, and now that it's finally here, she's on overload."

Barbara gave the girl an indulgent smile. "That's understandable. I'm a little on overload myself, and my only duty is to do the New Testament reading."

Angelica sniffed. "You've got it easy. I have those Old Testament names to stumble over in mine."

"I think what our Haley needs right now is a distraction," Celeste offered. "I have a little gift for her. I had planned to make my presentation following the rehearsal, but I think I'll do it now. If that's all right with you, Caroline?"

"Please, be my guest."

Celeste walked up the aisle between two blocks of white folding chairs and stood beneath the large metal arch that the florist would cover in flowers tomorrow morning. She lifted her voice and announced, "Excuse me. May I have everyone's attention for just a few minutes before we get started? If everyone but the bride, groom, and flower girl will please take a seat. Caroline, I need you, Jackson, and Haley up here with me. I have gifts for you."

"Gifts?" Haley repeated, immediately distracted from her missing-sock meltdown.

Jackson threw Celeste a grateful look, then took his daughter's right hand and led her over to Caroline, who took hold of her left. Together, the trio walked up the aisle, Haley whispering loudly, "I don't see any boxes or gift bags."

The sound of Celeste's laughter chimed like church bells in the summer air. "Oh, my child. As you grow, you will learn that many of the best gifts life has to offer us do not come in packages wrapped up with a bow. That said, I happen to have three of these with me."

From the pocket of the light jacket she wore, Celeste pulled out a small square box wrapped in white paper and tied with a sparkling gold bow. Haley's eyes lit, and she clapped her hands. "That's pretty."

"Before I give it to you, I need to make a little speech."

"That's okay," Haley said, which caused Tucker and most of the rest of the wedding party audience to smile.

"Some of you know this story, but most of our visitors from Texas likely do not. I moved to Eternity Springs and established Angel's Rest Healing Center and Spa because this valley that cradles our little town is a special place with a unique, healing energy. Eternity Springs is where broken hearts come to heal, but that healing does not happen overnight. Nor does it happen without work. Usually, hard work."

Celeste shifted her focus to Haley as she continued, "Now, I've had many different careers in my long life, and in one of them, I was a schoolteacher."

"You were a teacher?" Haley asked. "What grade did you teach?"

"Well, I taught almost every grade, but my favorite grade to teach was second."

"I just finished second grade."

"I know that. Did your second-grade teacher give you awards for accomplishments?"

"Do you mean like stickers? She had a chart on the wall, and we got stickers when we completed a task."

"There you go. When I was a teacher, I gave stickers too. I'm a big believer in awards. That's why I created a very special award that I give to very special people."

"Like me? I'm special. Everybody says so."

Everybody listening laughed. "Yes, like you." Celeste pulled up a chair and sat in front of Haley. She handed her the box. "Open it, sweetheart."

It took the little girl mere seconds to tear off the bow and paper and flip up the lid on the white velvet jeweler's box. "It's pretty! It's a necklace for me to wear?"

"This is the official Angel's Rest blazon, awarded to those who have accepted love's healing grace."

"I don't understand what that means," Haley said.

"You will someday, love. Right now, wear your new necklace because it's pretty."

"I will. Thank you."

"You're very welcome." Celeste stood and handed a box to Caroline and one to Jackson.

Standing next to Tucker, Boone leaned over and murmured, "That's the original Eternity Springs status symbol. I really want one of those."

Celeste continued. "You may have done your healing in Texas, but you are celebrating the start of your new life here with us, so I decided that qualifies for a blazon. Caroline, life has tested you, but never forget that climbing this mountain of trial has been aerobic exercise. It has made your heart strong. Wear your pendant proudly."

"Thank you, Celeste. I will."

Celeste turned to Jackson. "Ernest Hemingway said that the world breaks everyone, and afterward, some are strong at the broken places. You are strong at the broken places, Jackson, your heart and your ears. Your music is your angel talking to you. Congratulations."

"Thank you, Celeste." Jackson accepted the box, then leaned over and kissed her on the cheek. "I've admired Brick's pendant, and he's told me how much the Angel's Rest blazon means to those who have earned it. I'll be honored to wear one of my own."

"Excellent. Now, I suspect we should get on with the rehearsal, shall we not?" She turned to the ceremony's officiant and added, "Reverend, do you want to take it from here?"

Later, after the meal and the speeches and watching a seemingly happy-as-a-clam Gillian talk with everyone at the party but him, Tucker needed a few minutes to himself. He slipped away down to the lake, where he walked along the bank, lost in thought.

He didn't see the figure until she spoke from out of the shadows. "Searching for peace for your troubled soul, Tucker?" Celeste asked.

"Oh. Hello. Yeah, I guess I could use a dose of Enchanted Canyon right about now."

"Your angel dust is Texas red dirt, isn't it?"

"I don't know about that, but red has become my favorite color of late." Tucker's mouth twisted with a crooked smile and he added, "Angelica has these spicy sprinkles she sometimes puts on her cookies. Calls it her devil dust."

"I think I'll pass on making a comment about that. Beyond a general observation, anyway." Celeste clicked her tongue, took his arm, and started walking with him. "Cousins can be a trial, can't they?"

"That's no lie."

"But they are certainly treasures too."

"Yes."

They strolled together in silence for a few moments. Tucker was in no hurry to end the walk. Something about Celeste Blessing was as soothing as a long hike in the canyon at the end of a busy week.

She gave a long, contented sigh. "Listen to the night, Tucker. If you indulge my literary mood, I'd like to share something of the poet John Keble. 'Peace is the first thing the angels sang.' Isn't that a lovely thought?"

"It is."

"It's lovely, and there is a lesson there. If you open yourself to the song your angels are singing, you will find your peace."

He lifted his gaze to the starlit heavens. "I don't know that I have much of a relationship with angels."

"Now, that's where you're wrong." She halted and gave his arm a squeeze. "When you are lost in the wilderness, sometimes you need to take a leap of faith. Your angels are singing, Tucker McBride. Listen to them. Listen to them, and let go. It's the only way to fly."

Then, she turned and faded away into the shadows.

Tucker sighed and faced the lake. He filled his lungs with mountain-scented air and exhaled in a rush. "Angels?" he scoffed. "I ain't got no blessed angels."

What whispered to him was a conscience. It had nagged him for days now, ever since the argument he and Gillian had at her camp in the canyon. It's what had put him in such a lousy mood and put his trigger on "hair."

Gillian wasn't ready to be his wife. He was beginning to believe that she'd never be ready to be his wife.

His angels—such as they were—were singing loud and clear.

Gillian watched Tucker slip away from the celebration, and her throat went tight. Could she be any more miserable? She was trying to hide it, trying to pretend that all was well, and she thought she'd fooled everyone. Well, everyone except for Mom. Mom knew her too well.

She'd fielded a few questions about hers and Tucker's tempestuous arrival back at the North Forty. She'd mixed a little truth with some fiction, and blamed it on travel fatigue and a clash of tempers.

She knew that Caroline and Maisy thought her blues were Jeremy related. They couldn't be more wrong. Her mood wasn't wedding related. It was all about divorce.

Nevertheless, she'd done her bridesmaid duty and soldiered on. She'd made a lovely, heartfelt bridesmaid's speech, and she'd managed to forget her own problems and insecurities for a little while as she basked in the positive energy of the love in evidence at an Eternity Springs wedding weekend.

But now, Coco was about to sing. Gillian didn't have the heart to stick around to be entertained. She needed some time to herself, time to think about these doubts she was having about her doubts. Maybe she should let herself have one more good cry, after all. She could use her eye drops and the emergency mask in her makeup case before going to sleep, and she'd look all right in the morning.

The question was where to go. The last thing Gillian needed was to run into Tucker. He'd appeared to be headed down toward the lake. She'd go in the opposite direction.

She'd thought she made a stealthy escape, but her mother appeared out of nowhere and stopped her by grabbing her hand. Barbara led her away from the milling crowd, then asked, "Gillian, what's going on with you and Tucker?"

Gillian opened her mouth, the words of a confession hanging on her tongue. However, this was not the time or place or way to spring this sort of news on her mother. She swallowed and produced new words, honest words, if not all the words that needed to be said. "It's a long story, Mom, and this isn't the place to tell it, but, well, we've been seeing each other."

"I suspected as much."

"You did?"

"I know you pretty well, Gillian." She paused a moment, then added, "I like Tucker. So does your father."

"I do too, Mom."

"Do you think there's a chance that—"

"Excuse me," Gillian interrupted. "I need to powder my nose."

She fled and did a pit stop at the ladies' room in the dining hall because she really was done with lying to her mother. Then as Coco's heavenly voice rose on the night air singing the hit song "Wishes for My Angel" that she'd co-written with Jackson, Gillian took the path leading away from the lake. It took her toward the tree house that Haley had declared was her favorite place in Colorado. Gillian paused beside the ladder and gazed up at the trilevel structure that had a platform above the tree line for stargazing.

It was a perfect place to hide. The ideal place to think about lowering her guard and trusting versus letting him walk away.

She kicked off her heeled, slippery-soled sandals and climbed the ladder to the first level, then the second, and finally to the platform—where she discovered she wasn't alone.

"Hello, dear," Angelica said. "Did you come to share my sky?"

"Yes, if that's all right." What else could she say? *No, I wanted to be alone so I could have a pity party cryfest all by myself?* Even if she thought to be that rude, she knew better than to say something like that to Angelica. The Fallen Angel innkeeper would give her a well-deserved verbal beatdown.

It turned out Gillian didn't have to say much of anything to get that. She'd no sooner stretched out on her back beside Angelica and begun to seek the constellations she could identify when her friend said, "What is wrong with you, girl?"

"I'm sorry?"

"I should say so. I've never seen a woman so durn sorry in all my life. You have happiness at your fingertips, but it appears you're ready to throw it all away."

Gillian came up on her elbows and asked with suspicion in her tone. "What do you know?"

"'There are more things in heaven and earth, Horatio, than are dreamt of in your philosophy.'"

"From 'so durn sorry' to quoting Shakespeare to me?"

"I'm diverse, and my cousin got me started down a literary path with her Hemingway quote. But here is what I know, Gillian. Allowing fear to rule your actions is like wrapping weight bands around your ankles. Thick ankles are not a good look for you. Your heart will never fly free carrying that extra load."

"Now you sound like Celeste too," Gillian grumbled.

"Well, as much as I hate to admit it, the old girl makes a lot of sense when she's not making sense. Let me put this to you in Angelica fashion—you need to pull your head out of your bloomers. He's a good man, and he loves you!"

"Tucker told you about us?" *Who hasn't he told?*

"He hasn't said a word—with his mouth, anyways. His eyes speak volumes. The fact that he's in love with you is written all over that big, broad, beautiful body of his. I can't believe no one else has noticed."

"I think my mother has," Gillian grumbled. But it sounded like Angelica didn't know about the Las Vegas wedding either, so Tucker hadn't blabbed to everyone. If Angelica knew, she'd darned sure say something about it.

"Of course, the same message is written all over you too."

"It is?"

"Yep. It's just not as clear because you're transmitting other messages as well, so things get a bit mixed up. What is wrong with you, Gillian? What fears are the pellets in your ankle weights?"

She wasn't going to try to deny it. She was tired of trying to hide. Tired of lying, mostly by omission, but lies were lies, and they didn't rest well on her soul. According to Angelica and Celeste, Enchanted Canyon was where troubled souls found peace. Angelica was the closest thing to Enchanted Canyon around here at the moment. *Who knows, maybe she can help me?*

"It's not fear. It's trust. A lack of trust. In myself.

How do I know these feelings are real? I came within a one-night stand of marrying a man who, only a few months later, I don't even like, much less love. Makes one wonder if I ever loved Jeremy. Tucker doesn't like it when I bring Jeremy into our relationship—"

"I can understand why."

"But the man is part of me, part of who I am today. He changed me, and I'm trying to figure out who the new me is."

"You've been hanging out in the self-help aisle in Caroline's bookstore, haven't you? Listen to me, honey-child. I'm gonna speak frank. Okay?"

"Okay."

"That's bull. The only way a man has the power to change you is if you cede your power to him. You didn't do that with the eighteen-hole wonder. You won't do it with Tucker. You had a life experience, and you think you have to make it into this big woo-woo project."

"I don't think—"

"I've been doing woo-woo from way back," Angelica interrupted. "This ain't it. Save yourself and Tucker and everybody else you care about from the self-discovery chase because you're going looking for answers to something you already know."

"I don't know the answers! That's the problem!"

"Sure you do. At the center of your soul, you know who you are, and what you want. You've allowed distrust—which is just another way to say fear—to hide that knowledge from yourself. You're trying to peel those layers back, one at a time, when all you need to do is take a broom to 'em. Or, maybe a baseball bat. Just git 'er done, Gillian. Unbuckle those ankle weights. Because while you're going all Magellan inside your psyche, time is passing you by. Time is your most precious resource, your most valuable asset. Use it wisely. Don't let life pass you by."

With that, Angelica rolled gracefully to her feet, crossed to the access hatch and ladder, and began her descent from the stargazing platform. Just before her head disappeared, she paused and offered one last piece of Angelica advice. "Life is hard. Wear a helmet. Don't be a wuss."

Gillian stayed in the tree house gazing up at the star-filled summer sky long into the night, thinking. Peeling away. Using a broom, a baseball bat, golf cleats, and an acronym or two.

When she saw the shooting star streaking across the heavens, the job was done. She knew who she was and what she wanted.

Forget *S.U.R.V.I.V.A.L.*

As of this moment, she was all about *L.I.V.I.N.G.*

Chapter Twenty

The wedding went off perfectly. The bride was a vision in her dream gown from Bliss Bridal Salon, and the sight of his bride marching toward him brought tears to the groom's eyes. The flower girl all but stole the show, cute as a six-month-old puppy with a ball of yarn, as she carefully dispatched rose petals all the way up the aisle. Even River Dog the ring bearer cooperated, his most-excellent training on display as he walked beside Haley, and then took his seat at Angelica's feet.

Tucker and Gillian survived the awkward moment when they met to walk together up the aisle as groomsman and bridesmaid. It helped that he'd knocked on her door first thing that morning and suggested they cry peace for the day and leave their personal baggage locked away. Gillian had gratefully agreed. They'd even danced together at the reception. The only tricky moment came when Gillian accidentally caught Caroline's bouquet.

Now, they were back in Texas, and the time had come for Tucker to own up to his angels. Like it or not, he knew what he had to do.

On Monday evening, sitting at the dance hall bar

and nursing a beer, he fingered the engraving on his pocket watch. *To my love.* He closed his eyes, returned the watch to his pocket, and pulled out his phone. He sent Gillian a text. *"Can I see you sometime tomorrow? We need to talk."*

Three long minutes later, she responded. *"Tomorrow works for me. I agree."*

"Your place? After work?"

This time he waited almost five minutes for her reply. *"I have the afternoon off. How about I bring lunch to you—Taco Tuesday—and afterward we hike up to the cave? I would like to get the wedding dress for Bliss."*

That surprised him. What Gillian proposed sounded more like a date than a "talk," but he had nothing against the idea. *"Sounds good."*

"Your usual?"

"Yes, please."

She posted a thumbs-up emoticon. *"See you tomorrow. Twelve thirty-ish."*

He went to bed that evening feeling lonely and depressed, and his mood didn't improve when he awoke the following day. He spent the morning doing research and making calls and arrangements, carrying around a dust cloud of blue mood à la Pigpen in the comic strip *Peanuts.* The process depressed him. The plan dejected him.

At twenty after twelve, the perk of River's ears signaled Gillian's approach. He opened the trailer door and stepped outside to meet her, his cousin's dog at his heels. Moments later, Gillian climbed out of the car carrying Peaches and a white paper sack.

Tucker welcomed her with a genuine smile. "That smells great."

She handed him the bag. "I got you pulled pork

tacos, regular charro beans, and corn in a cup as requested. I also ordered you your own side of guac since you're always trying to filch some of mine."

"Good thinking. Want to eat here or take it with us?"

"Here, please. It was all I could do not to break into the bag on the drive out here."

He got them each a bottle of Topo Chico mineral water, and they made small talk while they ate. She asked if there'd been any word from the honeymooners, and he told her Jackson had called him last night to see how River had managed the flight home. He asked her how Peaches had made out at the dog sitter's while she'd been gone.

"She wasn't very pleased with me," Gillian said, dipping a chip into her guacamole. "Hopefully this hike will win me back into her good graces."

"I know the feeling," Tucker murmured. He was tempted to go ahead and put his plan on the table alongside the chips and salsa. Get it over with. Without thinking it through, he asked, "Do you want to have our relationship talk now or later?"

She sat back in her chair and considered the question. "Let's walk off our lunch first. Might end up with indigestion otherwise."

He nodded. She had a point.

After loading up the dogs and backpacks in the MULE, he drove to the trailhead, where Gillian muted her phone and stowed it inside her pack while explaining, "I learn from my mistakes."

They did little talking on the way to the cave, though he did point out where she'd gone off-trail on her solo trip.

"Oh, wow," she said. "I must have totally zoned

out on the *R*. I didn't remember where I was, because now I remember you telling me that trail led down to a spring." She paused, gave him a look he couldn't read, and added, "That won't happen again. I've been working on my acronyms."

"Good." He guessed it was good, anyway. He didn't know what the heck she was talking about. Gillian was in a strange mood today, but he imagined she might be thinking the same thing about him.

They set a good pace and arrived at the cave entrance sooner than Tucker had expected. For the first time on the hike, Peaches balked. She wasn't interested in going inside the cave. Her dog's reaction gave Gillian second thoughts. "Maybe she senses something or smells something inside. You'd better check."

Tucker smirked. "What would you have done if you two had made it here by yourselves that day, and she reacted this way then?"

She folded her arms. "I guess we'll never know, will we?"

Grinning, he shrugged off his backpack and reached for the small flashlight he carried on his belt. He'd started to duck into the cave when Gillian grabbed hold of his sleeve and stopped him. "Wait!"

He arched a curious brow. She slipped off her backpack and fished the flashlight from inside. Grimly, she announced, "I'll do it."

"Gillian, wait a minute," Tucker began.

"No. No, I'm going to do it. It's part of my new strategy."

Strategy? What strategy? He was the one who had a strategy. "Strategy for what?"

"Here. Hold my dog." She handed him Peaches'

leash, switched on the light, drew a deep breath, and ducked into the cave. Peaches whimpered. River followed on her heels. Moments later, Gillian called happily, "All clear."

Bemused, Tucker ducked into the shadowed cave.

Damned if she didn't meet him with a kiss.

It was the first kiss they'd shared since their canyon fight, and after the initial moment of shock, he went all in. He kissed her back hard, pouring all the pent-up sadness and frustration that he'd been feeling for more than a week into the effort, groaning against her mouth as she responded in kind. He'd missed her. Missed this. Hell, he'd been missing this all his life.

He didn't want to lose it. He didn't want to lose her.

She delved her fingers into his hair. He released her mouth and feathered kisses across her face to that spot on her neck just below her ear that always made her shudder. Hearing her moan his name sent a shot of heat racing through him like fine Kentucky bourbon. Biting, licking, and tasting, he let her scent wash over him and wanted to drown.

Then Peaches decided she wanted some attention and threaded herself between their legs. At the same time, River spotted a lizard and went on the hunt, sideswiping Tucker in the process. "Dammit," he muttered as he lost his balance and came close to taking them both down. Gillian stepped back and steadied him. Her eyes were laughing as she said, "Those darned kids."

"We'll have to send them to bed without their suppers," Tucker replied, then wished he hadn't said the *B* word. He cleared his throat. "I'll light the lanterns, though I'm sort of surprised they didn't burst into flame all on their own from all the heat we just generated."

"No kidding."

While he set about doing that, she knelt beside the trunk and lifted the lid. Her fingers trailed across the fabric of the wedding gown. "This is so beautiful."

"So are you. Beautiful inside and out, Glory."

She lifted the dress from the trunk, held it by its shoulders, and studied it. "I still wonder what its story is. I wish we had some way to discover it. Was this gown worn to her wedding to the love of her life, the father of her fourteen children?"

"Fourteen?"

"Life before birth control. Or did a villain steal this dress before she had the chance to wear it? Did a stagecoach robber steal her dream? I really wish we knew."

A stagecoach robber stealing dreams.

"I've been wearing the black hat," Tucker murmured.

"I'm sorry?"

Tucker simply shook his head and smiled.

Gillian removed a folded dress bag sporting the Bliss Bridal logo from her backpack. Carefully, tenderly, and respectfully, she packed the antique wedding gown inside. When the bag's zipper stuck, she picked away loose threads, and Tucker helped by giving it a good yank.

Then she lifted it, folded it over her arms, and faced him. "You ready for that talk now?"

No. Never. "Sure. There's a good spot just up the trail a little ways. Let me . . ."

A notion had occurred to him as he'd watched her take that gown from the trunk. It was a little weird, bordering on woo-woo, but if either Celeste

or Angelica stood beside him, he knew in his gut that
they'd tell him to go with it.

He pulled his pocket watch from his pocket, placed
it in the trunk, then shut the lid, and turned to go.

Gillian watched him quizzically. "Why did you do
that?"

"Time," he said. "The watch came to me for a
reason. I'm tucking it away as a promise."

He picked up his pack and led her from the shadows of the cave into the light, bright summer afternoon.

They hiked farther up the trail, beyond the cave. In
less than five minutes, they reached Tucker's goal—a
large, flat-topped boulder that offered a bird's-eye
view of most of the canyon. He took the wedding
gown from her arms and set it aside, then he placed
his hands around her waist and lifted her up and onto
the rock. "Stay," he commanded to both dogs in a tone
of voice that demanded he be obeyed. "Sit."

The dogs sat.

Tucker climbed up on the rock and sat beside his
wife. "Look." He pointed out the landmarks in the
canyon below. "There's the inn, and to the south,
Ruin. To the north lies Redemption."

"It's a pretty view," Gillian said. "Tucker, I need to
tell you—"

"Please," he interrupted. "Let me go first. I need
to go first, because I think what I have to say will
probably change whatever it is you intend to tell me."

"All right."

Tucker drew a deep breath, exhaled in a rush, and
abandoned his planned, canned speech and instead,
spoke from his heart. "The way I see it, I'm meta-
phorically sitting on the front porch of the inn, half-

way between Ruin and Redemption with a choice to make. I know what the choice needs to be. I've known it for a while now, which has been a reason why I've been as grumpy as Branch Callahan when the Cowboys lose to the Eagles."

"I understand that he does like his Cowboys."

"He's a maniac. He's older than dirt and swears he's not kicking up his boots until they win another Super Bowl."

"Your whole family will probably always root for the Cowboys' opponent in that case. I saw at the wedding how much everyone loves him."

"We do. And speaking of love . . ." He took her hand in his and brought it up to his mouth. He pressed a kiss against first her knuckles and then the heart of her palm. "I love you, Gillian, and I owe you an apology. I was wrong to pressure you into going public about our marriage. I'd promised you time, and I tried to change the rules on you. I shouldn't have done that."

"Thank you."

"In my defense, I've never been in love before, so I'll invariably make some training mistakes."

"Training mistakes?" she repeated, a smile hovering on her lips.

"It's a woman's job to train the men in their lives. Boone's sisters spout off about that all the time."

"I see. So, you're saying this whole argument between us was my fault for not properly training you?"

"Would I get away with that?"

"Not on your life."

"Didn't figure so. Here's the deal, Glory. I don't want to wear the black hat anymore. I choose to take the road to Redemption. You deserve to write the story you want to write, the one of the bride living her dream with her mother looking on, not the version where a robber with a six-shooter has held the bride up and stolen her dress. In that case, it's time for us to turn the page."

"I like the sound of this, Tucker, but how do you propose we do it?"

"We proceed as planned. I'm packed for the desert. My plane leaves tonight."

She blinked and went stiff. "Wait. What? You're leaving? Already? Without our discussing it?"

"We still have six weeks to eight weeks to discuss it, honey. I spoke with my buddy last night. We needed to make the call on who would be working where."

"So you chose Death Valley?"

"To be totally transparent, a portion of what we do is in an air-conditioned classroom in Las Vegas. We're not in the desert for the entire time, and we'll only be in the park itself for a portion of that."

"The park?"

"Death Valley is a national park."

"I didn't know that. But . . . you'll be gone. To Nevada. With a residence."

"I can file for divorce the first week of August."

"But . . . but . . . what about the plan?"

"What plan?"

"The one to win my heart!"

"Oh. That plan." He took hold of her hand, brought it to his mouth, and kissed her knuckles. "It's in the bag."

She relaxed a bit and arched her brows. Her lips twitched. "You think so, hmm?"

"I do. This isn't surrender, my love. This isn't even

strategic retreat. What I'm doing is clearing the way so the wedding planner can do her thing—when she so chooses."

"Are you asking me to marry you, Tucker?"

"Right now?" He rubbed his chin and considered the question a moment before shaking his head. "Well, no. Last time I did that in a shopping mall. I'm thinking next time around should involve some real romance. I'll be back in Texas in August, honey. I'm predicting a whirlwind romance that culminates with an engagement ring and a wedding date that's as soon as the wedding planner and her mom can make it happen."

"You want to divorce me so you can marry me?"

"No. What I want is for you to realize you can trust what is already in your heart. It will happen, and I can wait for it. Then, when the time is right, I'll watch you walk up the aisle to me wearing the wedding dress of your dreams on the arm of your proud father and with your happy mother dabbing her tears with a handkerchief in the front row." He turned her hand over and kissed the center of her palm.

"I will wait for you, Gillian. I'm sorry I let my impatience get the best of me. No more pressure. I've learned my lesson."

Gillian exhaled a heavy breath. Her voice was a little shaky when she said, "Well. Okay. Wow. You've blindsided me with this, Tucker. This is not at all what I was expecting. I need to think about this and figure out if it changes what I had intended to say to you today."

"Take your time. Tell you what, why don't we head back to the MULE and return to my place. We could go for a swim. You can tell me what you need to tell me when you're ready." He hopped down from the boulder and turned to help her. "I've got time. My plane doesn't leave until eleven forty."

Tucker carried the wedding gown as they hiked back to the utility vehicle. They kept conversation to a minimum. Gillian's expression was pensive, her thoughts obviously turned inward. Only when he loaded the dogs up into the MULE did she ask a question. "What are you going to do with River? Aren't you supposed to dog sit for the entire month that Jackson and Caroline are on their honeymoon?"

"Angelica said he can stay with her at the inn. Now that we've built the innkeeper's cottage, she has a way to keep him separate from guests who aren't dog lovers."

While Gillian seemed weighted by the revelation of Tucker's plan, he felt about a million times better. His Pigpen cloud had dissipated. The gloom surrounding him had lifted. The choir of angels creating a racket inside him had zipped their heavenly lips.

He didn't look forward to the sixty days in the desert, but he was a professional, and the reward would be worth it.

Back at the trailer, he placed the wedding gown across the back seat of her car, while she went inside to change into the swimsuit she kept here. He stripped down to his boxers and dove into the cool, refreshing water, where he swam underwater for three strong strokes. When he surfaced, he gave his head a fling to get the water out of his eyes. The sight that met him took his breath away.

Gillian had a new swimsuit. A teeny, tiny red bikini. Her mile-long legs carried her toward the fishing hole, her hips swayin' like church bells on Easter morn, and a hot time Saturday night look in her eyes. She'd painted her mouth vixen red.

Tucker thought it entirely possible that the sixty-nine-degree water surrounding him might just turn to steam.

"Mr. McBride, I have a counterproposal for you."

"Oh, yeah?"

"Oh, yeah. But first, I need to tell you something."

"Okay. Hurry up, though, because I need to get my hands on you bad."

"I'm counting on it." Poised at the edge of the swimming hole, ready to make her dive, Gillian lifted her lips in a temptress's smile that inexorably drew him forward. She signaled for him to stop at a point where his feet reached the rocky bottom.

She circled those luscious lips with her tongue. "At our Girls Getting Grubby weekend, you taught me three important survival rules. One." She held up her index finger. "Determine my need and develop a solution." She held up a second finger. "Continually work to improve my circumstances. And three." Up came the third finger. "Don't make my situation any worse. Based on those rules, I have developed a personal acronym."

She executed a graceful, shallow dive into the water and moments later, surfaced in front of him. Instinctively he reached for her, but again, she signaled him to stop. "Our acronym begins with *L*. I love you, Tucker McBride, with my whole heart. Not just my *entire* heart, but whole as in healed. I love you with my whole heart."

His own heart thudded. "Gillian—"

She cut him off. "No. My turn to talk. After *L* comes *I*, for invest. I am invested in this relationship. I am all in. That brings us to *V*. You have two *V*s in your *S.U.R.V.I.V.A.L.* acronym—vanquish fear and value living. I considered both, but I settled on Venus."

"A planet?"

She laughed. "The goddess of love. I intend to be your Venus, Tucker, because in addition to love, Venus's functions encompass desire, sex, fertility, prosperity, and victory."

"Fertility?"

"In due time, yes, fertility."

"I can work with that. So, you have *L.I.V.* . . . is the next one *E*?"

"Nope. Too short. We're going for the whole tamale, or gerund, as it were, so the next letter is another *I*. Infinite, for no boundaries. No boundaries in this love I give to you. *N* is for nanosecond. I'm not going to waste a nanosecond of loving you. Finally, *G*. *G* is for giggle, because laughter is vital to a life well lived."

"*L.I.V.I.N.G.* I love it. Can I kiss you now?"

"No, not yet.

"What about that nanosecond?"

"I have to summarize first. So, I determined my need, developed a solution, and I'm working to improve my circumstance without making it any worse. I'm committed to *L.I.V.I.N.G.*, which brings us to my counterproposal."

Gillian looped her arms over Tucker's shoulders and laced her fingers behind his neck. "Tucker McBride, will you repeat our wedding vows with me two months from Saturday? In Las Vegas?"

He blinked. Repeat their vows? No divorce! Tucker grinned as joy filled his heart. "A destination wedding? Really?"

"Really." Happiness sparkled in her eyes. "My mother will love it."

EIGHT WEEKS LATER

In the bride's room at the Chapel of Wedded Bliss, with a photographer clicking away and Maisy Baldwin, Caroline McBride, and the Blessing cousins looking on, Barbara Thacker buttoned the final button on Gillian's wedding gown and took a careful step away. She gazed at her daughter's reflection in the full-length mirror and then clapped both hands over her mouth. "It's perfect. Just perfect."

The gown featured an off-the-shoulder portrait neckline that Barbara had trimmed with beading and crystals. A dropped waist bodice and deep V-back gave way to a billowing ball gown skirt. Gillian met her mother's gaze in the mirror and sighed, "Oh, Mom. You're right. It *is* perfect. It's the wedding gown I've always dreamed of wearing."

Her mother's eyes gleamed with tears, and she blew Gillian a kiss. Gillian blew one back, then gave her reflection a critical once-over. "It's the right dress. Tucker is the right man."

"Reverend Mills is the right officiant," Celeste offered.

Angelica shrugged. "I understand Elvis was a little put out."

"He's going to play the piano as Gillian and her father walk up the aisle," Barbara said. "He's quite talented. I was impressed."

Gillian grinned. "We only pick the talented Elvis in Vegas, Mom."

A rap sounded on the door, and Maisy opened it to reveal Gillian's father and brother, each dressed in new gray suits and red ties. Mike winked at Gillian, blew her a kiss, then said, "I've been told to give you all a five-minute warning." As the Blessing cousins wished Gillian well and took their leave, William Thacker's gaze went past Maisy to his daughter. He pulled his handkerchief from his pocket and dabbed his eyes. "Oh, princess. You take my breath away."

"Thank you, Daddy."

"I wonder if Elvis knows CPR," Caroline mused as she picked up her bouquet and prepared to assemble in the back of the chapel. "Tucker is going to take one look at her, and his heart will stop."

Once the room was cleared but for her parents, Gillian attempted to put some of her emotions into words. "Mom. Dad. I want you both to know how much I love you, and how very much I appreciate how understanding you were about what happened in Vegas last time, and how much I value your part in making today a fairy-tale day for me. You are the best parents any girl could ever have."

Barbara took hold of her husband's hand and briefly leaned her head against his shoulder. In a voice that trembled with emotion, she said, "All we ever wanted was for you to be happy, Gillian. Tucker makes you happy."

"He does, Mom. More than I ever dreamed possible. I'm the happiest woman in the world—because of Tucker and Dad and you. And because I'm wearing my princess wedding gown."

Barbara grabbed her husband's handkerchief away from him and dabbed her eyes. "Well, then. No more of this or I'll cry, and my mascara will run. Let's get you into those skyscraper shoes of yours, and then I'll go do my MOB thing."

From a box on a dressing room chair, she picked up Gillian's wedding shoes—not the rhinestone embellished heels she always dreamed of wearing, but the red snakeskin Christian Louboutins she'd worn for her first wedding in Vegas.

Precisely at the top of the hour, on her father's arm and to the music of Beethoven's "Ode to Joy," Gillian picked up her fairy-tale castle purse and went off to marry the love of her life.

Again.